Strangers Brothers

a novel by

Raymond F. Flaherty
with **Pat McDonough**

Strangers Brothers

a novel by
Raymond F. Flaherty
with **Pat McDonough**

Terra Sancta Press
Melbourne, Florida 32935
2008

The original manuscript copyright © 2005 by Raymond F. Flaherty #TXu1-275-785 12/2/2005. This substantially revised book **Strangers Brothers** is Copyright © 2008 by Raymond F. Flaherty and Patricia A. McDonough d/b/a Terra Sancta Press. All rights are reserved. No part of this book may be copied or reproduced without permission of the publisher Terra Sancta Press. Although some of the events are based indirectly on actual experiences, the characters in the book are fictitious composites or are products of the authors' imaginations. Where names of actual people, living or dead, have been used, it does not have a bearing on the fictional nature of this story. The opinions expressed in this book are that of Raymond F. Flaherty and do not necessarily reflect the viewpoint of Terra Sancta Press. All rights to this book reside with Raymond F. Flaherty and Patricia A. McDonough d/b/a Terra Sancta Press. All rights to the bookcover, and cover art representation, and any derivatives in any form, reside with Patricia A. McDonough d/b/a Terra Sancta Press.

TITLE: **Strangers Brothers**
AUTHOR 1: Flaherty, Raymond F. (8/6/1927 - 9/11/2006)
AUTHOR 2: McDonough, Pat (9/2/1943 -)
EDITION: First Edition, First Printing
PRINT: 10 9 8 7 6 5 4 3 2   Printed in the USA
PRINT DATE: July 2008
RELEASE DATE & STREET DATE: September 1, 2008
ISBN: 978-0-9653467-8-8
LCCN: 2008906780
EAN BOOKLAND: 90000 $21.95 USD

1. **Strangers Brothers** (fictitious characters) —Fiction
2. Grenada (Military History)—Operation *Urgent Fury* —Fiction
3. U.S. Army Airborne Ranger (Military Science — Training) —Non-fiction
4. Paratroopers, parachute jumping (Military Science)— Non-fiction
5. Military Families

SUGGESTED BISAC: FIC032000, HIS027130
PUBLISHER ID NUMBER: SAN: 854-1388
PUBLISHER: **Terra Sancta Press**, 304 Royal Palm Dr., Melbourne FL 32935
           eMAIL: books4you@cfl.rr.com
           FAX: 321-259-9242 (24-hour number)
           PHONE: 321-254-9672 (11 am - 8 pm EST)
           WEBPAGES: http://www.terrasanctapress.com

Publisher's DOLR: 20080811

Publisher's Acknowledgments

Every book requires a team to bring the author's dream to fruition. Terra Sancta Press owes a special thank you to each of the following people:

★ Bill Coombs, Kevin "Hognose" O'Brien, R. Manning, Leamon Ratorreo and the SF Listeam house, and other SF friends who did not give their names, for their assistance in military fact verification, checking, and resources

★ Chuck James, Webmaster, website design, technical support, photographs from his personal file, and rave review

★ David Adams and MacAlan Thompson, technical support, photographs from their personal files and illustrations

★ Dale J. Muschamp, military munitions resource

★ Debbie Anderson and Kerry Goodier, military fact resource

★ Suzanne R. Witenhafer, Arrow Design Studios, Inc., of Rockledge Florida, bookcover design

★ Dennis & Carolyn Hamilton, R. Bradley Witenhafer, critical readers

★ Authors Richard Leonhart, Leila Harber, Zeta Gibbs, Joyce Henderson, and Mary Brotherton for in-depth review and critique

★ Mirinda Hartselle, Bob Golden, research

★ Claire Skiles, data entry, research, and proofreading

★ Marie E. Roman, fact checking, proofreading, and review

★ Sharon Flowers, medical resource

★ Carol Salzman, review

Publisher's Preface
& Permissions' Acknowledgments

We honor all the Airborne Rangers, and all the military services who were part of Operation *Urgent Fury* including the more than 200 women, who were later declared to have not served in combat and not to have been there.

As in the previous novel, **He Didn't Say** *Good-Bye* most of the things in this story really happened, but the characters and situations are composites. Where actual names may have been used unintentionally, it has no bearing on the fictional nature of this novel.

While Part I does recant events related in **He Didn't Say** *Good-Bye*, here it is usually from the perspective of another character.

An excerpt of Chapter 1, then called "Phin" was previously published in Space Coast Writer's Guild *Literary Liftoff* Magazine, June 2006, Melbourne, Florida 32901. Under the contract, *Literary Liftoff* was granted One Time First North American Serial Rights with the condition that after their publication of the story once, all Rights returned to the author Raymond F. Flaherty.

We owe special thanks for providing photographs of Operation *Urgent Fury* to David Adams, magazine editor; MacAlan Thompson; and webmaster Chuck James. Images were combined and digitized to create a new image for the bookcover. The cover image represents not only the characters in the book shaking hands, but further symbolizes that men of different races and ethnicity are bound as brothers by common cause and shared military tradition. The cover concept was Ray's vision created for Terra Sancta Press by Suzanne Witenhafer, Arrow Design Studios, Inc. of Rockledge, Florida.

Patricia A. McDonough

Author's Preface

Should any Rangers read this and take issue with one thing or another, please keep in mind that training has changed over the years. In later years beyond the scope of this story, the Desert Phase of Ranger Training was added. What occurred in one class did not necessarily occur in another. More importantly, this book is a work of fiction.

For purposes of this story, I have taken creative license by referring to **Go for Broke** by Chester Tanaka as if it had been available to read (published) by the 1980s when, in fact, it was apparently not published until the 1990s.

I have also taken creative license concerning the date of the formation of the 75th Regiment headquarters as if it occurred around 1981. I realize it was not officially established until the year following Operation *Urgent Fury*.

Ranger Ray Flaherty
9th Ranger Infantry Company, (Abn.) circa 1951

Dedication

Ray Flaherty had not completed this Dedication or the Author's Acknowledgments page before he died on Patriot Day, September 11, 2006, two days after he completed the majority of his edits on this story. Unfortunately, he took the passwords to his edited file with him, so pages concerning the rescue mission to Grenada and subsequent chapters were perfected after his death, as closely as possible to what he said he intended it to be.

On his behalf, we dedicate this book to his family and to the men and women with whom he served.

Patricia A. McDonough

Contents

Publisher's Acknowledgments .... -v-

Publisher's Preface & Permissions' Acknowledgments .... -vi-

Author's Preface .... -vii-

Dedication .... -viii-

PART I: Background in Laos 1
    CHAPTER 1: Ban Hin Leek Fai 1
    CHAPTER 2: U.S. Embassy, Vientiane 6
    CHAPTER 3: Paksanne 10
    CHAPTER 4: U.S. Embassy, Vientiane 11
    CHAPTER 5: Ban Hin Leek Fai 15
    CHAPTER 6: U.S. Embassy 17
    CHAPTER 7: Pak Kading 19
    CHAPTER 8: Vientiane 22

PART II: Georgia, USA 25
    CHAPTER 9: The CIA Office, Atlanta 25
    CHAPTER 10: The Marietta National Cemetery 28
    CHAPTER 11: The CIA Offices, Atlanta 36
        The CIA Safehouse 36
    CHAPTER 12: Adjusting to Life in Marietta 39
        Public Education 47
        The Tutor 52
    CHAPTER 13: Doug & Casey 65
    CHAPTER 14: The Superior Court of Cobb County 70
    CHAPTER 15: The U.S. Army Volunteer 77
        The Letter from Mitzi 77
    CHAPTER 16: The Departure 86

PART III Tom's U.S. Army Training 87
   CHAPTER 17: The Swearing In 87
   CHAPTER 18: Fort Jackson, South Carolina 89
      Basic Training 89
   CHAPTER 19: Fort Benning, Georgia 94
      Officer Candidate School 94
      Change of Plan 96
      O.C.S. Senior Candidate 99
      O.C.S. Graduation 102
   CHAPTER 20: On Leave 104
   CHAPTER 21: Return to Fort Benning 106
      Jump School: Ground Week 106
      The Mock-up Door 114
      Tower Jump Training 115
      Winn Army Community Hospital 120
      Live Parachute Jump Training 121
      Jump School Graduation 124
      The Talent Scout 125
      As a 'Tag On' 126
   CHAPTER 22: Ranger History & Traditions 129
        Abrams' Charter 136
   CHAPTER 23: Ranger Training 137
      Crawl Phase 138
      Test at Victory Pond 140
      Walk Phase: Mountaineering at Camp Darby 142
      Dahlonega, Georgia 143
      Run Phase: Swamp Training near Eglin Field 153

PART IV: The Fledgling Ranger 170
   CHAPTER 24: The 75th Regiment's Selection Board 170
      Fort Stewart, Georgia 173
        On Liberty 178
   CHAPTER 25: First Sergeant Beebe's Sermon 182
   CHAPTER 26: Prepare for Operation *Urgent Fury* 193
   CHAPTER 27: On the Move 199

CHAPTER 28: Roosevelt Roads Naval Hospital 204
CHAPTER 29: Winn Army Hospital 211
CHAPTER 30: Mary Monaghan & Brian McGlynn Bath 236
CHAPTER 31: Return to Active Duty 244

PART V: Family Matters 246
    CHAPTER 32: Convergence 246
    CHAPTER 33: Differing Cultural Perspectives 249
    CHAPTER 34: Atlanta Country Club Estates, Marietta 252
    CHAPTER 35: After the Encounter 258
    CHAPTER 36: Anne's Social Call 264
    CHAPTER 37: John and Anne McGlynn Bath 269
    CHAPTER 38: Finding the Facts 273
    CHAPTER 39: Brian and Mary 276
        Meeting the Families 282
    CHAPTER 40: Planning the Monaghan-Bath Wedding 295
        The Groom's Party 300
        The Nuptials 301
        The Wedding Reception 302

Appendix 308
    A. Original wording: "A Plan of Discipline by Major Robert Roger" 308
    B. Modern modified wording of "Rogers' Rangers Standing Orders" by Major Robert Rogers, 1759 313
    C. Ranger Creed 314
    D. The Airborne Creed 315
    In Memoriam 316

References & Resources 317

About Raymond F. Flaherty 319

About Pat McDonough 320

Terra Sancta Press Catalog 321

The *Strangers Brothers* Story 322

What others say 322

PART I: Background in Laos

CHAPTER 1: Ban Hin Leek Fai

Phin concentrated on the job at hand. She was tending to the records of her village of Ban Hin Leek Fai using the system her American husband had established when times were better for their family.

Her first husband, a Lao, had left her and their son, Kumpang, to fight in a war she didn't understand. If asked why she'd been left, or which side he had gone to fight for, she'd been too busy being a wife and a mother to worry about such things.

Fending for herself in the village, Phin had waited for him but he had not come home. After a while, she'd decided he had been killed in the fighting, and wept for him. She was lonely and struggling, but was determined to make it on her own.

Then, she heard rumors that he was alive and living with another woman in Vientiane, the big city on the Mekong. She was embarrassed for all the times the people in her village had seen her grieving, grieving for a man who didn't love her. She became angry with him for causing her such embarrassment. She vowed she'd never grieve for another man, and she kept her promise for a long time, that is, until she met the American. Her American had come from and returned to a place she knew nothing about. She didn't even know his surname, yet Phin's heart ached for him. He was a special man, so gentle, so loving, and here she was, wistfully thinking of the days they'd spent together.

Hearing the laughter of children, Phin rose and looked out onto the village square, hoping to see her daughter Sirion playing happily among them. Her daughter's long, reddish-brown hair shone lustrous when the sun hit it. The child stood sadly off to the side, watching as the black-haired children played. It had not been this way before Sirion's father, the American, had left.

They'd been a happy family: the American, Kumpang, Sirion, and herself. All four were the envy of the entire village and rightly so. Her American had shown prosperity to a village which had known only depression for many years. The men had gone off to war and only a few had returned, not enough to work the harvest of teakwood or to take it to the buyers in Thailand. If her American hadn't come, the village might have been lost to the surrounding jungle. His work had brought their village and the teak trade back to life.

Phin's reverie took her back to the day she first saw him. He'd been a wreck of a man plagued by dysentery and out of his mind with fever. She smiled, remembering the stirring in her when he became aroused as she bathed him. While others washed his clothing, she shielded his condition from their view and continued to wash the filth from his body. To this day, she didn't know why she'd chosen to go on the boat to bring him to the village. He'd been one of those who had taken peace from her village by waging war, and she'd despised him for it.

Why?, she asked herself. *Why did I help this man? Why did I take him into my hut and nurse him back to health? Why did I go to his bed and allow him to caress me as he did? Why?* She whimpered softly as the familiar stirring rose inside her.

Enough of this! she commanded herself. *I can't ever think about him. He came from another place. He didn't belong here, and now he's gone. He left the children and me. He left me!* Despite her resolve not to cry, tears ran from her eyes. Angrily she brushed them away.

She looked out at her daughter, standing alone, shunned by the other children. Phin knew they had been encouraged to do so by their elders. Phin saw the American's features in her daughter's young face and she wanted to cry again.

She moaned. *I've got to get away from here. I cannot tolerate the way my daughter is treated by these people I once called friends. It's not my village anymore.* Her jaw tightened. *But how can I leave, especially with two small children?*

Phin rubbed a loose strand of hair back into place. Maybe she could get away, to go down river on the Nam Muone to the town of Pak Kading on the great Mekong River. Pak Kading was the market place where the village floated the teak so they could purchase things not available in their village. (From there the logs were taken across the Mekong to be sold in Thailand.) Phin remembered the stories about the women in the towns and cities along the river. Sometimes, these women were sold into slavery, or had to sell their bodies for food and a place to sleep. Could she bring herself to do such a thing? She didn't know, but she was becoming more determined to leave as her thoughts unwound and her resentment grew.

"Yes," she said. "I could do such a thing *if* it would take the sadness from my children."

"What did you say?" asked Sirion, who had come into the hut unnoticed.

"Nothing, daughter," Phin replied as she reached and drew her beautiful child to her. She asked Sirion to help her with the evening meal. She tried to be a good friend to her daughter, but she knew that it didn't make up for the lack of attention from the village children. Phin even noticed that Kumpang was more attentive to Sirion than other older brothers typically were to their sisters. Kumpang recognized her pain, and as a result, he'd withdrawn from youngsters his age, too.

After they'd finished eating and the children were tucked in, Phin rested on her pallet, listening to the night sounds. She tried to relax, but her thoughts kept returning to her problems. Phin had to plan her escape from this non-caring place. She discarded one idea after another. She would be stopped. Since she was the only one who knew how to keep books the way the American had taught her, the elders just wouldn't let her go.

A scary thought came to her. *Why can't I leave like my American did?* She could still see him as he slipped from their pallet in the shadows of the night. He'd thought she was asleep, but she wasn't.

That night Phin had waited until he had left the hut, and then followed him. He put his equipment into the pirogue. In the shadows, she stood barely breathing. Phin didn't want to hold him to her if he didn't want to stay. He climbed into the boat and paddled away in silence. He looked back toward the village but didn't see her. She had wanted to scream *come back*, but she remained silent. Tears had blinded her.

It was not meant to be, she had reasoned. *He never belonged here. He is an American, and he belongs with Americans.* She'd stood there in the shadows for a long time, watching, letting her silent tears dry upon her face, hoping somehow he'd change his mind; but she knew, even that night, he wouldn't.

Phin changed positions on the pallet . . . again. *He has been gone a long time. Maybe something kept him from coming back. He wasn't like other Americans. He loved me; I know he did.*

I have to get away. Even if I don't find him, even if the American does not want me anymore, I can't stay here. I have to leave, but how can I do this thing?

She could rely on Kumpang to help her paddle the boat down the Nam Muone, but how would she find Pak Kading? She had never been there. Would this river take them there directly, or were there other rivers to take? She wasn't even sure what to do when they got there or to whom she would speak.

Her heart started pounding. Would her children be in danger? The doubts she was feeling began to crash in on her. She wept tears of frustration. She was so weary. Emotional exhaustion bore down on her, and she felt like giving up. Escape seemed impossible. With sadness, she knew she must slip back into the same life and accepted the routine she'd lived before her American had arrived. She used her fingers to wipe at her eyes. She did not know her son had heard her crying.

Kumpang heard her sniffle back her tears. He stared at the ceiling, silently promising himself he'd do all he could to bring joy to his mother's life. He wanted his family to be happy again. He listened to his watch tick on the arm which was folded under his head. The Seiko watch had belonged to his mother's American husband, a man he loved and respected as a father. He missed the American. He was still angry his mother would not tell him why the American had left, or why he wasn't coming back?

Kumpang understood his mother's sadness. He promised himself he'd figure a way to make things better for her and Sirion.

CHAPTER 2: U.S. Embassy, Vientiane

Pete Martin, the CIA's Chief of Station in Laos, sat at his desk in the predawn hours, having his first cup of coffee, as he went through the messages which had come in during the night.

He was tired and a little hung-over from last night's party, but he came to work as usual. Old habits were difficult to break. One often said he accomplished more in the morning than during the rest of the day. That's why he held to his routine in good times and bad.

His method was to scan his messages, organize them by order of importance, and act on them in like manner. He saw a message from Bert Scharff, who had been his partner on past missions. Pete started to put the message on a pile to work on later, but he noticed a name on the note which piqued his curiosity. He stretched an arm out to hold the message farther away. His eyes were beginning to show his age. He squinted, blinked, and went for his reading glasses in the top drawer of his desk. He decided to read it in detail, out of sequence, breaking a long-standing practice.

This was no ordinary message. A phrase with a name underlined stood out: Sergeant Major Thomas A. Noonan, previously known as Master Sergeant Thomas A. McGlynn.

RE: Sergeant Major Thomas A. Noonan, previously known as <u>Master Sergeant Thomas A. McGlynn</u>

Pete,

Sergeant Major Thomas A. Noonan and his pal just left after staying a few days. Good people. Was glad to be of assistance. Tom had a request that surprised me somewhat. I don't know if it's an attack of regret or guilt. I'll let you be the Judge.

He left a woman and two children in a village off the beaten path, and he's concerned about them. He claims the girl is his, but the older boy is not. I have no idea of the regulations concerning citizenship of the girl, but it should be looked into.

Noonan asked me to help set up something so he can send money to the woman or bring the family to the States or both. He told me his purpose is not, I say again, not marriage, but he feels he owes this woman. In the current political climate, she could be at risk because she helped an American. If caught, all three would be sent to Lao Family Prison. Tommy claims she was almost wholly responsible for his survival. Then, of course, he feels responsibility for the daughter but also has feelings for the son. I believe him.

I don't know if you are aware that he's terminal. I brought the Agency's Doctor Crosby in to have a look and the good doctor didn't like what he found. He said your friend's on his way out. I hate to give you that news if you didn't already know it. How long has he? Crosby wouldn't even venture a guess, but he was convinced Tom didn't have the chance of the proverbial snowball.

I was impressed with both of the sergeants you sent me, and I feel we should help Tom, if possible. I really hate dumping this on you, but you're there and I'm here.

Let me know what you think.

Her name is Phin Sangsuwan. She lives in the village of Ban Hin Leek Fai on the Nam Muone (a tributary of the Mekong Northeast of Paksanne). She and the two children have a working knowledge of English, which should be a plus. I wish I could tell you more, but that's all I have.

Good luck, friend. Keep me posted on your progress and let me know if you need anything from this end.

Bert

"Oh boy!" Pete said aloud. "Life sure does get complicated." He took a swallow of his coffee before getting up from his desk to check the map of Laos pinned to the wall. He found the village by tracing his finger along the Nam Thuen river until he found the Nam Muone and the village of Ban Hin Leek Fai.

"Ah, here it is. But what do I do now that I've found it?" He muttered as he stabbed his finger at the spot on the map.

He sighed. Sergeant Major Thomas A. Noonan, a.k.a. Sergeant Major Thomas A. McGlynn was a good man, a good soldier. He'd met him a couple of months ago.

He recalled the transcribed message:

> A MISSING AMERICAN SOLDIER HAS SUDDENLY RESURFACED— WITH HIS WEAPONS, NO LESS, WHICH HE INSISTS ON KEEPING UNTIL HE PERSONALLY SURRENDERS THEM TO THE MARINE GUARDS, WHO ARE NOW ON THEIR WAY BY HELICOPTER TO PICK HIM UP.

Back then, McGlynn had stopped the USAID Jeep on Lao Highway 13 the day before. They'd given him a ride to the USAID compound at Paksanne, where he'd spent the night and was treated by their medic, Doctor Jennifer.

Pete's mind wandered for just a moment as he thought of Doctor Jennifer. She was one good-looking woman. He wondered when she'd be coming into Vientiane again. He glanced up, halfway hoping to see her walk through the door, but he had no such luck. There'll be no Doctor Jennifer this morning.

He picked up his cup and drank the rest of the coffee. He could still remember what an ass Major Dutton had been. Dutton had been the Army Intelligence Officer assigned to the U.S. Embassy at the time. Dutton had been convinced that McGlynn was a turncoat who'd had his fill of whatever he'd been doing in Laos and was turning himself in to the Embassy for a free ticket home. Major Dutton couldn't have been more wrong.

The man Dutton thought was a traitor was actually a master sergeant from the Army's elite Special Forces. McGlynn, along with another man, had parachuted into the jungles of Laos to find and rescue a downed U.S.

Air Force pilot. In the fighting, McGlynn had received a head wound which triggered amnesia, and the amnesia had caused him to remain in Laos for a number of years unable to return to friendly lines. McGlynn was gone long enough to be officially declared dead, and his wife Anne remarried. However, his buddies had not forgotten him. Later, several of them came to Vientiane to help him return to where he belonged. Their presence was instrumental in an outcome favorable to McGlynn.

But did it really help the man? Does 'all's well that ends well' ever really work out? Pete wondered. McGlynn *was given a new identity, a promotion in rank, a proper discharge, a guarantee of benefits earned, and permission from his government to live out his life in the United States.* He slowly shook his head. Unfortunately, the U.S. government couldn't do anything to restore McGlynn's health, or return the wife and family which had been lost to him.

As cynical as Pete was inclined to be, he was sincerely glad that Tommy had gained what he had. However, losing one's family was bad enough, but worse were the lost years. Who could put a value on something so irreplaceable? There was no way to get time back. Pete was determined to do his best to see *all* of Tommy's wishes bear fruit.

Except for a stint at the Lao desk at Langley, Pete had been in Asia for close to 14 years now, alternating between assignments in Taipei and Bangkok before taking over as Chief of Station in Vientiane. He thought he could handle most situations which might surface, but he had been out of Field Ops for too long. In the 1960s, he had been a field officer with General Vang Pao and the Meo people in the mountains of northern Laos around the *Plaine de Jarres*, but his knowledge of the area surrounding Ban Hin Leek Fai was sketchy at best.

Who to call for help? he wondered as he studied the map. He snapped his fingers. *Bob Salzman, that's who!* Bob was the guy Tommy had handed himself over to. But first, Pete wanted to check with the visa people in the embassy to find out how to get the Lao woman and her children to the States.

Chapter 3: Paksanne

Bob Salzman, the USAID representative for the area encompassing Ban Hin Leek Fai, was just about to sit down to breakfast when he was called to the radio. It was Pete Martin, asking when he'd be making his next trip to Vientiane.

"What's up, Pete?" he asked.

"Something I'd like to discuss with you ASAP," Pete told him.

The hairs rose on the back of Bob's neck as he remembered the last time Pete Martin had discussed something. It was to finger a suspected communist infiltrator, and it damn near got both of them killed.

"Why do I suddenly wish I hadn't answered the radio?" Bob mumbled into the microphone.

He heard Pete laugh. "Really, Bob, you have nothing to worry about. This is just about a guy you introduced me to a short while back. A fellow named Tommy."

"Aaah, yes. How's he doing?" Bob asked as he quickly went over his schedule in his mind.

"Not too good. That's what I want to talk to you about," Pete answered.

"Really? Sorry to hear that . . . You want me there as soon as possible though? Okay, I'll be in on the next chopper. Be advised: Dinner at Suzanne's is on you," Bob said, as if he was warning him of some great danger.

Pete laughed again. "Roger that. Martin, out."

Bob ate a light breakfast. He planned to be very hungry by dinner time.

CHAPTER 4: U.S. Embassy, Vientiane

At Suzanne's Restaurant, Pete Martin and Bob Salzman found a table in the corner, where they were reasonably sure they'd have some privacy. They ordered and got down to business.

Pete leaned forward and spoke softly. "Bob, you remember Tommy McGlynn, the guy you brought us a little while ago?"

"Sure. I couldn't forget that man. It isn't everyday that some bandit-looking guy jumps out in front of your Jeep on your way from town. He scared the crap out of me. I won't forget him for a long time."

"I bet not."

"You should have seen him. He was bare-chested, with blood all over him where he had been attacked by a wild dog. He didn't have any weapons. As soon as I said, 'Get in,' he told me, 'Wait a minute, I've got to get my equipment.' Can you believe it? His equipment consisted of knives and firearms. If he hadn't offered to let me hold his M-49, I would have thought he was going to shoot me or take me hostage. He was wild-looking and desperate-sounding as well."

"You did a good thing by bringing him in. You know that, don't you?"

Bob nodded. "Yeah, he's good people. It's a shame that he was missing and then declared dead. He's one of the guys who slipped through the cracks. Our government owes him a lot."

"Well," Pete said, seeing his opportunity, "Tommy needs a favor, and from where I stand, you're the one who can deliver."

"Why do I suddenly feel my appetite fading?" Bob asked and then frowned.

"Easy, guy. I'm not going to ask you to parachute into Hanoi. Hear me out, okay?" Pete asked.

"I know I'm going to regret this, but okay, shoot," Bob reached for his can of Tuborg beer.

"Are you familiar with a village called Ban Hin Leek Fai?"

"No, not off hand." Bob thought for just a moment. "Wait! Yes. That's where our friend said he was all that time!"

"Right, you remember well. Now, do you think you could come up with a reason to visit Ban Hin Leek Fai?" Pete asked.

Bob turned the can up and drank half of its contents. He squared his jaw, then answered, "Probably. Who am I to assassinate?"

Pete laughed and held his hand up. "You are something else," he said. "Calm down. All I'd like you to do is contact a lady who lives there."

"And the lady is?"

"Tommy's Lao wife."

"And what am I supposed to do when I contact Tommy's Lao wife?" Bob asked, his interest stirred.

Pete knew he had a willing partner. He could read it on Bob's face. "Simply let her know that Tommy is concerned about her and for the children's welfare."

"That's all? You're not setting me up for something, are you?" Bob asked, as his eyebrows rose.

"No, it's just like I said. Tommy is worried about her and the children. He wants to get her some funds at least, or if she will, he wants her and the children in the States."

Bob thought a moment and then answered, "I can always find a reason to visit a village, but I'll have to go through the offices of the province and the district chiefs. Then, of course, they'll want to accompany me on the visit to make sure they get a cut of whatever pie they'll suspect I'm putting in the oven."

"I wouldn't want you to try to pass them by. It wouldn't be worth it," Pete advised.

"I know. If they ever caught me going behind their backs, I'd have to close shop, and then all the work I've done so far would go down the drain." He paused. "Okay, I'll do it. I'll start the ball rolling in the morning and let you know when it's set up. Do you want to go with me?"

"I don't think so. There's no sense in letting the Lao read anything more into this. They would if I went," Pete answered.

"You're probably right. I'll figure out a way to make it look like a routine visit."

The waitress brought their food, and Pete nodded his head at Bob while she placed the food on the table. Pete waited for her to leave before he said more. He told Bob the results of his visit to the visa section at the embassy. None of it was good.

He picked up his fork. "Bob, I feel badly for Tommy. He lost just about everything doing what he felt was his duty. Now, he wants to do something good. He feels responsible for them. Some guys might have forgotten about them, but I respect Tommy for not doing that." He forked in a bite of food, chewed and swallowed, before continuing. "I took the problem to the visa section this morning, expecting to be told there would be no problems. Not so, *tamadachi*. Tommy, the poor bastard, is once again about to be stonewalled by the government he swore to defend.

"In the first place," Pete continued, "paternity must be proven. Pay close attention to this now. Legally, Tom needs a Birth Certificate of the daughter naming him as the father, or a blood test, but that wouldn't be conclusive in a court of law. There are no birth certificates in a Lao village and a blood test is out of the question."

He paused for another bite of food. "Now, an investigation could be initiated, but it could take years. Even if we prove the daughter is a U.S. citizen, it wouldn't do much good. She would have to come alone. And that would leave mom out in the cold. She isn't old enough to claim her mother is dependent on her. And the brother? According to the embassy visa people, he doesn't stand a chance to get to the States. I even tried to bring up humanitarian issues. They don't apply. Sponsorship doesn't apply. Nothing seems to apply. Ah, shit! Sometimes, I hate this job, and this is one of those times."

"Pete, aren't you putting the cart before the horse? What if she does not want to leave the village?"

"Maybe so, but I'm one of those guys who likes to be prepared. If we can't make it happen, what's the use in asking?"

"Not much, but I guess I could get some money to her and the children so we can make their lives easier," Bob said.

"Even for that, I'll be grateful." Pete lifted his fork. "This is good chow, bud."

"Yep. At Suzanne's, it always is, but I'm glad you're buying."

Pete shrugged. The food was worth it, and so was having a good friend to share it with.

CHAPTER 5: Ban Hin Leek Fai

The Province and District Chiefs were waiting with their lackeys when Bob arrived at the helipad for the flight to Ban Hin Leek Fai. He knew they would be and had briefed Charlie, his Lao driver/interpreter, before they left the USAID compound in the city. Charlie had been with him for several years now, and he trusted him implicitly. He had to, because he knew if this mission were to be successful, Charlie would be one of the major factors in making it so.

"Charlie, do you remember the American we picked up when we were coming from Pak Kading several months ago?" Bob asked.

"Of course," Charlie said.

"Well, he's in the States now, and he's requested our assistance."

"And you want me to help." It was a statement, rather than a question, and Charlie listened patiently as the request was explained.

Charlie was quiet for a while as he formulated a simple plan for his American boss. They'd have to keep everything secret. If they did not, the Province and District Chiefs would cause problems for the woman, especially, if we'd found a way for her and the children to accompany them. Nevertheless, he thought he knew how to do it, and he told Bob about his ideas.

When Charlie was through, Bob was once again reminded of how lucky he was to have such a trustworthy driver who understood the culture of the people and how to manipulate things in our favor.

To go into a village by helicopter unannounced can be dangerous because the villagers tend to cluster around the strange machine before the rotor and stabilizer blades have a chance to wind down. People have been known to walk into the spinning blades and have suffered dearly for it. It was for this reason the pilot set his machine in the center of a dry rice paddy, a short distance away from the village, hoping for the best.

Charlie looked at the villagers as they gathered around the helicopter and spotted the girl he was looking for almost immediately.

Charlie tapped Bob and pointed. "There she is, Mr. Bob. The little girl standing alone, off to the right. Do you see her?"

As he dismounted the helicopter, Bob casually glanced in the direction his driver had indicated. There was no mistaking the identification. The auburn hair and the shape of her eyes were a dead give away.

The girl stood alone. *Where's her mother? Where's the woman called Phin?* he wondered, as he walked with the Province and District Chiefs to meet the Village Headman. Glancing back toward the helicopter, he saw the villagers gathering close to the machine, except for that one little girl who watched from a distance.

Chapter 6: U.S. Embassy

Later in the afternoon, Bob Salzman knocked on the doorjamb of Pete's office in the Embassy.

Peter Martin looked up from his papers. "Hey, Bob. How did it go?"

"Better than I expected," Bob answered, coming into the office. "We had no trouble at all getting to Tommy's Lao wife. It seems she's a key player in the village. From what I gather, Tommy set up a record-keeping system for the village which helped make the teakwood trade a success. Phin assumed his responsibilities when Tommy left. Man is she pissed!"

"How so?" Pete asked.

"Well, she's pissed because she's still there and he isn't. She told Charlie she's ready to leave and doesn't have anything to take with her except her children. She wanted to get on our helicopter and come with us! Luckily, Charlie talked her out of it. He told her it would cause too many problems. She'd never be able to get to the States unless she followed his instructions."

"Which were?" Pete asked.

"To get herself and the children to Pak Kading where she'll be contacted and brought to Vientiane. So the ball is in your court, buddy. It's up to you to get her out with the two children. One more thing, before I forget— Charlie feels strongly that the Village Headman will have someone with her to make sure she returns to the village," Bob said.

"Well, we'll just take the steps necessary to counter any move he makes. I don't think it will be as difficult to get her out as I originally thought, if all three can get there on their own. The Agency has a channel for people we want to get to the States. Since you left, I got permission to slide them into that expedited channel. All I have to do is get one of my people to pick her up in . . .ah, where was it you said?"

"Pak Kading. Where I picked Tommy up," Bob answered.

"Wherever. Did you happen to get her picture?"

"Yes, as a matter of fact, I have it right here." He took a picture from his briefcase and handed it to Pete. "I had a Polaroid with me."

Looking at the picture, Pete gave out a low whistle. "I don't blame our friend for falling for this one. She's quite a looker."

"Yep, I could have gone for her myself, although she impressed me as being a bit hard-nosed," Bob said. "Let's just see what you think when you meet her."

"Hopefully, I'll get the chance in a day or two. We'll put our plan into action," Pete agreed and then smiled mischievously as he pointed to the picture. "You two would make a good-looking couple." He ducked as Bob made a mock swing at him.

CHAPTER 7: Pak Kading

Unused to her surroundings, Phin took a quick look around the restaurant in Pak Kading, wondering about the person she was supposed to meet. Suddenly she shuddered. *What if they don't find us? What if I do everything I'm supposed to, but no one shows up?* She looked at her children sitting across the table as they enjoyed their lemonades. She felt such fear. *Am I doing the right thing?*

No. I will not waiver! Phin thought. *My daughter is very beautiful and my son is so handsome. How precious! I love them with my life.* Phin knew she would risk all for them. She had to take the chance—*for them and because of them.*

A stranger approached her table and interrupted her thoughts. "Are you the woman called Phin?" the stranger asked gently.

Phin hesitated before answering. *Have I been found out? Is he the one? Or has he been sent to bring us out?* She held her breath before finally nodding her head, and waited for him to say or do something.

"Were you followed?" the stranger asked.

Looking quickly about, and praying she wouldn't recognize anybody. "I don't know," she said, softly.

Hearing a slight tremor in her voice, "Don't be afraid. It's all right," the stranger said, in a calming voice. "Everything will be just fine. Wait until your children finish their drinks. Then, go out to the road and turn to the north. It is important none of you look back. Walk casually, as if you don't care that someone might be following. Don't look afraid. You don't want to look nervous. Do you understand?"

"Yes, but what then?" The tremble was still apparent in Phin's voice.

The stranger went on in the same soft, concerned voice. "I will watch, and then I'll follow. I have an auto, a *lote,* and we will ride away from this place. Do you have possessions to carry?"

"No," Phin replied. "We brought nothing."

"Good," he said and nodded. He left her and the children and he took up a vantage point where he could sip his lemonade and watch. He'd wait until they left.

Phin's untrained eye did not detect the man in the doorway, the man from her village sent to watch her.

Charlie, driving a Peugeot, watched the village man leave the shadows of the doorway across the street in an obvious attempt to follow Phin and the children.

She turned north as instructed and did not turn to look back even when she heard a commotion behind her. She held tightly her children's hands as she was walked on determinedly.

From his vantage point, Bob also identified the villager. He sighed. *Mr. Martin was correct in his assessment. But why do they put me against non-professionals?* Casually, Bob signaled his two men who were watching him. The signal was nothing more than scratching his head and a sly point to the villager, but it put a plan in motion to protect his charges.

Pete Martin had instructed the team that no violence would be tolerated. Their mission was to guide Phin and the children through any possible hindrances from her village's people. No more, no less.

The two men Bob alerted hurried so they could catch the man following Phin. They had to move in a way which wouldn't draw attention. They each greeted the villager as they would a long-lost friend while they hemmed him in between them.

As they did this, the man's protests could be heard. "I don't know you!" he shouted. "You mistake me for another!" As he attempted to worm his way through the insistent men, Bob saw the Peugeot slow to a stop. Phin and the children leapt into the back seat. As the sedan accelerated northward, Phin could still hear him shouting, "No! No!"

Just as abruptly, the two men, who had stopped him, apologized for their mistake. They turned to walk away, leaving him staring at the cloud of dust left by the Peugeot.

Bob smiled into his lemonade. *Piece of cake!* He smiled again and finished it.

CHAPTER 8: Vientiane

Pete Martin sat across the table from Phin in the Embassy's diningroom. She and the children had just finished eating. He smiled at the little girl sitting to his left.

She stared up at him, her questioning eyes boring into him.

He smiled at her again.

Surprising him, she returned his smile, but she continued to stare. He didn't know why but her stare made him feel uncomfortable. He tried to divert his attention by looking away, but he could still feel her eyes upon him.

He looked at Phin, and spoke slowly. "I understand you and your children speak English.

"Yes," Phin replied, a hint of pride in her voice. "My American husband taught us."

"Good. It will make things much easier. Now, do you mind if I ask you a few questions?"

"No, I will answer, if I can." Phin said, gaining confidence from the reassuring tone of Pete's voice.

"Do you understand you have the choice of receiving money, *or* leaving here and bringing your children to the United States?"

"Yes."

"What do you wish?" Pete pressed.

Phin didn't hesitate. "We wish to go to the United States!"

"Why?"

She paused awhile as she composed her thoughts. She glanced at her son before answering. "My son and I were left in our village when his father went off to war. He never returned. Why? It does not matter. Then came my American husband from a place we knew nothing about, and he brought happiness to our days. He became a father to my son and our daughter, and a husband to me. I don't understand what caused him to leave us; but I believe, when he did so, he felt he must. Perhaps he had some other duty."

She hesitated for a moment, and Pete started to say something, perhaps ask another question, but she held up her hand to stop him. "Please, allow me to continue. My family and the people of my village shun my daughter because she looks different. They forget about the good her father did for them. They remember him with scorn, and tolerate me only because I carried on the work he began. Now, I will gladly take my children and leave these ungrateful people. We are ready."

Pete was momentarily astonished by her candid declaration. He paused to light a cigarette to allow himself time to re-group his thoughts. He exhaled the smoke slowly, then looked at the boy.

"And you, son. Do you want to go to the United States?"

The boy held up his hand and pointed to the wristwatch Tommy had placed beside his pallet the night he left. "Yes, I would like to thank the man I called 'father' for leaving me his watch."

Grinding his unfinished cigarette into the ashtray, Pete looked at Phin and forced a smile past his frustration. "That's all I have. Do you wish to ask me any questions?"

Phin returned the look. "Don't you wish to question my daughter as well? Does she not matter?"

Once again, Phin had surprised him. He wasn't used to such a straight-forward woman. Phin was very intriguing. Pete lit another cigarette to cover his surprise.

He turned to the young girl and asked, "And you, young lady, what do you wish?"

There was no hesitation to her bold answer. "I wish to see my father."

"That is what I'm hoping to accomplish. Our next step will be to contact the people who will make it happen." He felt better than he had in years. It was good to be responsible for making a child's eyes light up as he had just done. He looked from the mother to the son, and back to the daughter. Today, he gotten to be the hero, and that was good for him.

Part II: Georgia, USA

Chapter 9: The CIA Office, Atlanta

How do I begin? This is a part of the job I don't care for. Bert Scharff took a deep breath. In the CIA office in Atlanta, he looked across his desk at the family of three Lao and wondered. *How will they react to the news?*

"My name is Bert Scharff. I'm a friend of Pete Martin, the man you met in Vientiane. . . . Er, . . . how do you wish to be called?" he asked.

"Phin, please," she replied. "Phin Sangsuwan."

"And your children?"

"This is my son, Kumpang, and my daughter, Sirion," Phin said proudly.

"The people who work here will help you settle in. We want to get your children into school in the Atlanta area." He took another deep breath. "But first, I have bad news to tell you." He watched as Phin's pleasant expression faded.

"Sergeant Major Noonan passed away while you were being processed to come here. He's to be buried in the Marietta National Cemetery tomorrow."

Bert expected some reaction but there was nothing but puzzled looks from the three, and then it dawned on him. *They don't know who I'm talking about. They don't know Tommy's assumed name.* "I mean, your daughter's father."

"What do you mean by 'passed away'?" Phin asked.

"He expired. He passed on."

Phin gasped. "You mean my husband has died?"

"I'm sorry. Yes."

The immediate silence was awkward for him. For a few seconds, the children stared open-mouthed at their mother, and then Sirion rushed to Phin's arms. Phin held her daughter and looked up at Bert. There was a controlled expression on her face. She asked, "Will you have to send us back to our country now?"

"No, not unless you want to go,"

The boy broke in, speaking to his mother in their native language.

She nodded to him. "Yes, we'll remain where *he* wanted us to be." Phin glanced at her daughter who nodded, too. She gave Bert her answer. "We would like to stay if it will be allowed."

Bert's gaze met hers. "Good. I'll call one of our people in and get you set up in your new home. Your husband will be buried tomorrow. Would you like to attend the service?"

"Is it permitted?" Phin asked. A tear slid down her cheek as she stoked her daughter's hair.

Bert answered, as he tried to make his voice sound gentle, comforting. "Of course, . . .I'll take you myself. Now, let me get my assistant in here, and she'll help you with whatever you need. Are you ready to live in America?"

Phin hesitated just long enough for Kumpang to answer for her, "Yes, we are!" His eagerness showed in his voice.

Bert lifted the phone and pushed a button before speaking into it. "Maria, would you like to meet our new arrivals?"

He paused and then said, "Yes, they're ready."

Maria Creamer is by no means an expert in the field of handling these newcomers, but she has compassion. That makes her the perfect candidate for the job. She's thorough, too. Once she accepted an assignment, she'd throw herself into it with contagious enthusiasm.

Everyone who knows her says Maria has one hell of a personality, which can put anyone at ease. It won't be long before Phin and the children trust and love her. Then, Bert reined in his enthusiasm for her.

When Maria Creamer learned of this assignment, she'd done her homework. She'd become familiar with the problems the newcomers might face, and then she studied methods which would help them adapt to their new surroundings.

Soon, Maria arranged for Phin and the children to have a modest, furnished house in Marietta, near the Agency's Marietta Towers. The Agency had arranged for Phin to have on-the-job training as a housekeeper there.

Maria furnished the house, and provided it with the basics: linens, towels, and necessary toiletries. At the supermarket, she did her best to buy food the family would like.

CHAPTER 10: The Marietta National Cemetery

Bert wondered if he had done the right thing when he asked Phin if she wanted to go to Tommy's funeral. *Tommy's second official funeral, that is*, he corrected himself. *Am I creating a problem that need not be created? How am I going to handle this?* he sighed. *It would have been simpler if Phin and the children had arrived after the funeral, but they're here now, and I figured they should at least see the guy into the ground.* It was also his hope that Tommy's American family wouldn't resent it too strongly, or better yet, wouldn't notice.

Maria was waiting outside her Atlanta apartment building when he pulled to the curb. He noticed her shapely leg as she got into his car. For a brief moment, he wished he wasn't her supervisor. She was a nice woman: pretty, intelligent, a great sense of humor; and he knew he'd like their relationship to be more personal. *If it weren't for those darn regulations that said this was a no, no. . . . Supervisors aren't allowed to fraternize.*

Bert spotted flashing lights in his rearview mirror as an ambulance sped along the express lane of I-285. Maria pointed to flashing blue lights ahead and cautioned Bert to slow down. "It looks like an accident, boss. We're going to be late."

"The traffic always backs up when there's an accident," he replied. "Too many are morbidly curious, huh?" He eased on the brake pedal, coming to a stop.

He turned on the car radio. "We might as well have some music to entertain us while we wait." He inwardly admired her silhouette. *Yes, I have a lovely woman sitting to my right.*

"I don't know why people always want to see if they can spot something gross," he said. "The worse the wreck is, the better they seem to like it." There were more flashing lights ahead.

She smiled when she relaxed into the seat, making herself comfortable for the wait in traffic. "It looks as if we may be here a while," Maria said, as she positioned herself on the seat to face him.

"Do you mind if I smoke?" she asked.

"Not at all." He took his own cigarettes from his pocket and pushed in the cigarette lighter. "Let me roll down the window."

They made small talk, aware of their closeness, each becoming more self-conscious, as the medics carted away the injured, and the police finally allowed traffic to resume.

"I hope we're not too late for the service," Bert said.

"That would be a shame," Maria nodded. "I honestly feel Phin really loved him, and the children seem to worship the ground he walked on."

"I got the same feeling. He must have been one hell of a guy from the input I have on him," Bert said.

"I sort of dread picking her up. I never really know what to say in situations like this." Maria inhaled her cigarette. "Women are supposed to have a magic power which lets them sympathize with other women, but I don't have it."

Bert looked over at her and saw that her skirt had shifted up higher. She had it all right, but sympathy wasn't what he had in mind. He ground his cigarette into the ash try and rolled up his window. *I can't let myself think like that. It isn't professional.* Bert gripped the steering wheel harder and kept his eyes on the road. *Maria's off limits.*

Phin stood in front of the modest home, tightly holding her children by the hand. She felt anxious as she waited for the American lady. She didn't know what she would do if she and her children were left alone to fend for themselves in this strange place. Phin had never been so afraid, at least not since the morning when her American had left her.

Kumpang, noticing his mother's anxiety, gently squeezed her hand to reassure her. "Don't worry, mother. Everything will be fine. Miss Creamer said she'd be here, and she will."

Phin smiled at her son and gently squeezed his hand in return. "Yes, I know I need patience." Her words sounded positive, but she continued to look anxiously at every approaching car. Not surprisingly, the occupants of the passing vehicles stared at the oddly dressed trio standing on the sidewalk.

All three were relieved when Bert finally pulled to the curb, and they recognized Maria sitting in the passenger's seat.

Maria got out of the car and apologized. She gave Phin a quick hug.

Phin stood stiffly. She was not used to this forward American custom of greeting. She brought her hands together and bowed in greeting.

"I'm sorry we are late. It was the freeway, the traffic. What a mess! We couldn't help the delay." Maria ushered them into the backseat of the Buick.

Bert turned around in his seat to look at Phin and the children. "We couldn't help it." He reaffirmed what Maria had just told them. Maria climbed in and shut the door.

"Is everybody ready?" Not waiting for an answer, Bert checked his rearview mirror and pulled away from the curb. "I hope everyone slept well. Are you all getting settled in? Have you had anything to eat this morning?"

"No." Phin answered, "We were too excited about this morning. It is a much more important thing we do. Is it not?"

Bert and Maria exchanged glances and Maria said. "It's also important to eat." She smiled at Phin and added, "I'll treat you to a good southern breakfast after the ceremony."

Phin and the children failed to understand the gesture, but Phin thanked her and did her best to relax while they rode to the cemetery. She wasn't used to seeing cars, or riding in them, for that matter. Phin had spent most of her time in her village, buried deep in the jungles of Laos. This was an entirely new world. The children loved the ride. For them, it was a great adventure, but to her, it didn't feel very safe.

Although there were no cemeteries in her village, Phin knew when they entered the cemetery grounds. She saw the cars that lined the narrow tree-lined drive which encircled the graves, and her heart began to pound. Somehow, she knew these cars belonged to those who had come to say good-bye to her husband. There were so many of them. These people had all known him, had loved him. They were part of his world, a world which she didn't know anything about. She wanted to yell out to the man who had brought her to this place, "Don't stop! Please don't stop! Go on! Please go on!" but she maintained her silence.

Bert continued along the lane, not because he sensed Phin's panic, but because he was looking for a place to park. He finally pulled to the side in front of the first car in line, leaving enough room for it to pull around him after the service. He shut off the engine and turned toward Phin and the children, intending to tell them they'd arrived, but he recognized the fear on Phin's face. *Damn! Looks like I screwed this one up*, he thought.

Maria saw Phin's fear and calmly pointed to a nearby rise. She suggested they watch the service from there.

By Western standards, Phin would not be considered an adherent of any particular religion, yet she believed strongly in *Phi* and *Kwan*. Her culture taught her the *Phi* spirits inhabited the universe and were present in the elements such as earth, heaven, fire, and water. She believed these spirits held great power over the destinies of men. On the other hand, the spirits called *Kwan* watched over her and her children. As a child, she'd been told all human beings are the union of 32 organs that the *Kwan* watch over, and constitute the spirit that activates the attributes of a person. Twenty of the *Kwan* are inherited from the father and 12 from the mother. At death, these specifically inherited *Kwan* fly from the body of the deceased to unite with other *Kwan*. Some eventually will reincarnate into other living people.

While Phin watched the ceremony being conducted, she willed the *Kwan* of her good husband to be spirited into Kumpang, so he would have the heart of a warrior, and she willed other *Kwan* into Sirion, so she would have her father's compassion.

Phin stood with her children. Without being able to understand the symbolism of the military service, Phin was confused by the actions of the soldiers while they carried out their rituals. When she realized the people gathered at the coffin were crying, she wondered why. This wasn't right. People were supposed to show the *Kwan* that they understood the departed's good fortune to be liberated from this life. Don't these sad people know they are supposed to linger, be patient, and joyful of heart, awaiting their own turn to die.

She jumped violently at the sound of the rifles firing in salute. She hadn't expected that. Then, she heard a sound which saddened her more than anything else she'd ever experienced. The bugler was blowing *Taps*, and to Phin, it sounded as if the instrument were crying. She somehow understood its intent: a last tribute, a finality.

When the people surrounding the coffin were leaving, Phin became alarmed. *They cannot go! They must wait until the coffin is opened for the final washing. His body has to be exposed to the open sky. Then, it must be cremated to placate the Phi!*

Phin tucked her arms around her children. These people were disrespecting her beloved husband. They were deserting him. How fast they would soon forget him. It was too quick, too final. Did they not celebrate his passing?

She didn't know they would gather again at the home of Anne McGlynn Bath, her husband's American wife, for food, drink, conversation, and to offer their condolences to the family.

This was all so different from the festivities she knew. *Where were the wrestling matches, buffalo fights, the music, and the dancing? . . . Americans do things so differently. It is a unique place, but is now a place we have entered into. The children and I were now a part of it, and we will adapt. We will find a way to become one with these people. . . . But I'd never intentionally offend the Phi and Kwan!*

Phin's thoughts were interrupted by the approach of two Asians. She saw a man dressed in a military uniform like the ones who had conducted the ceremony, and a woman dressed in the clothes of these Americans, her waist-length, jet-black hair worn in the fashion of the Vietnamese.

The man was the first to speak. "Hello, Mr. Scharff. It's good to see you again." He extended his right hand to him.

"Same here, Sergeant Major Mitzamuri. I wish it were under better circumstances, though. Is this lovely lady your wife?" Bert reached to shake hands with Mai Lin. Then, he introduced Maria Creamer, and she made the introductions of Phin and the children.

Phin was surprised when he put his hands together respectfully, nodded, and addressed them in their native tongue. *"Sabadee,"* he said. "Please, call me Mitzi."

Phin and the children placed their hands together in a like manner, raised them to their foreheads, and bowed. "Hello," they said in unison.

Sergeant Major Mitzamuri smiled warmly. "Hello, Phin. Tommy told me you spoke our language. Welcome to our country." Then, he shocked her by giving her an affectionate hug. "This is my wife, Mai Lin. She's from South Vietnam."

Mai Lin also grabbed her, and gave her the same big affectionate hug. Phin unintentionally took a step backward.

Mitzi turned to Kumpang and extended his hand. "You must be Kumpang. Tommy spoke well of you. . . . And you, young lady, must be Sirion. You certainly are pretty." He extended his hand to her. "Your father told me you were beautiful." He gave her a wink.

Sirion shyly bowed her head and accepted Mitzi's hand. "Thank you."

Mitzi turned back toward Phin. "I want to apologize for leaving so soon, but we have much to do before this day is over. Could I meet with you sometime tomorrow? I'd like to talk to you, if it is all right. I think I can answer some of the questions you might have about Tommy."

Phin looked questioningly toward Bert and Maria before answering. They each nodded their approval.

Phin smiled and said, "Yes, Mitzi, we'd like to see you tomorrow." Phin respectfully bowed her head.

Maria stepped forward and handed a business card to Mitzi. "This card has a number where I can be reached. Why don't you give me a call later today, and we'll arrange for a meeting sometime tomorrow." Maria didn't want to tell him that she had questions of her own and was looking forward to some answers.

Phin watched as Mitzi and Mai Lin walked away. She waved when Mitzi's car drove past, and patiently waited until almost everyone else left. She had her own good-byes to give. She went to where the coffin still rested on its catafalque as the workers made ready to lower it into the ground.

Bert motioned to the workers. "Please, wait a few minutes."

Phin and the children stepped closer to the grave site. The children stood on each side of their mother and they held hands. There was no outward display of sorrow, just three family members standing silently, all making promises to the man being laid to rest.

Phin looked at the strange coffin, steely-gray. Americans were an odd lot, with a mysterious culture. The man she had shared her bed with, had borne a child with, was from this alien world. It was part of him, her wonderful American, a man she remembered as generous loving —and living. It was hard for her to accept that he's dead. Phin was glad she'd made the vow to raise her children in this country, in the ways of his people. He would look down and be proud.

Her son, Kumpang, was making his own vow. He was almost a teenager, wise beyond his years, who was observant of his surroundings. He remembered during the service the soldiers who had carried out the ritual had given a boy about his age a folded American flag. Kumpang had correctly identified the boy as his father's other son, his true son, and perhaps the two girls standing beside that boy belonged to his father as well. These things had been easy to see. Things became clearer to him. That hadn't been difficult to decide: the older of the two girls had hair just like Sirion's. Yes, he was sure they were his father's children. He'd whispered as much to Sirion. He still wasn't certain who the other woman was. He had an idea, but he didn't want to think it. His father must have had an entire other family. As he thought about the other boy, Kumpang decided that he wanted to become like the other boy, only better. He would be *the best son.*

As Sirion stood by the grave, she made more of a wish than a vow to her father. Kumpang's whispered words had made her stare at the girls. She noticed the colorful bow in the youngest girl's hair and absently reached to touch her own hair which was unadorned and hung loosely to her shoulders. She noticed the older girl's elaborately braided hair. *I wish I looked as pretty. I must fix my hair like that*, she thought, *and wear nice American clothes.* Without conscious awareness, Sirion reached up again and touched her hair.

CHAPTER 11: The CIA Offices, Atlanta

On the telephone with Sergeant Major Mitzamuri, Maria gave him the address of the safehouse in Atlanta.

When she started to give him directions, Mitzi interrupted her. "I believe I know the building. Tommy and I were there at The Atlanta Towers as guests of The Agency, and spent a few days in Room 712. Just tell me what unit to go to and what time you would like me to be there."

"Would 9:00 a.m. be too early?" Maria asked.

"Not at all," Mitzi replied. "My wife would like to come, too, if it's all right."

"I'm sure she'll be more than welcome," Maria said. "Go to Room 712. We'll use that one, since you already know where it is, and it's not being used at the moment."

"Sounds good. We'll see you then," Mitzi replied and hung up.

THE CIA SAFEHOUSE, ATLANTA TOWERS

Mitzi could smell the coffee brewing as he entered Room 712. For a moment, he remembered a morning just a short while ago when he and Tommy were in this very room discussing Tommy's health. The thought saddened him, and he forced himself to not think about it. Losing his best friend was hard to take. He took Mai Lin's hand, glad she was with him.

Soon Tommy's Lao family arrived. The woman surprised him when she skipped the traditional Laotian greetings.

"Good morning, Mitzi," Phin said.

He had detected a slight pause between good morning and his name. *Is she self-conscious about the newness of the greeting or embarrassed by the familiarity of using my first name? In either case, I'd better put her at ease.*

Mitzi answered her greeting with the gusto of an old friend. "Good morning to you!" He stepped forward to hug Phin, but when she pulled back he shook hands with Kumpang and Sirion instead.

"And good morning to you, too," he said to Maria. "Is that coffee I smell?" he asked, and then smiled at Sirion.

Sirion shyly shrugged her shoulders while glancing in the direction of her mother for reassurance.

Maria went into the kitchen and put two mugs of steaming coffee on the counter for Mitzi and Mai Lin. "Do you use cream and sugar?"

She was the perfect hostess, just as Bert knew she would be. She fixed their coffee and brought it to the living room.

Mitzi was pleased with Maria and how she conducted their discussion. She knew the right questions to get the conversation going. He was also glad Mai Lin was with him, because she allayed some of their fears.

Mai Lin told them stories of her own experiences adjusting to her surroundings, to America and the people. Some of her examples were humorous, and he was glad to see that Phin and Kumpang had the capacity to laugh with her.

Maria outlined the plan she had in mind for Phin and the children. Maria's plan was for Phin to work for The Agency as a maid taking care of the apartments, similar to the one they were in, but at the Marietta Towers. There's an opening. This would give them an income. Maria would oversee their finances until Phin could assume the responsibilities on her own. Maria would teach Phin necessary skills such as how to use household appliances and purchase American clothing and groceries.

"Of course, we will need to enroll the children in school," Maria said.

Mitzi knew the family had a working knowledge of English. With no formal education, he realized Kumpang and Sirion would need help catching up to their age groups in school.

"Maria, if I may," he interrupted, as he turned toward Phin, "Tommy took out a life insurance policy when he got back to the States." Mitzi revealed the startling news. "I have the policy at home. If I'd known you were here, I would have brought it with me," he apologized. "Phin, you are the beneficiary. You're, by no means, a rich lady, but I think there will be more than enough money to help you get started and for you to hire a tutor for the children. They have so much to learn just to catch up."

He turned toward Maria. "I doubt very much that Phin understood everything I've said, but I know you'll have more time to explain it later. Mai Lin and I are leaving to go home tomorrow. The policy is for $25,000, if I'm correct. Considering that the average yearly income here is slightly less than $10,000, that's two years' maintenance. Please don't let her squander it. The policy should help them get started, and I hope you'll push for the tutor I suggested. I'll send the insurance policy by registered mail as soon as I get home. All I need is your address."

Maria nodded. "What you've just told us is wonderful news! You be sure we'll follow your suggestion. Do you have the business card I gave you yesterday? I'll just write my personal address on the back of it."

Mitzi gave her the card and watched her write on it in small, perfect letters. He could go back home knowing that Tommy's family would be all right because they are in such capable hands.

Mitzi could now concentrate on the healing from grieving for his much-loved friend. He would never forget his silly laughter or his quirky sense of humor. Tommy was a once-in-a-lifetime kind of friend.

CHAPTER 12: Adjusting to Life in Marietta

Initially, Phin and the children were shy and reserved. If it hadn't been for Maria Creamer, Phin and Sirion could have become two recluses, staying locked behind the doors of their house. But the same wasn't true of Kumpang.

He loved to explore his new world, taking long walks. Much to Phin's chagrin, he would venture farther away from their home with each successive walk, taking note of all he came upon.

Each outing became like an expedition. He noticed the hardness of the sidewalks and the paved streets, so unlike the dirt paths and trails of his village. Here vehicles traveled at speeds which seemed reckless and haphazard. He marveled at the many styles of housing: different sizes, materials, shapes, and colors. He also was fascinated by the number of shops and the variety of goods. He wanted to enter one of the stores to learn more about it, but hesitated, afraid he'd be unwelcome. He didn't understand their exchange system yet. Not barter.

As he wandered, he looked for something else, too. He hoped somehow to find the other family, to see how they lived. That way he might help his smaller family, and himself, become a part of this new world.

One day, he walked beside a high stone wall. When he found an open gate, he went inside to an expanse of green, a park. Large shade trees made it feel cooler, and the lawn sloped downhill to a pond. He felt overjoyed. He reveled in the freshness of the landscape, and he took off his shoes and enjoyed walking on soft grass among the trees. Of course, the trees here weren't as tall as the teak trees in Laos, but they were trees. He put his hand on the biggest tree to feel its strength. He had found old friends.

I must bring mother and Sirion to this place. They will like it here.

Thirsty and tired from walking, he'd have to suffer his thirst until he could get home. He didn't realize that the strange stone and metal box surrounded by a rock garden was a water fountain.

A few days later as he strolled along a pathway, he saw a man bend over a shiny pipe to drink water. He watched, trying not to be too obvious. When the man left the fountain, Kumpang bent over the fountain just as the man had done, but no water came up from the shiny pipe. He glanced about quickly, fearing he'd be in trouble for having broken this well. However, nobody seemed to notice him. He bent over again. Still no water and he was very thirsty. Wondering what he was doing wrong, he decided to do the smart thing. He went to a bench nearby so he could wait until someone else came along to drink from the well. He would learn how to do this wondrous thing.

Soon another man approached the fountain. Kumpang watched closely as the man bent forward and was amazed as the water once again flowed from the shiny pipe allowing the man to drink his fill.

Kumpang waited until the man was out of sight before he approached the fountain again. He expected the water to gush forth, but still it failed him. He went back to the bench to think about it some more.

Had these men emptied out the water? Maybe the well had not filled up by my turn.

I'll just wait here until it fills back up, and then I will have my share of the water. While he waited, a woman approached the fountain with a child. He watched as the woman steadied the child. This time he noticed that she reached for a shiny handle on the side of the fountain and turned it. Water squirted the child. After the child had his fill, the woman bent, turned the handle again, and drank.

When they left the fountain, Kumpang bent over it and turned the handle. Water bubbled up toward him. It startled him when it spurted from the pipe squirting him from nose to chin. When he jumped back, the water stopped. After drawing his sleeved arm across his face to wipe off the water, he approached the fountain and gingerly turned the handle, adjusting the water's flow to a level where he could drink comfortably. He was pleased with himself for having conquered his new discovery and quenching his thirst. Now when he came to the park, he could stay longer. *This automatic water-well is a good thing!* He resumed his commune with nature but was eager to tell his mother and sister of today's adventure.

When he got home, his mother and Sirion were not there. His mother wouldn't leave his sister alone, so she'd taken Sirion to work with her.

Kumpang plopped onto the sofa to watch *The Brady Bunch*. He didn't quite understand the storyline, yet felt he benefitted from the lessons learned while watching. He noticed how the people were dressed, and how they used the appliances, strange to his family. Even Alice, the family housekeeper, was of interest to him as she performed mundane chores. He liked the way the Brady home was furnished and wanted his small house to look the same. He wanted to dress like Greg, who wore bell-bottoms and button-up shirts, and for Sirion to dress like Greg's younger sister, Cindy. Cindy was a cute little blonde-haired girl missing two front teeth who usually wore jumpers. Carol, the mother on the program, was Kumpang's idea of a typical American mother, and he wanted his own mother to have the same clothes and hairstyle. As the show's characters sang a song called "Time to Change," Kumpang listened attentively to the words to understand the song's meaning and how it applied to his own life. However, the Brady family's vocabulary was sometimes unintelligible to him. *What does "groovy" mean?*

He went into the kitchen. The appliances were new to him. Nevertheless, he was going through a ritual which was being echoed in houses throughout America: he was a teenager checking the fridge to see what there was to snack on. After he ate, he plopped down in front of the television, but turned the set off. He was half-asleep when he heard the door open. He looked up to see the happy faces of his mother and Sirion when she bounced into the room.

Sirion is very happy since we left Laos. She seems to have left her sadness behind.

"Hi, sis. Hello, mom. How was your day?" he asked in English. They'd agreed they would speak in the tongue of their adopted country as much as they could, because they thought it was the right thing to do.

"Can I help carry anything?" he asked.

Phin continued on toward the kitchen. "No, we got it." She put the bag down on the countertop before turning back to Kumpang. "I met a very nice lady today who helped me learn some of the new ways. Her skin was like ours, but she was from a place called Panama." Phin put groceries away as she spoke.

"Panama! That has a rhythmic sound." Sirion said. She walked to the TV and turned it on. She rotated the dial to see what was on each of the four channels. When she heard *The Beverly Hillbillies* theme song playing, she left the channel selector on that station, but the static hiss was so bad, at first she couldn't tell if the show was coming on or going off until she made out the word "Good-bye" in the song.

"Hey, Sirion. What does 'groovy' mean?"

"Neat," she replied. She noticed the blank look on her brother's face. "Uh, good. It means 'good.' Where'd you hear it?"

"In a song from *The Brady Bunch*."

"Why do you like that show? I learn a lot from *The Beverly Hillbillies*."

"What do you mean? They all talk funny. Besides, I like the girls on *The Brady Bunch* better."

"Yeah, right. But the Hillbillies are immigrants, like us, except they ended up in California, not Georgia. Have you noticed they have a Maria-type, a helper to interpret, just like we have."

"But they speak some foreign language."

"That's just it," she said. "English as a second language, like us." She went to the TV and turned the dial behind the tuner to make the black-and-white picture come in clearer. Then, she turned another knob to adjust the volume."

"It's still not right. Wiggle the rabbit ears."

She did. "I like *The Walton's* too."

"That's good," he said. "My favorite Walton is Elizabeth."

By the time they got the image adjusted, the CBS News Eye appeared followed by Walter Cronkite, who was adjusting his big, black glasses.

Phin called, "Dinner's ready."

Tom got up to turn off the set, when Phin said, "Leave alone. I want to know what happening in the *big* world." So they gathered at the kitchen table in a way to view the 13-inch TV screen in the living room, a typical American family.

Phin continued her tales of the day as she served the meal of rice and strips of seasoned beef, with green peppers, broccoli, and carrots. "You two should see the amazing machines the American women use. My new Panamanian friend taught us to use several today. These machines do some work." She used pantomime to show the motion, and described the use of a vacuum cleaner and its noise.

Kumpang listened, enraptured by such stories.

Soon they were cleaning up the dishes when the phone rang. "Hello," Kumpang said, when he placed the phone handset to his ear. (Maria had taught them how to use a telephone.)

"Hello, Kumpang. This is Maria Creamer. May I speak with your mother, please?"

He handed the phone to Phin and said, "It's Maria, mom."

She hesitated, because she was not yet comfortable using the phone. Phin spoke into the mouthpiece. "This is Phin."

"Hello, Phin, this is Maria. I've been getting some good reports from Esmerelda about your work."

"Yes, Esmerelda has been very . . . er . . . how do you say? Helpful to me. I am very happy."

"I'm glad, Phin. How are Kumpang and Sirion getting along?"

"They are very fine, thank you," Phin answered, warming up to the telephone.

"That's good. The reason I'm calling is because I received a letter from Sergeant Major Mitzamuri today. You remember him, don't you? He lives in Hawaii. Well, he sent the information on the insurance policy he told you about. I'd like to talk to you about it and a few other things tomorrow."

"Do I come to you?" Phin asked.

Maria chuckled. "No, Phin, I'll see you at work. I will come to the Marietta Towers. I'll see you in the morning. Bye, bye."

Phin, again, hesitantly spoke into the phone. "Bye . . . er, bye," but she was speaking into a dead receiver. Maria had already hung up.

The next morning, Phin took Sirion to work with her as usual.

Her mother had the vacuum cleaner going back and forth across the carpet. Sirion suffered the noise of it as she tried to watch television.

Neither of them heard the door open until Maria shouted above the racket, "Good morning."

Phin shut off the machine, pulled it to a coat closet by the door, and put it away.

"Sorry that I didn't hear you knock. I was working," she said. "Good morning to you, too." She gave a little bow to Maria.

"That's okay. I came on in because I knew you couldn't hear me. I used my Agency key." She held up a key ring with several keys on it. Then, Maria noticed Sirion. She walked over and squatted beside her.

"Sirion," she said to the smiling child, "What a nice surprise to find you here." Maria smiled at her as she lightly ran her hand over the child's auburn hair. "You look pretty this morning, honey."

"Thank you, honey," Sirion answered shyly.

Maria looked surprised. "You're welcome, dear." Maria stood and went into the kitchen. "Is there any more coffee?"

"Let me get a cup for you," Phin answered. She was embarrassed and somewhat afraid she'd be in trouble for having made coffee for herself while she was on the job and supposed to be working.

"I know where they are, honey. I'll get it. Why don't you sit at the dinette table. I'll get the papers I told you about, and we can look over them." She saw a cup of coffee on the counter. "Is this your coffee? I'll pour you a warm cup. Sit and rest. You are probably due for a break anyway."

Phin looked at Maria anxiously. "Is it all right if I drink coffee when I am working? I was afraid that I would get in trouble for it. I had it sitting over there so I could just take a sip now and then. I never had coffee until we moved, but I really do like it."

"Of course, it's all right, Phin." Maria grinned at her. "And I know what it means to be hooked on coffee." She reached to give Phin's hand a reassuring squeeze.

Maria placed the insurance papers on the table. She took a sip of coffee, and then she began to explain what the papers said. These papers were full of legal terms, so Maria took her time going through the papers line-by-line. When she finished reading them, she asked Phin if she understood.

"I do," Phin said, nodding.

"No questions?"

Phin shook her head no.

Maria slid the papers across the table to Phin as she uncapped her pen and pointed to a lined signature block.

"Just sign here."

There was a sudden embarrassed silence. "But, Maria, I don't know how to do this thing in American."

"Oh, you poor thing, whatever was I thinking? We need to do something about this. Would you like me to arrange it so that I can sign the papers for you?" Maria asked.

"Yes, please. There's so much I still have to learn." Phin blushed.

"It's all right, hon', I'll see to it. Now there's one more thing we have to talk about."

"What is that?"

"We have to enroll Kumpang and Sirion in school. I made an appointment with the school's Guidance Counselor for ten o'clock tomorrow morning," Maria answered.

"School? But school is for wealthy people."

"No, not in the United States. In fact, here it's the law. Children under sixteen must attend," Maria told her.

"Oh, we don't want to break the law. We must, how did you say, enroll?"

"I'll be there to help you."

"Thank you so much for being good to us," Phin said.

"It's my job. I am supposed to look out for you."

Phin shook her head no. "You are not giving yourself enough credit. You have been a good friend to me."

"Thanks, I want to be a good friend to you." Maria gave Phin a hug. She could tell by Phin's stiff demeanor that hugging wasn't customary for her, but Phin appeared to like it.

"Yes, I could use a friend here in the United States."

"Something tells me I'm not your only friend. Sergeant Major Mitzamuri and his wife Mai Lin want to be sure you are taken care of, too. You're a likeable person, Phin."

Phin bowed. "Thank you for saying so."

"It never hurts to say the truth. Now . . . I will pick you all up in the morning, and we'll get things going so you all don't have to worry yourselves about breaking the law."

Phin bowed again, and watched Maria leave. She got out the vacuum and continued her household duties. This time, however, she had a spring in her step. She loved America: a land of freedoms, good friends, and even education for her children.

PUBLIC EDUCATION

Early the following morning, Phin had the two children out of bed, bathed, fed, and dressed in their best clothes, to be ready for this important day. They would be presented at school for admittance. This was beyond anything that she could ever have imagined, but doubts formed in her head. *What if my children are not med worthy?*

"Mother, I'm going to take a walk," Kumpang said. "Do you want to come, Sirion?"

"No, you can't go," Phin said firmly. "You must wait for Miss Creamer. We can't be late. This is too important."

Kumpang shrugged. "Okay." He and Sirion went back to watching *The Brady Bunch*, trying to make sense of what was on the screen.

The doorbell rang.

"I'll get it," Kumpang said. He started for the door, glad for the diversion. The TV program was boring. "It's probably Maria."

"Kumpang!" his mother admonished. "It's disrespectful to call her by her first name. We must call her Miss Creamer. It is only right."

Kumpang nodded yes, but when he opened the door, he blurted, "Good morning, Maria." He didn't have to look at his mother to know that she would have an angry look on her face.

"Good morning." Maria smiled at him as she stepped inside. "Hi, Phin."

"*Sabadee*, good morning," Phin bowed, but wondered what the smiles meant and if she was supposed to smile back.

Maria nodded to Sirion. "My, don't you look pretty this morning, Sirion."

Sirion pondered whether this was a question.

"Would you like some coffee?" Phin asked Maria.

Glancing at her watch, Maria replied, "We don't have time this morning, Phin. Our appointment's at eight, and we don't want to be late."

"No, we don't want that," Phin agreed.

They hurried to Maria's car. Phin and the children swayed as Maria maneuvered through traffic. Maria's evasive moves made Phin think that she would never be able to drive a car herself. She finally gave up watching the road and closed her eyes to relieve stress.

At the school, they waited only a few minutes before the Guidance Counselor could see them. He opened his office door and ushered them inside. He stuck out his hand. "Mr. Currier," he said, giving everyone a quick, firm handshake.

"My name is Maria Creamer," Maria began. "We spoke on the phone the other day. This is Phin Sangsuwan, her son, Kumpang, and her daughter, Sirion. We are here to enroll the children in school."

Mr. Currier smiled. "I have already put together the necessary papers, but first, tell me about yourselves. The more I know, the more it will help with my recommendations."

With Maria's help, Phin told Mr. Currier essentially what she'd told Pete Martin and Bert Scharff. The children could understand basic spoken English, but neither one could read or write English. Maria had seen to it they got the inoculations required for school.

The counselor wasn't surprised. Maria had already told him as much on the phone. Normally, he would have suggested they take a placement test, but a written test was out of the question.

Mr. Currier made a decision based on the children's apparent determination to learn. Since Sirion was younger, she could start in the first grade in the elementary school, with children closer to her age. She'd have to do some catching up, but he was convinced that she could do it. He would place Kumpang in Middle School, not first grade, but not high school either.

Mr. Currier carefully explained the inner workings of the school system, stressing the normal method of promotion from grade to grade. He ended by apologizing to Kumpang for starting him with children who would be younger than he was. "But," the counselor told him, "we will make an exception for you. You can advance at your own speed, and I have no doubt that you'll be with your own age group in no time at all. Your progress will be entirely up to you." He met Kumpang's eyes. "Do you understand what I'm saying?"

"Yes, sir, I do. Maria, ah . . . , I mean Miss Creamer, has arranged a tutor for us and I intend to make the most of it," Kumpang replied.

Mr. Currier smiled. "I wish you luck, both of you. I'll be checking on your progress, but if you ever feel the need to speak with me concerning school, my door is always open to students."

Kumpang glanced at the closed door and then gave Mr. Currier a questioning look.

Mr. Currier nodded. "That's what we call a 'figure of speech,' Kumpang. It means, I'll be available if you need my assistance, even if the door is closed."

"A figure of speech. I have so much to learn," Kumpang said. However, Kumpang knew that he would learn it, because he had ambitions of his own. He would apply himself to schoolwork with diligence, and he'd insist his mother and sister learn right along with him. They would all excel. The faster they progressed, the more

American they'd be, and then they'd fit in better. They could also help each other learn American history to prepare to become U.S. Citizens.

After the meeting Kumpang went to class, anxious to get started. When he entered the classroom at the Middle School, he heard the teacher stop the lesson.

"Class, may I have your attention please." The teacher was standing in the front of the room. "We have a new student joining us today. His name is Kumpang Sangsuwan. He and his family came from a land that is halfway around the world, the country of Laos. I want everyone to welcome him," she said as she began clapping her hands.

Why is she clapping? Kumpang wondered, embarrassed by the sudden attention. *Why did she have to make an issue out of me being different?*

"Would you like to tell the class a little something about your country, Kumpang?" the teacher continued.

"That is not my country!" Kumpang exploded unexpectedly. "This is my country."

Embarrassed and shamed by his outburst, Kumpang put his hands together prayer-like and bowed toward the teacher. "I apologize for showing anger. I don't know why I did that. I am sorry."

"That's all right, Kumpang. I suppose there are things you want to forget."

"No, Miss. I do not want to forget, but my mother, sister, and I have begun a new life here. We want to be Americans like you," He made a sweeping gesture to encompass the students in the classroom. "We want to be the same, not different."

"I'm sure you and your family will adapt nicely. Our country is known as the melting pot. Different nationalities from all parts of the world and diverse cultures come here and become Americans. People of many origins contribute to make our country." She looked at him earnestly. "As you learn from us, we should also learn from you. You have lived where most of us in this room will only read about. . . .That is, if you don't allow us to share your experiences."

Kumpang looked at the floor but answered in a soft voice, "Yes, Miss."

"Now, call me Miss Minton, and please take that empty seat over there. I'll get your books for you, and we can get back to our lessons."

Kumpang went to his seat. He was unsure whether he was supposed to take the seat somewhere or sit in it. He sat down and flipped open the spiral notebook that Maria had bought him, although he didn't know how or what to write. He listened to Miss Minton, drinking in every word, and praying that he'd remember it all.

After giving more thought to her exchange with Kumpang, she could see that for some reason it had upset him.

Miss Minton determined her best approach would be to talk to him one-on-one. When the class was over she asked him to remain.

He said, "I can't."

Seeing how flustered he was, she was sorry she'd asked. "Is there a reason why you can't stay?"

"After school, I need to go get my sister to walk her home. This is her first day in school. She in first grade. Sirion doesn't know how to take care of herself here yet. Sirion could get lost or might get hurt. . . . I don't know what to do. Mr. Currier said that staying after school was punishment for doing wrong things. I didn't mean to do anything wrong. I have brought disappointment to my family. I am so sorry, but I must look out for my sister."

"No, Kumpang, you've done nothing wrong. I just wanted to know more about you so that I can help you advance. Really, it's all right. You go ahead now. But do you think you could meet me after school tomorrow after you get your sister? You can bring her here."

She saw him relax.

"Sure," he said, as he hurried out to meet Sirion.

THE TUTOR

That evening when Mr. Carlson, their tutor, asked Kumpang if he had any questions, Kumpang told him about his teacher asking him to stay after school so she could help him advance. Mr. Carlson asked if Kumpang wanted him to speak with the teacher on his behalf.

"No, thank you. I'll handle it," Kumpang said in a overly-confident tone.

However, the following day Mr. Carlson called Miss Minton. They discussed Kumpang's progress, and how they could work together to help the fledgling citizen find his place within the school system. Miss Minton told Mr. Carlson about Kumpang's reaction to the class when she had said that he was from Laos, and asked him to tell say something about it to the class.

Mr. Carlson chuckled. "Kumpang has made his mind up to become a solid U.S. citizen. He seems to have set himself a goal and is determined to reach it, come hell or high water. Just what his goal is, I've yet to figure out, but I agree when you say he has much to offer his classmates. I'd like to help you with this, but when I offered to intercede for him about staying after school, he told me he wanted to take care it himself."

Miss Minton nodded. "That's just what I've been seeing in class. I would like him to tell the class about his experiences living in Laos. What do you think?"

He smiled. "I think it would do him a world of good. Not only would the class learn about how other people live, but I feel it would give him a tremendous opportunity to develop his language skills." Mr. Carlson paused before adding, "Why don't we discuss this over lunch? We have a common interest and I'm sure Kumpang would benefit."

Miss Minton's answer was slow in coming. "Well, my lunch break is between 12 and 12:30. That doesn't allow much time to leave the school grounds. Perhaps we could eat in my classroom. Would that be all right?"

"Miss Minton, I happen to have the day free, but I'd rather not have Kumpang see us together. He's not supposed to know I talked to you. Could we meet later—away from school?"

"Good idea. There's a bookstore with a delightful coffee shop where we could meet. It's called *The Book Nook*. Oh, and call me Casey. Say, about seven."

"*The Book Nook?* Casey, are you by any chance referring to the one on Roswell?"

Astonished by his knowledge of the store, she said, "Why yes. Do you go there often?"

He chuckled. "It's one of my favorite places, and they do have good coffee. And by the way, call me Doug."

"Well, Doug, will wonders never cease? We both like the same bookstore. I bet we've seen each other before. This should be very interesting. Meet at 7:30 then?"

"Suits me."

"But how will I know you?" Casey smiled and winked.

He grinned, "I'll be the guy wearing glasses and carrying a stack of books." He coughed. "I'm sorry, no I won't. I'll be the guy with glasses, standing by the potted palm with my coffee in my left hand, gazing out the window at the parking lot as I look for your car."

"See you at 7:30. Don't be late, now."

"I won't," he told her.

Doug Carlson grabbed his dinner jacket and started out the doorway. A man never knew when it might come in handy. He smiled to himself. *I haven't had a date with a woman in a long time.*

Doug gave the pretty brunette the once over as she approached the bookstore. He liked what he saw. The woman has a nice body, which she carries well. She walked with confidence. Everything about her said, "Here I am world. Like me or not, you won't easily forget me."

He felt his heart speed up when the brunette turned toward the bookstore. However, when Casey came in and started to look around, he was suddenly unsure of himself.

He saw her smile and then, he felt the blood drain from his brain. A tingling sensations started at the nape of his neck and traveled to the ends of his toes. Every nerve, every particle of his essence came alive to voice one overwhelming phenomenon, and he knew that he was lost. He was in love. Love at first sight, though impossible, had become a certainty. It didn't make sense, but it was there, and he knew in that instant there would never be another. His voice failed him. How could one speak to such a vision who commanded his soul— a vision who was walking toward him.

"Doug?" she asked.

"M... m....m... Miss Minton?" he stammered.

"Casey, please," said the vision, as she extended her lovely hand in his direction.

"Casey . . . ," Doug gulped. He took her hand and gently guided her toward one of the tables. "I left a few things on a table over here to reserve it. I didn't want us to have coffee and conversation while standing at the window."

"This seems private enough," Casey said in approval, as she sat in the chair Doug had pulled out for her. "Is this coffee mine?"

"Yes, I took the liberty of getting a regular coffee, double cream. They serve it hot enough to scald a person, so I thought I'd give yours time to cool. Packets of sweeteners are on the counter in a little bowl. I'll get some if you'd like."

"That's okay. I know the coffee is hot, and where to find the sugar." A small frown creased her brow. "How did you know how I like my coffee? And what on earth am I supposed to do with this huge cinnamon bun?"

"Well," Doug replied, with a smile, "I couldn't very well eat mine alone, could I?" He gingerly picked up his bun and took a bite.

"But this bun is so fattening," she said, feigning shock, yet she broke off a small piece and took a dainty bite.

"Tomorrow morning's jog will take care of my calories," Doug said with a nonchalant wave of his hand. He took another huge bite.

They talked over coffee, between bites of their fresh, moist, cinnamon buns, and found they had more in common than Kumpang's Americanization.

Doug let Casey know he had left the classroom to study for his master's in education. When Casey told him that she was especially enthusiastic about her role helping her students in their formative years, Doug knew they were kindred spirits, and his love for her deepened.

Casey mentioned she was a single mother of a two-year-old daughter.

Married and divorced, Doug explained that his marriage had ended when his wife made it abundantly clear that she had no intention of waiting while he finished his education, accusing him of being a professional student. She said she wanted more out of life. When he found her with another man, he was devastated. He swore then that it wouldn't happen to him again. Doug looked into Casey's eyes and wondered, *How can I be here entertaining thoughts of romance with this beautiful woman I've only known for a few hours. I thought I was commitment shy.*

Casey was the first to notice the lights in the store going dim, a signal it was closing. She looked at her watch. "Oh, my God, it's almost ten. I told Kirsten I'd be home before nine."

"Who's Kirsten?"

"My babysitter. Kirsten's a high school student and her mother doesn't like her to be out this late on a school night. I'm in trouble."

"Get your things together while I call a taxi," he said.

Casey shrugged into her jacket. "You don't need to. I can walk home in the time it would take for a taxi to get here."

"Fine, but at least allow me to see you home safely." He stood up and began to gather his books under his arm.

"Oh, how gallant you are," she said, and gave a soft throaty laugh that ended in a smile which melted his heart.

He followed her out, enjoying the night air as he walked with the woman he now believed he was in love with.

They'd gone only a couple of blocks before she announced that she was home. They stood in front of her apartment building.

"Thank you for seeing me home."

"What about Kirsten?" Doug asked. "How will she get home?"

"Not to worry, she lives in the building."

"I guess my attempt at gallantry is over for this evening," Doug remarked, and then flashed her with his winning smile.

"I guess so, Doug," she told him. "I'd invite you in for coffee, but I'm afraid I'm coffee'd out."

"Me, too. It's late, but I'd like to see you again on a more personal note." He could feel his heart in his throat. He had said it, and now he was vulnerable to her immediate rejection.

She graced him with a beautiful smile. "I'd like that."

He could feel his heart going back to its normal place.

She smiled again. "You can call me. I'm in the book."

He nodded, but stood staring at her.

"Goodnight," she said.

"Goodnight," he said shyly. He watched the door close behind her.

SCHOOL LIFE

The next morning, Casey Minton met with Kumpang before class. He'd let her talk him into speaking to the student body about Laos. In the long run, he believed it was better to do what the teacher asked. *If the students get to know me, perhaps it will be easier to fit in.*

He told her he'd do it, but when he began his preparation, he became painfully aware of how little he knew about his native land beyond the boundaries of Ban Hin Leek Fai. Did Laos have a President? a King? Was it a democracy? He didn't know and it disturbed him. Here, he was determined to learn to be an American, but he didn't know much about the country he had left.

Well, I'll just have to learn, he promised himself as he took on another challenge. *I'll ask my mother for more information about Laos.* He still didn't know how to read or write, not in English. He was far behind his classmates academically, but he was driven to advance to his age group and beyond, to excel: to become what he thought the man he called Father had been and to be better than the man's true son.

He also decided his first talk would be about life in the village of Ban Hin Leek Fai and the beauty of the surrounding jungle.

When he discovered the public library, he was awe-struck. *There are so many books. If a person could learn to read, he could find a book to tell him almost any information he wanted to know.*

At the assembly, he spoke confidently of the process of harvesting teak. Thanks to his recent studies and the help of a Reference Librarian, he could tell them Asian teak is called *Tectona grandis* and was of a higher quality than other species.

His audience seemed impressed with his description of the huge elephants used to drag the cut trees to the river so the trees could be transported to the market. There wasn't any note passing or whispering. They sat quietly and listened to him, and when he was finished, several students asked him questions.

"How big are the trees?"

"How big are the elephants?"

"What did you feed them? Peanuts?"

"Did you get to ride the elephants?"

Kumpang loved the sudden feeling of importance he felt as he answered the innocuous questions.

As Kumpang progressed in his education, he was able to tell them more and more. It wasn't long before he became accustomed to speaking before the class, and his use of his adopted language almost equaled that of the native born. He not only spoke to his class, but to other classes within the school system. Everyone wanted to know about Laos, and he told them all he knew, except that he never spoke about the man he called Father. He realized one of Tommy McGlynn's children could be in the audience, and he didn't want to hurt them or their memory of their father.

He had started at the bottom of the educational ladder, learning his ABCs at the same time as his younger sister, but by no means at the same speed. Kumpang had even insisted that his mother learn. No one in his family was going to be left behind.

It was remarkable, but no surprise to Doug or Casey, that Kumpang advanced through the school system from a Grade Point Average of near zero to almost a perfect four.

This was beyond anything Phin could have imagined. Never before had a member of her family, or for that matter, anyone she had ever known, gone to a school of any kind, but here before her, her son was graduating from high school. If only her American husband could have shared this joy.

I know he wasn't Kumpang's real father, Phin thought. *But he raised and taught Kumpang. We owe more to that man than we do his real father who deserted us.* She looked at Sirion, and then once again at Kumpang. She was so proud of her two children she loved so much, it made her feel at peace with herself.

On graduation day, Phin sat in the high school auditorium beside Marie and Sirion. She waved to Doug and smiled at Casey. When she heard Kumpang Sangsuwan called by the man at the podium and Kumpang strode across the stage to accept his diploma, Phin smiled wide and felt she'd burst with pride.

When the ceremony ended, she followed Doug and Casey, Maria and Sirion, and Kumpang's girlfriend outside where Phin hugged her son and announced that she wanted to take them all to dinner at Kumpang's favorite restaurant. Doug protested at first, saying he worried about the expense, but Phin told him that she had been saving for this occasion and that it was her way of thanking them for assisting her son through to graduation.

She didn't want to hear any more argument.

They went to the restaurant and everyone ordered, but much to Phin's frustration, no one seemed to want the more expensive entrees. She let them know that she was wise to their scheme to save her money, but she finally gave up when everyone insisted they had ordered what they wanted. They ate and enjoyed light and happy dinner conversation.

The waitress was serving coffee when Kumpang changed the tone of the discussion to something more serious.

"Mother, I have something to tell you and Sirion."

"*Oh, no,*" Phin thought. She could detect something in Kumpang's tone. She sighed. *He's going to tell me he wants to marry the girl he calls his girlfriend.* It wasn't that she didn't like Patricia, or Patti, as the girl liked to be called. It was just that she wasn't quite ready to let her son go. Not yet.

"Yes, what is it that you want to tell me?" she finally asked.

"Well, actually, there are two things. First, I want to Americanize my name. To change it from what it is to my father's name, Thomas Aquinas. I think he'd like that," Kumpang said.

"But why? Kumpang Sangsuwan is a good name. It indicates that you are tied by blood to a noted Thai family. It is not a name to be ashamed of." Phin felt hurt, and a little shocked. This certainly wasn't what she had expected.

After taking a deep breath, Kumpang told his mother why. "Mother, I am not ashamed of my name, but I am determined to become a true American."

"But you are," Phin argued. "The three of us are now U.S. Citizens. We studied the history and laws. We learned the language and we were examined. We swore an Oath to this country. My son, you are an American! We are Americans!"

"Yes, I am, but I want an American name, too. And that's not all. I have more to tell you, mother."

Kumpang's square-set jaw showed her his determination.

Sirion touched Phin's arm, in a gesture to hold her back.

Phin decided to let him continue without interruption. She knew she wasn't going to like what he had to say, but she felt she had to hear him out, at least.

"Mother, I want to join the Army, to be like him, the man I called Father."

Fear gripped her heart, but she pushed it aside. She looked at him and nodded. She felt a great deal of pride in her boy-child. He wasn't a child any more, though. He was a man now, and she was glad that he wanted to walk in the shoes of the man she had loved so deeply. But she couldn't help feeling uneasy, a deep feeling that warriors always leave.

Who could blame Kumpang? His American father had loved him, just like he had loved his own daughter, Sirion. Who am I to stand in the way of such love and devotion?

After dinner, Tom dropped Phin and Sirion at their house. *Tom was the name that Kumpang insisted his school friends call him, since he had started thinking seriously of the name change.* He and his girlfriend drove to the park by Kennesaw Mountain. It was a favorite place for older high school and younger college students, a place to be alone with one's sweetheart.

He smelled the fragrance of the pretty girl sitting close to him and felt good about himself and everything around him.

The world is my oyster, he thought as he looked for a place to park away from the crowd. He wanted to celebrate with the rest of his graduating class, but he also wanted to be alone with Patti.

"I'm glad it's finally over," he sighed.

"What? School?" Patti asked.

"No, well, that too, but I was referring to the talk I had with my mom. I didn't know how she'd take it," Tom replied.

"Tom, honey, I think she was hurting, but she seemed to be proud of you at the same time," Patti told him.

He liked the sound of his chosen name much better than the nickname he had been saddled with. "Pang" didn't sound quite right. *Yes, Tom is a much better name to take into the Army.*

"What makes you think so?" he asked.

"Women know these things," she answered, squeezing his arm as she snuggled closer.

He put his arm around her and was about to kiss her when they heard the yelling.

They looked toward the sound. Nearby, a blonde-haired girl was trying to scurry out of a Ford convertible, but the car's driver was trying to force her back into it.

"Uh, oh, looks like she needs help," Tom said. He took his arm from around Patti and opened his car door.

"Be careful," Patti told him. She recognized the convertible and knew it belonged to a ruffian from their school. She opened the door on her side of the car. "That's Brandon Spears."

"I'll be careful," muttered Tom, wishing that he were tough enough that his girlfriend wouldn't worry.

As a rule, the Lao were a peace loving people, almost child-like. Being tough was against his nature. Tom didn't need to be tough, but he had adopted the name of a man who had been a warrior, and he had chosen to follow that man into the same arena.

I guess it's time for me to step up to the plate, he thought as took a deep breath and hurried to help the girl.

The girl was crying. Her dress had been ripped open, and she was clinging to the frayed material as she tried to cover her bra so that the gathering crowd wouldn't see.

Patti took her own sweater from around her shoulders and gave it to the girl.

"Are you all right?" Patti asked.

The girl was still weeping, but there was anger on her face now. "This clown doesn't understand No!" she yelled, as she pointed an accusing finger at Brandon.

"You've been askin' for it all night, bitch," Brandon accused.

"Watch your language," Tom told him.

"Oh yeah, punk? Whadda ya gonna do about it?"

Tom smelled the liquor on Brandon's breath. "You're drunk," he said. He turned toward the girl and asked, "Do you want us to take you home?"

"Leave my girl alone, damn you!" Brandon yelled, as he threw a punch that caught Tom on the side of his face, knocking him to the ground.

"I'm not your girl, damn it!" the blonde-haired girl cried out, but Tom could only vaguely hear her.

"Fight! Fight!" some of the kids yelled and the crowd grew larger.

Tom struggled to his feet and managed to steady himself for the onslaught he knew was coming. Brandon outweighed him by 15 or 20 pounds. Tom knew he didn't stand much of a chance. He wasn't used to fighting, but he bravely gave as good as he got until a few of the more sensitive spectators broke up the fight.

Brandon was still cursing, but he got into his car. He muttered threats for anyone who stood close enough to hear, and then he floored the convertible so it would sling gravel as he drove away.

Her fists were clinched. "Good riddance!" the blonde-haired girl screamed at Brandon's rapidly disappearing car. She walked to Tom's car and got in on the passenger's side.

Patti looked at Tom. "Are you all right, honey?"

He held his car door open for her so she could get in on his side. She slid across to the middle.

He pressed a handkerchief to his bleeding lower lip as he sat down behind the wheel.

"I'm okay," he answered, as he held the handkerchief firmly to his bleeding lip. He had almost stopped the bleeding. He could feel where he had been punched, now more than when the punches were landing, but he could feel something else, too. He had walked into the fire to protect a girl's honor, and he had not faltered. Yes, he felt good. Not that he wanted to seek out Brandon for another round or two, but he had proven something to himself.

"Where would you like us to drop you off, Miss?"

"Kim. My name is Kim, and I'd like to go home if you'll take me."

Turning the key in the ignition, he answered, " Just give us directions, and we'll have you there in no time." He backed the car away from what had been tonight's arena.

"What's your name?" the girl asked.

"I'm Tom, and this is Patricia."

"I really want to thank you for what you did. That Brandon was awful. I'm never talking to him again," Kim said.

"I certainly hope not, for your sake," Tom said, and then added, "And for my sake, too." He chuckled and the girls laughed with him.

When he pulled to the curb in front of Kim's house, he put the car into neutral, allowing the engine to idle.

"You want me to walk you to the door?" Patti asked her.

"No, I'll be all right, thank you. And thank you again, Tom, Patti, for rescuing me from that ass."

They waited as Kim walked to the house, climbed the steps, and entered the front door. When the porch light went out, Tom put the car into gear and pulled away from the curb.

"Hungry?" he asked, as he turned to drive to the *Dairy Queen* on Power Springs Street.

"Not really," Patti answered. "You might as well take me home. Mister Brandon Spears ruined what could have been a nice evening."

"Are you sure you don't want to go back to Kennesaw Mountain instead?" Tom gave Patti a wry smile.

"No, honey. I just want to go home. My nerves have had it."

He sighed. This night had been full of so much. He had graduated, faced his mom, and faced himself to prove he was a man. He supposed he had done enough for one day. He kissed Patti good night, and extra good this time, just to show her what she was missing by not going back to Kennesaw Mountain with him.

CHAPTER 13: Doug & Casey

Doug caressed Casey's hand as they sat on the sofa in the dim light. She smiled at him.

"From a young immigrant who couldn't read or write, to a high school graduate with a 3.98 Grade Point Average— quite an accomplishment for him," Casey said.

Doug could hear the pride in her voice. "And Sirion is doing well, too. Phin is no slouch either," he added.

"No, not by any means. I was pleased we were invited to Kumpang's graduation. I know I was his first teacher, but he didn't stay in my class that long. He moved up so quickly."

"I was really surprised that Phin took us to dinner," Casey said.

"That was nice. It surprised me, too. Weren't you shocked when he told his mother he wanted to change his name. I was."

"Yes, me too." Casey answered as she bent to remove her shoes.

"Would you like a glass of wine?" Doug stood and went into the kitchen. "I haven't told you the latest."

"What's that?" Casey drew her legs underneath her to make herself more comfortable.

"Kumpang asked me to help him find Tommy McGlynn's other family. Tommy was his American stepfather in Laos." Doug uncorked the wine.

"Oh? Why would he want to know?" Pausing for just a moment, then Casey continued, "My first thought is he ought to leave it alone. What did you tell him?"

Doug's reply was immediate. "I told him I'd help him. And why? Why would you think that?" he asked. "I doubt if he is capable of being anything other than what I think he is, a young energetic kid with ambition and willingness to work to attain his goals. Do you see something I don't?"

"No, and I really don't see anything malevolent. I like him, too, but I get uneasy about him wanting to intrude into the lives of others," Casey answered, as she accepted the offered glass of wine.

"Let me put your mind at ease," Doug offered. "Kumpang and I had a long talk, and I think he wants to know how they live so he can provide the same for Phin and Sirion. Do they deserve less because they're not legally considered Thomas McGlynn's immediate family? After all, the man Kumpang admired did in fact act as his father, sleep with his mother, and is Sirion's dad. Does it matter that it wasn't sanctioned by a court of law or by a church if Tommy McGlynn acknowledged the family and provided for them even after he died? I think not. In addition, if the case were to be judged on the goodness of those three gentle people, I feel strongly it would be ruled in their favor. Does that make any sense to you?"

"You like that family, don't you?"

"Guilty as charged. Initially, I took on the job of tutoring for the extra money, but over the years, I seem to have become more like an honorary uncle to the three of them."

Casey got up from the sofa and turned the stereo on before sitting back down.

"I can tell that you have something on your mind, a plan. What do you intend to do?" she asked.

"I was thinking of calling Maria Creamer to ask for the address of the father's buddy in Hawaii. What do you think?"

"That's as good a route as any, I guess." Casey purred as she snuggled closer, "Do you love me?"

He was glad Kumpang had brought them together. He had tried to help the lad, but in the end, Doug felt that Kumpang had given him the greater blessing in Casey Minton. All this made Doug even more determined to help Kumpang.

The next day, Doug wrote the letter to Sergeant Major Mitzamuri to see what he could find out.

Sergeant Major Mitzamuri,

I feel awkward writing you at this late stage. I probably should have been giving you periodic progress reports on the Sangsuwan family long before this, but I knew you were in contact with Maria Creamer and figured she kept you up to date.

At the risk of duplicating her reports to you, I'll take this opportunity to tell you about Kumpang. He recently graduated from Walton High School with a GPA of 3.98, which is exceptional for a youngster who could not read or write just a few years ago.

In fact, he is much in demand as a speaker. Kumpang addresses school children throughout the area about his native land, Laos. His talks are interesting, and the children warm to him.

The reason for this letter is to tell you about a conversation I had recently with Kumpang, who now prefers to be called Tom or Thomas Aquinas.

He asked my help in locating, for want of a better description, "the other family." His reason may surprise you. Believe me, there is no ulterior motive. He said he wants his mother and sister to have the same lifestyle as the other family, and he fully intends to provide the means.

Before I go further, I must tell you I agreed to help him, as is evidenced by this letter.

He is also in the process of having his name legally changed to Thomas Aquinas, the given names of his stepfather, Tommy McGlynn (a/k/a Tommy Noonan).

You may wonder how the boy found out about Tom's names. Almost unbelievably, he traveled the streets of Marietta until he found the National Cemetery where Sirion's father is buried. Please keep in mind that he'd been there only once before, several years ago, for the graveside ceremony. Kumpang found the grave site headstone with the name Thomas Aquinas McGlynn (a/k/a Thomas Aquinas Noonan). He copied down the name and began his search.

If and when his change of name is granted by the Court, young Tom intends to enlist in the U.S. Army to be like McGlynn. I, for one, applaud him for his accomplishments and wish him well. Right now, he's working in a fast food place.

You could assume there would be many ways for him to find the family on his own. The phonebook for one, but he doesn't know who to look for because Tommy McGlynn's former wife remarried. He doesn't know the family's last name now. I assume the children took the name of their new father. We know they are not using McGlynn or Noonan.

Kumpang doesn't plan to contact them. He doesn't want to cause any disruption in their lives. If I'd have felt there could be any threat to the well-being of the family, I wouldn't be writing this letter.

I hope you'll see fit to help by providing the last name of the family and thereby allowing the young man to go on to other things.

I've been closely associated with the Sangsuwan family for some time now and have grown very fond of them. I'm sure Kumpang will attain whatever goals he sets his eyes on and will one day make us proud to have known him.

He is a young man with high aspirations, and he will not be deterred. There's no doubt in my mind.

Sincerely,

Doug Carlson

P.S. If you are in contact with the other family, please, don't tell them about this letter. The Sangsuwan family prefers to remain in the background. As I mentioned, Kumpang assures me he will not contact them.

CHAPTER 14: The Superior Court of Cobb County

In June, right after graduation, Kumpang thought it would take no time at all for his name to be legally changed, but he was disappointed to find there was more involved than just asking. First, he had to wait until he was eighteen years old, or have his mother sign the papers. He hesitated to ask her because she still hadn't fully accepted the fact that he wanted his name changed, so he'd decided to wait.

October 19, 1981 was the day he'd waited for, and when it came, he was at the front door of the Cobb County Courthouse with the necessary documents to be filed and enough money to pay the filing fees. He was disappointed once again when he learned about the procedural requirements that would have to take place before he could even have a Hearing before a Judge.

His Notice of Request for a Change of Name must be published in the Public Records section of the local newspaper once a week for four weeks. Then, he'd have to wait another thirty days to assure the court that no objections had been filed. All this was necessary before the court would set a Date Certain for the Hearing.

Another young man may have been so frustrated, he'd have given up, but Kumpang became more determined to follow the rules to achieve his goal.

In December, the day for the Court Hearing finally came. The anxiety which he'd built up had him tossing and turning most of the night, but his morning shower helped to refresh him.

He took great care getting ready for his court appearance and put on his graduation suit and tie. He wanted to impress the people he'd stand before today that he was worthy of the name he was requesting.

When his name was called, Kumpang stood and faced Cobb County Superior Court Judge Thomas Morrison.

"Kumpang Sangsuwan," the Judge said. "Did I pronounce your name correctly?"

Kumpang nodded.

"It's a nice sounding name. It has a pleasant rhythm to it. Why would you want to change it?"

Judge Morrison paused a moment but spoke again before Kumpang could answer the question. Then, he read the Petition. "I have your reason for this Petition in legal terms, but I prefer to hear it in your own words. I want to be convinced I'll be doing the right thing when I make my decision. Do you understand what I mean, young man?"

Undaunted, Kumpang answered, "Yes, your Honor, I do." He began his explanation, "Your Honor, my mother, my sister, and I came to this country from the village of Ban Hin Leek Fai in the heartland of Laos, a village which has no running water, no paved roads or concrete sidewalks, and most importantly, did not have a school. If we'd stayed in that village, my sister, Sirion, and I wouldn't have had the opportunity to go to school. I'm now a high school graduate, and Sirion is a good student. We studied, were tested, and passed all our exams."

He met the Judge's eyes. "We have taken an oath to our new country. We are bona fide citizens of this great country, but I want to go a step further in my Americanization and adopt an American name. I intend to enlist in the United States Army, and I'd like to have the name I've chosen when I do."

Judge Morrison raised his hand to stop Kumpang. "Do you think having an American name will make you a better soldier?" He didn't give Kumpang the chance to answer. He continued, "Have you ever heard the phrase 'go for broke'?"

Crestfallen, sure now his Petition was about to be denied, Kumpang answered, "No, your Honor."

Judge Morrison paused to reach into a drawer. He brought out a book and held it so Kumpang could see the title on the cover: **Go for Broke**. "This book's title is a phrase that could mean 'to bet it all' or 'to take your best shot.' However, in this book, it means the men who were written about were to complete their assigned mission whatever the cost. In one battle, it was to rescue over two hundred members of my unit even though the enemy had us surrounded. We sustained over eight hundred casualties. We were completely cut off when they came to our rescue, but they came and at a high cost to them, and they completed their mission. This book, **Go For Broke**, was written by Chester Tanaka, a Japanese-American who was a member K Company, 442nd Infantry. It's a story of a certain U.S. Army unit which fought in Europe during World War II. With over 18,000 individual decorations earned, it became the most highly decorated unit in the history of the U.S. Armed Forces."

The Judge opened the book. "In it, there are names of Nisei, American men born of Japanese parents, like Sadao S. Munemori, who won the Congressional Medal of Honor, and others who were awarded the Distinguished Service Cross, men like Mikio Hasemoto, Shizuya Hayashi, Yeiki Kobashigawa, and others. The point is the story's written about men of great courage. Men with strange sounding names, foreign names, who also felt the need to serve this country but didn't feel it necessary to change their names in order to do so. Kumpang, it's not the name we carry that causes us to succeed. It's the heart, and the character of the man that counts.

This book is in the public library and may be checked out. You do have a Cobb County library card, don't you?"

Kumpang nodded, "Yes," meekly.

"Fine," Judge Morrison replied. "I'd like you to get a copy from the local library and read it. Then, I want you to think hard about this name change. You have a month before this Court reconvenes on the matter of your Petition to change your name. At that time, I will ask you whether you fully understand what you're asking. Understand this. I'm not suggesting you change your mind, only that you understand what you are asking. When you leave the courtroom, go see my Clerk to set a time for the Hearing."

"Your Honor, if the book is in the library, I'll get it when I leave here and be ready tomorrow," Kumpang responded.

"This is very well, but the Court acts with deliberate speed. Let me look at my calendar here. Hmmm, this case is continued for one month, until Wednesday, January 20th at ten o'clock. That is, if you think a month will be enough for you," the Judge said.

"Yes, your Honor. I'll be ready."

The following month on Wednesday, the 20th, Judge Morrison's Courtroom was called to order. "All rise. The honorable Thomas Morrison's Court is now in session." The Judge came in and stepped up onto the platform at the front of the Courtroom. After he took his seat and adjusted his robes, the Bailiff said, "All be seated." The Clerk called the first case. Kumpang stepped forward. Judge Morrison was pleased to see in the boy's hand a copy of the book he'd recommended.

"I see you have a copy of **Go For Broke** with you. Have you read it?"

"Yes, your Honor, I have. It was quite a story. I hope I can perform as well if the occasion ever arises," Kumpang answered.

"I'm sure you will. You appear to be a fine young man who seems to have a good sense of direction, which is, unfortunately, not true for some of our native-born youngsters." He paused, scanned the papers on his desk, and then asked, "Are you ready to elaborate why you are Petitioning this court to change your name?"

"Yes, your Honor, I am," Kumpang answered. He took a deep breath and began, "Last month I explained to the Court where my family came from. I'd like to go on from there, if I may."

"Please," Judge Morrison prompted.

"When I was a little boy, my uncle, who had been away during the war, returned to our village. My uncle asked the Village Headman for help to go after a foreigner he'd left in the jungle. The foreigner was very ill. There weren't many men in our village, so my mother volunteered. She left me with my aunt, and she brought back the foreigner."

"And this has to do with why you want your name changed?"

"Yes, your Honor."

"Go on, please."

"When the rescue party returned, my mother also was volunteered to nurse the stranger back to health. He stayed in our hut, and in time, he became the man I looked upon as my father. He did good things for us, for our village. In all, he stayed with us for about ten years, and we were a happy family, until the morning we awoke to find that he'd left us. We were crushed. My mother and my sister cried all of the time. It wasn't long before I resented him for deserting us as my real father also had; that is, until my mother convinced me of the good he had done for our family and our village. That's when I began wearing the watch again."

"The watch?" the Judge interrupted.

"Yes, your Honor," Kumpang answered. He held up his left arm to reveal the Seiko watch strapped around his wrist. I found it next to my pallet after he left us. It was his gift to me."

"Continue on," Judge Morrison prompted again.

"It wasn't until I began the journey to this country that I found out the true story of why he had been in our village in the first place. Tommy had suffered a serious head wound, and because of the trauma of the things he'd experienced in war, he had amnesia. That's why he had stayed in our village for so long.

When he finally regained his memory, Tommy returned to the United States. We didn't know it until then, but he had left behind a wife and three children. He had an entire other family, although he loved us and wanted better things for us. He was the reason we were able to come to America. He arranged it.

"Tommy, er . . . , Thomas Aquinas McGlynn. was an honorable man who loved both of his families. He didn't abandon us as I had, at first, thought. He had arranged it so we would be taken care of, because by this time, he was terminally ill.

"At the burial, we, my mother, my sister and I, stood off at a distance and watched. When Sergeant Major Thomas Aquinas McGlynn was buried, his other family stood right beside his grave at the service. I realize my family will always remain standing off in the distance, so to speak, but I want to honor him by bearing his name and perhaps by bringing more honor to it."

"Does the man's other family know you want to adopt his name?" Judge Morrison asked.

"No, your Honor. They don't even know we exist. And, oh, I see what you're asking. No, your Honor, I'm not adopting his full name, only his first and middle names," Kumpang replied.

"You're not asking for his last name?"

"No, your Honor, I have no need to," came the reply.

Looking at his watch, then at the Petitioner, Judge Morrison said, "I see no reason to delay this Petition any longer than we have to, but first, let's recess for fifteen minutes."

It was a long fifteen minutes out in the hall for Kumpang, but he was determined to *Go for broke*. He came back into the courtroom, looked around, but felt less confident when Judge Morrison resumed his seat on the bench.

"Do any of you have anything further to add before I hand down my decision?" he asked. The room was silent. Judge Morrison turned toward Kumpang's mother. "Mrs. Sangsuwan, do you have anything to add to the proceedings? Do you understand what your son is asking?"

"Yes, sir," she said. "Sir, I know what my son wants and why. When my family stood on the hill and we watched the service for that good man I loved, I wished for the *Kwan* to leave his body and enter my son's, so my son would have the heart of a warrior. Now I also wish his name for my son."

Shuffling the papers before him, Judge Morrison looked at Kumpang. "Son, I think you made a good case and will do the name you've chosen proud. This old Judge thinks you have the makings of the type of person who will bring honor to the name." The Judge noticed the grin on Kumpang's face. The Judge tapped his gavel. "Petition granted. This Court is adjourned."

Chapter 15: The U.S. Army Volunteer

After the court documents had become of record at the courthouse, Kumpang Sangsuwan was officially legally Thomas Aquinas, so Tom took his documentation to the U.S. Army Recruiter's storefront office in the mall.

"Can I help you?" the Sergeant asked.

"I'm here to join the U.S. Army," the newly-named Thomas Aquinas answered.

"That's what I'm here for. Have a seat." The Recruiter smiled. "What do you have in mind?"

"I want to be a Green Beret," Tom answered.

The Recruiter gave a soft whistle and handed him a list of requirements. Then they went over the schedule for Tom to take aptitude tests.

In the weeks that followed, Tom was kept quite busy balancing his job at a local fast food restaurant to earn funds for expenses until he could depart for Basic Training. Fortunately, his boss allowed him time to fill out forms, take aptitude tests, and go into Atlanta to take his pre-enlistment physical, and more tests.

The Letter from Mitzi

All the while, Tom waited for a letter from Mr. Mitzamuri with the information he'd asked for. One of the first things Tom did upon returning home from his physical in Atlanta was to call Doug Carlson to ask if the letter had come yet.

The answer was always a disappointing, "No, Tom, I'm sorry. Maybe tomorrow." Tom was beginning to doubt that his letter would ever be answered.

One evening, he came home from work, entered the house through the kitchen door, and greeted his mother with a kiss on the cheek. "Hello. How was your day?" he said before heading for the hallway and his bedroom. "Is Sirion home, yet?"

"Yes, she is. Can't you hear her music?" Phin said, somewhat annoyed.

Tom started to go on to his room, but she stopped him. "Kumpang, you have guest in the living room."

"Really," he said, raising his eyebrows. "Who?"

"You'll see," she said.

Tom went straight to the living room. Doug Carlson was waiting on the sofa. He stood up and held out his hand.

"Hi, Doug. What's up?" Tom asked as they shook hands.

"This is what's up." Doug pulled an envelope from his jacket pocket and held it up. "A letter from Mr. Mitzamuri."

"Did he send the information I asked for?"

Doug smiled and said, "See for yourself." He handed Tom the letter.

He resisted the urge to tear it open and read it. He had waited so long to find out, but instead he asked Doug to sit while he himself walked to the window where there was better light. He slowly withdrew the contents of the envelope, somehow fearful of what it might or might not contain.

Only the ticking of the grandfather clock in the hallway broke the silence of the room as Tom read the letter. Mitzi's letter answered all of his questions, and even provided some information that hadn't been asked, such as the family's street address and where the children went to school. The letter ended with a plea to not contact the family. It said that the family had grieved enough, had suffered enough, that they didn't need any reminders of what they'd lost.

Putting the pages in order, Tom slowly folded and returned them to the envelope. He turned toward Doug and asked, "Would you please allow me to answer this letter?"

"Of course. I'm sure the Sergeant Major would appreciate an answer if it came from you." Doug stood as if to leave. "Well, Tom, it's all up to you from here on out, but don't hesitate to call if you need help. Oh, by the way, when are you leaving for the Army?"

"I don't know the date, yet, but they told me it would be within the month. I'll let you know as soon as I get word."

"Please, do. Casey and I would like to see you before you leave, maybe take you and Patricia to dinner." Then, calling out to Phin who was still in the kitchen, Doug said, "Bye, Mrs. Sangsuwan. Give me a call when Sirion is ready to begin studying again."

"Good-bye, Mr. Carlson. I'll call you when she's ready. Say hello to Casey," Phin said, coming in from the kitchen as she wiped her hands on her apron.

"I will," Doug told her, and then he closed the door behind him.

As soon as the door shut, Tom grabbed the phone book so he could see if the name and address which Mitzamuri had given him was listed. It was. He felt excited. He put the phone book in his lap, wondering what he could or should do now. He wanted to get into his car and drive by the place, but dinner was almost ready. He'd have to wait. Dinner was the chosen time for his family to talk. They aired their problems and sometimes found solutions. For the first time since he made the decision to enlist in the Army, a cloud of doubt enveloped him. He would miss their nightly discussions.

"Kumpang, Sirion, come to dinner," his mother called from the kitchen.

Tom went to the table, but thinking about the address kept him from really enjoying the meal. He gave up on the conversation and decided to eat quickly.

"Why are you in such a hurry?" Phin asked, as she spooned another helping of rice onto her plate. "Are you going to see Patricia?"

"No, I'm sorry." Tom didn't want to tell her what he had found out. He turned to Sirion. "And how was your day, little sister?"

After dinner, Phin was busy wiping the table, stove, and countertop, while Sirion washed and Tom dried the dishes without rushing.

He was being slow on purpose, so he wouldn't upset her again.

He had one more thing to do. Tom was anxious to leave, but out of respect for his mother and her ways, he was dutifully patient to her traditions and customs.

After the dishes were put away, his mother burned joss sticks at the small family shrine to please the *Phi*. Phin said, "I was raised in a village influenced by Buddhist monks. We must follow what I was taught as much as we can here, but we don't have to do everything exactly as the monks did. The monks carried strainers to sieve the drinking water so they wouldn't accidentally ingest a living thing."

While Tom respected his mother's beliefs, he really didn't yet have a strong belief of his own. "The Buddhist ways seem old-fashioned to me, as if the monks lived in the past. I'm more concerned with the future, and our future in our adopted country," Tom said.

The aroma of incense was strong, and he could still smell it after he had left the house. The sweet scent lingered in his senses as he drove to the address Sergeant Major Mitzamuri had sent him.

Now, I'll begin to know his family, his other family after all this time. But the closer Tom got to his destination, the more anxious he became.

He was stunned when he matched the address to the house itself. He had spent so much time wondering about the people who belonged to his father, wanting to know them, wanting to be accepted by them, and for his family to become part of their family, all belonging to his father.

Of course, he'd promised not to intrude on their lives. But looking at their big house floored him. He had been here before! He had once rescued a blonde-haired girl, and this was where he had taken her home.

That girl was my sister! Well, she's not really my sister, but she's his daughter. That should count for something. Actually, she is Sirion's half-sister, that's what she is. So Kim's my sister's half-sister. And I know Kim has a sister named June and Brian is their brother. Does this make us related somehow? American kinship rules are so complicated. Why didn't I recognize her that evening? I'd seen them at the funeral.

He continued down the street, driving slowly as he looked for a place to turn around. He had to have another look. He stared at the house again as he passed it. There were lights on in the upstairs windows. He wondered if *his father's* children were studying in their bedrooms. They had a big brick house, and Tom wondered what it would be like to live in a house like that. Were they a happy family? Did they still or did they ever grieve for the man whose name he adopted?

Headlights suddenly startled him, and he swerved to avoid the oncoming pickup.

"Jerk!" someone in the truck shouted, as the vehicles passed within inches of each other.

Uh oh, Tom said to himself. *I have to pay better attention.* Before he headed to Patti's house, he glanced one last time in his rearview mirror to take in the details of the brick house with three car garage and well-landscaped lawn. The image in his mirror haunted him. He knew he'd never be able to get it out of his mind.

Tom and Patti sat on the porch swing. They held hands as they let the swing glide gently back and forth.

"Wow! Is it possible?" he wondered aloud as he stood up.

"What, honey?" Patti asked.

He didn't answer her. He was miles away, lost in deep thought.

"What is it, Tom?" she asked.

"Patti, I just remembered something, and I've got to leave. Do you mind if I take off? There's something I have to do," he said. He was excited now by what had occurred to him.

"What is it, honey? Is something wrong?" Patti stood up. "I just feel like something's wrong."

He smiled at her. "No, nothing's wrong. Something's right." Tom tried to sound reassuring.

"What do you have to do that's so important?"

He couldn't tell her about it, about the thing which had driven him to learn so much, that had pushed him toward success, was finally making sense. Now he felt as if he knew the children of the man he called Father. The pieces were falling into place, and he had a place to direct them. But he just wasn't ready to talk about it.

Later, Tom was lying on his bed, fingers laced behind his head, as he stared at the ceiling. He lay there remembering the day he had first run into Brian, not at the funeral, but several years later. It was when Kumpang had just finished a talk to the civics class about Laos, and was putting his notes into his backpack.

A student approached him. "Do you have a minute?" the student asked.

"Sure," he answered. "What's up?"

"You're the first guy I've ever met from Laos. Can we talk for a minute? I'd like to ask you a few questions."

"Sure," he answered. "Let's get a Coke and sit over on the bleachers. My mouth is dry from all that talking," Kumpang answered.

Smiling, Brian replied that he'd buy.

"My father, my real father, that is, served in Laos during the war," Brian began. "And I really didn't know anything about the country until your talk today. Was it the war that caused your family to come to the States?"

"Not really. Our coming here was arranged," Kumpang said hesitantly. He paused before deciding to mention a man that he had all but forgotten. "My real father also went off to the war."

"Did he come to the States with you?"

"No, he never came back from the war."

"Oh." At a loss for words, it was all the student could think of to say.

"Did your father come back?" Kumpang asked.

"Yes, but he died later."

"Oh."

The two boys sat and drank their Cokes, making small talk until the student asked him his name.

"I mean your whole name, your real name?"

"Kumpang Sangsuwan."

"Well, Kumpang, I'm Brian Bath. I enjoyed your talk about Laos, and I'm glad to have met you. I have to run or I'll be late for class." Brian shook hands with Tom, and then added, "Maybe we'll bump into each other when you come to Walton. I'm on the football team here, and if I can help you in any way, just say the word. You will be coming to Walton, won't you?"

When Tom had said he would, Brian asked. "Do you play football?"

Thinking Brian was referring to Soccer, Kumpang said he did.

"That's good. I'll be watching for you. Take care and remember what I said. If you need anything, just give me a shout. My dad liked your country and its people, and I'd like to help you if I can."

Tom remembered how he had taken to Brian right away. That had happened back when he was still in Middle School, long before he'd changed his name.

"There must have been a resemblance to my father I recognized," he muttered. "Maybe it was there, or just that I was so intimidated about starting high school."

Tom could recall himself thinking that he was glad that he'd already have a friend once he got to Walton. The friendship hadn't come to fruition, though. When Tom moved up to high school, Brian had already graduated and gone to Fort Belvoir in Virginia. Brian was training in preparation for West Point. Besides, by that time, Tom had gained the confidence he needed, and a challenge; he was beginning to excel in his studies.

So he'd met Brian once, and he'd rescued Kim. He was getting to know them. However, he wasn't ready to pass on what he knew to anyone else. He would keep *his* new family a secret for the time being. Tom reached to turn off the bedside lamp, feeling rather satisfied with the situation. He had spent several years wanting to know something, anything, and now it was falling into place.

He woke up early the following morning and left the house before his mother or Sirion awoke. He drove to the cemetery to say good-bye to his father.

Tom read the inscription on the headstone, etching it into his memory. It would be a long time before he'd be at home again. He took several items from a paper bag to perform a ritual, a religious memorial to his father. He knelt and placed a paper plate containing a portion of rice and a pineapple slice at the base of the headstone. He lit some joss sticks and held the unlit ends between his hands in prayer and spoke to the man buried there, the man he knew as "Father."

"I'm scheduled to leave for the Army tomorrow morning, and I don't know when I'll be able to come pay my respects again. I'm going to be a soldier just like you were. I promise I'll do everything in my power to bring honor to your name."

Planting the joss sticks into the ground in front of the paper plate, he rose, read the inscription on the headstone again, breathed deeply of the early morning air, and turned to go to his car.

It wasn't a bad good-bye ceremony. He had said it alone, and that somehow felt right. Tom drove off, praying he could fulfill his promise.

CHAPTER 16: The Departure

Tom asked Phin, Sirion, and Patti not to accompany him to the recruiting station. He was afraid they would cry or something, and he didn't want the recruiters to see that. Besides, good-byes were a private affair. He got up to go out the door. It was time.

He had been right, she was crying. He could hear her sniffles. He turned around when he felt his mother's arm on his shoulder.

The look on his mother's face floored him. He hadn't been prepared for how her response would affect him. The sadness in her eyes broke his heart. He wiped at the tears threatening to spill from his eyes. He loved her so much. How could he do this to her? She was his mom.

He put his arms around her. He had to go. He had already signed the papers. The only thing left was for him to be sworn in.

Thank the Lord that they weren't in front of the recruiters now. He would have never been able to live down the fact that he was bawling like a baby for his mommy.

"I'll be okay, mother. I'll call as soon as I get there, and I will write home every time I get the chance."

He felt her grip tighten. He had to pull her fingers away in order to break her grasp. He looked at Patti. Patti was crying, too, and so was Sirion.

The girls each kissed him on the cheek. He wanted to give Patti a real kiss, one to remember him by, but he didn't trust himself. If he didn't get out of there, he might back out completely. He went to the door without looking back. He knew that the women were clinging to each other for support.

"I'll call," he promised, and then he went out the door. He sighed. Saying good-bye was hard as hell sometimes, but he was a man now and he would have to toughen up.

PART III Tom's U.S. Army Training

CHAPTER 17: The Swearing In

The recruits were ushered to the back room in the Recruiting Station. After a few preliminaries, the Captain said, "Repeat after me."

Right hand raised, Tom followed the directions of the Captain standing in the front of the room. Tom took his Oath of Enlistment:

> I, Thomas Aquinas, do solemnly swear that I will support and defend the Constitution of the United States against all enemies, foreign and domestic; that I will bear true faith and allegiance to the same; that I will obey the orders of the President of the United States and the orders of the officers appointed over me, according to the regulations and the Uniform Code of Military Justice; So help me God.

Tom could feel his chest swell with pride.

He and the other recruits in the room lowered their right hands.

"Congratulations, men," the Captain told them. "You are now recruits in the United States Army. You'll soon begin the process of becoming soldiers. I wish you all good luck."

The Captain turned toward a nearby Sergeant. "Is the bus ready yet, Sergeant Morrell?"

The Sergeant looked at his wristwatch. "No, sir. It's not due to leave until 1400."

"Very well. Take charge of these men. Let them visit with their families until departure time but don't allow them to leave the building."

"Yes, sir!" Sergeant Morrell answered smartly, as the Captain turned to leave.

"Listen up, people," the Sergeant ordered. "At ease! Smoke 'em if you got 'em. You're free to visit with your friends or family who are here to see you off, but you are not, I say again, NOT to leave this building. We'll be loading the bus through that door over there." He pointed to the exit. "You'd better be in line at 1345. That's a quarter 'til two for you boneheads that don't know how to tell time yet! And people, don't miss this bus or your ass is grass."

Ass is grass? Tom wondered, as he looked for somewhere to sit. He would be ready. The Sergeant didn't have to worry about him. Tom did not intend to test the system. He would do as told and make the best of the situation. He'd been warned that training wasn't going to be easy.

His plan was to obey orders, stay in the background as much as possible, learn what they asked him to learn, and to survive Basic Training. He was the first in line for the bus, and the first one to get on it.

CHAPTER 18: Fort Jackson, South Carolina

BASIC TRAINING

The horseplay stopped and the recruits quieted as the bus pulled up to the main gate at Fort Jackson, South Carolina.

Private Thomas Aquinas awoke from a doze and looked out of the window. He could see a Sergeant in a crisply-starched fatigue uniform, wearing an olive-drab campaign hat tilted forward on his head.

The Sergeant held a clipboard as he boarded the bus. He leaned over the bus driver and directed him to pull the bus up a few blocks to where he wanted him to off-load the passengers.

Tom looked at the various cloth insignia sewn above the Sergeant's breast pockets. Displayed on the left side of the Sergeant's jacket was a Combat Infantry Badge below a Master Parachutist Badge. On the Sergeant's right breast was a foreign Parachutist Badge. Tom recognized them for what they were, because he had made himself aware of such things while he waited for his departure date. Tom thought they might have been awards from Vietnam. When the Sergeant turned, Tom saw a Special Forces patch sewn on the right shoulder of his jacket, which meant that the Sergeant had been in combat with the unit.

I hope he's my Drill Sergeant. If he is, I'll tell him that I enlisted to be in the Special Forces. Maybe he will help me learn to be a soldier like my father was.

When the bus finally stopped, the driver opened the door. Another man was waiting at the curb.

"Ready for the troops, Sergeant Scott?" asked the Sergeant standing by the driver.

"Ready, Sergeant Owens!" yelled the man outside the bus.

Sergeant Owens looked toward the rear of the bus and said in a strong voice, "Listen up! Can you hear me in the rear?"

Owens didn't wait for an answer. He continued in the same authoritative tone, although he wasn't yelling quite as loud, "As I call your name, get your belongings and exit the bus. Follow Sergeant Scott, that handsome devil standing in front of you, but remain seated until your name is called. Any questions? Good! It makes me happy to be understood the first time." He looked down at his clipboard.

"Aaron, Richard. Abbott, Christian. Ahmed, Mohammed. Aquinas, Thomas." Sergeant Owens went on calling names as Tom stood, grabbed his bag from the luggage rack above him, and then hurried to the exit.

As he stepped from the bus, he looked up into the face of the meanest looking black man that he had ever seen. Sergeant Scott was staring at him from under a campaign hat that was similar to the one Sergeant Owens wore.

Sergeant Scott growled, "What are you staring at, recruit? Get over there with the others. Move!" He pointed in the direction he wanted Tom to go.

Tom bowed his head and took off, almost running to where Sergeant Scott had pointed. He wasn't going to argue. *Guess training starts now and I don't want any part of this sergeant. Forget learning from him.* It didn't matter that Sergeant Scott also wore a Combat Infantry Badge sewn above a Master Parachutist Badge, or that he had a Special Forces patch stretched over his muscle-bound right shoulder. Tom thought Sergeant Scott had steely eyes so mean they could bore through a person.

But Tom managed, like so many before him, to survive his initial introduction to the military, Basic Training. The haircut they'd given him was outrageous, and he was lonely, but he wrote or called his family when he could.

He had to admit that he liked the discipline of the military, and he knew he had changed, had grown up. Some of the change was good and some was not really bad but different from what he had experienced before.

This was never so apparent as the day he caught his thumb in the receiver of his M-14 rifle just as the bolt slammed forward. "Mutha . . .", he started the curse word he had recently learned, then shook his hand in the air hoping to relieve the pain; but the pain was overshadowed by thoughts of his mother.

Why would I use such a phrase? It was an insult to my mother and all mothers. Along with learning how to be a soldier, I guess I've picked up a habit. I don't like it. I will stop cussing. He wanted to be a soldier like his father, but doubted his father would want him to emulate such language.

It was just that he was so tired. They had been on the rifle range all week, qualifying with their M-16 rifles during the day and maintaining a bivouac during the night. On bivouac, they slept two men to a pup tent that they'd erected themselves. Tom would have preferred sleeping under the stars just as he had done on many occasions in Laos, but he wanted to succeed in his venture so he followed the rules.

When the week ended, they packed up and marched 23 miles back to their company area. Tom never felt so tired. He could almost feel himself weaving back and forth, as he stood in formation at attention, waiting for Sergeant Owens to give further instructions.

"At ease!" Sergeant Owens ordered. Then, he read the announcements necessary to the function of the company. When he was finished, he dismissed the men, but told Tom to see him afterward. . . .

Sergeant Owens looked at him. "Aquinas, are you Hispanic?"

"No, Drill Sergeant Owens. I'm Lao."

Having served on Operation *White Star* in Laos while with the 7th Special Forces Group, Sergeant Owens looked incredulously at Tom. "You're what?" he asked.

"I'm Lao, Drill Sergeant," Tom told him again, but seeing the shock on his Sergeant's face, he was now concerned.

"Where did you live in Laos?" the Sergeant asked.

"Drill Sergeant, my village was called Ban Hin Leek Fai. It's on the Muone River, not far from the Mekong."

"I'll be damned. You sure had me fooled," the Sergeant said. "We have something in common. I served in Laos a long time ago." He smiled. "But that's not why I asked you to stay after the formation. I know that when you enlisted you wanted to go into Special Forces, but have you considered Officer Candidate School? I've looked at your test scores, and you qualify for O.C.S., you know."

Tom hesitated before answering, "Drill Sergeant, I've never given O.C.S. a thought. All I want is to go to Jump School and to be in the Special Forces."

"Sergeant Scott and I have had an eye on you since we learned you volunteered for Special Forces. We both think you have what it takes, but why don't you think of going to Officer Candidate School first? You'll still be qualified to go to Jump School as an officer after you finish."

"Because, Drill Sergeant, I want to be like the man I once called Father, the father of my sister, Sirion. Maybe you knew him; he was with Special Forces. His name was Thomas Aquinas McGlynn. He's buried at the National Cemetery in my home town."

"Marietta, Georgia?"

Tom was stunned. "Yes, how did you know?"

"Because," Sergeant Owens answered. "I was on the burial detail and was honored to be so. I was also with the group that went in for Tommy and Mitzi the night Tommy went missing."

"Wow," Tom said, forgetting to address his Drill Sergeant by his title, as all new enlistees were required to do. "I was there at his funeral, too." Tom added. He paled. "Sorry, ah, Drill Sergeant."

Sergeant Owens shrugged. "That's okay. I understand."

"Drill Sergeant, I made a promise a long time ago that I would be like him." He went on to tell Sergeant Owens the circumstances surrounding his relationship with Thomas McGlynn.

"Well, I am certain that if Tommy is looking down from wherever a person goes after they leave this world, he is proud of you, son. I've met very few recruits as dedicated as you are," said Sergeant Owens, as their meeting ended.

"Drill Sergeant, thank you. I appreciate that," Tom said. He came to attention and waited until Sergeant Owens dismissed him. He went to bed that night with renewed optimism. He was glad that he had joined the Army. He was going to make it after all.

Tom decided to attend Officer Candidate School. O.C.S. and Special Forces training would each take a considerable amount of time, and he didn't know when he'd be able to come home next. En route to Fort Benning, Georgia, Tom had a short Leave to stop by his home in Marietta.

Phin was surprised to see how much her son had grown in just a couple of months. He wasn't taller, but his shoulders had beefed up, and his neck was thicker. He didn't look like a boy at all. It also surprised her that he awoke early every morning and went to the high school track to run and workout. He told her he wanted to maintain his physical condition because he knew what he'd be in for once he reached Fort Benning.

One thing did bother Phin, her son seemed to look for any excuse to visit Patti. Phin couldn't help feeling a little jealous that he wanted to spend more time with his girlfriend than with his family. Where did that leave her and Sirion? Phin hoped that he wasn't yet thinking about getting married. She had worried about that before, and now she was convinced that her worries would come true.

But when it came time for him to leave for Fort Benning, he left without Patti, and Phin was glad that he had decided to wait a while longer.

Chapter 19: Fort Benning, Georgia

Officer Candidate School

Reporting to his company at Fort Benning was a lot different than reporting to the reception station for Basic Training at Fort Jackson. At Fort Benning, despite still being considered a recruit, Tom was treated with a modicum of dignity. As soon as he arrived, the tactical officers, called TACs, and the Senior Candidates descended upon the new arrivals.

"What's your name, candidate?" one shouted. Tom couldn't tell if it was a TAC or a Senior Candidate who had asked.

It didn't matter, not really. Tom was required to stand at attention, eyes straight to the front, and answer in a set manner.

"Sir, Candidate Aquinas. My name is Thomas Aquinas, sir!"

"Why?" another voice demanded.

Why? he thought. How could anyone answer a question like that, never mind ask it?

"I asked you a question, Candidate Aquinas. Are you related to the saint?" the voice persisted.

"Sir, Candidate Aquinas. No, sir!"

The harassment went on until they were finally assigned alphabetically to platoons and roll was called. They had to abandon their baggage on the company street to be marched to their noon meal.

At lunch, Tom could hear whispered talk between a few of the candidates who pointed toward an older candidate at a table by himself.

Someone whispered about a rumor that the older candidate had "hell-to-pay." It seems the older candidate was discovered to have beer on his breath when he reported to the Tactical Officer. The TAC Officer, in turn, told the Company Commander.

"As the story goes, the Company Commander counseled the older candidate at length, reminding him that although his Master Sergeant insignia was not on his uniform, he was still to be a role model for the younger candidates. Afterward he was marched to the mess hall and ordered to eat a large raw onion to mask the beer odor," the candidate said.

After eating the noon meal, Tom's platoon moved into a WW II-style barracks. They were broken into four squads, two squads to bunk on the first level and two on the second level. Tom and the others found out later the older master sergeant, called Frank, was from a regular unit.

Although a combat veteran, for this O.C.S. Training, regulations required that he remove his chevrons and all his awards and decorations before reporting to Officer Candidate School. It was a rule that all candidates begin training on an equal footing.

That evening Tom noticed Frank had been assigned to the same squad. Tom and some other recruits, Ben and Wade, were getting to know one another.

Frank joined in. After the introductions, Frank leaned toward them. "Guys," he said loudly enough for others to hear, "notice that high gloss on the floor. It took a lot of work to get it that way, and I suspect we'll be required to keep it shining. So, if I may suggest, let's remove our shoes and walk in our stocking feet whenever possible. That way we won't mark up the floor."

Word spread quickly and the agreement was unanimous, even on the floor above them, and the men quickly removed their footwear.

Tom noticed that Frank took a lot of hazing from the senior TAC Officers who supervised the freshman O.C.S. class. Generally, Frank just smiled at these bullies, but held his ground.

Throughout their training, they were required to march double-time everywhere they went. They came to a halt and saluted whenever they approached officers or senior candidates.

Sometimes, when a new candidate halted to greet an approaching officer, the candidate would be out of breath, but he still had to make himself heard. "Good morning, sir!" the candidate shouted.

"Good afternoon, stupid!" the officer replied because the clock had passed the noon hour.

Tom suffered ups and downs during his training. When a newly-made friend was dropped from the rolls for academic failure, or because he simply wasn't "officer material", the candidate would be there one day, and then suddenly be absent from training. The transfers were always kept quiet. Tom didn't like losing friends.

However, he didn't need to worry about academic failure or incompetence. He was confident he'd graduate, and he looked forward to Jump School and an assignment to a Special Forces unit.

Commissioning as a second lieutenant came after six months of adhering to discipline Tom hadn't believed possible, such as folding his Jockey Shorts into 4-1/4-inch by 6-3/4-inch rectangles, the size of the Field Manual for Drill and Ceremonies. The tiny rectangles of white cotton shorts lay in his footlocker, along with his T-shirts, larger rectangles, and tight rolls of socks aligned in perfect columns of six. Some might think such requirements went overboard, but they were breath to military life. Supreme attention to detail taught soldiers never to overlook anything, no matter how trivial.

CHANGE OF PLAN

Everything seemed to be going Tom's way until he received a letter from his sister, Sirion, who now knew about her father's other family. While he was on leave before coming to Fort Stewart, Tom had told her most of what he knew.

Sirion wasn't in direct contact with the other family, but the contents of her letter told Tom that she'd heard something. Her letter read, "Brian's been assigned to Fort Stewart with the 2nd Battalion of U.S. Army Airborne Rangers."

Tom took this news hard. *I'd planned to be assigned to Special Forces, but now I'll have to rethink my goals if I'm going to stay competitive with Brian. I still want to be like our father, but I had also made a promise to myself that I'd be better than his real son, Brian.*

Now Tom was in a difficult situation. To compete with Brian, he'd have need to be assigned to an Airborne Ranger Battalion, too, but that decision could keep him from being in the Special Forces training to be like Tommy McGlynn. He suddenly remembered that his father had been assigned to the 9th Airborne Ranger company during the Korean War. Tom Aquinas made a decision.

The Tactical Officer's door was ajar when Tom knocked on the doorjamb.

"Come in."

Tom entered, stood at attention, saluting. "Sir, Candidate Aquinas requests permission to speak to the Tactical Officer."

"Stand at ease, Candidate. Speak."

"Sir, before I was assigned to O.C.S., I volunteered for Airborne Training and the Special Forces. Is it too late to change?"

"Losing your nerve, Candidate Aquinas?"

"No, sir. I think I'd be better trained if I could take Ranger training first."

"Are you joking, Candidate? If you think O.C.S. is rough, the Rangers will chew you up and spit you out. What makes you think you're good enough to be a Ranger?!" the TAC officer said sarcastically.

Before Tom could answer, the TAC ordered, "Candidate, you have my permission to leave my office. Ranger indeed! I don't think you have what it takes. Leave my office now!"

Saluting smartly, Tom turned sharply on a toe and a heel, and marched out of the office.

Tom was really annoyed by the TAC Officer's remarks. For the rest of the day, it was all Tom could do to go through the motions of training. *What if I'm not even good enough to become an officer? Maybe I can't cut it.* That thought struck a nerve. . . . *If I can't cut it yet, I'll make myself learn how to cut it. I'm going to Ranger school even if I have to resign from O.C.S. and do it as an enlisted man. . . . I've taken my stepfather's name, I'll never dishonor it. I'll live up to it.*

That evening, returning to his bunk, he found several sheets of paper there which he picked up. Tom's spirits soared. The TAC officer had to have been the one who'd put the forms there. At that moment, Tom was sure he would graduate. An attached note read:

Candidate,

Here are the forms to apply for Jump School, and to change your intention from the Special Forces to the Airborne Rangers. Things are getting down to the wire. I expect these papers to be completed in full and on my desk when I return from dinner.

Good luck!

TAC

O.C.S. Senior Candidate

Important events occurred... Tom's O.C.S. class moved to Senior Status, just below Commissioned Officer. This entitled them to obtain the uniforms they would soon be entitled to wear. Ben, Wade, and Tom went to a uniform shop in nearby Columbus to be measured for the uniforms they would wear as commissioned Second Lieutenants.

After the Review on the main post was over, Tom went with his fellow Senior Candidates to a party at the club. Something had changed among the classmates. The Senior Candidates were now clannish. Those who had chosen the combat branches separated from those who had chosen the support services.

Tom found himself with the volunteers who after graduation would become the elite of the combat branches: Airborne, Ranger, and Special Forces. Of course, they hadn't proven themselves yet, and had to go for more training. But they were willing to try, and that put them a cut above the rest.

Several pressed Master Sergeant Frank for information.

"What's it like to jump from a plane?"

"Is Ranger training really rough?"

"How about Special Forces?"

"Do you think I've got what it takes?"

"What's combat really like?"

Master Sergeant Frank had lived with these young soldiers for almost six months, long enough to form an opinion of each one. Regardless, he answered all of their questions and offered encouragement.

"Sure, you'll make it," he said. "Just remember, it's mind over matter. Like they told us when we were sweating in the sawdust pit during PT: 'They don't mind and we don't matter'." He smiled. "Besides, if I can do it, you can, too."

One evening, Tom was sitting on his footlocker spit-shining his boots when Frank approached.

"Tom," Frank said as he sat down beside him. "I understand you knew McGlynn."

Tom looked up startled. "How did you know that?"

"You and I have mutual friends, young fella. Do you remember Sergeant Owens and Sergeant Scott?"

"Of course. They were my Drill Sergeants in Basic Training."

"Well, they asked me to keep an eye on you, and offer a helping hand or a kick in the ass, to get you through O.C.S. Don't worry. I told them that you didn't need either— which made them happy."

"But, er, . . . How did?" Tom stammered.

Frank smiled. "For cripes sake, stop stuttering. I was in the States, when the then Master Sergeants, Tommy McGlynn and Joseph Mitzamuri did their thing in Laos, . . . but I heard about them. When you know guys like Owens and Scott, you get to hear their war stories. From what I've heard, you've got one hell of a pair of shoes to fill. Don't worry, though. You'll do the job. I know you're going into the Rangers. I'm going back to Special Forces, but if we meet somewhere down the line, I'll buy you a beer or three." He grabbed Tom's hand and gave it a crushing shake. "Good luck, Kid."

Tom watched Master Sergeant Frank walk away.

It was true. They would have that drink together someday if they ran into each other. At that moment, Tom became aware that he'd somehow joined a close-knit fraternity of soldiers. He hoped he could live up to being a member.

The Senior Candidates' first orders were to be posted on the bulletin board during their twentieth week of training. These orders would assign some to schools for further training, and others to active units (where they would be expected by some to perform as "Shaved-tail second louies"). Some candidates would move on to satisfying careers, others would just put in their time and return to civilian life, and a few would fail miserably.

Thomas Aquinas was determined to be one who would succeed. Of course, he didn't know that, not at this stage in his career. He didn't even know if his application for Jump School had been approved. Everyday, when they were dismissed after the day's training, he and the other men in his company rushed to the bulletin board to see if for their orders had been posted. Night after night, the group of disappointed young men walked away, muttering among themselves, worrying, wondering if they'd been selected for what they'd chosen.

"I heard they were closing Jump School," someone said.

"No, they're not. It's being moved to Fort Campbell and Fort Bragg so the Airborne Divisions can conduct their own schools," came another rumor.

"Bullshit!" chimed in another. "They need 250-foot towers for training and the only ones the Army has are here at Fort Benning."

The discussions went on night after night until Friday of the 22nd week. Tom slowly walked toward the bulletin board fully expecting another disappointment. He heard Ben yell, "Aquinas! Better start practicing push-ups. We've got our orders!"

"All right!" Tom shouted to his classmate. He peered over the shoulders of those blocking his view. "Are we assigned to the same company?"

"Yeah, me, Wade, and you, all of our squad plus a bunch more from the rest of the company. Looks like we'll be sticking together for a few more weeks."

"That's great. Where's Wade? Does he know yet?" Tom asked.

"I do now," Wade shouted from the back of the group.

The three candidates stood there, high-fiving each other, glad they'd made it this far.

O.C.S. Graduation

Only one full-length mirror was attached to the barracks wall, and the men of the two squads jockeyed for position. Today was graduation day, and they wanted to be flawless. They checked themselves in the mirror admiring their new uniforms, and then checked each other. Some of them had family and/or sweethearts coming for the ceremony.

On this day, pride ran so deeply in the barracks, it would have taken a chain saw to cut through it. Pride seemed to emanate from the very air they breathed.

A hush fell on the group of candidates as they parted to gape at Frank as he approached the mirror. His uniform now sported Special Forces patches on each shoulder, and on his chest, he wore rows of colorful ribbons and blue-and-silver badges.

Wow! This guy is the real thing. Someday, I'll be able to wear a uniform like that! Tom adjusted his uniform, smoothing out imaginary wrinkles from the cloth. Then, he rubbed his chin to make sure his face had no stubble. It wasn't that he had a beard anyway. His Asian skin was smooth, except for the four or five stray whiskers that sometimes cropped out on his chin. He rubbed his chin again, just to make sure. There was nothing. He was 35-10, the Army's code for having one's uniform and person squared away, for being dressed to code.

Tom spotted Sirion. She smiled proudly as she waved. He looked through the crowd and saw his mother nearby. Doug and Casey were there, too, and this genuinely surprised him. Tom wanted to wave at them, but he couldn't, of course. He had to maintain his military bearing as he took his seat.

With monotonous speeches, several guest speakers congratulated the Candidates. It didn't matter; this was the day they'd all waited for. The TAC Officer suddenly called them to attention. They rose as one when their Company Commander walked to the front of the stage.

"Please raise your right hand and repeat after me," he said.

The Senior Candidates began the Oath of a Commissioned Officer, repeating the words after their Commander.

> I, Thomas Aquinas, having been appointed an officer in the Army of the United States, as indicated above in the grade of Second Lieutenant do solemnly swear that I will support and defend the constitution of the United States against all enemies, foreign or domestic, that I will bear true faith and allegiance to the same; that I take this obligation freely, without any mental reservations or purpose of evasion; and that I will well and faithfully discharge the duties of the office upon which I am about to enter; So help me God.

Phin swelled with pride. She wished her American husband were here with her. She was sure he would be surprised to see her son on this day, an American citizen, and a newly pledged officer of the U.S. Army, standing so handsome in his uniform. What would her American husband have to say? *Is he watching, too?* She closed her eyes for a moment to silently thank him for leaving his *Kwan* with Kumpang.

After they pledged, "So help me God" to complete their oath of office. the students let out a loud, ear-splitting roar.

Phin jumped, startled from her reverie by their noisy enthusiasm.

Chapter 20: On Leave

Later, as they drove back home to Marietta, Phin asked Tom, "Why did you give money to that soldier?"

"What?" Tom asked. "Oh, because he was the first soldier to salute me."

"Will you have to give money to every soldier who salutes you?"

Tom smiled. "No, mother. It's only given to the first man who salutes a new officer."

"But how much money did you give him?"

He laughed. "Only a dollar. It's customary."

"Oh," she said. "American customs are strange."

"Strange, maybe yes, but mostly just different."

Phin nodded and looked at her son, wondering if his training had changed him. He wasn't Lao any more. If they'd stayed in Laos, he might have grown up to be the Headman of the Village of Ban Hin Leek Fai, but here he was an American Second Lieutenant. This thought seemed strange to her, so different than what she had planned for him when she first held him as a babe in her arms.

Tom noticed her watching him, and smiled at her.

"I missed you," he said.

She looked away before he could see the tears forming in her eyes. "I missed you, too," she said quickly. "My job is keeping me so busy." She wanted to change the subject. "I like it, though."

"That's good," he said. He looked in the rearview mirror at his sister. "How about you, Sirion? How are you doing in school?"

Back home in Marietta, Tom was glad to have had a relaxing weekend with his family, and time with Patti. He even had the chance for a pleasant visit with Doug and Casey. Although he was pleased and proud of the way his life was going, he knew his greatest military challenges were still ahead. He had much more to accomplish.

CHAPTER 21: Return to Fort Benning

JUMP SCHOOL: GROUND WEEK

Tom, Ben, and Wade formed a pact to stick together at least until they finished Jump School. Their orders read: Report no later than 1200 on the 17th. They'd arranged to meet in nearby Columbus on the day before, so they could drive to Fort Benning together and report early on the sixteenth. They wanted to be ready and alert for their first roll call.

"I wonder when they issue us a parachute?" Wade turned his car down Riodan Street toward the headquarters of the Airborne school. They could see the jump towers across the field as they passed.

"Pull over!" Ben yelled excitedly.

"What's up?" Wade asked as he pulled the car to the side of the road.

"I just want to take a look," Ben told him.

The three newly commissioned Second Lieutenants stepped from the car to look across the field toward the towers. There were three 250-foot towers rising above the smaller 34-foot towers.

The three officers stood in silence for a minute or two until Ben said, "They're what's worrying me."

"What? The 250s?" Tom asked.

"No. The 34-footers," Ben answered.

"Hey, don't worry about the towers. I don't even think the 250s should bother us. On Coney Island, people pay to ride the tower, and here we'll be riding ours for free," Wade said. Then added, "I don't see how the 34-foot tower should bother you. It's only the height of a three-story building. Besides, Jump School should be a snap after all the crap we just went through."

Ben gave his buddy a frown. "I've heard that more people quit during tower week than any other part of the course, including jump week."

Draping his arms across the shoulders of his two companions, Tom reminded them of their pact. "Guys, we're going to graduate from this training. The three of us. Together. Then we're going to have one helluva party. Rumors of people quitting do not, I say again, do not apply to us." He let go of his friends and turned toward the car. "Now let's go to the 'O' club and have a sandwich before we sign in."

"Suits me," Wade said. He followed Tom and slid behind the steering wheel.

Ben slid into the backseat, but before they drove away, he looked at the towers again, and felt a foreboding. He wasn't used to failure. His father wouldn't allow it. He had spent his life striving to be the best, both as a student and an athlete, always driving himself to the limit, constantly struggling to please his father.

After he closed the car door, Ben shook his head. He wanted to erase the apprehension that looking at the towers brought on, but when he closed his eyes the image of the towers bored into him with a nagging fear, making him feel threatened. He wondered if he should admit to Wade and Tom that he was afraid of heights, but as he looked at his buddies sitting in the front seat, he could see their cool confidence, and he dismissed the idea.

I'll cross that bridge when I come to it, Ben thought. *Who knows . . . maybe this training will help me overcome my stupid fear. I'll learn to deal with it.*

Wade drove to the Officers' Club. "Sounds crazy, but I hope they stop us at the door to see if we're officers," he said.

"Me, too. I never thought I'd be a Second Lieutenant," Tom added.

They went inside and found a table. No one asked to see their ID cards, though.

"I guess they are used to seeing a lot of newbies reporting for Jump School," Wade remarked, but there was disappointment in his voice.

They each ordered a beer to wash down the sandwiches. The topic of conversation swung immediately to the day they'd reported to their O.C.S. company.

"Do you think we'll be eating onions after we report in for Jump School today —beer breath and all," Tom said. His brows were furrowed.

"Nope," Ben said. "It's a whole different ballgame here. Besides, you have to remember that we're officers now, and officers don't have to eat onions. Taints the breath. Makes one unkissable, don't ya know?"

The waitress returned to their table. "I forgot to ask if you wanted onions on your cheeseburgers," she said.

Ben gave her a serious look. "Yes, please. Covered in onions," he said.

The other two burst out laughing. The waitress gave them an odd look and walked away.

When they were through eating lunch, they reported for duty. The earlier they got it over with, the sooner they could get settled in.

Wade pulled into the parking lot of Building 2748. On the long wall of the single story building, there was a row of large colorful murals replicating the shoulder patches which the Airborne units wore, past and present. The murals were in numerical order: the blue patch of the 11th Airborne Division was first with its white wings and red circle, and a white number "11" centered in the insignia. Then the unicorn of the 13th, followed by the talons of the 17th, the AA of the 82nd, and the Screaming Eagle of the 101st.

"Take a good look at the history of the Airborne," Wade told his cohorts.

"Let's hope we can add to that history," Tom said in a half-mumble.

"What did you say, Tom?"

"What he said and what he meant were two different things," Ben answered for Tom. "The inscription over the Gates of Hell: *All hope abandon, all ye who enter here!* That's what he meant. A quote from Dante Alighieri's **The Divine Comedy**."

"Huh?" asked Tom.

"Would you rather have it in Italian? *Lasciate ogni speranza, voi ch'entrate*."

"What the hell are you talking about?" Wade asked.

"Damn, Wade. Didn't you go to school? Don't you read? Dante was one of history's greatest epic poets," Ben answered. "He wrote of places, called Hell, Purgatory, and Heaven. Appropriate, don't you think? 'Abandon hope'."

Opening the door to the building, Wade turned to Ben and asked quizzically, "Are you all right?" There was genuine concern in his voice.

But Ben didn't answer him. He just gave a shrug. Then they both entered the building and Tom followed them inside.

The next morning, the three young officers were eager to begin their training. The sun hadn't broken the horizon over Lawson Field, but they were already waiting in the company area. They were the first there, but lights shining from surrounding barracks assured them that they wouldn't be alone for long. Gradually, the other members of their class filtered in beside them.

"Let me have your attention. . . . Listen up over here!" came a booming voice from a short, muscular sergeant. He was standing at the top of the steps leading into the barracks. "Answer when I call your name, and then form up by Sergeant Roy over there on my left. Sergeant Roy!"

Sergeant Roy raised his right arm into the air and answered, "Yo!"

Hearing an answer from Roy, the Sergeant on the steps continued, "Major Gordon, Captain Askew, Lieutenant Adams," The roll call continued until the company for basic Airborne Training was formed.

There were 493 volunteers at the start of this grueling three-week course. That number would thin out in a matter of days. The Sergeant shouted, "Expect the sudden disappearance of any individual or a group of individuals. Only the best will wear the coveted Silver Wings of a paratrooper. It is the will of the Almighty. Those not worthy are destined to be 'ptewy-legged non-jumpers'."

"Company, attenshun!" yelled the Sergeant. The company snapped to attention. "Right face! Forward march!" Those who had thought their training had begun were in for a rude awakening. The start of their training waited in a parking lot by the 250-foot towers.

"Company halt! Left face!" Sergeant Roy barked the order, and when the class made the required movement and stood facing him, he walked away from the formation, leaving them standing at attention.

A few moments passed in silence until Tom heard the shuffling of feet and a few muttered remarks.

"What the hell is going on?"

"I wonder if we can smoke."

"Where the hell is everybody?"

But their wonderment came to an abrupt halt and apprehension settled in as commands were heard from behind the row of hedges to their front.

"Instructors, attenshun! Right face! Double time, march!"

From out of the corner of his eye, Tom could see the instructors as they rounded the hedge trotting toward his company. The instructors were dressed in starched fatigue trousers bloused and tucked into the

Corcoran Jump Boots. Their boots were spit-shined to a high gloss. The instructors wore T-shirts with each man's rank and name stenciled across the front, and on each man's head was a black baseball cap adorned with silver parachute wings centered on the front of the cap. These men were referred to as 'Black Hats.' Their one purpose in life was to train the volunteers to become paratroopers. They would train them or break them.

Individual Black Hats dropped out of their formation as they ran past the company. Each man then took a position at the head of each rank of trainees, standing shoulder to shoulder at arm's length apart.

One Black Hat was left. He trotted to stand in front of the company, centered on the formation, facing them. In a booming voice the Black Hat ordered, "Open ranks, march!"

When he saw that the other Black Hats at the end of each rank had properly aligned their rank, he ordered, "Ready, front!" and the inspection began.

The Black Hats could be heard as they meted out punishments for minor infractions.

"What did you shine your boots with, Lieutenant, a Hershey™ Bar? Drop and give me 25 push-ups!

"Have you ever heard of Brasso™, Sergeant? Your belt buckle is growing penicillin! Drop and give me 25!"

"Did you sleep in that uniform, Private? Drop and give me 25!"

Welcome to Jump School, Tom thought as a Black Hat stopped in front of him. He was confident nothing would be found to cause a caustic remark or push-ups.

The Black Hat looked at him. "Do I detect a smug attitude, Lieutenant? Are you so sure you'll make the grade to join our ranks? Drop and give me 25." He cleared his voice and added, "sir."

The Introduction to Airborne Training was being impressed upon this group of potentials. An additional impression would be made upon them when they listened to the welcoming speech given by a certain field grade officer, who spat on the ground every time he mentioned the phrase, "ptewy-legged non-jumper." A derisive remark of contempt reserved for those who flunked out of Jump School.

They were told during their welcome to take a good look at the men to their left and right. There was a good chance that the man standing next to them wouldn't be there for graduation ceremonies. The attrition rate, quitters, illness, and injuries averaged between 20 and 30 percent.

Tom was hesitant to look but could feel the eyes of others looking at him. He started to cut his eyes to the right, but suddenly he decided not to look. *I don't want any negativity to permeate my thoughts. I'm determined to graduate.*

He wouldn't let his mind become cluttered with self-doubt or worry about which of the others would or wouldn't make it. This attitude helped to keep him focused. Later, Tom even gave his two friends pep talks so they could finish what they'd started. It seemed to work, too.

All was going well for the three friends as the training progressed. Of course, the physical side of their training was no trouble after the six months of O.C.S. they had endured. Their O.C.S. training also helped them to privately laugh off the harassment that the Black Hats gave out. Of course one does not laugh at, nor challenge a Black Hat. To do so would be a ticket to the Officer "Ptewy-legged (spit, spit) non-jumper's' outfit and forfeit of the chance to wear the coveted Silver Wings".

The three young officers progressed through their first week of training, Ground Week, with relative ease. They were even able to offer encouragement and physical assistance to others in their company. On the first morning when they ran along the track surrounding the tower area, a classmate from O.C.S. running between Tom and Ben began to falter. Tom and Ben each grabbed the man's belt and managed to hold him in formation. The following morning the man again needed assistance, and they provided it, but after dinner that evening when Ben was returning to his quarters, he saw the classmate wearing civilian clothes and walking toward his car.

"Where are you off to, Dave?" Ben called.

"Town!" Dave yelled. "It's party time!" The classmate got into his car and drove off toward Columbus.

Later that night, Ben told Tom about it. "Tom, I saw Davidson earlier tonight. He was all dressed up in civvies and headed for town. He told me it was party time. Can you believe that crap? We carry his ass during the day, and he parties all night. I'm not doin' that any more, friend. If he can't make it on his own tomorrow, it's his problem. I ain't helping him."

"Maybe he had an appointment or something," Tom offered.

"Nope. He told me it was party time. Screw him. If we carry him now, somebody else is gonna to have to carry him somewhere else down the line, and that ain't gonna be on my conscience. Have you already forgotten the incident in the sawdust pit?"

"Do you mean when he spit?" Tom asked.

"That's just what I was referring to." Ben sounded angry. "Yes! And our Black Hat was livid! I remember him asking Dave, 'How would you like to roll around in some other guy's spit?' and the Black Hat made him get his spit out of the pit."

"I know," Tom said. "And when Dave tried to scoop it out with his hands, the Black Hat told him to get it out the same way he got it in. I thought it was gross to see Dave root around like a hog to get it back in his mouth so he could take it and spit it outside the pit. I, for one, felt sorry for him."

"Not me. Not to mention the fact that I didn't much care for Dave in O.C.S. He just didn't act like a team player then, either. I tell you, if he drops tomorrow, it's his problem. Screw him," Ben said with conviction.

Tom nodded silently in agreement.

On the next morning's run when Davidson showed signs of fatigue, Tom glanced at Ben, but neither one made a move to help. Tom ran on, thinking, *Everybody needs a helping hand now and then, but there comes a time . . .*

THE MOCK-UP DOOR

The First Week of Ground Training had two purposes. First, how to exit properly from an aircraft in flight, and second, how to land and roll on the ground to lessen the risk of breaking bones. This landing was called a "Parachute Landing Fall" or "PLF". The only way to learn PLF is through repetition.

They used a "Mock-up Door" training apparatus made of plywood. The mock-up was a long wooden hull simulating an airplane's fuselage. It stood about three feet off the ground. Students were required to shuffle, in a foot-sliding motion, along the length of the airplane as they approached the open door. This was known as the 'Airborne Shuffle.' It was mandatary in the aircraft so jumpers wouldn't get entangled in each other's equipment.

As each jumper reached the open door, he had to turn with military precision and slide the static line forcefully along the anchor line cable toward the tail of the airplane. The jumper then positioned himself to stand in the door for a short second as he placed his hands flat against the outside of the fuselage in order to propel himself vigorously up and out, to completely clear the airplane. At the same time, he had to assume a body position proven to be in the best interest of the jumper. Feet and knees together, elbows tight to the side, fingers widened and hands gripping the front of the reserve parachute, and chin touching the chest. Then the jumper had to start his count, loud and clear, "One thousand, two thousand, three thousand," to give his parachute time to open. If it wasn't open by the end of the count, he had been instructed to pull the aluminum handle of his reserve chute. If the jumper had exited the airplane as he'd been trained, and assumed the correct body position, the handle would be readily available under his right hand.

The Black Hats stood ready to ensure that students in their charge followed these set procedures to the letter, and prepared sufficiently to start training at the tower the following week. Consequently, the Black Hats aggressively admonished those who were slow to get the hang of the mock-up exercise.

"That was the sloppiest door exit I've seen in all my time in this school. Drop and give me twenty-five! Then take your place in line and do it again!"

"Number one-one-seven, you'll do it again and again until you get it right or wear out the ground with pushups."

"Good exit, number one-two-four! Get back in line and try it again—just to make sure that wasn't a fluke. I want to be sure you're becoming proficient, but in the meantime, give me twenty-five. I don't want you to get a swollen head!"

It was a No Win when it came to pleasing one of the Black Hats.

Tom and Wade had avoided mentioning the 34-foot towers whenever they were with Ben, but the problem was not to be avoided for long. Tower week started Monday, although it would begin without Lieutenant Davidson. No one had seen him since he'd dropped from the run a few days before. It had happened just like the sergeant had warned them the first day. One day, Davidson was in formation, the next day he wasn't.

TOWER JUMP TRAINING

Class numbers were issued alphabetically by surname. Tom was given a lower number than Ben or Wade, so Tom was the first of the three to go to the 34-foot tower.

During early instruction there, Tom was worried about Ben. He'd allowed his mind to wander during the instruction and the demonstration of procedures. Now he'd have to pay for his lack of focus.

"Where is your mind this morning, Lieutenant? On your sweetheart at home? Or have you fallen in love with some floozy on Front Street?" the Black Hat, Sergeant Bass, roared at him. "Did you take part in this training as part of some suicide pact? You're being trained in what can become a very hazardous occupation for you, and more importantly, dangerous for those you will command— that is, *if* you happen to make the grade. Give me twenty-five, sir. And please, count loud enough so they can hear you on the main post. Then, and only then, will I allow you to climb the tower again!"

Tom did the 25 push-ups, counting loudly, and then he rushed to stand once again in front of the Black Hat so he could be outfitted with the harness needed for the tower jump. As he attached the harness to his body, he saw Ben running up the stairs to the platform at the top of the tower. Suddenly afraid for his friend, he stopped what he was doing and held his breath, watching and waiting for Ben to jump.

His wait was short-lived. The Black Hat in front of him shouted, "Have you lost it entirely, Lieutenant? Are you waiting for an invitation to join this training? Or is it that you like doing push-ups for me? Give me 25, sir, and this time I want the count heard in downtown Columbus. When you finish, report back to me and no one else. Do you understand? No one else."

As he was counting his push-ups in a voice loud enough to satisfy the Black Hat, Tom recognized Ben's voice counting as he exited the tower above. Tom quickened his pace. He was glad that his friend had been wrong in his prediction of failing the tower. He did his twenty-fifth push-up, suddenly realizing that he'd allowed himself to fall into this predicament. He needed to get back on track.

Tom reported to the Black Hat and was taken aside and questioned at length about his mental attitude. The parachute school didn't want to graduate any student they determined would be a danger to themselves or others. Tom answered the questions and was surprised when the Black Hat told him to go to the tower. Apparently, he was now satisfied with Tom's answers.

"I'll be keeping an eye on you, Lieutenant, and I strongly suggest you get your ducks in a row. Concentrate on the matter at hand and that's all! Now, double time it and take your place in line!"

"Yes, Sergeant Bass!" Tom answered briskly. He turned and ran to the tower to wait his turn. He stood there, as his harness was inspected, before climbing the steps on the double. His heart was pounding by the time he reached the top. He stopped, suddenly unsure of himself. He handed the risers of his harness to the Black Hat, who was waiting at the top of the tower. The Black Hat hooked them to the device that would stop Tom's fall and carry him safely down the cable.

"Get ready!" yelled the Black Hat.

Tom looked upward, studiously avoiding a glance toward the ground three stories below.

"Lieutenant, when you are ordered to 'Stand in the Door,' make eye contact with the instructor sitting below and sound off with your number so he can hear you," ordered the Black Hat. "Ready? Stand in the Door!"

"Number twenty-seven!" Tom yelled as he made eye contact with the Black Hat who would be grading him.

Tom felt a twinge of vertigo, but he reacted to the shouted order and the expected slap on the back of his leg. He leaped from the tower without hesitation. He counted loud and clear. He was rewarded by hearing the metal "Klang" when the risers' connecting links banged into the back of his helmet—which knocked his helmet askew.

A Black Hat below called to him, "Check your canopy number twenty-seven! Check your canopy!"

He ignored his lopsided helmet, and with both hands up on the risers, he looked above him where the parachute canopy would be if this had been a live jump. He slid down the cable until his forward motion was stopped suddenly after the risers made contact with the arresting cable.

Tom could feel sweat running down his back. *What an experience!* he thought. *I wonder how many times I get to do that? What a ride!*

Another student, standing on top of the beam, unhooked him from the cable, and Tom double-timed back to stand in front of the Black Hat who was grading him. He wasn't worried about the grade, about the possibility of push-ups, or the 250-foot tower jumps. He and his friends had done this one. They would make it. He was happy for Ben, Wade, and himself.

The three friends decided to celebrate. They ordered a pizza and bought a six-pack to take back to the Bachelor Officers' Quarters (B.O.Q.). Tomorrow, they'd have a chance to experience a real parachute landing. They would be dropped from the 250-foot tower. Now that they were looking forward to it, it was just about all they talked about—although the name of a female or two entered into the conversations.

Tom had already had his turn at being dropped from the 250 and was sitting in the stands with the rest of the company members who had been on the tower. He saw Ben's parachute canopy being attached to the cable and huge ring that would take him to the top.

Tom flashed Ben a thumbs up signal. "We've got it made now, buddy," Tom said aloud.

Ben had seen the "thumbs up" sign Tom had flashed him, and he wanted to return the same sign, but he knew better.

Tom watched as three men were lifted into the air on tower arms one, two, and three. Ben was using tower arm one. The fourth arm hung unused for two reasons: it was broken but also because it was on today's windward side.

Having been dropped from the tower previously, Tom now knew what to expect.

Ben was lifted almost to the top, but stop temporarily about ten feet below the arm of number one until the Black Hat with the megaphone told him, "Number One, unhook your safety line." Then, the Black Hat beckoned him to look around at the surrounding countryside from that high vantage point. "You're hanging from the tallest structure on Fort Benning, the home of the Infantry, birthplace of the Airborne! From where you are hanging, you can see the Brevard Fault Zone. You can look across the beautiful Chattahoochee River to see the State of Alabama on the other river bank."

Ben followed instructions and endured the tour-guide spiel from the Black Hat on the bullhorn, but he kept his eyes closed, except for a squinted peek at the countryside. *I have to settle down if I'm was going to get through this.* He swallowed and felt himself calm down a little. He took a deep breath. That helped, too.

After that, the Black Hat gave Ben his final instructions. "Arm Number One, reach well up on your front risers and prepare for a front slip. You want to stay away from the cold steel of the tower to your rear." Seeing his order had been obeyed and the safety line unhooked, the Black Hat gave the order, "Release arm one! Release number one!"

Ben was brought up the last ten feet to be released so he could float gently to earth.

Ben knew there was a strict procedure to follow, and he wanted to follow it to the letter. But when Ben felt himself pulled up the additional ten feet to the top of the tower, his heart beat in a vicious drum roll. That is, until he was taken higher and higher, and his fear of heights took hold of him. There was a swishing and a clicking sound when his canopy was released from the cable and ring.

He thought about the nylon harness from which he was hanging. *The harness is only a few nylon straps an inch and a half wide holding me up.* Ben gritted his teeth and remained silent.

He had friends some 200 feet below he'd not disappoint; but his mind raced: *What am I doing here? What am I trying to prove? And to whom?* It took all of his reserves not to cry out, BRING ME DOWN! *I DON'T WANT TO BE HERE! IT'S ALL A BIG MISTAKE!*

Then, he no longer cared if his friends were disappointed. His stomach gave a flip-over. They weren't in his thoughts. For the first time,

Ben knew pure terror. He panicked and dropped into nothingness. He lost his grip on the front risers. In his haste to regain his grasp, he panicked. His arms flailed about. Then, he felt what he mistook to be his front risers in his hands. He had actually found his rear risers and held them with a death grip as he vigorously worked them, driving himself into the tower.

The students on arms three and two had just been released and as they fell beneath full canopies, a problem developed on arm one.

"JUMPER IN THE TOWER!" the Black Hat yelled into his megaphone.

The rest of the Black Hats sprang into action. They climbed the steel quickly to where Ben was tangled, and first, secured him to the tower so his parachute canopy would not disengage from whatever was holding it, causing him to be dragged abruptly and painfully to the ground. Then, keeping him in his harness, they released him from his parachute's canopy, and let it drop to the ground before his injuries could be assessed.

Now surprisingly calm, Ben answered the questions asked of him.

"Where are you hurt?"

"My back and my left leg," he said with a grimace.

"Hang on; we'll have you down in a few."

"Damn, I really screwed up, huh?"

"Don't worry about it," the Black Hat lied. "It happens all the time," as he hooked Ben's parachute harness to the same cable that, just moments before, had taken him to the top. This time, he was lowered to ground, loaded on a stretcher and carried to an awaiting ambulance.

WINN ARMY COMMUNITY HOSPITAL

Later that evening, Tom and Wade made a trip to visit their friend who was in Winn Army Community Hospital at Fort Stewart. He was encased in a plaster cast from neck to groin. His left leg was also in a cast and suspended from a trapeze attached to the bed. His upper body was in considerable pain and he didn't seem to make much sense when he tried to explain what had happened.

The two attributed that to the painkillers Ben was probably getting. They didn't stay long, but they promised to return the following night.

When they did return, the room was empty. They asked at the Nurses Station, and a nurse, Captain Monaghan explained. "Your friend Ben has been transferred to Walter Reed Army Medical Center in D.C." She lowered her voice, "They're doing research to help people with Ben's type of injuries."

Tom and Wade were speechless. They thanked her and couldn't get out of the hospital fast enough.

Now that their trio had been separated, things just weren't the same. Ben had been the glue that kept them banded together. Tom and Wade were still able to progress through training, but it was different.

LIVE PARACHUTE JUMP TRAINING

A few days later, Tom stood in line with his company. They were being issued parachutes for their first live parachute jump. A Black Hat separated the company into groups who would fly together for the jump. He brought a Master Sergeant over to Tom's plane load and placed him in line with two PFCs. The PFCs were brothers attending Jump School together. One of the guys in his group told Tom that the Master Sergeant was a qualified parachutist and that he was also the older brother of the two PFCs. The Master Sergeant, although assigned to another Airborne unit, would accompany his brothers on their first jump.

Second Lieutenant Thomas Aquinas, Number 27, sat across from the three brothers in the C-130 as the whine of the four Allison engines changed from a high pitch to a roar. The airplane sped down the runway of Lawson Field.

Tom envied the banter between the brothers and thought it might be nice to have a brother. He remembered Brian McGlynn Bath and wondered, for a moment, if Brian would ever call him brother.

Tom looked toward the Black Hat, wearing a free-fall-style parachute, as he held onto the anchor line cable. He was talking to the Master Sergeant.

"Sure," said the Master Sergeant to the Black Hat. The Master Sergeant nodded his head and then undid his seat belt and stood. He turned and pointed to his brothers and smiled. Then he yelled to the Black Hat above the roar of the engines so the rest of the men would hear him, "If either of these two clowns hesitates, you have my permission to kick their asses out the door."

The Black Hat smiled back and answered he would. He had the Master Sergeant hook his static line to the anchor-line cable and check his equipment.

When the Master Sergeant seemed satisfied that all was well, the Black Hat left him to go to the starboard door and check the outside of the plane before beckoning his volunteer wind-dummy to Stand in the Door. Tom noticed the red light glowing beside the door and was somewhat surprised the Master Sergeant was following the same procedures they'd been taught. He thought because of the Master Sergeant's rank and advanced qualification, the Master Sergeant would be above the rules. Tom was wrong. The rules governing military parachute jumping were etched in stone and would be modified for no man, private, master sergeant, or general.

Tom was fascinated as he watched the Master Sergeant standing in the open door. The man alternated his gaze between the outside and inside of the airplane. When the Master Sergeant looked outside of the plane, the pressure of the rushing wind distorted his face, but as he looked inside to check the light, his face returned to normal.

Tom stared as the red light to the left of the door went out, and the green light above it flashed on, indicating the airplane was at the correct altitude and over the drop zone (DZ). The man who had been standing there suddenly was gone. He'd disappeared from his position in the open door.

My God! Tom thought. *Is that what will happen to me?*

There it was, all that they had been trained to do, the Airborne Shuffle, all of it. The Black Hat ordered them to stand up, hook up, check their equipment, and sound off the equipment checks. He followed the precision commands, time-tested and true. It was now Tom's turn.

"Stand in the Door!" came the Black Hat's call to him.

Tom slid his static line forcefully toward the rear of the anchor line cable. He pivoted nicely and stood with the toe of his right foot extended slightly beyond the edge of the doorway. Momentarily pleased with himself, he was startled by the slap on the back of his leg and found himself falling outside the airplane. Above the wind, he shouted the required count, "ONE THOUSAND! TWO THOUSAND! THREE THOUSAND!" His parachute pulled from its bag and he kept falling. Then with little warning, his canopy blossomed above him, and with a sudden jerk, dramatically slowed his fall. His twisted risers unwound, slowly spinning him in his descent.

How did that happen? he wondered momentarily, thinking he had done something wrong, yet at the same time, realizing he had done it right.

My God, I did it right! He had jumped without hesitation. His parachute deployed as it was supposed to, and he was soon to make a perfect PLF. When he looked down, the ground was coming up faster than he'd anticipated. Instead of landing in the prescribed manner called "feet, calf, thigh, buttocks, and push-up muscle." (It requires bending the knees, turning to the side, rolling on calf, thigh then buttocks.)

However, he landed in what had become the joking standard for a PLF, "heels, ass, and head."

Because of his bad landing, a Black Hat took him to task, and had him do twenty-five, as a reminder. Tom didn't care, though. He was happy. He'd jumped and landed safely! He could have done push-ups until the sun came up if the Black Hat demanded.

What did it matter? He had survived falling from the edge of the atmosphere to claim earth as his own. Now he was a jumper, a paratrooper. How many Americans could say that? At barely 20 years of age, he'd accomplished so much. Just thinking what the future has in store for him was overwhelming. He figured that Thomas Aquinas was a man to be reckoned with, for sure.

JUMP SCHOOL GRADUATION

By chance, the Rangers of the Korean War were having a reunion in nearby Columbus when Tom's class had their graduation ceremonies. These Airborne veterans were invited to pin the newly-earned wings on the jumpers.

Tom stood at attention, worried his pride would burst the buttons from his uniform as one of the tough-looking Ranger veterans pinned the coveted Silver Wings above his left breast pocket.

The Ranger smiled and congratulated Tom, but the newly winged paratrooper was shocked when he looked into the Ranger's eyes. Seeing eyes like that made Tom shiver. There was something awful in those eyes. They had a haunted quality— of eyes that had seen the hells of combat.

Tom no longer felt so proud of himself. In fact, he wondered if he had it in him to graduate to *another* level in his military career—the level of the man who had just pinned his parachute wings on him.

With haunted eyes, the Ranger smiled at him. He wished Tom luck, then walked away.

Tom stood there watching him. *I'll never forget how, with only a look, that man made me feel so humble. I'm reminded of how much I have to live up to, not just living up to the military record of Thomas Aquinas McGlynn, but also to those others in the elite ranks of Special*

Forces and Rangers, as well as to the scores of other men who have sacrificed for their country.

THE TALENT SCOUT

Tom wasn't so hungry. He picked at the food the waitress placed in front of him, but his thoughts were elsewhere. He failed to notice the Major standing by his table, until he asked for the second time, "Do you mind if I join you, Lieutenant?"

Momentarily confused by the request, Tom looked up and saw the gold leaf on the Major's collar and almost knocked his chair over when he stood. "Not at all, sir, please," Tom said, as he gestured toward the vacant chair.

"You seemed to be in deep thought," the Major said, as he reached for a menu. "Are you having a problem of some kind?"

Tom started to say that everything was fine, until he noticed the scroll of the 75th Ranger Regiment on the Major's left shoulder.

"Well, sir, I am a little frustrated. Initially, I volunteered for Special Forces but I changed my mind while I was at O.C.S. Instead, I've now volunteered for Ranger training and for assignment to a Ranger unit. I graduated from Jump School three weeks ago, but I *still* don't have any orders.

"My entire class had assignments before we graduated, and they are all gone now. It's hard to keep myself busy while I wait to find out where I am going."

Suddenly, the Major had a spark in his eyes. He held up two fingers, "I have two questions, Lieutenant. One: why did you decide to volunteer for the Rangers instead of Special Forces? Two: what are you doing to keep busy?"

Before Tom could answer him, a waitress interrupted to take the Major's order. He ordered a beer, asked the waitress to bring a refill for the Lieutenant, and then ordered a sandwich.

After she left to fill his order, the Major said, "Lieutenant, you don't have to answer if you'd rather not. It's just that I'm interested, and you never know when you might meet someone who can help you."

The Major's demeanor caused Tom to tell him the real reason why he had changed his mind. He told him all of it, about his father also being a Ranger in the Korean War and his decision to be a Ranger as well.

The Major was silent for a moment after Tom finished his story, and then he asked, "What languages do you speak?"

"Lao, of course. Some Thai, and with a refresher, I should be able to make myself understood in French."

"Do you have a security clearance?" the Major asked.

"Yes, sir. I'm cleared for Secret."

"Good," the Major replied, as he took a notebook and ballpoint pen from his uniform pocket. He passed it to Tom, telling him to print his full name, social security number, telephone number, and designation of his current rank and unit. Then, satisfied he could read what Tom wrote, he put notebook and pen back into his pocket and reached for the beer that had just been delivered.

"Cheers," he said, lifting the bottle to his lips and Tom followed suit.

AS A 'TAG ON'

Tom had all but forgotten his meeting with the Major as he went about helping in the company. He did enjoy the atmosphere of Jump School and opportunities to jump with the students as a space-available 'Tag on.' His confidence increased with every jump. He would miss the camaraderie of the Black Hats. Now he even had a black hat of his own. But he had a bigger goal now, and he wanted to move on. Even the men he worked with were well aware of his goal and silently applauded him for his tenacity.

The following week, Tom was called to go before the First Sergeant. He figured it was for a routine visit, but he hoped he'd get his orders.

The First Sergeant smiled at him as he entered the Corpsman Room. "Lieutenant, this seems to be your lucky day." He handed Tom the papers.

"Orders?" Tom asked.

"Yes, sir, to Ranger School."

Tom glanced down at the papers and quickly scanned them and absorbed most of what he read. Tom stiffened his jaw. "Thank you, First Sergeant."

Tom walked away so he could read in detail the papers he had been handed. He'd expected to be excited by the news, but doubt came again from out of nowhere. *What if I don't have what it takes to be like him?*

The cover sheet read: "Ranger candidates should not report for training until they have demonstrated proficiency in all Ranger Course Prerequisites."

The next paragraph listed the candidates' commander's responsibilities to ensure that applicants were proficient in physical and soldierly requirements, known as "common tasks" in order to enter training.

Another page described the function of the Ranger course: To develop combat-related skills for volunteers eligible for assignments to units whose primary mission is to engage in close combat.

The top graduates of this training had the best chances to be assigned to the 75th Ranger Regiment, or to Special Forces for 'A' Team level. If they were willing to volunteer for such assignments, it would make them a "Triple Volunteer." A volunteer: 1. For the Army; 2. For parachute training; and 3. for the units that would be the vanguard in any future conflict (as they had been on the beaches of Normandy and the jungles of Southeast Asia.)

Tom volunteered for units requiring higher physical and mental aptitudes than any other group and most other schools in the military of the day.

Page 3 outlined those prerequisite military skills: Knowledge of weapons; Use of maps to direct supporting fire; Day and night land navigation. The physical requirements included: a 15-meter swim, fully-clothed and with boots and weapon; a five-mile run, fully-clothed, in under 40 minutes. The runners would be fully-clothed, but not in shorts and track shoes as they would be in sporting events.

The prerequisites mandated a candidate must have intelligence, proficiency, and cross-training in many specific skills such as:

1. The medical training to treat the wounded in the absence of doctors,
2. Knowledge of antenna lengths for communication in remote areas,
3. An ability to function in the absence of leaders, and
4. Mental and physical capability to parachute, using a 40-pound rig, into absolute darkness from various altitudes; Static line or free fall, carrying 100 pounds of equipment; and, travel on foot, carrying this equipment into the battle area, and still have the stamina to fight upon arrival.

CHAPTER 22: Ranger History & Traditions

"Lieutenant Aquinas?"

Tom looked up to see the First Sergeant standing before him.

"Mind if I ask you a question, sir?" the NCO asked.

"Not at all, First Sergeant. Shoot."

"What's the deal about you wanting to join the Rangers?"

Tom hesitated, but answered, "It's a personal goal I set for myself, to be part of the best."

"You seemed to like it in Parachute School, and you've gained a good reputation in the short time you've been with us. Why don't you stay?" the First Sergeant asked.

"I'd like to stay, in a way, but I've got to take the challenge."

"I thought you might say something like that, so I took the liberty of getting something for you from a buddy in the Rangers. It may prove to be interesting reading." He handed Tom a small stack of papers. "Good luck, Lieutenant," he said, and left to go back to his office.

That night, Tom sat in the Officers' Quarters and read through the papers he'd been given, along with four copies of his orders to Ranger School. The batch of papers contained information and orientation. One page caught his eye almost immediately: *Ranger History.*

What do I know about being a Ranger? What is it really? If I don't know, then how can I be good enough to be one? he asked himself.

As he lay across his bed, he read up on the subject. According to the material:

The fellowship of Rangers was not a concept of modern warfare. Units had been designated as Rangers as far back as the 1600s. Under Captain Benjamin Church, Rangers fought in a conflict known as "King Philip's War" against Chief Metacomet (1639-1676). Metacomet was a

Wampanoag Indian Chief, who gave himself an English name, "King Philip." He fought hard to regain and retain regional territory for the Indians.

Later, Major Robert Rogers (1731-1795) of New Hampshire organized nine companies of Rangers of American colonists to fight for the British during the French and Indian War. He incorporated the inherent characteristics of the frontiersmen into military doctrine. He recorded his insights in a journal which was later excerpted and published in 1769 in Dublin, as "A Plan of Discipline" from the **Journals of Major Robert Rogers,** now called **Rogers' Rangers Standing Orders.**

Tom had already seen the short form of it handed out on a small card for soldiers to carry in Vietnam, so his curiosity lead him to the library to read the original 1769 version. [*See Appendix for both versions.*] He compared the two versions of the Standing Orders. He realized they didn't contradict the way a Lao soldier would think about military tactics out in the woods.

He took a walk to enjoy the night air. Tom realized that becoming a Ranger was not simply an act of volunteering; It was a commitment to carry on a tradition bathed in blood. Back in the B.O.Q., he picked up the material to resume reading:

In June 1775, the Continental Congress decreed that six companies of expert riflemen be raised immediately (two each from Pennsylvania, Maryland, and Virginia) because of impending war with England. These volunteers organized under the command of General Daniel Morgan (1736-1802). General George Washington, himself, designated this organization as "The Corps of Rangers." Washington's adversary, British Brigadier-General John Burgoyne (1722-1792) called them, "the most famous corps of the Continental Army." (Burgoyne had introduced light cavalry to the British Army.)

Another group, The Connecticut Rangers were used primarily for reconnaissance; About 150 men served under the command of Thomas Knowlton. Knowlton was killed-in-action leading his men in the Battle of Harlem Heights, New York.

During the American Civil War, both sides realized the value of Ranger units. Confederate cavalry officer Colonel John Singleton Moseby (1833-1916) began with a three-man reconnaissance unit in 1862, which grew to eight companies by 1865. He instructed his Rangers to attack, then blend in with the local people— 'like a grey ghost.'

Colonel Turner Ashby, Jr., known as "the black knight of the Confederacy," was a Virginian known for his daring attitude toward his command. He commanded another unit of Confederate Rangers. Although not as well known as Colonel Moseby's Rangers, Ashby's unit was equally effective.

Not to be outdone, the Union Army had a Ranger unit, made famous for the capture of the ammunition train of Confederate General James Longstreet (1821-1904). Those Union Rangers even captured an element of the Moseby's Ranger force.

Tom was puzzled by the absence of mention of Ranger units during World War I, but he continued to read.

Six Ranger Battalions were formed early in World War II, on the recommendation of Major General Lucian King Truscott. Truscott proposed to General George Catlett Marshall (1880-1959) that an American unit be formed along the lines of the British Commandos. He chose the name of this new unit to be Rangers to honor those past heroes in American history who had exemplified courage, initiative, determination, ruggedness, fighting ability, and achievement.

Colonel O. Darby, a West Point graduate from Fort Smith, Arkansas, was stationed in Northern Ireland with General Russell P. Hartle's staff. Darby was selected to be Commander of the 1st Ranger Battalion formed there June 19, 1942. Darby's handpicked officers interviewed thousands of volunteers from among the American units stationed in Northern

Ireland. After a weeding out program, the chosen were initiated into the 1st Ranger Battalion at Carrickfergus.

This was also the first Ranger Battalion since the American Civil War to be under the supervision of battle-seasoned Commando instructors from their training center at Achnacarry, Scotland. Five hundred men of the 600 men which Darby had brought to Scotland completed their training successfully.

When they joined with British and Canadian Commandos for a raid on Dieppe, France, 44 enlisted men and five officers from the 1st Ranger Battalion were the first American ground soldiers to see action against the Germans. The 1st Ranger Battalion also spearheaded the invasion of North Africa. As campaign ribbons were added to their unit's colors, their reputation grew, and their ranks swelled with new volunteers.

Two more battalions joined Darby's force. The Rangers went on to Sicily and the Italian campaign, where they sustained heavy casualties.

At Anzio, the Rangers penetrated the German frontline positions and advanced five miles. Surrounded by the Germans and running low on ammunition, the Rangers fought as they waited for supporting units who could not break through the strong German positions. Although suffering heavy losses, they thwarted Hitler's planned German counterattack, known as: *Push the Allies into the Sea*.

When elements from his division were pinned down by murderous crossfire on the Normandy beachhead, General Norman D. "Dutch" Cota (1893-1971) gave an order that became a rallying cry for Rangers, then and now: *Rangers, Lead the Way!*

The Rangers did. They advanced through withering fire, four miles to the key town of Veirville, France, and continued on through Europe.

Commander Darby described Rangers in his farewell speech to his men said, "Commanding the Rangers was like driving a team of very high-spirited horses. No effort was needed to get them to go forward. The problem was to hold them in check."

Tom fell asleep with the book on his chest. The following morning after doing his assigned chores, he continued reading his homework.

Another, the 6th Ranger battalion, was formed at Port Moresby, Australia, for duty in the Pacific. The 5307th Composite Unit (Provisional), later known as Merrill's Marauders formed to spearhead the Chinese army into Burma. The 6th Ranger Battalion became the first American force to return to The Philippines, while Merrill's Marauders operated behind enemy lines for extended periods of time in the jungles of India and Burma.

On April 10, 1944, the 5307th was combined with the 475th Infantry. On June 21, 1954, this force was redesignated as the 75th Infantry Regiment. The 75th Ranger Regiment of today traces its lineage to what was once Merrill's Marauders.

Then, on September 2, 1945, Cessation of Hostilities officially came when the Japanese signed a surrender agreement aboard the USS *Missouri*, anchored in Tokyo Bay. The war was over. The Allied forces had defeated the forces of the Axis powers, and the world finally was at peace once again. So it was believed there would be no need for Ranger-type units any more. *Or was there?*

On June 25, 1950, a well-prepared North Korean army crossed the 38th parallel to invade South Korea. The American units called upon to halt the attack were poorly-trained and ill-equipped. After all, we were thought to be at peace with the world.

We assumed as victors of WWII that we deserved to rest on our laurels. *Or could we?*

At the time, Major General John G. Van Houten was first commander of the Ranger Training Command. While he had supervised the formation and training of 14 Ranger companies which served in Korea, he himself had not undergone the Ranger training.

In September 1950, he was called to Washington and told that training for Ranger-type units would begin at Fort Benning, Georgia on the earliest possible date. Colonel Edwin Walker, a combat veteran of the 1st Special Service Force, was assigned to be his deputy. A call went out in the Army for "volunteers to do extremely hazardous duty in combat zones" without revealing the destination was to be Korea and the Far East.

The response from the U.S. Army's 82nd Airborne Division was astounding. Approximately 5,000 experienced, well-trained, regular-Army paratroopers volunteered— some of whom had fought as Rangers during World War II.

Wherever possible, selection of the men was done directly by the officers chosen to lead the new units. On October 9, 1950, training began with four Ranger companies which would be designated as Ranger Infantry Companies (Airborne).

These companies would be trained exclusively to be warriors. There would be no clerks, cooks or bottle washers. All would be capable of being delivered into combat by parachute. They were assigned to companies of 112 men, in infantry divisions of 18,000, to perform "out front missions," such as scouting and patrolling, as well as spearhead attacks in raids and ambushes. At the time, three of the companies were composed of white soldiers and one company of black soldiers, all parachute qualified.

Men who had fought as Rangers, Marauders, or OSS during World War II were to train them. Training was extremely rigorous and basically followed what had been taught to Rangers in past conflicts, with the addition of night, low-level parachute jumps.

After Korea, Major General Van Houton would become known as the father of the U.S. Army Ranger School. Van Houten made it possible for individuals to receive training and return as Rangers to serve in their original units. This approach recognized that having Rangers serving throughout the Army would raise the overall standards.

However, after the Korean War, for a short time, the U.S. Army Ranger program was disbanded for political and budgetary reasons by the Department of the Army. All Ranger companies ceased to exist. *What the enemy couldn't do, our own leaders in the Pentagon could do and did. The Rangers were erased.* Servicemen heard only rumors about the rationalization for it. It was said that division commanders had misused them, that they'd suffered too many casualties. Moreover, because these men had volunteered for the Rangers, they'd left behind vacancies in their original units which needed men of the same caliber.

During World War II, Rangers also experienced, in one form or another, the jealousy of other units. Because the elite Rangers had been so successful in combat, their pride caused many to gloat about it, to think and act as if they were better than the rest (which of course they were—they had to be.)

However, an underlying reason for the military reorganization was not exactly to abolish the Rangers, but that General Matthew Ridgeway, the Supreme Commander of the United Nations Forces in Korea (who had been a paratrooper during World War II), wanted the Rangers assimilated into the 187th Airborne Infantry Regimental Combat Team. This move permitted him to have a stronger 'unified' Airborne force to use as an effective "swift strike force."

This type strike force was later needed for Long Range Patrol Units during the Vietnam War, to gather first-hand intelligence. "Small patrols were inserted at night by whatever means available: helicopter, air boat, Navy swift boat, or on foot."

Sometimes a patrol was purposely left behind when their unit moved. When that happened, their mission became to locate Viet Cong and North Vietnamese units—not to engage in battle, but to pinpoint enemy locations, and relay them to the U.S. Commander.

These units were Ranger volunteers, but unlike the Rangers of the Korean War who had trained at Fort Benning, these U.S. soldiers were recruited while on duty in Vietnam, and trained and tested on actual combat patrols. For these units, there were no graduation ceremonies or parades. Their diploma was acceptance by their peers, men who would willingly walk into harm's way beside them, knowing these Rangers were dependable and highly trained.

In 1974, Army Chief of Staff General Creighton Abrams recognized a need for a light mobile force which could be moved quickly to any trouble spot. Consequently, the Rangers were back in business. They started out as one battalion, but soon grew to be the 75th Ranger Regiment, with battalions at Forts Benning and Stewart in Georgia, and Fort Lewis, Washington. Reborn, if you will, but with the same one caveat that is still their standard to this day, according to *Abrams' Charter*.

ABRAMS' CHARTER

The Ranger battalion is to be an elite, light, and most-proficient infantry battalion in the world. A battalion that can do things with its hands and weapons better than anyone. The battalion will not contain any "Hoodlums" or "Brigands" and if the battalion is formed of such persons, it will be disbanded. Wherever the battalion goes, it will be apparent that it is the best.

Chapter 23: Ranger Training

When Tom reported for Ranger Orientation, the TAC was there to greet them. "Attention! You men have volunteered for training to become U.S. Army Rangers. I'm here to tell you, few will graduate. If you fuck up, we don't let you try again. So do it right the first time." The TAC paced, rapping his knuckles on the back of his clipboard. "I don't want to hear complaining. You guys are the lucky ones with only three phases to Ranger Training. At the end of 58 days, you will know how to 'walk, crawl, climb mountains, lasso submarines, and move silently through the jungle' or you will have disappeared back to your original units. However, anyone who tries this next year will have 65 days of training and learn to survive in the desert. So, no complaints. This year, you have it easy on the mountain or by the water."

He handed the clipboard to the Sergeant beside him. "Sergeant, call the roll!"

After roll call, three men were not present. "Corporal Hauk, take this list to the gate. Tell the guard these men are ordered to return to their units and will not proceed to Crawl Phase. No excuses accepted!"

"Yes, sir." Corporal Hauk took the list and left.

The TAC continued. "Any infraction, no matter how minor, *will*, I say WILL DISQUALIFY YOU from this training. If your hair is a fraction too long, or your fatigue uniform displays an insignia, without further consideration, you are OUT. No recourse. You're gone.

"This program is to train good soldiers to be the best of the best. If a soldier can't even follow simple instructions, this proves his inability to pay attention to detail, an unpardonable sin."

Those of you who remain, MUST prove to the Ranger school your confidence, your military skills, your physical and mental endurance, stamina, and ability to absorb new information quickly. All this WILL BE needed in the future. Most of all, it testifies to your determination, desire, and ability to become a Ranger. If your desire isn't strong enough, YOU WILL BE DISMISSED."

CRAWL PHASE

According to his Orders, Tom reported at the appointed time and appointed place at the Harmony Church area of Fort Benning.

He had already removed the patches and rank insignia from his three fatigue uniforms. Only his nametags were left, just as was mandated by the Letter of Instruction he'd received. He brought the equipment he had been instructed to bring with him. But the boots? He had been told to bring two pair of well-worn boots. They were supposed to be boots which he didn't intend to wear again. He had correctly reasoned the absence of rank from his uniforms, knowing that this would cause all students to be treated equally. He remembered that from O.C.S., but his mind couldn't adjust to bringing well-worn boots, not ones which he didn't intend to wear again, especially after O.C.S. and Jump School where their Corcoran jump boots had to be spit-shined to a high gloss. Of course, he'd soon find out the reason for these orders.

At 0400, Tom's class of 248 men began the first run of the day. They ran a half mile, followed by 30 minutes of physical training in the Army's daily-dozen exercises, and then they went on another run. Each day their distance was increased by a half mile until they could reach a three-mile plateau. Once there, the distance would be increased a mile a day until they reached five. Thereafter, they would run for three miles in full uniform while wearing full packs.

They would conduct the runs and other training fully-clothed, rather than in shorts and T-shirts. The Ranger course was combat oriented. In combat, there are no timeouts for the combatants to change into comfortable clothing.

Breakfast was at 0530, and it wasn't unusual for a man to order a half-dozen eggs or to see a man with food piled high upon his tray. The dictum was: TAKE ALL YOU WANT. EAT ALL YOU TAKE. To reinforce the rule, a Cadre was posted at the garbage can to ensure nothing edible was thrown away.

After meals, the students were allowed to walk back to their barracks. This was the only time they were allowed to walk. They ran everywhere else. Of course, those who couldn't meet the rigors of the set standards were soon gone.

Classes were held a half mile away from the barracks area. The class would run cross-country to the classroom for 50 minutes of training, and then run to another area for full contact hand-to-hand combat or bayonet training. Once finished, they would get a ten-minute break before running back to the classroom. They underwent day and night training in scouting and patrolling, land navigation and compass courses. It was do-or-die for all, pass and continue, falter and be recycled, or drop from the course to be returned to your unit.

Living in the barracks as they were, with no sign of rank on anyone, the normal form of address was "Ranger." However, as they became more familiar with each other, they switched to last names.

There were those who wondered about rank, but if they inquired, they were told, "Don't worry about it. There's no such thing as 'Rank Has Its Privileges (RHIP)' during this training. That's for the outside world. Here you are all 'Rangers.' All officers and enlisted men will be addressed as 'Ranger' and treated as you perform: respect for those who do well, distaste for those who don't cut it."

The students wore their hair cut close to the scalp and were dressed in similar fatigue uniforms, except for the students from the Marine Corps who were allowed to wear camouflage fatigues. Naturally, this wasn't a good thing, because it marked them as 'outsiders.'

Before long, Tom found the reason for having two pair of well-worn boots and plenty of good socks. It had to do with having to slog across country on extended compass marches and through knee to waist deep Georgia swamplands. Tom was wise enough to listen to an older and more experienced student who advised carrying extra socks to change into when he had a chance. It was impractical to carry an extra pair of boots, but knowing he had a dry pair waiting for him in the barracks made life more tolerable.

TEST AT VICTORY POND

Tom had an advantage over some of the other students. His entire military career had been spent in some type of training. He was used to the discipline of O.C.S. and the physical and mental challenges of Jump School. He thought, at times, he was merely in a continuation of the two. He faced each day as a challenge. His excellent physical condition helped him.

At Victory Pond, each man had to pass a swim test before he could move on to the second half of Phase I training.

Tom almost failed, because he couldn't swim in the prescribed manner. As a boy, he'd spent time in the Muone river with the other children, but it was to bathe or cool off from the heat of the day, sometimes to frolic, but never to swim. His swimming style was a dog paddle, with his head held high and both arms paddling swiftly to keep from sinking.

The day of the test, Tom stood fully-clothed on a platform six feet above Victory Pond. He held his dummy weapon with a death grip. He knew that to drop the weapon would automatically cause him to fail, and the nasty word 'fail' was not in his vocabulary. He took several deep breaths, willing himself not to panic and pushing down his fear; then he jumped in.

He held his breath as he flailed frantically until he could break the water's surface to get his head up. He opened his eyes. Up ahead, his goal was in sight. He struggled to breathe quickly by keeping his head up, as it awkwardly turtled up and out of the water. He was almost there. He dog paddled furiously onward. When he made it all the way, without drowning, he was quite pleased with himself.

But his Instructor loomed over him. "What's the problem, Ranger? Can't you swim?" he said sarcastically.

"I made it, didn't I?" Tom asked, still breathing heavily.

"Don't be a wiseass," the Instructor said, and then added with a sardonic smile, "Would you like to try the swim again?"

"If it would please you, sir."

"Hit the platform, Ranger. And on the way, elevate your feet!"

"Yes, sir!" Tom hotly replied, becoming angrier by the minute.

He rested his ankles on the nearby railing, performed his push-ups, and then headed for the six-foot platform.

"Make way for Ranger Aquinas. He's gonna demonstrate his swimming technique for us," the Instructor announced, drawing attention to Tom.

Tom gritted his teeth as he went toward the platform. However, under his breath, he muttered, "Fuck you, Instructor, sir. I'll drown before I let you get the best of me." Then breathing deeply, as before, he heard the Instructor yelling at him.

"What are you waiting for, Ranger? An invitation? Just jump!"

At the order, Tom jumped in again and found himself struggling to the surface just as he had the first time. This time, however, when he broke the surface, his anger had elevated his adrenalin. It was much easier. In fact, this time he was swimming and using his legs more than paddling or flailing his arms. For a brief moment, Tom wondered if there could be method to his instructor's madness. He paddle-swam until he reached the edge of the water.

"Much better, Ranger Aquinas, but not enough to keep you out of the Weak-Swimmer category. You'll be required to sew three 'Ranger eyes' to the back of your patrol cap."

"Yes, sir," was all Tom could say, but he thought, *I made it, weak swimmer or not. I'll sew a dozen 'Ranger eyes' on the back of my cap if it means I can still pass.*

Tom knew that "Ranger Eyes" were not to single out individuals for ridicule. They had a practical purpose. The "Ranger Eyes" were two luminous rectangles sewn on the back of the cap which enabled men to follow the man in front of them in the dark. However, three "Ranger Eyes" on a cap identified the man in front as a weak swimmer, so the person following could be prepared to provide assistance, or to be extra cautious when working in swamps or on other water exercises.

WALK PHASE: MOUNTAINEERING AT CAMP DARBY

Camp Darby was named for Commander Darby of the first Ranger unit in World War II.

At Camp Darby, training would become even more stringent and intense. Individual responsibilities became more apparent and important. The men would sleep in two-men pup tents and learned to rest where they could. Here Tom appreciated the value of a catnap, even for just those few precious moments of a ten-minute break, instead of as others might waste time with a cigarette.

On the first day at Camp Darby, Tom heard Hognose say, "Today is a Category-4 Heat day! That's as hot as a freshly-emptied pistol." The phrase stuck in his head all morning. Later, Tom and his class formed at 1300 to make the legendary 15-mile, long-distance, forced march, known as "the Darby Queen" march. The route was indicated only by the compass directions.

Tom was two-thirds back in the formation. His heart was pounding in the heat, but he kept pushing himself. He was puffing to get air and eating the dust stirred into the air by those ahead of him when he blacked out.

When he came to momentarily, he felt the shock of cold water stinging his skin. A fireman from the fire truck, which followed such marches, was hosing him down with cold water.

The next thing he knew, Tom awoke in Martin Army Community Hospital, fully-clothed and immersed in a tub of freezing water with ice bobbing around him. Not only that, Tom couldn't remember anything about his ride in the ambulance Jeep.

A Ranger Medic Makowski had been placed there to monitor him. When Tom regained consciousness, the medic informed him, "You've had a heat stroke. You have 72 hours here to pull yourself together and return to duty, or you'll be recycled."

"Then, I'd better get going." Tom tried to get out of the tub, but was unceremoniously pushed back in the water.

"No you don't," the medic admonished him. "Cool it, Ranger. I said 72 hours! Make damn sure you're ready, before you get out of that tub, or you're gonna find your ass back at Day One, Phase I."

Still shivering, Tom attempted a reply, but his teeth were chattering, so he gave up and let himself sink down into the freezing water. As the ice stuck to the bare skin on his arms, Tom wondered if he really wanted to continue Ranger school. Maybe he couldn't hack it after all. He closed his eyes and brushed the ice away.

I still have to try, and I'll make it. I have to make it. Tom bucked himself up to the job.

In Ranger school, the attrition rate was obvious with the absence of many familiar faces—as men without the necessary grit or skills continued to disappeared.

Dahlonega, Georgia

Dahlonega was a quiet town in the foothills of Georgia's share of the Blue Ridge Mountain Range, less than 200 miles North of Fort Benning.

The uncomfortable ride in the two-and-a-half-ton trucks made it seem much farther. Very few of the passengers were interested in the countryside. Those who had learned the value of rest were napping.

The trainees were directed to sit on the open bleachers. After a brief instruction covering mountain climbing terminology and knot tying, two instructors put on an awesome climbing demonstration to show what the trainees would be expected to learn.

Attached by a long rope, the instructors began their ascent on a vertical cliff which Tom guesstimated to be as high as a ten-story building. Despite the effortless appearance, Tom knew the climb was a well-orchestrated demonstration.

Next, the class' attention was directed to another rock formation where two men were free climbing, as individuals rather than as a team. They used hand and toeholds to cling to the rock face. When the climbers reached the top of their respective cliffs, they sat on the edge with feet dangling, resting for a few moments, before moving out of sight. Tom noticed the absence of any rope that would normally connect the two men, and he marveled at their skill. The narration continued.

The class' attention was directed to the taller palisade where ropes were being thrown from the top. When the ropes hung almost motionless, a squad of men appeared at the top edge. Each man grabbed a rope to back off the cliff. To avoid the danger of falling, but unknown to those who watched, each man wore a *Swiss seat* fashioned from a 12-foot-long 5/8-inch rope looped around his legs and buttocks. The rope was knotted on the side at each man's waist. The seat was attached to the dangling rope in a double loop through a snap link, called a *carabineer*.

When the instructors began to rappel down the cliff face, there was a noticeable gasp from the spectators. The men slid rapidly down their ropes, stopping at intervals to push off the face of the precipice to continue descent. On reaching the ground, they detached from the ropes, un-slung their weapons, and moved quickly into the woods where they fired blank ammunition in a mock raid.

At the sound of the gunfire, movement could be seen atop the second cliff. Two men appeared backing to the edge with a stretcher between them. A man was strapped to the stretcher.

They watched the men step backward over the edge, taking the stretcher with them in a slow descent. They controlled the stretcher while rappelling to the bottom.

"It must be a dummy," Tom heard someone say.

"How many of you agree it's a dummy in the stretcher?" the narrator asked, as the class watched in awe. Hands shot into the air as the two stretcher-bearers unhooked themselves from their ropes and un-strapped their "patient" from the stretcher. The patient stood to his feet as the spectators applauded.

Walk Phase of Mountaineering Training was every bit as demanding as Crawl Phase had been during the first 21 days, but the students had now become more accustomed to the rigors. They welcomed the cooler climate of the mountains as relief from the sweltering heat of Fort Benning. However, some of the trainees found it was harder to breathe in the thinner air of the upper atmosphere, especially those who smoked, but Tom didn't. He even thought the morning PT was more invigorating.

2What he felt was an uneasy knowing, a sense that men had died on this mountain. He focused on the morning PT to keep his mind off thoughts of any warrior *Kwan* that might still linger on the mountain. Tom was surprised since he had never thought of his mother's Buddhist beliefs before. The landscape was inspiring, and he enjoyed each new challenge as their climbs became higher, steeper and more difficult.

Tom was especially impressed with the Sergeant First Class in charge of the mule team, a Sergeant who referred to himself as a 'muleskinner.' He wore riding boots and breeches, chewed tobacco, spoke as if he belonged in a western movie, and was fiercely loyal to his mules. In his introduction to the use of mules, he threatened the class with bodily harm if any of them mistreated *his* mules. "But if any of these jug-heads gits cantankerous, why you jest bite down right hard on his ear. That'll settle the critter down fer ye. Now, do any of you young fellers have any questions?"

"Yes, Sergeant. Can we ride these mules?" one of the trainees asked.

Muleskinner suppressed a smile. "Why shore, sonny. Pick one and climb aboard. . . ."

The young Ranger approached a mule as the rest of the class looked on, somewhat amused. He took a firm grip on the mule's lead rope and the apparatus attached to the mule's back and vaulted aboard for a ride.

"By the way, that ain't one of them fancy riding saddles she's a wearin.' It be made of steel."

The class erupted into loud guffaws and cries of "Ride 'em, cowboy!" as the mule began to buck and kick. The pale young Ranger held a death grip on his steel saddle.

The mule decided to take his passenger for a tour. He galloped across the field, ignoring the cries of "Whoa, damn it! Whoa!"

The rest of the class roared with laughter.

When the Ranger flew off, the mule was without a rider. The hapless wanna-be cowboy tumbled, trying unsuccessfully to execute some type of parachute landing fall to lessen his chance of broken bones.

"Is that what you damn fools who jump outta airplanes call a PLF?" Muleskinner asked.

Laughter and applause sounded from the bleachers.

A few of the trainees rose to go to the assistance of the thrown rider but were stopped by Muleskinner. "You ride out and you ride back; or you walk back alone. . . . He'll be sore, but the walk will do him good. The damn fool ought not to have ridden Mildred anyhow. . . . Now, as I was sayin'," and he went on with his instructions, while the rider limped slowly back to the area, nursing his bruised body and ego, and not caring where the mule had gone.

The skinner looked at the rider as he stumbled past him. "Sonny, back in the old days, that trick would a cost you every stripe you wore on your sleeve, and any damages to the mule would a come out a your pay. Now, you jest climb back up to your seat there and listen to what I have to say." He paused for just a moment, and smiled. "Unless, of course, you'd rather stand."

The young man did climb the bleachers carefully, and he sat down in a way that let everyone know that sitting wasn't his choice, but he was through making waves. His smart attitude had been bucked out of him.

After watching this demonstration, Tom couldn't help but to imagine this military training if in Laos, given by a mahout. How would the recruit have managed on an elephant?

The trainees settled down and listened as they were taught details of rope climbing to climb up and down rock formations by employing ropes. In descent they were taught *rappelling*. Practice helped them control their descent, using ropes to slide down, and by bringing the ropes tight to their body for braking.

At one point, the Instructor led the class to a cliff face to look over the edge. It was more than 100-feet, straight down to the ground. Here they'd have the opportunity to prove how well they'd paid attention. The Instructor explained, "Hopefully, this cliff will teach you some confidence."

While he stood nervously at the cliff's edge, Tom was tied into his Swiss seat, while he attached to the rope by his carabineer. Then he waited his turn.

The Instructor pointed to a small ledge about halfway down and smiled. "Do you all see that outcrop below you?" Not waiting for an answer, he continued, "It's about three by three feet. Do any of you think you can land on it?"

Accepting the challenge, despite his apprehension, Tom answered in a loud voice, "Yes, Sergeant!"

"All right, Ranger. Your orders are to hit that outcrop without braking and to kick off and continue to the bottom again without braking. Whenever you're ready, go."

Accepting the dare, Tom pulled the ropes taut against their anchor and backed to the edge. He looked backward, behind himself to estimate the distance to the ledge. He took a deep breath, kicked out and adjusted his position, increasing his speed as he slid down the ropes. He moved the ropes close to his body, instead of braking, slowing himself only enough to land safely on the ledge. Feeling he had somehow cheated by the way he had slowed himself down, he kicked off the ledge and purposely held the ropes away from his body, which caused him to hit the ground hard enough to jar his teeth.

He managed to stay upright as he disengaged from the ropes and gave a quick smile to the Instructor standing up top. Tom sent a message to him, "Didn't think I could do it, did you?"

Seeing the surprise on the Instructor's face, Tom quit smiling. No need to rub it in, and make an enemy. It was better to stay in the background and remain one of the team.

Rangers were expected to be well-versed in such subjects as patrolling, land navigation, and the conduct of battle in varied situations over unfavorable terrain. The trainees were also expected to sit for hours of sometimes monotonous classroom instruction, or they were marched to on-site demonstrations.

Tom was not surprised when his group was gathered for a night patrol. The patrol had a hot meal early in the afternoon, and the food was sitting heavily on his stomach. For once, he was glad that it wasn't his turn to be in a leadership position.

Before leaving, a briefing was called so the group would know where they were going and what they were expected to do once they arrived. Patrol orders were issued, plans were made, individual responsibilities were assigned, and camouflage paint was applied to exposed body parts. The group was given opportunity for a final cigarette for the night. A distant rumble of thunder sounded. Mother Nature was warning them that they could expect a nasty, wet patrol.

The trainees crossed their line of departure as scheduled. It was shortly after dusk, with no promise of a moon; the thickening clouds would obscure it. Tonight, they'd be patrolling in silence and in pitch dark. Just as they started climbing a fairly steep slope, the rain began. Near the back of the group, Tom was determined as he sought hand and footholds. He paused for just a moment to catch his breath, when he heard a cry . . .

"Falling!" came the yell.

It broke the silence that the patrol was trying to maintain.

Then Tom heard someone sliding toward him. Tom instinctively reached into the dark in a futile attempt to grab hold of him, but he missed. Tom held his breath, listening, praying to hear the sound of the man sliding to a safe stop. The sound didn't come. Instead, he heard the pitiful sound of a bone snapping, followed by a mournful moan.

Tom followed his instincts. He carefully headed toward the sound. Above and below him, he could hear men whispering. "Who fell?" "Where is he?"

Tom got to the man first and did something that felt natural. He took charge. "I'm calling an emergency halt to this patrol. Gather over here all of you. And watch your step!" Tom ordered.

The patrol gathered around the injured man. The Ranger Cadre, there to grade the trainees, came over to assess the situation.

"What next, Ranger?" a Cadre asked the trainee who had been the designated patrol leader.

But the Patrol Leader just stood there. He couldn't come up with an answer.

Tom knew, with an injured man on the ground, this wasn't the time to hesitate. The wheels in his head had started to churn. Right or wrong, he was going to do something. "James!" Tom called out in his most authoritative voice.

"Yo!"

"Aren't you a medic?" Tom asked.

"Sure am," James answered, as he bent toward the injured man.

"Is that you, Aquinas?" one of the Cadre asked.

"Yes, Sergeant," Tom said, stiffly.

"What are your responsibilities as a Ranger?" the Cadre asked.

Tom's answer was immediate. "First to the mission, second to higher headquarters, third to my fellow Rangers, and fourth to myself."

"Are you following those responsibilities tonight?" the Cadre asked. "You halted your mission because of a man who fell and made a hell of a lot of noise in doing so."

"But it's a training mission, and this man's injured."

"Ranger Aquinas, every patrol you are on as a Ranger is a true mission whether it's at Fort Benning or some war-torn nation. We train to become better at what we do; to beat an opponent; to survive. To win! There will be no halt to this mission, emergency, administrative, or otherwise." Then loud enough for all to hear, "You seem to have forgotten basic patrol techniques."

"Aquinas, you are now Patrol Leader." The Cadre leader asked, "What are your actions? Think!"

Tom took just a moment to let the situation sink in and began his orders. "James, do what you have to do as a medic. Johnson, you, Mac, and Stevens erect a shelter for Carter and James. They'll stay here, and we'll pick them up on the way back." Then turning to James, he continued, "James, can you put together some type of litter to carry

Carter? Do you have what he'll need for pain? Do you need anything else?"

James' answer was immediate, "Negative, we'll be all right until you get back. Happy hunting."

Taking out his compass, Tom sighted before calling the man he had now selected to lead the patrol, "Gus, take the point and be especially alert for any ambush. We made a hell of a noise taking this break, and if the Cadre has anything planned for us, we'd better be ready. Any questions?"

Tom took his place in line where he could best control the mission. "Okay, move out and let's keep noise to a minimum."

A sudden bolt of lightning overhead momentarily blinded Tom. Seconds later the ground vibrated as thunder echoed in a rumble that Tom could feel in his rib cage.

"Move out," Tom reaffirmed. The rain hit in huge splatters as the patrol once again began to climb. As they neared the crest, the cloud to ground lightning continued to flash in bright hot bolts. It struck some trees along the top of the cliff.

It was then two of the Ranger Cadre stopped the patrol for a class on actions to be taken when encountering lightning this intense.

The Cadre told Tom to continue.

This time, he did so following the instructions given in the Lightning Hazard class. Tom moved his men off the hill, caching equipment which might attract lightning. Radios and explosive devices were left and would be picked up when the worst of the storm abated. They would continue the mission then, but for now, they were to take cover. The undue risk to his men would be jeopardizing the success of the mission. The mission always came first.

Tom spread out his men for increased safety, and they waited. A few of the men took advantage of the break, and although soaking wet, made themselves as comfortable as possible and dozed.

Tom used his time to his advantage by reviewing the intent of the patrol and how he would bring it to a successful conclusion. He also went over in his mind what he perceived to be the strengths and weaknesses of the men with him. He'd use them to the mission's advantage.

As soon as the lightning moved off, Tom alerted his people. He sent men to retrieve the radios and gear. Then he led the patrol up the mountain. Soon after, the mission was concluded, and designated 'a successful training mission.'

More importantly, Tom had proven to himself that he could be an officer.

Tom wasn't aware of it, but he was being observed and tested as a candidate for the prestigious Ralph Puckett Award, and possible acceptance into the active 75th Ranger Regiment. Tom's take-charge actions at "Lightning Hill" had not gone unnoticed.

Ranger Ralph Puckett, Jr., is an officer who'd distinguished himself in Korea, Vietnam, and elsewhere. The Ralph Puckett Award was to be given in recognition of "Excellence exhibited by a graduate while undergoing training."

Tom went to bed no longer worrying if he'd be able to pass to the next phase of his training. He would do it. He had stamina. He remembered the toughness that his mother possessed. She had always met every challenge. She had survived when her husband didn't come back from war. She had taken care of a sick foreigner. She had been the first woman in their village to take part in the teakwood trade. She'd orchestrated their escape, come to America, learned a new language, and adapted to a new culture. She had raised two children alone. She was even talking about starting her own business.

Tom realized for the first time how awesome his mother was. He had always looked up to his American father as a man who had grit. His father was a 'Green Beret.' He had left a legacy that made men of honor remember Thomas Aquinas McGlynn, but Tom felt that his mother was also courageous, strong and resilient.

Second Lieutenant Thomas Aquinas decided he came from good stock. He'd never sell himself short again.

RUN PHASE: SWAMP TRAINING NEAR EGLIN FIELD

Bone tired the following morning, Tom sat through yet another briefing for the final phase of training. Completing three strenuous weeks of mountain training, today they received orders to report for three weeks of jungle training in the swamplands and coastal waters of Florida. He learned he'd be the Jumpmaster for the evening's parachute drop into Eglin Field, Florida. Their arrival itself would be a training exercise.

The parachute-qualified students would jump into one of the auxiliary fields at Eglin, "to establish an airhead." Tom's team was to assault and secure "the enemy's" communications' building.

The next team would attack the control tower. Another team was to set up radar beacons to guide C-130s which were bringing the non-jumpers into the airfield.

Their parachute drop into Auxiliary Field Number 6 at Eglin Field went well with relatively few injuries, all minor. The jumpers dispersed to carry out specific mission assignments to secure the landing strip for the incoming C-130s which would carry the non-jumpers. These non-jumpers also had missions to complete before all would be secure. The deadline was to get to Camp Rudder by 0330. Then, after a short rest there, they'd begin another period of rigorous training.

Tom and his mates, like others who had gone before them and those who would come after, found the training more demanding than that at Benning or Dahlonega. They traversed alligator and snake-infested swamps and waterways in the dark. Here, mental attitude came into play fearing and occasionally encountering other creatures of the night.

On patrols in Florida, the value of the "Ranger Eyes" sewn on the back of their patrol caps became even more evident to Tom as they crossed waterway after waterway. At times, they'd navigate in chest-deep water, trying desperately to keep weapons and equipment as dry as possible and remain relatively silent.

Tom was probably five or six feet behind a man as they moved slowly in the darkness. He was aware of the faint luminous glow being given off by the man's three "Ranger Eyes" when suddenly the "eyes" disappeared. The man had stepped into deeper water and vanished.

I guess that Ranger turned a corner. Uh, oh . . . There's no corners out here! I need to take action, Tom thought.

Although Tom was designated as a weak swimmer, he shed his rucksack and weapon, and dove underwater. He groped frantically in the darkness, his lungs threatening to burst, until his hand brushed against the submerged man. He grabbed the foundering Ranger's webbing harness and kicked vigorously to the surface.

When his head came out of the water, Tom gasped for air and yanked the Ranger to the surface to find his breath. Other members of the patrol grabbed them both.

"Are you okay?" one Ranger asked, as he pulled Tom toward the shallows.

When he found his footing, Tom replied, "I'm okay. I just need to catch my breath. I'm not sure about the other guy." He rested only a minute or two. Then, he took a deep breath, and went underwater again to search for his weapon and equipment— for to lose either would be to fail. He'd come too far to fail. Luckily, his hands found both items. He struggled to get into shallower water and find firm footing. There another member of the patrol helped him out of the wet harness of webbing that held his other gear.

As Tom slogged out of the water, the Ranger he'd rescued approached Tom, and shook his hand. "Thanks, man. You save my life!"

"Hey, no problem. Are you alright?" Tom asked.

"Shaken but unharmed. I owe you one," Kelly replied.

They'd both be soaking wet until tomorrow. Tom looked forward to tomorrow when the warm Florida sun could allow his body heat to dry him out, but it didn't matter. He was in good spirits for having done the right thing. His teammate, Kelly, could have drowned.

Tom suddenly felt more like a true Ranger, and this feeling drew him closer in spirit to the man he called Father.

Tom had little experience in swamplands, but he was a natural when it came to the woods. He seemed to know his way about instinctively, and where others depended heavily on their proficiency with a compass, he always knew where he was or could find his way with or without a compass. Because of this, the other students were drawn to him. He could lead them out when the situation called for it.

The incident in the swamp magnified Tom's reputation. Everyone knew he was a weak swimmer. The three "eyes" on the back of his cap reminded them. When word was passed that he'd saved a patrol member from drowning, his popularity soared.

Small Boat Training was the next skill to be learned. For that training, the class was trucked over to a beach on the Gulf of Mexico. They spent the first day learning to handle the rubber boats they'd be using for their final exercise in the Florida phase. During this exercise, they were to work with a Navy SEAL Team in a Joint Waterborne Assault. The SEAL Team would go ashore first to place the signal lights which would guide the boats to shore.

The trainees slept close to the beach that night, and the surf breaking on the shore had a lulling effect on everyone, including the security guards who had been posted. It wasn't long before the mosquitoes were ignored and sound sleep overtook them all—until the Ranger Cadre attacked just shortly after midnight, firing blanks at them.

The attack didn't last long. Cadre attacks seldom did. These attacks were used as a means to keep the trainees alert. It worked, even if it kept the trainees from having restful sleep.

Soon things quieted down, but the trainees were put on 100% Alert. They lay there listening to the surf which drummed a peaceful rhythm that said, "Sleep, sleep, sleep."

The trainees dreamily blinked their eyes open and closed, lulled by the sound.

The Designated Company Commander for the day stood up. He went to check the perimeter around their camp. He figured the Cadre might try another attack. Why else would they put them all on Alert?

When he returned, most of the men were asleep. He tapped Tom. "We've been sleep deprived for so long, how can I keep these guys awake? I don't know how I'm going to do it."

Before Tom could answer, the Cadre attacked again from a different direction, firing blank ammunition. Everyone was awake then!

"Oh shit! There'll be no sleep again tonight," the Designated Commander said.

"Hang in there, big guy. This is the final test." Tom tried to encourage him, giving his fellow trainee a friendly clap on the shoulder as he left for his firing position.

That was the way it went all night long. Just before dawn, the bleary-eyed trainees were ferried by LST, a relic from World War II, to two troop-carrying submarines just offshore. The carriers were attack subs, also from the World War II era, but they had been restructured to carry troops.

Once aboard their assigned sub, the trainees were taken below deck to wait until they could begin a Wet and Dry Launch Training.

A *wet launch* was where boats were put into the water, and then the troops were expected to reach the rubber boats by climbing down a cargo net draped from the side of the idling submarine.

A *dry launch* was even more interesting. The rubber boats remained on the deck of the submarine. The troops got into them and took rowing positions to be prepared to paddle away as soon as the sea broke over the deck of their submerging submarine. For the submarine to submerge, it had to blow the stale air from its tanks. Unfortunately, the troops in the boats waiting to paddle away were sitting above where the stale air vented, causing them to suffer the foul odor until their rubber boat was well away from the sub. This added to their sense of urgency when they paddled, furiously, to get away from the smell.

At sea, they had two methods of returning to the Navy submarine. One method, the easiest, was to row to the waiting submarine and merely climb aboard using the same cargo net they'd used when they'd left.

The second method was more dangerous and only to be used when there was a danger of losing the sub to enemy fire or if the sub's presence compromised the troops' mission. When this happened, the troops would paddle to a predetermined spot in the ocean at a predetermined time where the submerged sub would be waiting for them. The sub would use its periscope to watch for the rubber boats to appear. When the boats were spotted, the submarine commander would maneuver his sub to pass just below the surface, beneath each of the rubber boats. Of course, the sub would only be going forward very slowly. It was important for the periscope to avoid poking a hole in the bottom of any of the rubber boats!

It was the responsibility of each person in charge of a rubber boat to maneuver it over the sub, where a designated man in the rubber boat could lasso the submarine's periscope with a rope. Ropes on the periscope made it possible for the sub to tow the rubber boats out to open water far enough to be clear of enemy detection, or beyond enemy fire. Out there, they'd safely board the submarine.

When this training finished for the day and the troops were brought below deck, the sub's crew secured the rubber boats for the night. Once below deck, a member of the crew, a young Petty Officer, briefed Tom's group. He explained the rules of living aboard "his submarine" and told them not to be alarmed when they heard the klaxon horn signaling that they were submerging. The sub was to submerge, and remain so, until it was time to set out on their next training mission.

The Petty Officer explained, "The sub's crew is also in a training phase." He pointed toward a wire stretched taut across their sleeping area. "Pay close attention to it. If you watch the wire, you will be able to see the pressure that the submarine's hull has to deal with when it's submerged."

The trainees weren't quite sure what he meant, but the Petty Officer said they'd soon understand. Before leaving their sleeping quarters, he said, "I'll be in the area if you deign to have any more questions."

"Where else could he go?" one of the troops wise-cracked .

Tom chuckled softly as he dug into his still damp rucksack and pulled out a can of C-rations. He wanted to eat before taking a nap. They'd already been briefed on tonight's mission, and he knew that he had better eat and get some rest quickly while he had the chance. It promised to be another long night.

The klaxon horn sounded, and the overhead lights flickered as the electrical system switched to the redness of night-vision lighting. The trainees' attention all went to the stretched wire. Tom watched, fascinated, and more concerned, as slack in the wire became more evident.

"Holy shit!" somebody shouted.

Then another voice came from the semi-darkness. "And that, gentlemen, is why *I'm* in the Army instead of the fucking Navy. There's just no place here to dig a foxhole."

No one said a word to refute that. Someone always had a wise crack to make, but those words rang true for too many of them.

Tom was awakened by a gentle shake on his shoulder. "Piss call, Tom," Sergeant First Class Dan Moorman said. "We'll be going topside shortly. I thought you might like to throw some cold water on your face."

"Yeah, thanks," Tom replied, as he dreamily wiped the sleep from his eyes. He shook his head. He suddenly remembered that he was on a submarine someplace in the Gulf of Mexico, not in Marietta as he had been dreaming.

The sub had surfaced as the troops slept. Four swimmers from the SEAL Team, assisted by members of the crew, were readying their equipment and the boat that would take them closer to shore.

The swimmers, the Navy's version of Pathfinders, rolled into the sea from the boat as it sped parallel to the shoreline. They planned to swim in and set signals to guide the Rangers to the right spot. There would be a strict timetable between the time that the Navy SEAL Team would leave the sub until the time that the Rangers would leave it to follow them. Timing would be critical for the mission to be successful.

The Petty Officer, who'd briefed them earlier, entered the compartment, and Tom could feel the engines stop.

"Let me have your attention," the Petty Officer announced. "Form up just like you practiced earlier. When your boat number is called, follow your boat captain topside. Because of the number of boats we're putting into the water tonight, it will be a *wet launch*. There's a good moon so you'll be able to see, which means that you won't have any excuse for falling into the water. Everybody ready?"

"Yeah," a few answered, but most were busy getting into their gear. The Rangers knew this wasn't the real thing, but their adrenaline levels elevated when the muffled order came.

"Boats one and two, report to your boat stations!" came the order.

Eager to get started, Tom's element waited by their boat station until the others were brought up from below. The order was given to "Man the boats." The loading began with little noise or confusion. The moon was bright enough just as the Petty Officer had reported, and there were no incidents of any of the Rangers falling into the water, although the climb down the cargo nets was clumsy because they were carrying all their combat gear.

Tom settled into his boat and made himself as comfortable as he could. He gripped a paddle and rested it in the gunwale while they waited for the next order.

Dan Moorman, the trainee designated to be the rubber boat captain, gave the order, and they was rowed away from the sub. The crew paddled in a slow, rhythmic cadence toward the far shore.

Although there was no way for Dan to judge the distance to the shore, when he heard over his radio that the SEALs had begun their swim, he felt a sense of urgency. He urged his boat crew to put more muscle into their paddling. "The swimmers are in the water. We've got to get in there," he urged, and he took another compass sighting.

It was definitely a team effort. Ten young men paddled as one. It didn't take the paddlers long before they started to feel tired. The three-foot seas were making some work for these greenhorns, but they couldn't ease up. There was too much danger of breaching, of being at an incorrect angle to the oncoming waves, which would cause the boat to be swamped. It was here, now more than ever, that Tom promised himself he'd learn to swim proficiently at the next opportunity; Then, he prayed that the opportunity wouldn't come tonight.

Tom's thoughts were interrupted by a subdued shout, "There's the signal light!"

"Where?" inquired another voice.

"Off to the right," came an answer.

As the boat rode onto the crest of a wave, the light was clearly visible to the paddlers. The sight of it gave them renewed vigor. They paddled the boat safely through the pounding surf to get to the beach.

One by one, they dropped to the sandy beach to relax their aching muscles. Some sat in the sand, others sprawled across it, all waiting for the rest of the boats to arrive. This had been just another test in their training. They had made it to shore.

In the distance, out in the surf, Tom heard someone shouting. A boat had breached and turned over, spilling its exhausted passengers into the water.

"Damn it, there are guys in the water," Dan said. He sighed and looked at his crew resting on the beach. "Let's go guys. There are people in trouble." His crew stood up to help, but just as they did, the breached boat tumbled to the shore with Rangers still holding on.

Tom found the boat's captain. "Woody, are all your people accounted for?"

"I think so," Woody said, looking dazed.

"You'd better have a head count," Tom said. "You have to make sure."

Woody assembled his crew on the dark beach and called off names, but there was no answer from Kelly. He called the name again, but there was still no response.

By this time, several of the instructors had gathered around. Woody asked for assistance in organizing a search along the beach, hoping that Kelly had made it to shore. The Cadre took immediate control and started the search along the water's edge. The men yelled out Kelly's name as they searched the beach. When it was soon apparent Kelly hadn't made it to land and was in trouble, the trainees formed a human chain at the shore. They spread apart just enough to maintain a three-foot interval, and waded into the pounding surf to waist deep searching for him. After several unsuccessful attempts, groups of men stood on the beach in somber conversation in place of the normal congratulatory backslapping at having finished their training. They were exhausted, but pushed out again to find him.

Suddenly a voice boomed from the darkness. "Here's Kelly! I need some help over here!"

Men ran to the sound. They found one of their mates pulling the lifeless body up onto the sand.

"Who knows CPR?"

"I do," Dan yelled. "Let me through. Get out of the way!" Onlookers were pushed aside to make room. Another man joined Dan, and they worked on him to establish an open airway, chest compressions, pinched his nose and puffed breath into Kelly's opened mouth.

Radio communication had already been established with headquarters at Camp Rudder to notify them of the missing man. Now they sent a new message that he'd been found. A helicopter was requested to transport him to the base hospital at Eglin.

Dan and his partner worked tirelessly administering CPR until the helicopter, directed by flashlights, landed in a clear area of the beach. They put Kelly on a stretcher and placed it aboard, as the two men stayed alongside to continue chest compressions and puffs of air without breaking their rhythm. They accompanied Kelly all the way to the ER. They'd be able to rejoin their class later.

RETURN TO FORT BENNING

The flight back to Fort Benning from Elgin usually took about an hour, but the crew of the C-130 was being trained in cross-country flying, so the route included taking them over Mississippi and Alabama. If they avoided any turbulence, the two-and-a-half-hour ride would be comfortable for their passengers. The crew didn't want airsick paratroopers messing up their training passenger compartment. After clearing the turbulence, the plane headed for Fort Benning. When the jump doors were opened, the trainees prepared to jump from the C-130 in mid-flight.

Confirming their thoughts, Dan, today's Jumpmaster in Tom's plane, stood and tightened the loose straps of his parachute harness, and he signaled the rest to do the same. When he was finished, he put on his steel helmet and fastened its chin straps, and then watched the others follow suit.

The crew chief, in contact with the plane's pilot through his headset, told Dan the plane was five minutes out from Fryar Field, their DZ for their return to Benning.

Brian held his hand up, five fingers extended, and shouted, "Five minutes!" before hooking his static line to the anchor line cable and going to one of the open doors. He held on to the sides of the door as he leaned out to make sure there were no planes below them, or anything else outside the plane, which could be a danger to the jumpers. Satisfied, he pulled back into the plane so he could shout orders to the jumpers.

The passengers could feel the plane slow to jump speed. Brian raised both hands, palms to the front, and shouted, "Get ready!" Then he moved both arms in a lifting motion, and yelled, "Stand up!"

All of the jumpers stood. Dan continued his commands with accompanying hand movements, pausing between each command.

"Hook up. . . ."

"Check your equipment."

"Sound off for equipment check!"

Dan watched and heard the voices, start at the front of the plane and come down each side, as each man in turn slapped the leg of the man to his front and shouted his number.

As the shouts got closer, he heard, "Five okay."

"Four okay."

"Three okay."

"Two okay."

Finally, "One okay." This came from Tom, who happened to be the lead man *at the stick*, a term referring to the men in front of each of two lines of jumpers on the opposite sides of the plane.

"Stand in the Door!" Dan finally shouted the order. He saw Tom forcefully slide his static line along the static line cable and pivot to stand in the open door on his side.

Satisfied, Dan did the same, and stood holding onto the sides of the opened doorway as he watched the ground pass below.

Dan, the Jumpmaster, yelled out the different checkpoints leading to the drop zone until the plane crossed over the edge of the zone. He alternated his gaze between the ground below and the glowing red lamp by the door. Suddenly, the red lamp went out and the green light above it flashed on. Dan shouted his final command. "Let's go!" and he leapt up and out from the plane.

Tom did the same from the opposite door. Each was followed by the troopers behind, until the plane was emptied of its passengers. Tom looked up and saw a full canopy above him. Then, he looked below. He could see trucks parked in a line and realized they were his group's transportation back to the Harmony Church area.

Dan was not far from him, so Tom yelled, "I'm heading for the trucks, Dan. Coming?" Then Tom reached up on his risers to guide himself in that direction— so he'd have a shorter walk after landing. After all, he had a full rucksack and a 40-pound parachute to carry to the turn-in point at the trucks.

Training is over! We have survived. On the ground, Tom and his buddies were giving each other high-fives. We're Rangers now, bona-fide Rangers! The truck full of happy paratroopers departed.

When they reached their billets, their joy had just begun. The class had been given free time, but would have to return by 1600.

After eating lunch, they returned to their area so they could finish cleaning their gear and turn it in to the supply room. After they cleaned up the barracks, Tom and a few of his classmates decided to visit the Post Exchange for a few items.

Later back at the barracks, Tom, Wade and Kelly sat around making small talk, waiting for 1600 to come.

At 1600, it was announced that the Rangers were now permitted to go to the Officers' Club (the 'O' Club) for a hearty graduation dinner. The men were pleased to sit around tables covered with white linen, a welcome change.

Afterward, they meandered back to the barracks.

Soon one of the Ranger Cadre entered, carrying a stack of papers. "Gentlemen, I have your diplomas and the orders awarding you your Ranger tabs."

Conversation ceased. The class gathered around the Cadre as he called names and passed out the papers.

Seventy-four men out of the initial 248-man class graduated and were presented with the coveted Ranger Tab to be worn above unit patches for as long as the Ranger remained in the Army. *Once a Ranger, always a Ranger.* The tabs and diplomas might have seemed trivial to some people who'd never earned the black-and-gold RANGER tab, but to these men whose names were being called, it meant they'd passed beyond being ordinary soldiers. They had earned, through their determination, the right to be called 'Rangers.'

In the barracks, the men heartily congratulated each other. The issuance of the *tab* —a distinctive rectangle of cloth with the word 'RANGER' stenciled on it—sparked their mood of laughter and jubilation.

Despite the hardships and harassment they'd just passed through, most of them would miss the camaraderie, and closeness they felt depending on one another to survive the rigors. The 74 Rangers were to graduate the following day, and afterward travel to their separate parent units. But tonight, they'd drink beer and party, wanting this moment to go on forever. Tomorrow after graduation, they'd be breaking away from friendships which were meant to last a lifetime, not unlike those friendships forged in combat.

Later that evening, a beer bust was held at Victory Lodge for the men who had completed the training. There was plenty of food and drink. The party was going strong, but Tom was not much of a drinker. He stood alone, watching the celebration and taking only an occasional sip of the beer that he nursed in a plastic cup.

He saw a captain walking toward him. Tom wondered what he wanted, but the Captain just stood beside him for a few minutes as he, too, watched the crowd.

He looked hard at Tom. "Yep, you're the one. You're the guy who crapped-out on the Darby Queen march. How the hell did you make it all the way through the course? I would have dropped your ass then and there. We seem to be graduating pussies nowadays."

Tom didn't answer. He took another sip of his beer, emptying his cup. When he took the cup from his lips, he saw that one of his classmates had joined them. The classmate had overheard the Captain.

"Do you have a problem with Lieutenant Aquinas, Captain?"

The answer was quick and given in a nasty manner. "Who the hell are you?"

"I'm Captain Robert Elmer, and I've observed Lieutenant Aquinas for the past few weeks. In the time I've come to know him, I think he is a fine young officer who has more than earned the right to call himself a Ranger. Now, I'm telling you to back off, or do you want to compare dates of rank?"

"Stick your date of rank," the obnoxious Captain fumed. He pointed his finger in Tom's face. "I'm not through with you, Aquinas!"

Before Tom knew what had happened, Captain Elmer had decked the other Captain. He looked down at the Captain on the floor. "Yes, you're through, you dip-shit," Elmer said.

When he got up from the floor, without dusting his uniform, he glared at the man who had punched him, and walked away.

"I wish you hadn't done that, Captain Elmer," Tom said. "I've been trying to get into the Ranger Regiment. I guess I can forget about it now."

"Tom, that jerk isn't in the Regiment. We wouldn't have him, and when his commanding officer gets the report I've already written on him, he won't be here much longer, either. I don't know how he slipped through the cracks, but he's definitely not an officer, despite his captain's bars. And, if he were the Ranger he thinks he is, he'd have been off the floor and on my ass in a heartbeat, not skulking off like the snake that he is. Forget about him; he's no threat to you."

Tom had picked up on one thing. "You're assigned to the Regiment?" There was awe in Tom's voice.

"Yep," Captain Elmer said, and then smiled. "And there's somebody else you know from the Regiment, Major Clement. The Major was just telling me over a drink which we had earlier, that he intends to congratulate you on being selected for the Colonel Ralph Puckett Award." Captain Elmer looked at his watch. "In fact, the Major should be here, by now."

It was then that Dan Moorman, a Sergeant First Class, walked up to them. "Tom, I mean, sir, I never would have believed you were a second lieutenant. I thought for sure you were an enlisted slob. At least an E-5, though." It was meant as a compliment and Tom took it as such. He smiled and thanked him, and the Captain laughed at their humor.

They were interrupted when Major Clement came up to them. "I understand congratulations are in order, Lieutenant," the Major said, as he offered his hand to Tom.

"Yes, sir. I guess I got lucky," Tom answered, shyly.

"Luck had nothing to do with it, young man. You earned it." The Major turned to Captain Elmer. "How did you like the course, Bob?" and Bob Elmer and the Captain became involved in their own conversation.

Dan gave Tom a shrug and started to leave, but the Major stopped him. "No need to leave, Sergeant. I only stopped by to have a drink with these two, not to interrupt anything." He looked at Tom and added, "You seem to have made quite an impression during your training. Congratulations. What are your plans now?"

"I have no idea, sir. Every time I run into you, I'm in a rut without any orders." He sighed. "I sometimes think I'll never leave Benning."

"How would you like an assignment with the 75th Regiment? It's not a done deal, and you'll have to go before a selection board to get assigned, but from what I hear, you stand a very good chance."

"Major, I haven't thanked you, yet, for getting me into Ranger School. I am grateful, but you don't know how much I'd appreciate it if you gave your recommendation to the 75th."

"Being a good Ranger officer will be thanks enough, Lieutenant."

Dan interrupted the Major before he could go on. "Excuse me, sir, but can the 75th use a good sergeant first class? Lieutenant Aquinas and I make a good team, sir."

As he did when he first met Tom, the Major took a notebook and ballpoint pen from his pocket and handed it to Dan. "Let me have your full name, rank, serial number, and the unit you're assigned to. I'll have a Letter of Acceptance sent, and you can initiate the papers in your parent unit."

Dan grinned broadly. "Yes, sir! Thank you, Major."

"Sergeant, my thanks will be in seeing you as a good Ranger. Good luck to the both of you."

The following morning, Tom's class stood in formation waiting to pass in review, while the instructors from the Ranger HALO (high-altitude, low-level opening) parachute department exited an airplane above them at 14,000 feet. Each of the jumpers had a smoke grenade taped to one boot so they could be seen as they crisscrossed high above. The band broke out into *"The Ballad of the Green Berets,"* much to the amazement of the dignitaries present.

Later, they learned that a Special Forces officer from Tom's class had bribed the bandmaster to play it–to steal some thunder. There would have been hell to pay if the guilty party had been found out earlier, but after passing in review, the class was dismissed. Most said their good-byes, got into their private vehicles, and headed back to their parent units. All but Tom. He still didn't have any orders. He was waiting to go before the 75th Regiment Selection Board at Fort Benning.

PART IV: The Fledgling Ranger

CHAPTER 24: The 75th Regiment's Selection Board

Tom confidently walked up to the conference room table where the 75th Regiment Board members were assembled. He faced a senior officer, a Lieutenant Colonel, one of the battalion commanders of the regiment.

"Second Lieutenant Thomas Aquinas reporting as ordered, sir!" Tom rendered a snappy salute.

"Please be seated, Lieutenant," the Senior Officer told him. "Lieutenant Aquinas, do you know why you were instructed to report before this Board?"

"I believe it's to be interviewed for possible acceptance into the 75th Ranger Regiment, sir." Tom answered.

"Good." Noticing Tom's stiffness, the Colonel went on, "Lieutenant Aquinas, please relax. The purpose of this Board is not to intimidate you in any way. It's simply a method of getting to know you and to determine if you know what will be required of you as a Ranger officer. Do you understand?"

The Colonel's voice had a calming effect on Tom, and he confidently answered, "Yes, sir, I do." Then he waited for the questions to start.

"Why do you want to be assigned to the Ranger Regiment?" the Captain sitting at the far left of the Colonel asked.

Tom thought it more of a challenge than a question, but he maintained his composure. "Captain, I want to be one of the best that the Army has to offer."

The next question, from another Colonel, came on the heels of his answer. "Lieutenant, there are a good many people who would like to be one of the best. The question is: Do you have what it takes to be an officer in our regiment?"

Determined now, no longer fearful of being rejected, Tom thought back to the courtroom in Marietta and decided *to go for broke*. He answered with confidence, "Yes, sir, I do!"

Then a question came from the other end of the table, this time from a Major. "Lieutenant Aquinas, your name suggests you are Hispanic, but I read here in your records that you speak Lao fluently and have a working knowledge of Thai and French. Please explain."

Tom, once again faced with telling his story, took a moment to gather his thoughts. He started at the beginning, telling it almost word for word as he had told it in the courtroom when he'd petitioned for his name change. Members of the Board listened patiently. After Tom finished, they sat quietly for just a moment. Then, the questions began anew.

"You hold this American soldier in high regard. Am I correct in assuming he's the reason you're here?" the Senior Officer asked.

Tom started to mention Thomas McGlynn's other son, but didn't. *The panel won't understand and might not accept me. How can I explain my need to be as good as the other son?* Instead, he answered, "Yes, sir, he is the reason. In the time I knew him, he showed me what an honorable man was. Unknowingly, he set a standard I've tried to maintain. I feel I've been successful in holding on to his values, and I would like to go this one step further."

"By becoming a member of this regiment?"

"Yes, sir, by serving as a Ranger in the 75th."

"But you're already a Ranger. You graduated from Ranger training. Reading the recommendations of those who vouched for you to come before this panel, I can see you've done quite well." He added, "But if you are accepted into the 75th Regiment, you'll find your duties will be more demanding than anything you've ever experienced. We have an outstanding Regiment, which requires you give all you're able to, and then, even more. We have no part-time jobs in our unit." Looking at the other members of the Board, he said, "I have no further questions. Gentlemen?"

The panel had nothing else to ask.

"Lieutenant Aquinas, the Board will meet again in a day or two to select those of you who will be chosen to join the 75th. Thank you for volunteering, our Army needs more men like you. You'll hear the results of this interview within the week."

Tom left, knowing he'd spend many anxious hours awaiting their decision.

Tom picked up the phone on the second ring. "Lieutenant Aquinas here."

"Hi, Tom, this is Captain Elmer. I've got some good new for you. You made a good impression on the Board. You'll have your orders in a day or two. How does that sound?"

"I like it fine, Captain," Tom answered. "But I understood the Board wouldn't make a decision for another day or two."

"Major Clement commands a lot of respect within the Regiment, and when he recommends a man or an idea, it's just about a done deal. You can consider yourself fortunate for landing on his good side. From what I've observed over the past few weeks, he picked another winner. One more thing, Tom, the regiment doesn't normally accept second lieutenants, we prefer more experienced people. It won't be easy. You've got a lot of work ahead of you, young man."

"I hope I won't disappoint any one. I will try my best."

"You'll do fine, Tom. By the way, it looks like you'll be leaving Benning after all. I recommended you to Captain Carvell, the C.O. of a company in the Regiment's battalion at Fort Stewart. You'll find him to be a demanding commander, but one who is fair and will ask nothing of you that he hasn't done or won't do himself. He's a fine officer, and I'm sure you'll benefit from the assignment."

"I won't let you down, Captain Elmer. Thanks for the good word, and thanks for letting me know this soon. I was really sweating it out."

"No problem, Tom." the Captain said, then he chuckled. " And, oh, I would suggest you get a close-to-the-scalp haircut before you report in to the battalion. You have a reputation to uphold. Good night, Tom, and good luck."

Tom started to thank him again but realized he was speaking to a dial tone so he hung up the phone.

FORT STEWART, GEORGIA

Orders in hand, Tom hesitantly knocked on the door of the Battalion's Corpsman Room at Fort Stewart.

"Enter!"

Tom went in. A non-com was sitting behind the desk.

"Can I help you, Lieutenant?"

Looking at the stripes on the man's sleeve, he noticed the diamond signifying he was the man in charge. Tom replied, "Yes, First Sergeant. I'm Lieutenant Aquinas, and I have orders to report to your company." He passed a manila envelope across the First Sergeant's desk.

The First Sergeant Donner stood and received the envelope with his left hand and offered his right hand to Tom. "Glad to meet you, Lieutenant. Captain Carvell and his Executive Officer (X.O.) First Lieutenant Golden, are expecting you. I'll let the Captain know you're here."

The First Sergeant went to the door of the adjoining office, tapped on the door facing, and entered. "Captain, Lieutenant Aquinas is here, sir."

"Good. Have him come in. And First Sergeant, will you please have Sergeant Henning meet us in the mess hall? He might as well have a cup of coffee with us and meet his new platoon leader."

"Yes, sir."

The Captain was courteous and welcomed Tom to the company. He also introduced him to Executive Officer Golden, who was sitting in his office.

"We were just going for coffee, and I've asked for Sergeant Henning, who'll be your platoon sergeant, to meet us in the mess hall. You two can get to know each other. Sergeant Henning is one of our best NCOs. You can learn a lot from him. He's been to the wars, Lieutenant. He has 'seen the elephant'."

Tom was being told that he was here to learn, and Sergeant Henning would be his teacher. But Tom was puzzled. *What does he mean by about having seen the elephant. I've seen more than one elephant but can't understand how it would make a man any different or better than others.* He decided to ask Captain Elmer, later. No sense in showing these men that he was a "dumb-ass butter-bar, second louie" when they had just been introduced.

He liked Sergeant Henning from the moment they were introduced, and the Sergeant gave him a firm handshake and a cheerful greeting.

"Glad to meet you, Lieutenant. When are you going to sign for the platoon equipment?" The question had been said with a jesting tone, but it also showed Tom that Sergeant Henning was all business, too.

Tom smiled. He sat down at the table impressed with the Sergeant's demeanor and appearance. He was definitely a professional. The Master Parachutist Wings and the Combat Infantryman's Badge that were sewn above the man's left breast pocket helped in this assessment. It hadn't taken long in Tom's military career for him to understand that men who wore badges like that were men with whom he wanted to serve.

Yes, he thought. *I can learn from this man. As the saying goes, 'he seems to have his shit together.'*

As nervous as Tom had been with the prospect of joining this elite unit, of meeting the people with whom he'd serve, wondering if he'd live up to their expectations and determining what he envisioned as his own, he quickly felt at ease with these men. They were warriors, indeed, but they were also just regular guys, talking and joking as they sipped the blacker-than-black chow-hall coffee. Not only that, but Tom now understood what his new Commander had said earlier, about him learning a lot from his Platoon Sergeant.

Tom's first impression was reaffirmed when Sergeant Henning addressed his Company Commander. "Sir, if you'll excuse us, I'd like to show Lieutenant Aquinas around and introduce him to his platoon."

My platoon, Tom thought. *My platoon*. Tom felt quite good about himself, but just for a moment. *Not yet, Kumpang. Not yet. It's Sergeant Henning's platoon until you earn their respect.*

As the days wore on, Lieutenant Tom Aquinas became comfortable in his role as a fledgling Ranger Platoon Leader. He enjoyed garrison life but felt more comfortable in the field, and his men could sense his comfort. He found Sergeant Henning to be a great teacher. Tom learned how to lead a Ranger platoon, and before long, he and his Platoon Sergeant were a good team.

In fact, Tom told himself, *they were in the best damn platoon in the battalion, the regiment. No! In the entire Army! And life is good!* Good, that was, until he overheard a conversation between members of his platoon. He was stunned by it.

Tom recognized the voice of Corporal Garcia when he said, "You think Lieutenant Aquinas is Hispanic? Bullshit! I said a few words to him in Spanish, and he just looked at me like I was from Mars. I think he's a fucking 'gook'."

Never having been called 'a gook' before, Tom was in shock. *People used it against the North Vietnamese during the Vietnam War. Every American knew that. But I'm not North Vietnamese. No one had ever called me that, at least not to my face.* And he hadn't missed the derogatory tone Corporal Garcia had used either. Tom decided to let the incident pass. *Small minds have small opinions.* He'd keep an eye on Corporal Garcia, but he would let this time pass.

However, the next day word about the racial slur had somehow gotten back to Sergeant Henning. Then, Sergeant Henning actually got into a fight with Corporal Garcia about his attitude toward their platoon leader.

Initially, Tom felt good that his Platoon Sergeant had stood up for him, but he was concerned about the way it had been handled. Sergeant Henning had risked his rank fighting Corporal Garcia, even if he had whipped him. Tom wondered if he should take some type of action against the Sergeant and Corporal since he was the Platoon Leader. He had been taught that dissension in the ranks could fester until the unit became totally ineffective. Finally, he decided to approach Sergeant Henning about it. He invited him for a cup of coffee.

"Sergeant Henning, I hear you had a bit of trouble with Corporal Garcia."

"No trouble at all, Lieutenant. He has a big mouth that occasionally spouts too much crap. I didn't like something he said, and he wouldn't listen to reason, so I kicked his ass to remind him to think before he speaks," the Henning explained.

"Do you mind telling me what he was spouting off about?"

"Sir, what he spouted off about isn't important. What's important, and needed to be addressed, was that he did it in the first place."

"Do you think it wise for you to settle it with your fists?" Tom challenged.

"Lieutenant, I went to war with a man who taught me more than a few things. Two things stuck with me more than the others. One, don't send a man where you can send a round. Second, as a leader, I'm responsible for the actions of my men. If it takes holding his hand to get the job done, I won't hesitate to hold it. But if I think it takes an ass kicking, I'll not hesitate there, either. Corporal Garcia is a good Ranger and a super machine gunner. His problem is he doesn't think before he opens his mouth. He'll have to learn. And become a better man for it."

Tom replied, "I find it hard to argue that, but I'd rather not see you jeopardize yourself. If the wrong people found out about your giving lessons with your fists, it could prove costly."

Deciding not to pursue the matter, Henning simply said, "Yes, sir," and took another sip of his coffee.

The First Sergeant Beebe came up to their table.

"Morning, First Sergeant," Tom said.

"Good morning, Lieutenant. Captain Carvell is at battalion and wants his officers to wait for him to get back. Something's up," the first shirt advised.

"Does he want us to wait in his office?"

"Yes, sir. X.O. Golden is in there now. Maybe he knows what's going on." he answered. Then as an afterthought, he added, "When you find out, I'd appreciate it if you'd let me know."

The junior officers stood at attention as their Company Commander entered his office followed by the First Sergeant. The Company Commander pulled his chair out and sat down.

"You'd better sit down for this one, gentlemen. It's doozie." He gestured toward the chairs which had been added to his office. "It seems we've been asked to go into harm's way again, and it looks as though we'll be going in half-cocked . . . again."

He gave the men a frown before continuing, "You may consider this a warning Order. We are going to be put on Alert. It will be our job to rescue another nation from communist threat. The Colonel is at a briefing up at Bragg now. Have any of you heard of an island named Grenada? Have any of you been to the Caribbean? Anywhere in the Caribbean?"

Getting no response, he continued, "No? Well, I'm afraid you are going to find out where it is. From what I've been told so far, we'll be going in cold. There's little or no intelligence on the island, and if I understand correctly, headquarters is having a hard time even getting maps of the place."

He shook his head slowly, and smiled sheepishly. "For our planning purposes, we may have to use tourist maps, brochures, whatever. Does that remind you of anything, First Sergeant?"

"Yes, sir. It sure does. The maps we used in Vietnam, if you'll excuse my French, weren't worth a shit, but they got us to where we wanted to be, sir. I'm sure we'll get the job done with or without military maps."

"That we will, First Sergeant, that we will. Gentlemen, as of now, all leaves, extended passes and the like are cancelled. The troops aren't to be alerted yet, but I expect we'll be going into quarantine soon. When the orders come down, we will move to Hunter Army Airfield outside Fort Stewart. There we will meet up with the 2nd Battalion from Fort Benning."

He stood up. "That's all for now, people, and as they said in the Indian Wars, 'See to your weapons and stand by your horses.' You'll know more when I do, so please hold your questions. First Sergeant, I need you to wait up a minute."

Before leaving the office, Tom looked at the plaque on the wall behind his Company Commander's desk, and read it once more, trying to commit it to his memory.

On Liberty

War is an ugly thing, but not the ugliest of things. The decayed and degraded state of moral and patriotic feeling which thinks that nothing is worth war, is much worse. A man who has nothing for which he is willing to fight, nothing which is more important than his own personal safety, is a miserable creature and has no chance of being free unless made and kept so by the exertions of better men than himself.

John Stuart Mill

Captain Carvell opened the lower drawer of his desk and took out a bottle of Jack Daniel's sipping whiskey and two glasses. He poured three fingers of the spirits into each glass and passed one to his First Sergeant. He took a sip of his own.

"What do you think, Don?"

"Captain, we've both been in similar situations in the past, and for one reason or another, we've gotten the job done. We have one helluva good company of Rangers. I have no doubt in my military mind that we'll accomplish any mission they assign to us, maps or no maps. Just give these Rangers a mission, point them in the direction, and stand back."

"You seem pretty confident," the Captain said. "What's your read on our officers?"

Taking a sip, the senior NCO thought a moment before answering. "Ah, youth. I like what I see, Captain. Compared with the other companies in the battalion, I think we're fortunate to have those we do; But, then again, we won't know "until they see the elephant," will we?"

The Captain smiled as he remembered his own baptism of fire. "I feel the same, but I'm sure they'll be up to the task."

The First Sergeant Beebe waited a moment to see if his Company Commander would say anything else. "Do you have anything else, Captain?"

"Not yet, but I expect the order to come at any moment."

"Good. I've got something to do," the First Sergeant Beebe said, his determination suddenly becoming evident.

"Anything that needs my attention?"

"No, sir, just a young Ranger who wants to get married."

"Anything I should know?"

"No, sir, not really. I just want to talk to him the way I wish someone had talked to me a few years back, before I went to Vietnam the first time."

"Bad marriage?"

"Unfortunately, yes, sir, and then some."

"Sorry to hear it."

"It took me a while, but I got over it," As an afterthought, the First Sergeant Beebe added, "but for a while, I thought my military career was damn near trashed."

"I, for one, am damn glad it wasn't," Captain Carvell told him in a complimentary tone.

The First Sergeant asked as he stood up, "Is there anything else, Captain? I have the NCOs standing by for a meeting."

The Captain finished his drink. "Nothing else. Good luck with your young trooper and don't be surprised if you get a phone call to your quarters in the middle of the night."

"It seems to be an occupational hazard, Captain," the First Sergeant said. He could hear the Captain chuckle as he left the room.

First Sergeant Donald Beebe told his NCOs essentially what his Company Commander had told the officers, but knowing most of his NCOs had combat experience from Vietnam, he went further.

"People, you know we've got good officers, but frankly, we won't know how good they are until they've been shot at a time or two. I'm afraid it falls on us to carry the load again. Make sure your troops realize that whatever task we're assigned is "The Real World." This won't be a training mission. It is essential for them to have their equipment ready." He smiled, and then added, "As Captain Carvell told me earlier, don't be surprised if you get a phone call in the middle of the night to go meet up with the other battalions before we move out."

He looked at Sergeant Henning. "I need you to stay after the briefing." Then, to the rest, he said, "See to your Rangers. I'll see you when the balloon goes up, if not sooner."

CHAPTER 25: First Sergeant Beebe's Sermon

First Sergeant Beebe waited until the rest of the NCOs had left the room, and then he pointed to a chair beside his desk. "Have a seat," he told Sergeant Henning.

Sergeant Henning obeyed, and as he sat down he let out a long sigh. His all-business demeanor relaxed. "What's up, 'Top'?"

"Bob, could you spare Corporal Rooney for an hour or so? I want to try to talk him out of this marriage crap he seems set on. Just before being sent out, isn't the best timing for falling in love or whatever it's called nowadays."

Sergeant Henning nodded. "Sure. What do you have in mind?" He chuckled. "An ass kicking?"

"No," the First Sergeant answered. "I intend to tell him about how I almost lost everything years ago, because I thought I wanted to get married when I was on orders for my first tour in Vietnam." He shook his head. "But, if he repeats my story to a soul, I might have to resort to kicking his ass anyway, just as you said."

"I'd help you out, 'Top'," Sergeant Henning added.

The First Sergeant continued, "I wish now somebody had taken me aside and talked me out of it. Not that I would have listened, I guess, but I hope Rooney does."

"I wish you luck. Rooney's a good Ranger, and I'd rather have him with his mind on fighting instead of worrying about his sweetie at home. After you talk to him, could you let me know how it went?"

"You'll be the first to know. How about sending him to the Corpsman Room, so I can get started on him?"

Sergeant Henning stood up. "I happen to know where he is. I'll have him here in a minute or two."

"Great," the First Sergeant Beebe said. Then, he pulled out a notepad and began making himself notes. He heard Henning shut the door behind him as he wrote:

- Get personal field gear ready-to-go.
- Ask the company clerk to verify duty roster phone numbers.
- Call the dog kennel to house Max.
- Pick up dress greens from cleaners.
- Get hair cut.

There was a knock on the Corpsman Room door. "Come in!" First Sergeant Beebe ordered.

"You wanted to see me, First Sergeant?"

"Yes, Corporal Rooney, I do. Are you involved in anything at the moment? Anything you can't tear yourself away from?" he asked, knowing that the Corporal wouldn't dare tell him that he was too busy to talk to his First Sergeant. However, he'd asked as a way of saying this conversation was going to be of a more personal nature.

"No, First Sergeant. Nothing."

"Good." Then he looked over at his company clerk. "Mac, I need you to do me a favor.

"Sure, First Sergeant," the Spec 4 said.

"I want you to get the duty roster and the call roster, and verify that the phone numbers are all correct. I'd also like for you to hold down the fort. I'll be back in about an hour. You know where I'll be if you need me."

The First Sergeant saw a confused look on Corporal Rooney's face. It wasn't every day that a person was called to the First Sergeant's office, especially when the First Sergeant had just said that he'd be leaving the office.

"I want you to come with me," he told Rooney.

"Yes, First Sergeant. May I ask what's up?"

"Nothing much. I just thought I'd take you out and buy you a beer or three. You do drink beer, don't you?"

"Huh?" Rooney hadn't expected this. First Sergeants don't normally buy beer for junior NCOs. Rooney's mind was spinning as he wondered if he had screwed up in some way. He could see a definite red flag. First Sergeant Beebe was known to throw a punch or two when he felt it was warranted, and Rooney had a strange feeling he was being "taken out behind the wood shed."

Nah, he thought, as he tried to calm his nerves. *I haven't done anything to piss him off that much. He must need me for something. But what?* He reminded himself, *I'll soon find out.*

They got into Beebe's car and headed along Highway 27 toward Columbus. Rooney was sweating bullets, so he asked the First Sergeant, "Do you mind if I let in some air?"

"No problem," Beebe answered. He glanced at Rooney for a second. "How do you like your new platoon leader?"

Aha, he wants information on Lieutenant Aquinas, Rooney thought as he cranked the window down a few inches. . . . *But why?*

"He seems like a good officer, First Sergeant," Rooney answered. "He pretty much follows Sergeant Henning's lead. He didn't get here from Ranger School all piss-and-vinegar like some of the officers I've seen."

The First Sergeant began to talk to him about the other platoon leaders and some of the other company and battalion officers; however, to Corporal Rooney, the talk seemed very generalized, like the First Sergeant was just making small talk.

They turned into a bar's parking lot.

"Here we are," said the First Sergeant. "I didn't feel like going to the NCOs' Club."

Rooney wondered why not, and the only answer that he could think of worried him even more. *Because he wants a private talk with me, that's why.*

The First Sergeant got out of the car, and Rooney followed him inside. The bar seemed almost deserted. Beebe selected a table in the back.

"Draft beer okay with you, Rooney?"

"Suits me, First Sergeant."

"Rooney, until we get back to the company area, we can dispense with military protocol. I left my rank at the door, I'll pick it up on the way out."

Holding up two fingers, Beebe signaled the waitress.

She went behind the bar and began to draw the beers. When she finished, she brought them over.

"Thanks, Cynthia," the First Sergeant said.

"As always, sweetie," she answered and gave the First Sergeant a wink.

"Have you ever been here, Rooney? They claim to have the coldest beer in town."

Feeling as though he was treading on thin ice with the suspension of military protocol, Rooney avoided calling his First Sergeant by name. He answered, "No I haven't. Not a bad looking place, and I could use a cold beer."

Beebe paid for the beers and sucked part of the foam off his beer. Then, he put down his glass.

"I suppose you're wondering why I invited you for a beer."

Rooney thought, *Uh oh, here it comes.* But he forced a smile, and then answered, "As a matter of fact . . ." Leaving the sentence unfinished, he took a swallow of his beer and waited for the explanation.

Beebe pointed toward the door. "I said I left my rank at the door, but as part of this conversation we're about to have, I have one more condition. And it isn't up for discussion. What we say here stays here. Agreed?"

Still somewhat confused about what was going on, Rooney agreed.

"Okay, now a question. What's this about you wanting to get married?"

Rooney was stunned by the question. He hesitated. *This isn't about my platoon leader. It's about me!* Gape-mouthed, he looked at his First Sergeant, who was still waiting for an answer.

"Yes, I do. I want to get married," he answered,

"Have you got the young lady in a family way?"

Slightly angered by the question, Rooney shot back, "That's personal, First Sergeant."

"Well, pregnancy usually is, Rooney."

Rooney looked hard at his First Sergeant. There was sincerity in his eyes. The First Sergeant was attacking him. He could tell that now.

"No, she's not pregnant." He put his beer glass down hard.

"Then, why the rush to get married now? Can't you wait a while?

"We want to start a family."

"Oh, really? How the hell are you going to start a family with her here and you off doing the Ranger thing in Grenada? You're a Ranger, you know. Do you earn enough to start a family? Don't you think it may be wise to wait until you're promoted to at least E-5? Or are you planning to quit the Rangers and get one of those jobs where you can homestead, or maybe get out of the Army?"

"No, I'll stay with the Rangers. Cathy and I have everything worked out. We can make it."

Beebe held up two fingers toward the bar and, like a trooper, Cynthia went to the beer tap.

"Rooney, I'm going to tell you a story. It's a personal story, and I expect you to honor this condition. What we say remains here. If I find out that even part of what we said makes it out that door, I'm gonna be pissed, and you really don't want to see me pissed.'

"I know how to be discrete. You have nothing to be concerned about," Rooney told him. He couldn't help but feel curious, though, because his First Sergeant was being so secretive.

Cynthia brought their beer to them. Beebe reached in his pocket to pay her, but Rooney waved him off.

"I'll get this round," he said.

"No, I said I was going to buy, and that means I am going to buy. You can leave the tip if you want, but the beer is on me, Rooney."

Cynthia grinned at the two men. "You can both leave me a tip," she said smartly.

Beebe swatted her behind, and she blushed, but Rooney could tell that she liked it. There was a special closeness between Cynthia and his First Sergeant which went beyond barmaid and customer. She walked away still giggling.

Beebe once again sucked the foam off his beer, and then he downed a big portion of the glass.

"Where were we?" he asked.

"You were going to tell me a story."

"Yeah, right. Well, back in '63, I was in Special Forces at Fort Bragg and going steady with a sweetheart up in Baltimore. I used to go see her on weekends, except when we were out in the field for training. I tell you I was in love, Rooney, just like you are. Except I was a Sergeant First Class, and could afford to support a wife and start a family."

He swigged down another sip of beer. "By that time, I'd already spent a 6-month temporary duty tour in Laos with 'Operation *White Star*' and was ripe for an assignment to Vietnam. I knew it would mean I'd be gone for a year. The Army was my life and everything was going right for me. I made E-7. I had the time in grade, and a good reputation. Rooney, I can honestly say without bragging, I was a good soldier.

"Well, while I waited on my orders to come down from headquarters, I continued my weekend drives to Baltimore to see the love of my life. When my orders finally came down, Jane and I decided to get married. I didn't think twice about it. Her father was a career soldier, so she knew what she'd be in for as a soldier's wife. She had a good government job at Fort Meade, and we wanted to start a family. Just like you and Cathy, right?"

Beebe didn't wait for an answer. "Jane got the license in Baltimore and had everything ready when I got there. We drove to Elkton to the quickie Justice of the Peace, a stranger. We were so eager, we interrupted the JP and his wife's family dinner to get him to marry us. We went alone, without our family or friends. Some marriage, huh? A fuckin' shame!"

Rooney could hear bitterness in his First Sergeant's voice as he described leaving his new wife behind the day he left for Vietnam.

"I looked back at my new bride, after handing my ticket to the agent, and I saw her crying. Crying because I was leaving to go off and fight a war. Suddenly, I didn't want to go. I felt like hell. I wanted to quit the Army, to desert the only job that I had ever loved. I was willing to do anything just to stay with her, to dry her tears, to hold her and never leave her again." Beebe stiffened his jaw and said, "But, being the soldier that I am, I turned away from her and walked to the plane."

He turned his glass up and killed the rest of his beer. He belched loudly, then went on with his tale. "It was a good year. I spent it with an 'A' Team in the Delta. We didn't drive the VC out, but we more or less held our own and brought some measure of comfort to the local villagers."

Beebe held up his hand to flag Cynthia, but continued, "Mail from Jane was regular, full of love and all that crap— for a while, that is. Then the frequency of letters slowed down. I guess I'd slacked off writing myself, but the people who were trying to kill my ass were keeping me busy. On the other hand, I guess my letters didn't contain that lovey-dopey stuff she needed.

"I was promoted about half-way through the tour. When I got close to rotating home, I was asked to extend. I considered it. Hell, I knew I was needed, and it would be a definite boost for my career, but again like you, I was in love and wanted to get home to my little woman. It had been a full year and then some."

Cynthia brought two more beers, and Rooney chugged down the rest of his first beer. He now had two full glasses sitting in front of him.

"You don't drink too much, do you?" Beebe asked.

"Depends," he answered. "I do drink, but I am a little slower."

"You're just not a sot," Cynthia quipped. This time she side stepped Beebe's swat to the rump, but as she walked away she stuck her booty out and let it swish from side-to-side in a teasing manner.

"Damn, what an ass," Beebe remarked.

"You have something going with Cynthia?"

"Hell, boy, I got something going with more than one Cynthia. And it ain't something that I hide from any of them," he giggled at himself. "I am strictly a career man now."

"Because you grew apart from Jane while you were in Vietnam?"

"No. Our real problems didn't even start until I got home. That's where my story begins. The other stuff was just history." Beebe shrugged. "I came home and she was so happy to see me, or so I thought.

"A couple of days after I got home, we went to see my family. I wanted to show off my beautiful bride, and they loved her. Great! Now, I was certain that I'd made the right decision not to extend my tour of duty. I thought everything was great. I was in heaven. It was on the drive home to Baltimore, when she broke the news. Jane said, 'I've spoken with my mother to ask her advice. Mom said to keep my mouth shut, but

I think too much of you to do that. I need to tell you something. I'm pregnant.'

She came right out and told me she was pregnant! I nearly drove the car off the road! Amazing! . . . My wife was pregnant and had gotten that way without me! Her husband! Of course, she told me getting pregnant was an accident and all that crap. She'd gone to a polo match and the victory party afterward, and had too much to drink. Like it was the most reasonable thing in the world, like drinking too much would automatically make you pregnant.

"The next day I found out I was also broke. The allotment, plus the extra money I'd sent home, was all gone. I was devastated. My bubble had burst right before my eyes. My little flower had done this to me. They say you can tell things about people— that some people are just naturally so good they don't have it in them to do something like that. That's what I'd have said about Jane. Not Jane, she wouldn't do that! But I tell you, you never know.

"It just about killed me, too. Part of her was under my skin. I slipped into an 'I don't give a shit about anything' mode. My world was shattered. I tried to transfer back to Vietnam, the hotter the area the better. I was in the mood to slam some people up, to take out my frustrations by shooting people, and the VC were available for the shooting." Beebe took a drink of his beer, and then, wiped his mouth with the back of his hand.

Rooney could see that these memories were hard for First Sergeant Beebe to talk about.

Beebe was making the sacrifice trying to save Rooney from making the same mistake. He felt like he was doing something noble.

Beebe swallowed the beer hard. "She continued to get my allotment until the divorce became final. It didn't break me, because I'd already been broken. Until I was finally free of her, I jeopardized my career and myself with stupidity. Luckily, some people cut me some slack when I screwed up. My attitude wasn't the best, but because of their generosity, I survived. Eventually, I realized that the pain wasn't so bad any more.

"Oh, I went back for another tour in Vietnam, but the Good Lord above saw to it that I didn't go until my anger had subsided, which was a good thing, because I was better able to do my job.

"Do you wonder why I told you this? It's because I wish someone had talked to me and explained how this could happen to anybody. And I mean *anybody*. I'm just like you. I'm an average Joe. I didn't do anything to bring this on myself. I didn't think it could happen to me, not my Jane.

"Now, I want to ask you two questions,. . . which you don't have to answer. Just think on them. . . . Do you think it was the first time that ever happened? And if you asked any guy this has ever happened to if he thought his sweet flower would do this, do you think he'd say yes? I made the same mistake as thousands of other guys have made. It nearly ruined my career. It nearly ruined me."

Rooney looked away, not ready to say anything to his First Sergeant, and embarrassed by the whole encounter.

"I realize now how lucky I am the marriage ended when it did," Beebe said. "What if we'd had children, and then, she decided to be unfaithful? It could have been disastrous. I thank God no children were involved." He smirked. "I mean children of my own, not another guy's."

"But I know Cathy's not like that," Rooney objected.

"Hell, Rooney. I didn't say I knew she was. The point I'm making is that if Jane and I had waited, it would have been an entirely different ballgame. Less damage done. If you decide to wait, will it make that much difference? Will she not be there when you come back? I'm telling you that if she isn't willing to wait, then she probably wouldn't be willing to wait if you were married either. A: You get married and all is well. B: You get married, and it sucks. C: You wait and all is well once you come back. A and C are the same thing. They have the same results, but if you chose C, you won't risk having to go through option B, and you can have more time to talk things through. You have time to have extended conversations through your letters.

"Another thing, while I have the floor. I've learned a soldier cannot serve two masters. It takes a very strong man to not worry about a wife and kiddies while he's fighting a war. Being distracted like that can make it dangerous. A man in combat, especially, one who is responsible for others in battle, can't afford for his mind to be on anything but the matter at hand."

He sighed, and then, cleared his throat. "Don't let this go to your head, Rooney, but there's something I see in you that reminds me of myself years ago. You're a good Ranger. You have potential. I'm not the only one who would hate to see that potential wasted. Think about it. You may need all your faculties sooner than you think. Now, drink up. I'm about finished with my third beer, and we'd better be getting back."

"First Sergeant, do you know something that I don't?"

"You'll know soon enough." The smile on Beebe's face was the smile of a warrior.

CHAPTER 26: Prepare for Operation *Urgent Fury*

While Sergeant Beebe and other platoon leaders began their preparations, Tom visited the post library to learn what he could about Grenada. He checked out as many books on the subject as the library allowed, and photocopied a small map of the Caribbean Sea including the Islands of Grenada.

Later that night, Tom sat on his bed in the B.O.Q. with the books and reports spread out around him.

He read, 'The country of Grenada is made up of three islands, one of which is the island also called Grenada. The country is under the British Commonwealth." He glanced at the photocopy of the map. Tracing his finger across the paper, he found a small oval island labeled Grenada, located southeast of Puerto Rico and north of Venezuela. "Grenada is the southernmost of the Windward Islands, a chain of small islands in the Caribbean Sea that formed a barrier to the Atlantic Ocean." Using the map key, Tom figured the Island named Grenada is only about 12 miles wide and 21 miles long. *That's only about 133 square miles.*

The description in a travelogue indicated a year-around population of just over 90,000 people. It described "beautiful white sandy beaches surrounding a mountainous inland covered with spice trees. Mt. St. Catherine is the highest peak at 2,757 feet."

Oh crap! Mountains again! He thought back to Dahlonega and the rigors of Ranger training on that little Georgia mountain. He closed his eyes for a moment and tried to block the memory. Instead he saw the three "Ranger Eyes" of a weak swimmer. He shook his head to clear his mind and went back to the reading— "A lush tropical island nicknamed 'The Isle of Spice,' Grenada is known for its export of nutmeg and cloves."

"Weather in summer is very hot, and all islands in the Caribbean are subject to tropical storms which usually blow in across the Atlantic from the Cape Verde Islands and the West Coast of Africa."

Then, Tom came across some typewritten pages stapled together as some sort of recent report. It indicated "Grenada has been a peaceful island, but recent reports suggested it has been infiltrated by Cuban soldiers." Tom wondered if they were regulars or soldiers of fortune. "A coup toppled the government in March, 1983, allowing Cubans a foothold in the island. Their military strength and popular support are unknown at the present time."

He closed the report, and neatly stacked the books and reports on his nightstand, and turned out the light. *How could war visit such a peaceful island paradise?* Grenada sounded like Hawaii or Jamaica or some other vacation dreamland.

Tom stretched out on the bed and closed his eyes. He was tired and he dreamily wandered toward sleep.

Suddenly, he opened his eyes. *I'm responsible for the lives of the men in my platoon. What will I do if we have to go to war?*

His heart was pounding. *Will I be able to cope with seeing my men die? Blood and guts? Screams of agony? My men looking to me for direction to keep them . . . from what?*

When the phone rang, he jumped and nearly fell out of bed. He reached for the lamp, his hands shaking as he picked up the telephone receiver. "Aquinas here."

"Lieutenant, this is Sergeant Henning. Are you awake?"

"Yes, what's up?"

"This is not a drill, Lieutenant. I say again, THIS IS NOT A DRILL. Do you understand?"

His heart racing, he answered, "Roger that." He took a deep breath.

"We've been placed on Alert and will be going into Isolation shortly. Bring your equipment, sir. We may be gone a while."

"How soon?"

"ASAP, Lieutenant. All off-post personnel are being called in as we speak. The troops are working on their gear now and should be ready for inspection by the time you get here."

"Thanks, Sergeant Henning. I'm on my way."

Tom and his Platoon Sergeant had completed inspection of their platoon, which had gone well. In the mess hall over coffee, they waited for Captain Chervil to return from battalion headquarters. Several junior officers and senior NCOs sat at Tom's table making small talk, nervous about being put on Alert, but avoiding the subject until they received more information.

As Captain Chervil entered, one of the Sergeants called, "Attention," and they stood.

"As you were!" Captain Chervil said.

The men returned to their coffees, but all eyes remained on their commander. He approached and sat at Tom's table. The First Sergeant went to the coffee machine and brought coffee for the Captain.

"Thank you, First Sergeant. How about clearing the mess hall of nonessentials," he said.

The few other men who were in the mess hall had heard him. They dropped off their trays and cleared out without being told to.

"Come in a little closer, people. I've got some news," Captain Chervil said. "Looks like everyone's here, so I might as well get started." He stood up. "Gentlemen, the 1st Battalion from Fort Benning, the 2nd Battalion from Fort Stewart, and some from Hunter, will be going into Grenada. Some from the Battalion Headquarters will be going, too.

"Vice Admiral Joseph Metcalf III is in charge of Operation *Urgent Fury*, as it's now called, and Operation *Just Cause*. For tactical purposes, he's divided the island horizontally, across in the middle. The USS *Guam* will be the flag ship of the operation. Our Ranger units are assigned to the south. Some Marines and the Navy SEALs, including Seal Team Six, will come in after dark from the south end of the island. Other Marines will come into the North.

"The SEALs are to land in the sea, come ashore and get to Point Salines Airport to set radar homing devices. Four hours after the SEALs have landed, we Rangers are to follow the radar beacons into Point Salines and take the airport. So far as we know, it's not guarded. Then go up Richmond Hill to shut down the New JEWEL Movement center. They're a bunch of hard-core Marxists. Neutralize any resistance. Gather as much intelligence as you can, and sent up communications back to the rest of us. As much as possible, we are to secure the peace, and definitely rescue any American students and their families. It's still up in the air as to whether it will be a jump in or an air landing. Any questions?"

"What's this about jewels?" a Ranger asked. There was a chuckle in the room.

"The J.E.W.E.L. in the New JEWEL Movement stands for 'Joint Endeavor for the Welfare, Education, and Liberation Movement'—but that's more than you need to remember. Under a Cuban General, they've taken over the government and are holding a British governor official captive, if he's still alive. There may others." Captain Chervil replied.

As an after thought, he added, "Unfortunately, we don't yet have any maps of Grenada."

Chervil heard the questioning, "Huhs?" and the "What the hells," but he ignored them.

Tom said, "Permission to speak, sir?"

"Permission granted."

"Sir, I have a travelogue map I copied at the library."

"Let me see that."

"Tom handed over his folded Xerox copy."

"Good work, Lieutenant." Chervil handed the paper to the man beside him. "Get this photocopied immediately. Get as many as you can. At least, be certain all the pilots get copies."

Captain Chervil straightened his uniform jacket, and turned back to face the men. "We don't expect any opposition at the Salines International Airport since it has been out of service while the runway is being extended. By the time you get near it, the SEALs will have set homing devices at the airport, and at the New JEWEL headquarters on the hill.

"After you've landed, we have a *specific mission* to support Delta in an attack on Grenada's Richmond Hill Prison to free political prisoners being held there. If the British Governor General Scoon is there, rescue him, too. It's up to you to figure which building is the prison. A prison looks like a prison. We'll be part of a Task Force of 160, along with members of the Delta Force and the SEALs. While we support Delta on their mission, the SEALs will have two separate missions as well. The SEALs will have a 4 hour lead to make ready for our insertion. The Navy will have a sizeable flotilla off shore. The Ranger Reaction Force from 2nd Battalion will be standing by to medevac as needed.

"In about an hour, I'll be assigning platoon missions in my office. I can't give you a specific schedule until I get word from Battalion headquarters. They're still in the planning stage themselves. Needless to say, we're now quarantined. There'll be no calls out to wives or sweethearts. This must be kept in the strictest confidence. Gentlemen, we're about to earn our pay. That's all I have for the moment. I expect your Rangers to be ready on a moment's notice."

At the next meeting, the Company Commander spelled out plans in greater detail."SEALs will go in from the beach four hours ahead of your teams and elements of SEAL Team SIX will plant radar beacons. Rangers are to take control of the Salines airfield, then split off to take Richmond Hill to neutralize the hard-core cell of Marxists. You should find them in and around the New Jewel Movement headquarters and a nearby villa. If necessary, neutralize. Take over communications. It goes without saying, you should gather intelligence."

Afterward, the Company Commander briefed his officers and top NCOs as they sat around a table in the mess hall. When he was finished, those attending the briefing stood, pushing in their chairs. Tom flinched at the scraping sounds of their chairs made sliding back.

When the First Sergeant heard the grating sound of their chairs scraping the floor as the meeting ended, he began to recite the Ranger Creed aloud, so it could be heard outside as well, and be repeated by any within earshot, "Recognizing I volunteered as a Ranger. . . ." [*See Appendix.*]

Caught up in the spirit of the men, Tom and the others recited the Creed with pride. When the final words were said, he realized the gravity of the words he spoke, " . . . complete the mission, though I be the lone survivor."

Then someone shouted, "Rangers, lead the way!"

He felt good, his fears somewhat allayed. He was part of something bigger than himself, part of a brotherhood.

Chapter 27: On the Move

Tom's company joined Task Force 160 and they flew to Barbados in a C-5A *Galaxy* accompanied by Black Hawk helicopters from the 160th Special Operations Aviation Regiment. From there, it was less than an hour's flying time to Grenada. Most of the company was upset at being detached from their battalion. They would rather have made a parachute jump into Grenada with the others.

Tom and his Rangers had been briefed and now assigned to Black Hawk helicopters by one of the regiment's staff officers.

As they waited for their mission to begin, there wasn't much for the men to do, except tend to their equipment and watch the Black Hawk helicopters, which were being unloaded and hustled back into flying condition to transport the Rangers.

Some men offered suggestions to the crew chiefs. "Make sure you tighten all those nuts and bolts. I have an aversion to falling from the sky without a parachute strapped to my ass."

Or, "Make sure you check the oil in that there machine."

"Do you know what you're doing, crew chief? Did you go to school for that stuff?"

The mechanic doing the work, feeling as though he'd had enough prodding, used the back of his sleeve to swipe the stinging sweat from his eyes before climbing from his perch. He pulled a grease rag from his hip pocket and began to wipe off a heavy wrench, where all could see.

He looked at the Rangers. "Guys, yes, I went to school, and I know what I'm doing." He tapped the wrench onto the palm of his other hand, and shook his head. "You can bet your-sweet-ass I'll be making sure all the nuts are tight, because I'll be riding the son-of-a-bitch with you. It's my job to man that M-60 machine gun mounted at the door. I'll be looking out for any of those assholes shooting at you, so you better be nice to me. Now, I'd appreciate it if you wise asses would shut-up and let me do my job."

The Rangers stood and applauded as the mechanic returned to his job. They knew and respected the fact he was a volunteer serving in the helicopter unit known as *Night Stalkers*. The Night Stalkers flew support missions for Special Operations and had a reputation for being daring and reliable. Their motto said it all: *"Night Stalkers don't quit!"*

When the mission was finally set to go, helicopters took off in line from Barbados for the 45-minute flight. They trailed each other until they crossed the coast of Grenada. There, Black Hawk troopcarriers broke formation to let four carry a Navy SEAL Team to their missions. Two Black Hawk helicopters would transport Tom and the members of his platoon to their objective at Salines Airport. These would be followed by two more choppers with supplies. The other helicopters, carrying Delta and their supporting Rangers, headed toward Richmond Prison; to the Government House to ensure the Governor-General's safety; to seize and control the transmitting station for a radio-free Grenada; and rescue any American medical students and their families.

While all have the assignment to evacuate American medical students and their families, none of the troops were specifically told where on the island the American medical students or their families might be, or even where the schools were located.

Tom unhooked his seat belt and knelt behind Pilot Hedley's compartment where he could look through the windscreen to watch their approach to the target area.

"Damn!" Tom said, looking at the target.

"You got that right, Lieutenant. There's not enough room for both helicopters. We either go in one at a time, or you can rope down," the Pilot Hedley told him. "I'm trying to find the signals the SEALs planted."

Without another thought, Tom turned toward his men and shouted, "Rig for fast rope!" Then he looked back at the Pilot. "Notify the other helicopter."

"Already did," the Pilot answered. He eased back on his cyclic and at the same time lowered his collective, adjusting it delicately to maintain the necessary RPM to keep his machine in the air. Hedley did this while working the rudder pedals keeping a correct heading to allow his passengers time to get ready. As the helicopter made the slower approach, the pilot strained his neck to look until he found a spot that would give the Rangers an advantage, and then he headed toward it.

Satisfied he was where he wanted to be, the Pilot asked the Crew Chief, "Give me directions while I lower the helicopter. Release the ropes so the Rangers can hang down freely from each side of the chopper so as to be in the down blast. Let the bottom of the hanging ropes lay a few feet along the ground so the Rangers won't run out of rope on their way down."

When he was in the best position and at the proper altitude, he selected a point on the horizon and focused on it while he brought his machine to a hover. His actions in the next few minutes would require all of his attention to control this Black Hawk and allow his passengers to exit safely. He had to keep "motionless in the sky" in order for the Rangers to slide to the ground.

The pilot felt the shift in weight, and he made adjustments with his controls. Having flown other Special Operation units in training, he used a gentle touch in his adjustments in order for his passengers to reach the ground safely. Any sudden movement on his part could cause a whip action in the dangling ropes that could snap a man into a free fall, causing serious injury or death. A change to a higher altitude could also cause the ropes to dangle above the ground and again present danger to the troops—making the men hanging targets.

Given the signal, Tom checked to see if the men at the other side were ready before he led the way out the right door. He gripped the rope with gloved hands and began his slide. He had just cleared the threshold of the helicopter doorway when he felt the rope vibrate in his hands, and a millisecond later he heard the chatter of machine gun fire from the door of the helicopter. Bullets fired from the ground made snapping sounds as the bullets whizzed passed him. For a fraction of a second, he wanted to release his grip to speed his descent, until he caught a glimpse of a falling body. When Tom was halfway to the ground, suddenly something had changed. He was falling despite his firm grip.

Oh shit! The helicopter's been hit.

The Pilot concentrated on fine-tuning his adjustments, using both hands and feet in sync. He stared in disbelief as bullets fired from below shattered his windscreen, and his control over the aircraft disintegrated. That's when he saw the other chopper. That machine was falling! *Both* choppers were falling and there was nothing either pilot could do.

Tom couldn't remember the fall or the confusion of the battle. He only knew he heard something bad, then he fell, hit the ground hard enough to knock the wind out of him. There was gunfire all around him. Instantly, the heat of it caused him to feel sunburned. Chunks of metal fell on and around him.

Back at battalion headquarters, the battalion staff members were monitoring the actions of elements of their command, ready to respond with a Reaction Force if needed. They heard the radio transmissions of the Black Hawk helicopters. Were both shot from the sky?

With the sense of urgency apparent in his voice, the Battalion Commander asked, "Who has the Reaction Force?"

"I do, sir," Lieutenant Brian Bath answered.

"Get to the situation map. Now!"

On this day, Brian was responsible for this Reaction Force and had to know the mission of each element within the team. He strode over to the situation wall expecting to see a big map. Instead he found a letter-sized page tacked up with gray push pins.

When the Colonel joined Lieutenant Bath at the map, he asked, "Lieutenant, are your troops ready?"

"Yes, sir. They're aboard the helicopters and eager to get into the fight."

"Have you been monitoring the radio? You are aware of Lieutenant Aquinas' platoon's situation?"

"Yes, sir, I am." Brian answered.

"What's your plan?"

"Sergeant Groves is attempting radio contact with Lieutenant Aquinas' platoon now, Colonel." Brian answered, as he pointed to a spot on the map. "I intend to land my people here, somewhat removed from the action, then go to the crash site as fast as we can. We'll take action as the situation permits, sir," Brian answered.

The Colonel thought for just a moment as he studied the map. "Not much detail on this map. No elevations," he muttered to himself. Then, turning to Brian, he said, "Get moving, Lieutenant, and good luck! You've got some Rangers depending on you."

Someone was tugging on him, and Tom looked up to see the blackened face of Corporal Garcia. Tom tried to follow Corporal Garcia, because the direction was taking him away from the heat.

"What the hell happened?" Tom asked him.

Corporal Garcia ignored the question. "Are you hurt, Lieutenant?"

Tom moaned. "What happened? What happened to our target? Who else is injured?" and then he fell unconscious. Someone moved metal. They had to field dress his wounds before they could pull him out.

CHAPTER 28: Roosevelt Roads Naval Hospital

Dr. John stood his ground as the X.O. shoved a leather-bound volume in his face.

"You must follow the Emergency War Time Procedures! They're right here in the operations' manual," the X.O. said.

The Commanding Officer (C.O.) came in right behind him with another copy of the manual. "Yes, we have to go by the book, and it tells how to triage the wounded. You know, how to decide who to treat first and how much."

Doctor John's face turned purple. "I know exactly what *triage* is and I know exactly what to do." The veins in Doctor John's neck protruded. "What you just read in the book is ten years out of date! Besides, the first steps of triage take place before the patients arrive here. See the clipboard on each gurney?"

Ten more gurneys were wheeled into the Emergency Room (ER).

"This is the Navy and you'll act according to the operations' manual. I'll keep reading . . . ," the X.O. said in a loud voice.

Dr. John pulled back a sheet. "Get this man to surgery. . . ." Then he shouted, "Close this facility to all civilians who do not have life-threatening emergencies. Cancel all routine medical appointments. . . . Send out a page for Trauma Team personnel to the ER now!"

"But the Manual specifically says if you are in the ER, you must put paper booties over your dress shoes. You aren't wearing dress shoes and you aren't wearing the paper booties. No one in here is! Furthermore, you need to put a paper coat over your lab coat," the X.O. pontificated.

"Good thing you're not here on 'casual Friday' to see everyone wearing little floral-print-cotton caps! Good for our *esprit de corps,* don't you think?" he said sarcastically. Getting serious again, Dr. John reminded everyone, "Be sure you change gloves as often as you can."

When the X.O. tried to push the leather-bound tome into Dr. John's gloved hand, Dr. John yelled, "I've had two years' experience in a metropolitan hospital triage unit! Now I may be a shrink but, in my professional opinion, your damn military operations' manual is the crazy!"

He waved to the medics. "Tell the honorable X.O. and C.O. to take their paper booties, their procedures' books and shove . . ." he hesitated, "And get-the-hell-out-of *my* ER!" Looking the C.O. right in the eye, he said. "Ever hear, 'Lead, follow, or get out of the way?' The answer is, YOU ARE IN THE WAY, sir. Please leave at once! This is a construction zone and you aren't wearing a helmet!" Then, Dr. John mouthed to the Medics, *"Get them out of here."*

The medics understood completely. Four Navy Medics grabbed the two officers, still clutching the operations' manuals, lifted them by the elbows, and removed them both from the ER and took them down the long hall.

"Okay staff, we may be Navy, but today, we're running this ER like the big city. Now hustle!"

"Who are these civilians? I said no civilians!"

"They're wounded from the mental hospital. It got bombed by mistake —The Cubans put their flag on the hospital's roof and moved the Red Cross flag to the top of the JEWEL's headquarters," Corporal Garcia said.

"We bombed a mental hospital?" Dr. John asked, but the Corporal had left to get another gurney.

Dr. John turned to the next gurney. "We've given you painkillers and stopped the bleeding."

"Doctor, do I have my legs?"

"I'm so sorry. No."

"Oh, that's bad. That's bad," he said. "Do I have my balls?" The doctor lifted the sheet to look.

"No. I'm sorry." Dr. John didn't have time to wonder how he'd lost both legs and his genitals, yet made it to the ER.

"Ooh, that's bad. But, am I gonna live?"

"Yeah, I think you're going to make it. When the wounds heal, you'll be fitted for new legs and be walking in no time." He moved to the next gurney.

"Glory halleluia!" the wounded man shouted. "Did you hear that!!! I'm gonna live! Praise God! Praise the Doc, and some of you all, too!"

The trauma team nurses and doctors flooded into the ER in response to Dr. John's earlier page.

Nurse Manning immediately came alongside Dr. John and began to roll an injured man onto his side when she found a rifle under his leg.

"He's got a rifle. Help!" Nurse Manning grabbed the rifle with her free hand gave it to Dr. John who pushed it into the hands of Navy Medic Makowski who was just walking by the cart to go get more gloves.

Medic Makowski looked astounded. "Eee gads! It's Russian. Is this guy Russian?" My Russian isn't too good. He tried to sound out a Russian greeting to the patient. *"Kock bozheviachet?* How are you?"

The patient groaned the traditional response. *"Ochin horoshaw.* Fine, thank you."

Dr. John shook his head. The Russian patient didn't look 'fine.'

Medic Makowski removed the clip and unfolded the stock on the semi-automatic rifle. "This is a newer Kalashnikov AK74."

"How did we get a Russian here?" Nurse Manning persisted.

"Forget it. Treat whoever is here." Dr. John said, then he shouted, "Check every patient here for weapons—*before* they come in the door!"

The staff began pulling back sheets and turning patients. "Over here! This Cuban has a gun," Medic McCue yelled.

"Cuban? Russian? Mental hospital? . . . What kind of battle was this?" Dr. John asked.

In broken English, the Cuban pleaded, "No! Not take my pistol. I *must* have it. Big trouble if I lose my weapon."

"Forget it! You aren't going back for a long time. Do you want to live, or do you want to hold on to your gun?"

"Aaah," he hesitated. "I have to keep my gun or I'll be a dead man."

Hearing what was going on, Corporal Garcia walked over and grabbed the Cuban's gun, and unloaded the clip. "Nice piece," he said. "Dr. John, what do you want me to do with this old TT-33?"

The doctor looked confused until Garcia said, "The Tokarev pistol?"

"Get it out of here. Now!"

Corporal Garcia nodded, pocketed the pistol, and went out the double door to off-load another wounded man from the *Guam*.

A lean young man walked into the ER with his right arm in a sling and a soccer ball under the left arm.

"No civilians today," Dr. John shouted over the bedlam.

"I'm an American medical student from Grenada. Something broke my arm. I need the bone set." And he kept talking, "I was playing a game of soccer, by the Salines Airport, against Cuban workmen's team, when all hell broke lose. Anti-aircraft artillery came out of nowhere, guns blazing. U.S. Choppers were falling, flaming. Tan tanks —Russian troop carriers— pulled up. I ran for cover as fast as I could, but shrapnel or something, broke my arm."

"Somebody take him to xray." Doctor Shih intervened.

Navy Nurse Manning looked quizzically at the student. "I thought American medical students needed to be rescued?"

Corporal Garcia came back into the ER. "Yeah, we rescued 'em, *after* we were ambushed at the airfield."

"Ambushed?" a Navy SEAL on a gurney said. "We ran into patrol boats. After we cut the engines, the damned outboards wouldn't restart. We were caught in a rip current and taken out to sea. When we tried to beach again, we were ambushed, our boats swamped, and the current was pulling us out again. Four guys I knew didn't make it."

On the next gurney lay another Navy SEAL patient. He groaned. "We were pinned down on the Western beach. Why did they air-drop us into the ocean on that side of the mountain, 40 kilometers away from the airport? Planning allowed us 4 hours to land and hack our way up a mountain through jungle over-growth of brush, vines, snakes, even cactus! Supposed to spot the airport and enemy headquarters through that, then hack our way down the other side to get there. A damned SNAFU! We never reached Richmond Hill or the airfield. A four hour mission, my ass!"

"Maybe Admirals haven't climbed mountains in the tropics. . . . I'm asking, why no 'lessons-learned' from D-Day? — Hey, men wearing full packs sink! They oughta know by now. And why drop us in a rip current?"

The first SEAL continued his rant. "The damned outboards on the rubber boats— We had to row through the surf with whatever we had." He gasped another breath. "All the time we were under fire. Somebody knew we were coming! Rubber boats don't deflect gunshells." Then he was rolled out to surgery.

All the while, the man with the soccer ball kept talking. "I spoke to classmates on my cellphone. They were holed up on other parts of the island. Said Cuban military men ordered 'em to get inside buildings or be shot on sight. They were on lockdown when I talked to them. They said, 'Dead bodies are all over the streets in the cities.' . . . Out at the airport, we weren't worried, us being soccer friends with the construction workers, uh, soldiers, I mean. We played almost every day — we didn't feel we were at risk.

"I guess your arm says otherwise," Medic Makowski said. He escorted the medical student down the long hall to xray. "Well, some guys made it in an air drop. They say we got everyone out. That's the important thing. I guess the mission was a success."

"I'm glad they got me out!"

Corpsman Washington brought Dr. John reports of more incoming wounded. Without hesitation, the Doctor prioritized each injury and shouted the orders for each new patient.

A second later, he came to Tom's gurney and put his hand on Tom's shoulder. "I'm Doctor John and we're taking good care of you." He took a penlight and checked Tom's pupils, waking him up. "You're going to be okay. You're cut up and have some burns, but with a few stitches and two weeks' rest, you'll almost be ready to jump out of airplanes again. Nothing looks broken," Dr. John reassured him, then went to the next patient.

"Thanks, doc. That's good news." Tom smiled.

When Garcia heard Tom's voice, he came over to him.

Tom asked, "Where am I? What happened?"

"You're at Roosey Roads. That's Roosevelt Roads Naval Hospital in Puerto Rico. You've been unconscious. Brian and I got you out of the wreckage, and you were flown to the USS *Guam* which transported you here."

"Brian?" His question went unanswered.

"You'll be fine." Dr. John told Tom, "I'm just going to give you a shot to relax you. You'll go for xrays in a few minutes. Nothing looks broken. If the xrays confirm that, I'll stitch you up."

A Medic brought a syringe over to give Tom a shot.

"I don't want a shot of anything!— at least, not until I find out about my men," Tom insisted.

Corporal Garcia grabbed the Medic's hand. "Look at his collar. He's already had a shot! Get away from him."

The Medic glared at the Corporal, but took his syringe and went hunting for another patient's arm to inject with morphine.

"Incoming wounded!"

Tom thought he recognized Sergeant Henning's voice across the room.

Sergeant Henning came into the ER and asked in a loud voice, "Has anyone seen the C.O. or the X.O.?"

Four Medics grinned, exchanged knowing looks, but said nothing.

"I said, 'Has anyone seen the C.O. or the X.O.'?"

This time a Corpsman smiled. "I think they're detained on business at the far end of the building."

Henning replied, "If it's like most military hospitals, that's over a mile away! Anyone have a helicopter or a golf cart to get me there?"

"Sergeant, you're in the wrong place for a chopper. This is the ER."

Sergeant Henning left to get directions to administrative wing to find their office.

"Sergeant Hen-n-in?" Tom called weakly. Henning didn't answer. He'd already left.

"It's all right, Lieutenant. I'll fill you in after you get taken care of. Just do as the doctor says," Corporal Garcia said, as a Medic Makowski arrived to take Tom to xray.

CHAPTER 29: Winn Army Hospital

Some of Tom's platoon members were gathered in their 2nd Lieutenant's hospital room at Winn Army Hospital, Hinesville at Fort Stewart. They wanted to offer their support to the young officer, suggesting he get his ass out of bed and get back to the unit.

Tom appreciated that Sergeant Henning had come with the guys to visit him. *Maybe I somehow managed to impress the Sergeant enough to get his approval,* Tom speculated. He looked about the room, and his eyes came to rest on his rescuer, Garcia, who now wore a third stripe, showing him now a Buck Sergeant.

"I understand congratulations are in order, Sergeant Garcia,"

"I didn't do much. While I was moving stuff to get to you, Trujillo pulled three men out of the other burning chopper. He's the real hero."

"You saved me, so that means you're a hero to me." Tom said. "Thanks for getting me out from under the helicopter. I owe you one." Tom reached for Garcia's hand. "How about holding off on the promotion party until I get out of this place?

"Hell, Lieutenant, you better save your thanks for Sergeant Henning. He's the one who saved all of us," Garcia said.

"Damn it, Sergeant Garcia. Knock it off!" Sergeant Henning burst out.

"Sorry, but the Lieutenant should know." Sergeant Garcia continued, "Sergeant Henning was on the helicopter that took us out to the hospital ship. When the Navy refused permission to land, he went ape-shit. Henning, a lowly Army Sergeant First Class, ordered the lady pilot, who was, by the way, a Captain, 'Land your fucking machine on the ship's landing pad whether they said Okay or not!' He grabbed her microphone. 'Captain, I'll take it from there'. I guess he scared the shit out of the Captain because the Pilot ignored the ship's radio messages saying, 'Do not to land,' and the wave-offs of the ship's crew. She landed the chopper on the moving deck perfectly. . . .It seems the landing was 'against Naval regulation,' because the Army pilot hadn't been trained by the Navy in the Navy's procedures for landing aboard a ship at sea. We probably could have gotten them on gender discrimination as well."

Incredulous as the story sounded, Tom believed it. He glanced toward his Platoon Sergeant with a questioning look. "Did you get into any trouble?" Tom asked.

Sergeant Henning smiled slyly. "No, sir. I just explained nicely to the whatever-he-was in a jumpsuit greeting us, that we had injured aboard, and since our ships at sea accepted the Vietnamese helicopters that evacuated Saigon back in Vietnam, he'd better damn-sure accept ours now!" Henning grinned again. "He *finally* agreed with me."

"Tell the Lieutenant about the Marine," Garcia prompted.

When Henning seemed reluctant to talk about that particular story, Tom urged him on. "What are you hiding? I knew it! You did get into trouble over this!" Tom said.

"No, sir. It's just that some Marine, all shined up in a fancy uniform, started to take issue with us coming aboard. I pointed a grubby finger at him and told him, 'Don't even think about interfering!' and he backed off. It was as simple as that."

"You backed him off just by pointing a finger?" Tom furrowed his brows. "Come to think of it, you are a mean looking SOB—and you didn't get into *any* trouble? Really?" Tom asked again.

"No, sir." Henning said. "In fact, our Colonel laughed his ass off when I explained what I'd done."

The visitors were laughing when a cute nurse in an Army uniform came in to check Tom's vital signs. He thought he recognized her from somewhere.

Sergeant Henning noticed how tired Tom looked, so he motioned to the guys it was time to leave.

"We'll be back soon," Hognose said.

Garcia waved, "Speedy recovery, Lieutenant."

The following day, First Lieutenant Brian McGlynn Bath entered the hospital room and approached the bed. "How are you doing, Tom?"

"Not bad, considering it could have been much worse," Tom answered.

"Are you up to reading? I brought a few books you might find interesting. If you don't feel like it, I can hold on to them until later."

"No, I'm glad you brought them. I appreciate the thought, Lieutenant. They'll help break some of the boredom. I'm sick of just laying here but my doctor says I'll be up and around in no time at all."

"Nobody will tell me about my men or what really happened. Tell me what you know," Tom asked.

"Okay, but hey, don't call me 'lieutenant.' You know my name," Brian said. "I'll tell you what I can, but then you have to answer something for me." Brian looked down and took a deep breath. "Not all the reports are in yet, but we think what happened was that Cuban regulars who'd taken over Grenada got word we were coming. It wasn't us. Washington says something was said or somebody blurted out something at an Organization of American States (OAS) or Organization of Eastern American States (OEAS) or something, and word got to Cuba and to Grenada. Some say Reagan got a phone call after this meeting asking for an invasion, and maybe just a plea from a student asking for help to get back home. It's unclear whether the rescue mission was planned before or as a result of the OEAS meeting. In any case, President Reagan made the final decision about the same time that the Cubans or Russians found out it was being contemplated, so the secret mission wasn't really a secret mission! History will have to sort it all out in about 25 years. Most of what I've gleaned, I got from the guys I was pulling out afterward, or my buddies who were with me the year I went to West Point.

In any case, SEALs were washed out to sea. Some were rescued and dropped in all over again. At the beach, the rest were pinned down under fire and didn't make it to the airfield to be sure it was clear, or set radar beacons for our aircraft. . . . We were supposed to come in unnoticed. However Salines Airport was surrounded by uniformed Cuban soldiers with ZU-23 anti-aircraft artillery, some Russian soldiers armed with and some shoulder-fired missile launchers."

"Wait a minute," Tom said. "You were at West Point?" The wheels in Tom's brain began to spin. *Do I have to try to get into West Point now?*

"Yeah, I was. But I didn't graduate. I took my dad's death pretty hard and couldn't concentrate when I got there. It was right after high school. So I didn't stay there."

Tom's thoughts settled down.

"Meanwhile, back to the story. In Grenada, as your platoon was coming down the ropes from the chopper, they let loose with anti-aircraft fire. Your chopper was hit first. Parts of the flaming wreckage came down on you.

"But here's where the story has a public and a private version." Brian lowered his voice. "What didn't make it into the news was that when your chopper was hit, Pilot Hedley tried hard to control it, but then the two Black Hawks collided with each other and burst into flames. It's a miracle you're alive."

"But the others? What about them?"

"We know of thirteen or fourteen who didn't make it: Grenier, Kelly, Lannon, Rooney, one pilot and at least four men from SEAL Team Six. I'll bring you a list of names when I can. Not everyone is accounted for yet. Worse, there's a suspicion some of the injured didn't have a 'pin in their label' and so may have gotten more than one dose of painkillers, and died later.

"You know how it is, there's the official version and then there's the rumor mill. We may never really know. . . . Both women pilots made it back safely, but now, the Pentagon is saying, 'Women, what women? We never have women in combat.'

"But my men, nobody made it?"

"Do the math. Eleven men and a pilot on each chopper. Garcia and I pulled out a couple, and Stephen Trujillo alone pulled three out. He went right into the fire. So, some did, I'm just not sure who. They were taken to different hospitals."

The color drained from Tom's face as he realized most of his men were killed. He felt a wave of survivor's guilt sweep over him.

Brian stood up and walked over to the window to give Tom time to compose himself. "I'd like to tell you more, but that's really all I know so far."

"Sergeant Garcia and I were with the Reaction Force bringing out the wounded. I haven't had a chance to sit down with the other guys to hear how the fight went. We did see two big transports land. When we left, some units of SEALs and Marines were still there fighting. Probably still are. When the Rangers of the 75th Regiment completed their part of the mission, we were pulled back to post. I think the American medical students and their families have all been rescued, but no one told us ahead of time that there were three different medical schools."

"Yeah, I saw some students playing soccer by the airfield when we flew in," Tom said. "One was in the ER with me. I remember him, the soccer-doctor. American medical students vs. Cuban military construction-worker soldiers."

"I spoke to some others we pulled out of another location. They said, after the coup, the head of government was executed by the JEWEL Movement forces. American students were ordered to get inside a building and stay out of sight or be shot. There was martial law and a round the clock curfew. Anyone found outside was mowed down."

Brian looked up when the nurse brought in a carafe of ice water and a tray of glasses.

She gave Brian the once over before handing Tom a glass of water. "Drink up, soldier," she smiled, and left the room.

"Anyway, the American med students couldn't thank us enough for pulling them out. They were badly shaken and still remembered to thank us!"

After Tom put his glass down, Brian picked up a chair and moved it closer to the bed.

"Brian, there's a favor I'd like to ask. Could you get my library books from my room at the B.O.Q. and return them for me? They're in a stack next to the bunk."

"Yeah, sure. I'll try. . . . I have, uh, something to ask you." Brian put the books he'd brought on Tom's bedside table, and continued, "When you were being evacuated, you kept talking about something . . . something about us being brothers? . . .It was pretty strange. What did you mean?"

"Huh?" Tom asked. "Were you there?"

"Yes, I saw you at the Aid Station before the medevac chopper took you to *The Guam*. You rambled. Said something personal to me. . . about my having another sister? . . . one I didn't know anything about. . . . And you said you and I are brothers? What the heck is that about?"

"I'm afraid I was sedated. I shouldn't have said it." Tom looked away.

Brian leaned closer to Tom. "But you *did* say it, and I think you owe me an explanation."

Unnerved that a long-kept secret was revealed, Tom looked at the ceiling as if the words might be written there. He wondered about the impact it would have on the two families. He cleared his throat. "My mother met a man in Laos," he began, knowing there was no turning back now. Tom struggled in his mind to find the right words in English. "I knew your father," he finally said. Tom turned so he could see Brian.

"What? How?" Brian stammered. "How could you have known *my* father?" Brian scooted his chair up to Tom's bed.

The two officers sat in silence, each waiting for the other to say something, anything, until neither could stand the silence any longer.

Tom answered with a question, "Do you know your father's middle name?"

"Of course! Aquinas." Then Brian's tone softened as he continued slowly, "Thomas Aquinas McGlynn, Thomas Aquinas. . . . Is that a coincidence or is there a connection?"

"Are you sure you want to hear what I have to say?"

"Oh, hell, yeah. You've already opened a door. Let's have it." Brian crossed his arms and leaned back slowly, feeling a mixture of anger and curiosity.

Tom began the long story. "I first met your father when my uncle brought him to our village in Laos. The American soldier had suffered a head wound and was very sick with a fever and dysentery. My mother was asked to take care of him. After he was cleaned up, our Village Headman placed your father in our hut so my mother could use herbs and poultices to nurse him back to health."

Tom breathed deeply and continued, "After your father got better physically, he had almost no memory of who he was although he could still speak Lao and American words. His head hurt him a lot. . . . As the American got stronger, he began to improve things in our village, to improve our living conditions. He was good for our village. He continued to stay in our hut and became my father, and soon my sister Sirion was born. Then one . . ."

"Hold it! Back up! He became *your* father? I thought you were there when he was brought into the village?"

"Oh, he wasn't my real father. Years before, my first father went off to fight in the war and didn't return when the other soldiers from our village came back. Your father took his place in our family."

"And you're saying he fathered a child with your mother?" Brian asked, incredulously.

"Yes, my sister, Sirion."

Brian rose from his chair and began to pace. The two young men remained silent for long moments as Brian tried to absorb what Tom had just revealed. He finally came back to the chair and sat down.

"I suddenly have a thousand-and-one questions," Brian said. "To begin with, when we met after you gave the talk at Walton High, you told me your name was 'Kump' something or other. A few days ago, at the Aid Station, I saw the name on your dogtag was Thomas Aquinas. How the hell did that happen? Did you falsify records to get into the Army?"

"Negative. Let me explain, please." First, Tom told him about standing with his mother and little sister on a knoll at the Marietta National Cemetery watching the American man they loved being put to rest. Tom spoke of learning to live in America, having to adapt to the safehouse in Atlanta, and then to their new home in Marietta. He told how he'd wanted to follow in the footsteps of Thomas Aquinas McGlynn, the man he loved as a father, the man who'd given him the Seiko watch, taught him to speak American, and given him goals and aspirations. The same man who was also Brian's real father.

"Watch? What watch? What the hell are you talking about?"

"Your father left his watch for me when he left us. I still have it."

Suddenly angry, Brian lashed out, "You lay all this crap on me about my father being *your wonderful father*, and you expect me to just accept it? And that he left you his watch! He never gave *me* a fucking watch. He never gave me or my family anything but heartache!" With that said, Brian stormed out of the room without a backward glance.

How could I have handled that so badly? Tom asked himself. He rolled over to face the wall, regret filling him. *I really wanted Brian to be my friend, my brother.*

In the hallway of the hospital, Brian paced. "What in hell does this guy want? What could he want? I'll fix his fucking wagon! Brother, my ass!" Brian said loudly.

Several members of the hospital staff were looking apprehensively at him.

Brian punched at the cement block wall. He felt the sting of skinned knuckles, but he didn't care. He gave the nurse standing behind the Nurses' Station a mean look, slowly shook his head, and walked away.

Later at the B.O.Q. Brian lay in bed waiting for sleep. He thought about his father, and what Sergeant Major Mitzamuri had said about him at the funeral. *How did he put it?* His mind went back over the years. *Damn it! Mitzi did mention my dad suffered from amnesia after he was wounded! In the eulogy, Mitzi said: "In Laos, Tom lived a primitive life, but he survived, and found a way to return to us due to his strength of character."*

Brian reached for the telephone book and found the number for Winn Army Community Hospital. He dialed the phone number. When the call was answered, Brian asked to be connected to Lieutenant Aquinas' room.

The answer came in a monotone that infuriated him. "I'm sorry, sir, but we don't accept incoming calls to patients after 2100. Please call back in the morning."

He attempted to tell the operator about the urgency of the call, but no one heard his plea. The operator had already disconnected.

Rules are rules, and there were no exceptions, period. This was the Army.

"Crap!" He slammed down the phone handset. He got out of bed, got dressed, and went into his bathroom to throw water on his face. He'd make himself look presentable, go see Aquinas, and make things right.

At Winn, Brian stepped off the elevator onto the fifth floor. The hallway was dimly lit by night-lights. As he approached Tom's room, the nurse stopped him.

"May I help you?" she asked.

"No, problem, ma'am. I'm just going in to see Lieutenant Aquinas."

"I'm sorry but visiting hours are over." She looked at her watch before continuing, "They were over exactly two hours and twenty-three minutes ago. You'll have to leave."

Brian noticed the Army nurse's rank, but protested anyway. "But Captain, you don't understand. I was here earlier to see Kumpang, er, I mean Tom, but I couldn't understand what he was trying to tell me. He's my brother—I can't let him spend the night feeling I rejected him."

"You're Lieutenant Aquinas' brother? Heh! You sure don't look it!" the Captain said.

Brian put on his sweetest smile and shook his head. "Ma'am, it's a long complicated story."

Concerned their conversation would disturb her patients, the nurse asked Brian to accompany her to the Nurses' Station.

Realizing that no matter how good his explanation would be, she wasn't going to let him see Tom. Brian decided to try something else. "Ma'am, will Lieutenant Aquinas be getting medication tonight?"

"Yes, at midnight."

"When you wake him up, would you *please* tell him his brother Brian was here to see him, and that I'll be back in the morning? *Please.* It's very important he knows."

"I'll tell him, but visiting hours are from 1400 to 1600 tomorrow. Not tomorrow morning! I suggest you come between those hours—*not* in the morning."

"Yes, ma'am, I will. Just tell him." He turned and pushed the elevator button.

The following morning, Brian placed a call to his mother to run Tom's story by her, and to see what she thought or might know. When their usual pleasantries were finished, Brian asked her to sit down, that he had some news.

Laughing, Anne replied, "Don't tell me that you got married."

"No, mom. I'm not married. I'll never find a girl who'll put up with me. This is more serious."

"Oh, then maybe I'd better sit. Okay, I'm sitting. Shoot."

Brian told her about what had happened.

Anne was silent for just a moment, then asked, "Do you believe him?"

His answer was immediate. "I have no reason not to, mom. I never would have believed that dad could do something like that, but then I remembered that Uncle Mitzi said dad had amnesia for a long time."

When she didn't say anything, Brian was starting to get worried about his mother.

Finally, she asked, "What do you think we should do, Brian?"

She's asking me what to do. She is asking me like I'm an adult on her level. She's never done that. To mom, I'm still her little boy. Lord, she must really be confused and worried about what to do. Brian rubbed at his temple. . . . "Would you want to meet him, or them?"

"Oh, God, honey, I don't know. Let me sleep on it and get back to you."

"Okay, mom. We don't have to figure this out today. We've gone this long without knowing about it. We're scheduled to go on field maneuvers for a couple of days, and I won't be able to call for a week or so. Say hello to everybody back home. Try not to worry, mom. I love you."

"I love you, too, Brian. Be careful. Bye, Bye."

"Bye, mom."

The following afternoon, Brian tapped softly on the door of Tom's hospital room. "May I come in?" he asked.

Tom recognized Brian's voice. He put down the book he was reading. "Door's open," Tom said in a tone that implied he wasn't that happy to see him.

"I take it the night nurse didn't tell you I was here after visiting hours last night," Brian said, and walked to the foot of Tom's bed.

"She told me. . . . But I also heard you yelling in the hallway after you'd left my room."

"Oh." Brian raised his brows. "I'm really sorry I blew up yesterday, Tom. You've got to admit that it isn't every day a person finds out that his father had another family. It was a real shocker for me."

"And now, all of a sudden you believe me? An overnight revelation?" Tom asked, sounding miffed.

"In a way, I guess you could say that. After I went home last night, I remembered something Uncle Mitzi told me: that my Dad had gotten amnesia from head trauma. Once I thought about it, things sort of fell into place. I also remembered what Mitzi said about their friendship and Army days, about Dad's strength of character and dependability. Like a fog clearing, I began to realize there's nothing wrong with this picture. In a sense, Dad lived two lives, one in which he loved our family and one in which he loved yours." Brian paused. "Does that make sense to you?"

Tom didn't answer him. He looked away for a moment.

Brian made himself comfortable in the stiff bedside chair. He sat silently, giving both of them time to think things over.

When Tom finally looked at Brian, and said, "Brian, I lost my father, my American father, when I was still pretty young. And because of it, I also lost a major part of my boyhood. If you think about it, I lost my father to you. He left us because he finally remembered who he was, and when he did, he chose you over us. That was very hard for me. I never could understand why. It made me feel there had to be something about him that I didn't understand. I questioned whether I ever knew him at all."

Brian's eyes met Tom's. "I know you must have felt that way. For me, I wonder what happened while he was gone. . . I was a little kid when he left for Laos. I never got to know him *at all*. Maybe you could share what you know, and I could do the same. Would you mind telling me about him? How it was growing up with him as your father figure? Did he ever mention us? My mother, my two sisters June and Kim, or me? It's important for me to know."

Tom saw the sincerity in his question. "Let me answer your last question first. No, I don't recall him ever mentioning them. It was like his life began when he came to our village. There was nothing before that for him. It's important to me that you understand. At that point, he had *no* memories. . . .

Tom took a sip of water. "Remember, he wasn't the first father that I'd lost. I also lost the father of my birth. I was so young when he left, I don't even remember what he looked like. If he were to walk through that door right now, he'd be a stranger to me. Like your dad, he went off to war, but he wasn't in the regular Army like your dad was. I don't know why mine went or which side he fought for." Tom continued, "He never came back. My mother and I lived alone in a small rural village. I tell you this to explain my family's situation when your father was rescued.

"Brian, when I first met your father, he was very sick with dysentery and burning up with a fever. He smelled terrible. His U.S. Army clothing was torn and filthy. Wrapped around his head was a rag, caked with dried blood.

"I'd never seen an American. I was more curious than anything else, especially, when I found out that he'd been placed in my mother's care and moved into our hut. Although it was difficult, my mother took her responsibility to heart, and your dad got better everyday. Soon, he was up and about, not full-speed, mind you, but well enough to hold some food in his stomach.

"In no time, he started walking freely about the village, usually with me as his guide. He and I became friends because we communicated by teaching each other our languages. As his health improved and he learned more about our village, he began suggesting improvements to help our community run better. You know, sanitary conditions and such. He was a whiz at stuff like that. Before long, he even took control of the village's work force to harvest teak and to transport it to Thailand for sale. The more involved he became, the better the village prospered."

Tom grinned, and then continued. "But more importantly, the village people all seemed happier. There was laughter among them again. And my mother was a part of that. Before, she had been bitter, probably from being abandoned and having to raise me alone. But now she smiled a lot. I knew why. She was in love with your father. You should have seen how happy she was when she realized she was pregnant with my sister, Sirion.

"We were a happy family, living a simple life in a small village in Laos. There was no contact with the outside world, no radio, TV, or movies, but we weren't bored. It was a pure kind of happiness, coexisting with each other, and nature, being a family just as Our Maker intended."

Brian saw a nostalgic look on Tom's face and correctly read the sincerity in his voice. *This guy is sad that things changed. He wants to go back to those days. I think he really cared for my father*, Brian told himself.

Tom continued. "One morning, I woke up and found a Seiko wristwatch laying beside my pallet. His sleeping mat was rolled up. He was gone. Gone! And we didn't know why. My entire family was devastated. I would catch my mother crying at the oddest times. I couldn't help it, but there were times that I hated him for hurting her that way.

"To make matters worse, people in our village treated us as outcasts. They were angry because he'd deserted the village, and left our village economy in the teakwood trade to founder. We lost our position in the village. Before, we were respected for having such an important person in our hut. Now, we were just the family who had been deserted by a foreigner. Children would not have anything to do with my mixed-race sister or me. I could not understand it, and wondered what we had done to be so mistreated. My mother continued the work that he'd initiated, to keep the village records as your father had, but things were just not the same.

"One day, my mother told Sirion and me we were going on a little holiday. She took us by boat to Pak Kading, a city on the Mekong River.

"Brian, I've got to tell you, I was in no mood for a holiday of any sort, but I jumped at the chance to see my mother and sister have a get-away, even for a little while. We left with only the clothes we were wearing.

"As it happened, we were met by a man unknown to me who whisked us away in a car to Vientiane— never to return to our village. The ride in the car was unbelievable. You may not realize it, but none of us had ever seen an automobile, never mind ridden in one.

"We were taken to the U.S. Embassy. That's where I found out my mother had planned this escape from our village. This was to be no holiday. Somehow, we were scheduled to leave for America, courtesy of your father.

"Was I 'surprised' to learn this? No. 'Shocked' was the word. When I found out that your father had arranged it—the man I believed had deserted us, I was really confused. Once I found out, I was miserable for having been so upset with him. I will never forgive myself for leaving the watch that he left me behind in our village hut."

"The watch?" Brian asked.

"Yes, the watch you got so upset about yesterday. This watch." Tom raised his left arm and pointed to the Seiko on his wrist.

"You just said you left it behind."

"I did, but my mother brought it along and later gave it back to me. Once I found out that he'd arranged for us to come to America, I realized that he really did care for us. Eventually, I understood my anger had been because I loved him so much. Once I learned he'd never truly forsaken us, I vowed to be like him. He was a good man.

"I couldn't wait to get to America. I had to see him. I missed him so much. I couldn't wait for us all to be a family again. We were on our way to see him again, but he died several days before we got to America.

"The CIA arranged for my mother, sister, and me to get to Marietta in time for the funeral. Our first experience with America was his military ceremony with the guns and everything. We stood and watched from a distance on the hillside. I saw the officer present you with his flag.

"When the ceremony was over, I watched as you walked to the limo holding the flag to your chest. I was jealous, I couldn't help it. I wanted to be the one to hold on to his flag."

Tom turned to look out the window. He wasn't looking at anything in particular. His vision had misted over, and he didn't want Brian to see this. He blinked until the tears left his eyes. . . .

"When he left, I felt rejected. I was jealous. I wanted his love and approval. And I thought I knew how to get it. I had to be to a better son than you." Tom said. "And it was then that I promised myself to follow in his footsteps whatever the cost."

"Huh?" Brian's jaw dropped but he couldn't find any words.

Then Tom mentioned how Sergeant Major Mitzamuri had arranged for them to receive insurance money that his father wanted to be used for his and Sirion's education. He explained how he'd graduated with a 3.8 grade point average."

Brian put his hand up to interrupt. In an elevated voice he said, "Give me a minute here. What'd you say? You *know* Uncle Mitzi?"

"Please, let me finish telling you how I thought I could get my father's approval. I promise to explain it all."

Brian paused a moment. "Okay, I'm listening, but this is a lot to take in."

"At Walton High," Tom said, "I was really disappointed I didn't make the football team, because you had been a star there. I wanted to do it all, to do everything you could. But I had to settle for not being as athletic as you were. . . .

"By the way, Uncle Mitzi let me know something you'll want to know. Before he died, your father was brought by ambulance to watch you play the homecoming game at Walton. They permitted him to have a last wish to watch the game. Because he was quarantined with infection, he had to remain isolated in the ambulance. The ambulance parked by the end of the football field where he could watch the game and also see your mom and sisters watching the game, too."

Brian was speechless. His eyes were welling up.

Tom continued, "Of course, someone was looking out for us, because if I hadn't been trying to get on the team, I wouldn't have been there the day Brandon Spears attacked Kim."

"Whoa! . . .Were you the guy who stopped it? Why didn't you say something before now?"

"I didn't know who Kim was at the time. My girlfriend was with me, and after I fought off Spears, we just drove Kim home. She thanked us and that was it. I didn't figure out that Kim was the girl I'd helped until later when you told me about how your sister had been attacked and who the boy was. Then I knew that Kim was the girl."

"When I found out about it," Brian said, "I looked for Brandon and gave him an ass kicking he'd never forget. I told him, if he so much as looked at Kim again, he'd get worse the next time."

Tom laughed. "Yeah, I heard you did."

Brian stood up and walked to the window. "That's quite a story about my father, and also about you wanting to be better than me— when I didn't even know you," Brian said, his back still turned to Tom.

"Why do you think I'm here? A Ranger officer! A clod from some far-off village making the big time? What do you think caused me to get this far?" Not waiting for an answer, Tom continued, "Because you led the way, Lieutenant Brian McGlynn Bath. You set the standards that I would have been lost without. Now, please, sit and let me finish my story."

Brian shrugged and went back to his chair. "Isn't it time for the nurse to bring in the pitcher of ice water?"

Tom didn't answer Brian's query. "You wondered about my name? Well, I'm here to tell you it was all done legally. After my family and I got our U.S. citizenship, and I'd graduated from Walton High, I petitioned the Cobb County Court to have my name changed. I wanted to be closer to your father, and I thought if I carried part of his name, it would do the job. I wanted an American name before I went into the Army. Can you imagine the nicknames I'd be called if I'd kept the Lao name, Kumpang?"

"Why didn't you adopt his whole name then, to include McGlynn?"

Tom smiled. "Look at me, Brian. Do I look like anything even resembling a Mic? a McGlynn?" He chuckled, but suddenly turned serious. "Truly, it was really because I didn't want to draw any attention from your family. My name change was a matter of Public Record, and was published in the Cobb County weekly and *Atlanta Journal* legals. Now, I guess you know everything."

"Not everything. How do you know Uncle Mitzi?"

"Well, we met Sergeant Major Mitzamuri before your father's funeral, and he and his wife Mai Lin have been a tremendous help since. She understood what immigrants might need."

Tom then described some of the ways they'd helped his family. "I've got to add that they were also very protective of your family. He and your father must have been through a lot together."

"Tom, I'm a bit ashamed of myself for losing it yesterday, especially, now, after hearing your well-told history. Are we brothers? I don't know. Not by blood or by any legal definitions, but I guess you could safely say that we've been made something by circumstances beyond our control. Fate, if you will." Brian reached to shake Tom's hand and asked, "Friends?"

Tom's smile was answer enough.

There was a soft tap on the door. The same nurse, who'd asked Brian to leave the night before came into the room carrying a small tray.

"Time for you-know-what, Lieutenant," the Captain said in a cheerful tone. "Please, lower your you-know-what and roll onto your stomach." Then, as though noticing Brian for the first time, she said, "Oh, it's you, again. I see you came during visiting hours for a change."

Brian asked in mocked remorse, "Why do you hate me so? All I wanted to do was speak to my long lost bud, but you wouldn't allow me to. Is there anything I can do to atone for any sin I might have committed? Take you to dinner perhaps? What time do you get off duty?"

"Midnight, Lieutenant. Do your parents allow you to stay up that late?" The nurse gave him a teasing smile. She administered the injection. Then she gave Tom's hip a playful slap when she'd finished.

Brian ignored the fact that she was paying attention to Tom. "Perhaps an early breakfast?" he asked.

She didn't answer. She'd finished her duties, picked up her equipment, and walked to the door. Opening the door, she turned toward Brian and gave him a coy wink, and then vanished into the hallway.

Brian looked at Tom. "Tom, I'm in love." For the first time in two days, the two young men laughed.

Before leaving the hospital, Brian decided to stop by the Nurses' Station. He saw her there, busy with paperwork.

"Ma'am, my name is Brian Bath, and I was serious about the dinner invitation."

"Only if you promise not to call me 'ma'am'. Every time someone calls me 'ma'am', I get afraid to look into the mirror at night. Afraid I'll see wrinkles and liver spots." She smiled at him. "My name is Mary. Mary Margaret Monaghan."

Brian gave her an odd look. "That's my mother's name— There must be some reason why the name is synonymous with beauty? It is, you know."

Thinking for a moment that Brian was toying with her, she stood up. Mary said, "Lieutenant, you're probably not going to believe this, but my father's name is Brian. Brian Patrick Monaghan. And over the years, I've found his name to be synonymous with 'shooter of the bull.' Are you by any chance Irish?"

"Yes, ma'am. It's a McGlynn, I am!" Brian said in an Irish brogue imitating his grandfather's accent.

"Damn it, Brian McGlynn," Mary whispered threateningly as she dug her fingers into his arm with a fairly strong grip. "What did I tell you about calling me 'ma'am'. My name is 'Mary', not 'ma'am', not 'Captain', but 'Mary'."

"Okay, okay, I get the message." He rubbed at his arm. "Damn, that hurt."

"Has the big bad Ranger got a boo-boo?" She smiled sweetly. "An Irish Ranger. What is the world coming to?" she said mocking his Irish brogue.

Suddenly serious, Brian asked, "Mary, I want to get your phone number. I have to get back to my company, but I'd really like to see you again, away from here, that is."

"You haven't asked if I'm married."

Her reply stunned him. "Are you?" Disappointment furrowed his brows.

"No, Brian McGlynn. And I'd also like to see you away from," she made quotation marks in the air, "'this place'. But I have a question. Is your name Bath or McGlynn? On the phone you said . . ."

He cut her off. "Yes. It's a long, complicated story that I promise to tell you over dinner."

"I'm going to hold you to that," she answered, as she wrote her telephone number on a prescription pad. Passing the top sheet of the pad to him she said, "You seem to have a lot of 'long complicated stories,' Irishman. And if you call me 'Captain' or 'ma'am' when you call, you can forget you ever had this number."

Brian smiled as he watched her walk away. Her walk was worth smiling over. His spirits suddenly felt very high. He left the hospital thinking how well his visit with Tom had gone and feeling as if he'd had met the woman he would always love. Was there love at first sight? Maybe. It sure felt like it to him.

Down the hallway, Tom felt bored. No matter how many times he looked at the wall clock, it seemed the hands were creeping in slow motion. He couldn't wait for visiting hours tomorrow. Brian had promised to come see him again.

The phone rang. "Aquinas here."

"Tom, this is Brian. Sorry pal, but I won't be able to make it for visiting hours tomorrow. I completely forgot that our company is going on field maneuvers. We'll be gone for a week."

"A week?"

"Yeah. We're jumping into Taylor Creek DZ at 'zero-dark-thirty' tomorrow. We'll be running in the woods for awhile."

"I wish I was going. This place is getting on my nerves," Tom said. "Oh, before I hang up, my nurse has been asking about you. You must have impressed her."

"I hope so. And speaking of our nurse, I've got to call her next. See you when we come in from the woods. In the meantime, I'd appreciate it if you'd say nice things about me to *our* nurse while I'm gone."

"No problem."

Tom hung up and picked up the book he'd been reading. He glanced at the cover. It didn't even look remotely interesting to him. He was tired of reading. His door opened.

Tom's friend, Dan Motorman, who'd gone through Ranger training and applied for the 75th Regiment with him, stuck his head through the doorway. "Does my Ranger-buddy Lieutenant Aquinas live here?"

"Dan! Come in! Come in! Have a seat and tell me what you're doing here."

Dan slid into the bedside chair, then asked how Tom was feeling. "I'm sorry you got hurt. I was late getting signed into the Regiment. If I had been here earlier, maybe at least I could've been in on the rescue. But I did make it to the 75th Regiment, Lieutenant. I called Captain Elmer, and luckily, there was a slot for me in your company."

Then came a conversation not uncommon with soldiers. "I want you to tell me everything. How was it in Grenada? How were you hurt? How bad? When will you be up and around, and back to duty? Are they gonna let you stay on Jump Status?" And finally, Dan asked what Tom thought of the unit.

"Whoa, fella," Tom said, and chuckled. "Slow down. One question at a time. First, I got cut up when our Black Hawk helicopter was hit while we were fast-roping from it. It plummeted. When parts of the chopper fell on me, I got deep lacerations on my thighs and butt, and some burns and minor cuts on my stomach. Of course, I was bruised all over. Luckily, no broken bones, but they tell me I lost a lot of blood. From what I understand, as soon as my cuts heal and the bruises are gone, I'll be out of here, and back on Jump Status."

"That sounds pretty rough," Dan replied.

"It bothers me that I still haven't 'seen the elephant'," Tom lamented.

"Seen the elephant?" Dan asked. "You just came back from combat! The old guys are always talking about that. I don't know if it means much to the rest of us. What's it mean, anyway."

"Uh, I don't really feel like I've been tested in combat. . . . It's a phrase I didn't understand until Sergeant Henning, my platoon sergeant, explained it to me," Tom said. "It seems that on the cattle drives of the old West, near the end of the Santa Fe Trail, there was a rock formation that looked like an elephant. In the late 1840s and early 1850s, anyone who made it that far was said to have 'seen the elephant.' It carried over into the U.S. Civil War, when troops who fought and didn't run, were said to have 'seen the elephant'. However, in my culture, the expression would mean how you respond when a raging elephant is charging toward you. . . .In Grenada, while everyone else was taking care of the mission, I was on the ground, helpless, pinned by chunks of helicopter. I still don't know how I'd react under fire.

"As for the unit? Second Lieutenants aren't usually assigned here, but my Platoon Sergeant, Sergeant Henning, took care of things and I'm glad. Since then, it's been a smooth ride. The good officers, good NCOs, and good troops are without equal. An invisible bond exists which ties us all, officers and enlisted men, into a tough family with a 'We are the best there is!' attitude."

"I'll second that," Dan agreed.

Captain Monaghan came into the room with a small paper cup of pills.

"Time for meds, Lieutenant."

Tom started to slide his pajama bottoms down and roll onto his stomach.

"You just have pills this time. Don't bare your butt to me," she said with a wicked gleam in her eye.

"No shot?"

"Nope. I've seen the last of your rosy cheeks." Captain Monaghan smiled innocently. "The doctor changed your orders. You should be getting your sutures removed next week. Your wounds are healing well."

"Really?"

"Yep, you're on the mend. Before long, you'll be doing whatever people like you do for enjoyment, like walking through the woods, communing with nature, or 'jumping out of perfectly good airplanes'."

"Oh, have you heard from Brian?" she asked, casually.

"Yes, he called and told me he was about to call you. He won't be coming over tomorrow. His company is going into the field."

"That's odd. He didn't call."

"He asked me to put in a good word whenever I saw you," Tom told her, and then added, "It seems he's fallen for you."

Her cheeks flushed and she looked away. When she turned back toward him, she was all business.

"Have you been out of bed today? The doctor wants you to start walking."

"Yes, ma'am. They had me out of bed earlier, but I felt weak at first. I had to use the walker. Later, I was able to venture out into the hallway without the walker. It felt good to be on my feet again."

"Good for you. You'll feel much better as you go along. Do you need anything?"

"No thanks."

"If you do, buzz me. You won't be getting any more meds tonight so I probably won't see you again unless you need me. If Brian calls, tell him I said, 'Hello'."

"I will," Tom said.

Captain Monaghan left the room.

"Lieutenant, that is one very pretty nurse," Dan said. "But who is Brian?"

"That, my friend, is a long, complicated story. I'll save it for a later date when I know where all of this is headed."

Dan took his cue. He stood, looked at his watch, and told Tom he had some errands to run and phone calls to make. "I don't know what my schedule will be yet, but I'll be back when I get a chance. Is there anything I can get you or do for you while you're in here? A book, maybe?"

"No, thanks. I've got more books than I want to read. I've got the TV over there, and if I get hungry or want a Coke or anything, all I have to do is buzz the corpsman." Tom smiled, then continued, "They treat me like I am the only guy who is paying the bills."

"That's not such a bad thing, Lieutenant. You better rest up while you have the opportunity."

"Yeah, but all of this resting up is making me soft. I'm not used to laying around," Tom said.

"Just get well, sir. I will talk at you later." Dan then left Tom to deal with another boring evening confined to a hospital room that was getting smaller by the hour.

Chapter 30: Mary Monaghan & Brian McGlynn Bath

A week later, Captain Mary Monaghan stood at the foot of Tom's hospital bed in her crisply-starched white nurse's uniform.

Tom looked up from his book. "Why, hello, Captain Monaghan. I didn't hear you come in. Is it already time for my meds?"

"No medicines, Lieutenant. I just came on duty and thought I'd say hello to my favorite patient. What are you reading?"

"A very good book, *A Bridge Too Far* by Cornelius Ryan. It's about the Allies jumping into Holland during World War II."

They passed small talk, until she offered the real reason for her visit. "Is Brian back from the field yet?"

Tom could see something in her eyes. She was fishing for an answer. He decided to give her one. "Yes, his battalion came in yesterday. Brian stopped by to see me earlier today."

"And left before I came on duty." Her voice had a soft sound, and Tom saw tears beginning to form.

"I guess Brian is the wrong guy," she answered. "He told me he'd call when he came in from the field. Have I been waiting for a call that's never going to come? If he visited you, but left before I came on duty, he's avoiding me."

"I'm sure there is a misunderstanding." Tom replied. "You were all he talked about before he went to the field. I thought the first thing he'd do when he came back would be to call you. There's something wrong with the picture I'm getting. Do you want me to ask him?"

Mary hesitated before answering, "No, thank you." She immediately turned and left his room.

Tom promised himself he'd ask Brian when he came in the next day.

His chance came early in the morning when Brian slipped in to visit.

"Hi, Tom. Feeling better today?"

"Hey, Brian, pull up a seat. I'm glad you are here. We've got to talk."

"Sounds serious," Brian said as he sat down. "What's up?"

"Captain Monaghan came by last night."

"So?"

"She's hurt that you haven't called her. She knows you came in from the field."

"She's hurt, is she?" Brian asked with more than a hint of bitterness in his voice. "I called and a man answered. How do you like them apples?"

Tom was stunned, but he quickly regained his composure. "She's hurt because she doesn't know you called. Maybe there was a reason that a man answered her phone. Maybe you had the wrong number. I don't know. What I do know is that she's a good woman. She deserves at least some type of answer. You need to find out the whole situation and not jump to conclusions."

"What would a man be doing in her quarters? Do you have an answer for that?"

"No, but I'll bet a month's pay that *she* has. Besides, I've already approved her as my sister-in-law." He gave Brian a pleading look. "Why don't you wait until she comes on duty and give her a chance to explain?"

"Thanks, but no thanks. I think I'll just move on with my life."

"I'll check with her and see what I can find out. You know, about a man answering her phone."

"Whatever floats your boat, Tom."

"I'm going to, you know."

"Whatever." Brian shrugged. He left before Mary came on duty.

Tom was even more determined to rectify the situation. He could hardly wait until her next shift. He'd confront her directly. He picked up a book to pass the time, but after a few hours, he realized that Mary was now avoiding his room.

Tom pressed the nurse's call button beside his bed and waited for her to answer.

Instead, Corpsmen Mitchell answered, "What do you need, soldier?" a deep raspy voice asked.

"I need the nurse," Tom told him.

"She's busy with another patient. What can I do to help you?" The Corpsman persisted.

"Would you please ask Captain Monaghan to come by when she has a minute?"

Corpsman Mitchell didn't respond, so Tom assumed that everything was okay. Another hour passed. She'd had a reasonable amount of time at least to stick her head in his door. He pressed the call button.

"Do you need something?" It was Captain Monaghan's voice.

"Captain, are you busy?"

"I'm always busy," she said dryly.

"Can you spare me a minute or two?" he asked.

"Do you have a problem?"

"Negative. I just have some information for you."

"All right, I'll be there in a minute."

There was a tap on his door. "What do you want to talk about, Lieutenant?"

"Brian."

"I'm not sure I want to hear what you have to say about him," she answered, but she didn't leave. She folded her arms and gave him a look that said, "This had better be good."

"I asked Brian what his problem was in not calling you."

"And?" She cocked a thinly-arched eyebrow.

"He said he did call you when he came back from the field."

"Is that what he told you?"

"Brian said when he called, a man answered the phone so he just hung up. He was hurt . . . He was hurting— because he'd already fallen in love with you."

"Wh . . . what? He called my quarters and a man answered? Impossible! He must have dialed the wrong number."

"He told me he checked your number and dialed again, and the same man answered."

"Impossible! There was no man in my quarters to answer the telephone!" Her voice trailed off as she thought for a moment. "Uh, it could have been, but I really doubt it . . . it could have been my little brother. But he is barely a teenager. He doesn't even sound like a man. His voice is still changing. Billy was with my parents when they came to visit. I guess it could have happened. Maybe Billy sounded like a man. It's just he didn't tell me about any calls."

"Probably, because they were hang-up calls your brother didn't attach any importance to them. Why don't you give Brian a call? Tell him about your family's visit. It's sad that a simple misunderstanding could separate two people who obviously care for each other. Fix it. Call Brian and explain."

"He should have known better. It seems he doesn't care as much about me as I thought he did. Besides, I don't have his number."

"But you'll call if I give you the number?" He scribbled Brian's number on a scrap of paper and handed it to her.

"I'll think about it," she said over her shoulder, and left the room.

She couldn't concentrate on the rest of her rounds. She went to the Nurses' Station and plopped down on a stool in the corner to do her charting, but in her mind she went over the conversation. *Call Brian. Explain the problem, Tom said. Tom doesn't understand the situation. How could Brian think I had a man in my quarters?!*

"Damn it!" she muttered as she searched her pockets for the telephone number. She dialed and hung up immediately.

She redialed and let the phone ring eight or nine times before she hung up, concluding that Brian was either out on a date or at the Officers' Club with his Ranger buddies.

The following morning she called Brian's unit. The phone was answered on the first ring.

"Sergeant Morrow speaking, sir."

Mary cleared her throat. "This is Captain Monaghan. May I speak with Lieutenant Bath?"

She heard the muffled conversation through a partially covered mouthpiece. "Lieutenant, it's for you. A Captain Monaghan."

"Tell her I'm not here."

Sergeant Morrow came back on the phone. "I'm sorry, ma'am. He's not in the area."

Stunned, Mary thanked the Sergeant and hung up. Her shock was short-lived as her Irish temper flared. "'Tell her I'm not here', is it?" she said aloud. "How dare he! How dare he! Damn you, Brian McGlynn, or Bath, or whatever your name is," getting louder as her anger mounted higher.

A plan began to formulate in her mind. Brian had once told her that he slept late on Saturday mornings when he could. She hoped he'd be sleeping late this coming Saturday. She would take care of him.

"'Tell her I'm not here', indeed," she said as she slammed down a chart.

Corpsman Mitchell gave her a funny look and then took off in the opposite direction.

"Men! What is wrong with the male population? Are they all afraid of confrontation?"

On Saturday, Captain Monaghan had a leisurely breakfast. She pulled on a pair of snug jeans and a peasant-style, powder-blue blouse. She looked comfortable, but the off-shoulder shirt drew attention to her creamy shoulders and revealed a hint of cleavage. She would look good enough to make him feel sorry that he had blown her off. She dabbed on perfume and makeup.

After checking herself in the mirror, she tucked her blouse into the Levi's, satisfied with her trim figure. Then she fluffed her hair and put on soft pink lipstick. She took a deep breath and left her quarters.

Mary went to his B.O.Q., where she paused long enough to look at the directory to locate Brian's room. She took long, confident strides until she came to stand in front of First Lieutenant Brian Bath's room.

Brian's muffled voice responded to her knock, "Go away, I'm sleeping."

Mary knocked again and again, despite Brian's replies until she heard the rustle of his bedding.

"Who-the-hell is it?" he asked.

Mary remained silent until his door opened.

"Who-the-hell . . .is . . .it?" his voice had trailed off when he saw who had disturbed his sleep.

Mary didn't give him a chance. She pushed into the room as she slammed the door behind her.

"'Tell her I'm not here', is it? 'Tell her I'm not here'? How dare you dismiss me like a common whore."

"But . . ." Brian looked dumbfounded, standing there in his briefs and T-shirt.

"Don't you dare try to '*but*' me. Do you understand? How could you mistake a boy's voice for a man's? Yes! A boy's voice! My family came to visit while you were in the field. My little brother answered the phone. But that's not important. What's important is that you thought the worst of me." Hot tears of anger ran down her cheeks, unbidden.

"I know." Brian managed to say, reaching for her. He wanted to hold her, to comfort her, but she angrily pushed him away.

"You know what?" she asked.

"I know now it was your brother who answered the phone," he said, quietly.

"You knew?" she whispered. "How?"

"Tom called and told me."

"But you continued to avoid me."

"Because I'm ashamed of myself, ashamed for the way I acted. I felt like a dumb-ass and I couldn't face you," he explained.

Mary noticed his legs. "You could at least put your pants on."

He looked down and blushed.

Mary suppressed a smile at the thought of how cute he looked staring at her standing in his underwear.

"Well?"

"I'm sorry," he stammered. He grabbed his pants and hurriedly put them on.

"Mary, I've been miserable without you."

She nodded. "I know the feeling."

"Please, forgive me," he mumbled as he stepped closer to her.

Mary wanted to laugh at his shyness as she backed away from him. "If you're not a sight, Brian Bath, I don't know what you are. You should have seen yourself when you opened the door to find me standing there. You were in your underwear, wide-eyed, with your chin hanging down to your chest. It was almost funny, but I was so angry at the time, I didn't laugh at you. I was angry. Angry as hell."

"Does that mean you're not angry any more? Am I forgiven?"

"Not by a long shot, Lieutenant. Not by a long shot. It'll be a while before I let you off the hook."

He smelled the sweetness of her perfume. He took her into his arms, not giving her the opportunity to object, but she turned away when he tried to kiss her. He used his hands to gently guide her face back toward him. This time, he didn't try to kiss her lips. He kissed at her tears.

"Mary, would you give me another chance? I fell in love with you when we first met. I don't want this to end."

Mary started to say something, but instead, she offered her lips, lost in the softness of his mouth on hers. The kiss deepened and became a kiss shared between two people in love, a kiss that said, "All is forgiven, I love you."

CHAPTER 31: Return to Active Duty

Sergeant Henning knocked on Tom's hospital room door.

"Good morning, Lieutenant. I heard you were being discharged today and figured you'd need a ride back to the company area."

"You heard right. You've got perfect timing. I was just about to call a taxi."

"It's your Platoon Sergeant's place to know what's going on. Where are your bags?"

"This is all I have," Tom said, as he held up a small overnight bag. "But I'd appreciate it if you'd stop at my B.O.Q. to give me time to put on a presentable uniform."

"No problem, sir."

Sergeant Henning made small talk on the way back to the company area as he brought Tom, his Platoon Leader, up to speed on what had happened in his absence. Sergeant Henning glanced at Tom. "First Sergeant Beebe took Rooney's death kinda hard. Did you know that he had talked Rooney out of getting married before we went into Grenada?"

"No."

"First Sergeant Beebe told me that he and Rooney went to the *Beer Barrel* and had a couple of beers. He told Rooney to wait until he got a few more stripes and a raise in pay. Now he feels guilty about doing that. It bothered him so badly that he took a short leave and went to see the girl Rooney wanted to marry. He apologized to her for interfering with their marriage plans. Then he went to some little town in Ohio, I think, to see Rooney's parents. He stayed up there for close to a week."

"Is he all right now?" Tom asked.

"Yes, sir, I think he is. He acts like he's back to his old ass-kickin' self," Sergeant Henning said and then chuckled. "But I've known First Sergeant Beebe for a long time, and even though I was afraid he'd had enough war, he didn't go off the deep end or anything like that. He just bounced back, resilient old fool that he is."

Tom raised an eyebrow. "Well, it proves that he really cares for his troops."

"You can bet on that, Lieutenant."

First Sergeants don't usually stand when junior officers enter their Corpsman Rooms. They only stand when their company commander enters or a higher-ranking officer comes in, but First Sergeant Beebe stood when Tom walked into his office.

"Lieutenant Aquinas! We heard you were getting out of the hospital today. Welcome home." He offered Tom his hand.

"Thanks. I am feeling a lot better now."

"Well, I hope so. I've got a job for you," said a voice from behind him, and Tom felt a hand on his shoulder.

Tom recognized the voice of his company commander, Captain Chervil. He turned around to look at him. "Good morning, sir."

"You look fit, Lieutenant. Are you ready for duty or have you been put on a temporary profile?"

"I am fit, Captain. I am ready, willing, and able for duty. I am sick of laying up in a hospital room."

"Good! Let's go down to the mess hall. Let's talk over a cup of coffee. I need to bring you up to date. The 75th Regiment is going to expand at the Regimental headquarters and we have some new positions being created. Apparently you scored some points with the travel map of Grenada!"

PART V: Family Matters

CHAPTER 32: Convergence

Tom had been back to duty a week when Brian phoned.

"Would you like to drive up to Marietta together next weekend?" Brian asked. "I'd like to bring the two families together."

However, Tom was worried about how his mother would react. She had always been clear that she didn't want to interfere with Brian's family.

However, they agreed that Brian would pick up Tom Friday afternoon.

As he drove his convertible onto the westbound lanes of I-16, Brian asked, "Tom, is your family aware that you and I know about each other? Have you talked to them at all?"

"No, I didn't know how to tell them."

"Just tell your mother what happened. You met me, we talked, and although we're not related by blood, we have a father we both loved. Tell your mother the truth."

Tom didn't want to tell him how hard that would be for him. Instead, he decided to put Brian on the spot. "Have you told your family?"

"Yeah."

"When?" asked Tom. He was shocked that Brian found telling his family so easy.

"As soon as I believed you were telling me the truth."

"How did your family take it?"

Brian laughed softly. "Sitting down, Tom. They took it sitting down."

"Huh?. . . What's 'take it sitting down' mean? I'm serious, Brian. What did they say?"

Brian shrugged his shoulders. "Mom said she'd sleep on it."

"'Sleep on it'? What does that mean?" Tom asked.

"Well. . . Basically, it means she'd consider what I told her, and take some time to decide what she should do, if anything."

"Oh. . . . " Tom thought about it for a while. "It would probably be better if you just dropped me off near my house. Otherwise, my mother will see you and wonder why I didn't invite one of my Army buddies in to meet her. I would invite you in but I don't think it would be comfortable for either of us, considering what I have to tell her. I have no idea how my mother's going to take it."

"I guess you're right." As they passed through Atlanta, Brian asked directions to Tom's house. "We'll be in Marietta in a half hour, and I don't know where you live. Tell me how to get there. And I'll drop you at your house and pick you up later." We'd better swap phone numbers. I'd like to maintain some sort of contact."

Tom wrote Brian's number down, and then wrote his own number for Brian. "Here's mine. I expect to stay at home all weekend."

"What about your sweetheart?"

"I think I'll be too busy trying to convince my mother that this is a good thing we're doing. . . .As for my girlfriend, I feel different since Grenada. I need some time to think."

They were nearing his home. Tom reached into the back seat and got his overnight bag as Brian pulled to the curb.

"Suit yourself, but she might be upset when she finds out you were here and didn't see her."

"No, I've already called her to explain the situation. "There may not be enough time for Patti. Maybe the next weekend we come up," Tom told him.

Then Tom got out of the car, smiled at Brian and said, "Maybe if things go well, we can all get together." He smiled and added, "If so, maybe Patti and I can sneak out for a drive up to Kennesaw Mountain."

Brian gave Tom a nod and drove away. In spite of acting confidently, he too was worried about how things would turn out for the two families. He had spoken to his mother, but the phone call had been short. Now that he was going home, Brian would see what her real reaction was.

CHAPTER 33: Differing Cultural Perspectives

Tom's mother didn't like surprises. "Kumpang! Why didn't you tell me you were coming?" Phin asked, as she wrapped her son in her arms. "I've missed you so much." She gave him a loud kiss on his cheek.

"I've missed you too, mom." Tom returned the hug and kiss. "Where's Sirion?"

"She went to the movies with a couple of her friends."

Damn. Now I have to wait until Sirion comes home so I can break the news about Brian to both of them. There's no sense in having to tell it twice. Besides, I'd hoped Sirion would be here to give me some much-needed support.

"I wasn't expecting you," his mother said. "Is there a special reason that you showed up on my doorstep?"

"Oh, a friend was coming up so I got a ride with him."

"But where is your friend? Why didn't you bring him to meet me?"

"He was in a hurry to get home, but maybe you'll meet him sometime this weekend."

She grinned and patted his shoulder. "I am so glad that you came. I've really missed you. Have you eaten, yet?"

"Yes, we stopped along the way."

"Mother, where's Sirion?" he asked again.

"What is wrong, Kumpang? I told you she went to the movies."

"Oh," he said.

"Are you in trouble?" Phin asked.

"No, why do you ask?"

"Because, I've known you long enough to be able to tell when you have something on your mind. I can tell it just by the way you're acting. All you can do is pace. There's no smile on your face, and you just came home to see the mother you adore."

Realizing he wasn't fooling his mother, Tom decided not to wait for his sister. He held nothing back. He began with the vow he made at his father's funeral to be better than Brian, to be the best son possible. He would join the U.S. Army, be an Airborne Ranger, and make his father happy in the afterlife. He finished by telling her about being injured and about telling Brian that he had a half-sister.

"You told him about Sirion?" his mother asked in a half-whisper. "What if they take Sirion away from me? What if I end up being alone?" Tears began to glide down her cheeks.

"Oh, mother," Tom put his arms around her. "They won't do that. Brian's family wouldn't."

The door behind him opened, and he heard Sirion gasp.

She rushed past Tom to her mother. "What is it, mother? Why are you crying?" Sirion glared at her brother, then looked back to her mother. "Kumpang, what did you say to her?"

Before he could answer, Phin burst into a fresh round of tears. "They're going to take you away from me," Phin sobbed.

"Who's going to take me away? Why?" She turned toward her brother. "Kumpang, what's going on?"

"I'll tell you in a minute, Sirion," Tom said. He was more concerned with calming his mother.

After a few minutes, the three of them sat at the kitchen table, sipping Oolong tea, while Tom repeated the entire story to Phin and Sirion.

Sirion listened without interruption. In truth, her heart was pounding, but her face was solemn. She waited until Tom had finished.

"Who are these people? What is their name?" she asked.

"Their last name is Bath, and they live over in the Estates."

"You mean Kim and June Bath are my sisters?"

"Do you know them?" Tom asked.

"Well, I know Kim. She's one year ahead of me, but we're on the cheerleading squad together. That's how I met her sister, June. And I've also met their mother. She chaperoned a dance at school." She looked at her mother. "Why would they want to take me away from you?"

Tom interrupted. "They don't. But mom's afraid they might want to."

Sirion went to her mother and hugged her hard. "I would never leave you. If they wanted me to live with them, I would refuse."

Phin held on to her daughter. *I'm glad Sirion feels such loyalty, but I'm afraid it can happen. The other woman was First Wife. There's no one from our village to defend us. I have no way to hire a lawyer to keep it from happening in America.* She stroked Sirion's hair. *You're my baby. If anyone tries to take you away. . . . Somehow I'll fight. I'll never give you up without a fight! . . . Leaving Ban Hin Leek Fai to come here was my way to protect you. I'll protect you again, however I must.*

CHAPTER 34: Atlanta Country Club Estates, Marietta

Brian drove to his parents' house in the Atlanta Country Club Estates in Marietta. When he turned into his driveway, he saw the lights were lit in the kitchen and living room.

Looks like there's going to be another one of our famous family meetings, he thought.

Brian was so absorbed with what might be said that it took him a moment to realize someone had opened the front door before he'd even reached for the knob.

Kim stood before him. She had a grin that said she was happy to see him.

"Hey, big brother. How's my favorite soldier?" she asked, and then gave him a hug and kissed his cheek.

"Hi, yourself. Were you on your way somewhere?"

"No, I heard you pull into the driveway. I thought I'd greet you at the door."

"What did I do to deserve this V.I.P. treatment?" Brian asked.

"Just being you makes you a V.I.P., Brian."

"How's that?"

"Little sisters always adore their big brothers." She gave him a mock slap on his shoulder and giggled.

Brian followed her into the living room. His stepfather was sitting in a winged-back chair by the fireplace. He rose and they shook hands.

"Hi, dad." He pointed at John's mid-section. "It looks like mom's still the best cook in town."

Brian's mother and his other sister, June, came into the room.

"Hi, mom," he said as he went to get a customary hug and kiss from them both.

"How's school going, June?"

"Not bad, Brian. Not bad at all."

"Where's the love of your life? I expected to see him hanging around you and drooling."

June gave him a teasing laugh. "I told him since we had a family discussion planned, he could take the weekend off."

Brian took off his jacket before he sat on the piano bench.

"Have you eaten, honey?" his mother asked.

"Yes, ma'am. Tom and I stopped and had a bite on the way up."

"Isn't he the one who knew dad?" June asked.

"He's the one." Brian answered.

June grabbed a sandwich and headed for the family room.

Brian paused a moment, then asked, "Have you slept on this long enough, mom?"

"Not really. What is it you want us to do?"

"Nothing more than to accept them as extended family."

"Nothing more? Extended family!" Anne stammered, red in the face.

Brian kept on. "I was angry when Tom first told me, but I've come to know him and think he's a nice guy, actually. I've got to respect him for his accomplishments. The road wasn't always easy, but look where he is: a Ranger officer. A damn good one. Oh, one thing I failed to mention when I first told you about Tom—his real name is Kumpang Sangsuwan, but he had his name legally changed to Thomas Aquinas before going into the Army."

Anne paled. "Oh—my—God. That's your father's first and middle names."

"Yep! He thought so much of dad he wanted to be as much like him as he possibly could."

"But he didn't take the McGlynn name?" she asked.

"No, he knew it would be Public Record, and it might cause us some concern if we read about it in the newspaper. Uncle Mitzamuri advised him not to interfere in our lives. We'd suffered enough," Brian said.

"He knows Uncle Mitzi and has known about us all this time?" Anne's voice grew louder.

"He met Mitzi at dad's funeral, mom. He knew we existed and lived somewhere in Marietta but nothing beyond that."

"Why do you think he told you?" asked John. "Knowing who and where we are, would he have anything to gain from our family?"

"I don't think so. When he first told me I had a half-sister, I got mad. He was really hurt. Besides, I honestly think he wanted me to know so if anything happened to him and his mother, the girl wouldn't be set adrift. She'd still have family."

"That makes sense," John agreed.

"I asked him to drop by some time tomorrow afternoon to meet you, and of course, so you can meet him."

The color drained from Anne's face. She looked toward John and asked, "What do you think, dear?"

John paused before offering his opinion. "Honey, the possibility exists that the young man is really concerned his sister would be set adrift without resources, in the event something happened to him or his mother. It indicates to me that he's a caring young man. I haven't given the situation much thought, but, to be honest, I don't see an ulterior motive in meeting us and letting us know about her."

The next morning, Anne found it difficult to relax. She was aware she was doing things just to be doing them. She wanted to make sure everything was right for her guests.

She was smoothing an imagined wrinkle when she asked herself, *Why am I doing this?. . . Why am I so concerned about pleasing my former husband's bastard child? . . . Does the word 'stepmother' feel threatening?*

Anne poured herself a cup of coffee and thought of nothing but what she was doing as she spooned the sweetener into the cup and slowly stirred it into the coffee. Taking her cup, she walked into the living room, put her cup and saucer on the end table and sat on the sofa.

"It's about time." John remarked.

"What, honey?" She adjusted a throw pillow behind her back.

"What's gotten into you this morning? I said, it's about time you sat and relaxed, read the paper, and had your coffee," John said.

"You know I like a tidy house." Anne explained.

"I know, but don't you think you've been over-doing it a bit?"

Anne glared at her husband before answering sharply, "A bit critical, aren't we? Didn't you sleep well last night? Why can't you understand?"

Anne stood and taking her coffee with her, she walked to the kitchen. After pouring her coffee down the drain, she put the cup and saucer in the sink. She noticed how her hand shook as she did, and realized how unfair she had been to her husband. She could feel the tears forming as she walked back to the living room and sat on the sofa close enough for John to take her hand in his. "Honey. I'm sorry. I had no business using the tone of voice I did. I've been on edge since Brian told me about these people from Laos and now it's coming to a head." Reaching to dry her tears, Anne continued. "The illegitimate daughter of my former husband is coming to our home, and I don't feel I can do anything about it— except try to be gracious."

John started to speak, to comfort the woman he loved, but Anne was not to be denied and he wisely remained silent.

"When I think of the hell the children and I went through, beginning with the night the Colonel came to the house to tell me Tom was missing and I fainted and lost my baby. Then I almost lost my mind, I was so sick with worry. I had three children to care for, and I prayed every night for the strength. I prayed that Tom would be safe and return to us—only now to find, all the time, he'd been living with another woman, in another land, and even making babies with her!" Her voice rose in anger as she spoke. Finished, Anne's tears flowed freely.

John waited, once again feeling the touch of jealousy for the man McGlynn, now dead.

He sat and watched Anne until he felt he could speak. "Honey, Tommy suffered from amnesia. He must have been in a world of his own. I don't think he could have known right from wrong. I would think he lived from day to day and followed his instincts." He paused for a moment before continuing, "I could fill the air with platitudes and give advice until I'm blue in the face, but the truth is, I don't feel it necessary. You've always been a strong and fair woman. I know when you open the door to welcome those two young people, it will be done with grace."

He gently squeezed her hand and waited.

"Thank you for understanding, John."

June and Kim came down the stairs and into the living room and Kim asked, "They're not here yet?"

"No, sugar, Brian just left about fifteen minutes ago to pick them up. They should be here any moment now."

The room became uncomfortably quiet when June asked, "Mom, have you been crying?"

"I was just in one of my melancholy moods, honey. It's over now." Anne answered, as she wiped her eyes.

"Mother? You're upset with *those people* who are coming here today, aren't you?"

"No, honey, I'm not and don't you dare be rude to them when they arrive. You understand?"

June hesitated, then answered with a half-hearted, "Yes, ma'am."

"I'd better freshen up before they get here," Anne told John.

"Are you going to be all right, honey?" He asked, still holding her hand.

She slid her hand from his. "Yes, sweetheart." She rose from the couch. "I'll only be a minute."

Anne was applying fresh make-up when she heard the chimes of the front doorbell. She gave herself a critical look in the mirror and decided any evidence that she'd been crying was sufficiently covered up.

She looked up and said, "Tommy McGlynn, wherever you are, please help me through this afternoon."

CHAPTER 35: After the Encounter

June and Kim were already asleep. Brian was on his way back to Fort Stewart. The house was silent except for Anne's muffled footfalls on the carpeted stairs. As she entered the living room, she sighed.

John looked up and saw her walking toward him. He marked the place in his book and laid it on the table beside him.

"Are the girls asleep yet?" he asked.

"Both are tucked in for the night," Anne replied. She always checked on her children after they'd gone to bed, although she no longer helped them say their nightly prayers as she had when they were younger.

John thought that the girls were too old to tuck in, but he said nothing to Anne. He knew she still needed to mother them.

"What did you think of our guests, Tom and Sirion?" John asked.

Anne made herself comfortable on the couch. "I don't know whether or not to be angry with Mitzi. He and Mai Lin have been good friends. But Mitzi apparently knew all about Tommy's Sangsuwan family, yet he and Mai Lin never said a word to us. I wonder why?" Anne asked.

"You could call him and ask, but my guess would be he wanted to spare you and the children any more grief," John said.

"You're probably right, but I think I'll call. I'll feel things out, then I'll casually mention the visit just to see what they say. I'll act as if I knew about them all along," she said calmly.

"Sounds like a plan," he said. However, John noticed she was picking lint from her skirt and wringing her hands.

Anne gave him a nod. "Getting back to your question—our visitors made a good first impression. When Brian told us he had invited . . . that boy and girl, I didn't know what to expect. Uh, I don't know what to call them. I don't even remember the boy's real name. For some reason, I'm reluctant to call him 'Tom.' Somehow it doesn't feel right." She shook her head, trying to shake off the odd feeling.

"I suppose it must feel uncomfortable." John adjusted his bifocals and tried to return to the sports page.

"It does. I didn't want to, but I did like both of them, especially the girl," Anne said.

"I thought she was cute. Did you see the shy wave to Kimmie when they recognized each other? They were both such polite people, and I was impressed with the young man. He was very well-mannered and answered our questions directly. He seemed truthful."

"Their love for Tommy was obvious." Anne paused briefly to think about it, and then continued, "Yes, I liked them, but I must admit, I was uncomfortable about the girl and couldn't quite shake the uneasy feelings. . . . I think I saw the resemblance to Tommy in her face and it startled me."

"Why? Why be uncomfortable? What's done is done."

"I suppose it's because she's Tommy's daughter. If she affected me that way, then I'll be a wreck if or when I meet their mother—the woman who took my place in Tommy's heart!" Anne swallowed. "Do you detect a note of resentment? I'm not sure, but maybe I resent the life they were having with Tommy while the children and I mourned him here. Is it so awful for me to feel that way, John? I waited so long."

"Honey, I'm really surprised that you do," her husband replied, with a hint of disappointment in his voice. He got up and went to the kitchen and poured them each a mug of coffee and brought the mugs to the coffee table. "You sound as though you've been wronged, that Tommy had a hand in what happened. It wasn't McGlynn's fault he got shot, got amnesia, or got liver fluke disease from the polluted water. Someone had to take care of him. Regardless of what happened between them, she did keep him alive, and he made it back."

John paced back and forth in front of the coffee table. "Do you honestly believe he and the woman have somehow sinned against you? Do you doubt his amnesia?" He brushed his hand through his hair and sat down. "When will you accept the fact that the circumstances surrounding that period of your life were beyond your control, even beyond Tommy's control? It's over! He's been dead and buried *twice* for heaven's sake. And it was years ago! What's done is done. Let it pass." John's annoyance was palpable.

He took a deep breath, then his voice softened. "Anne when I found you again and you said you'd marry me, I thought I'd won back the love I'd lost so many years ago. I guess I didn't. Maybe I only had you back because of the disappearance and being declared dead of the one man I'd been so jealous of since you left Atlanta with him years before. I can't tell you how happy I was I had found you again, that you'd date me again, that you'd marry me. I was even happier when I realized my love encompassed your three children, Brian, Kim, and June. It was great. We settled into what I thought was a complete family. Then *he* came back — alive— and disrupted our lives. But I stuck with you. Even though it stirred my old jealousies, I was actually happy you and the children had found him. I still felt secure in our marriage." He took a long drink of coffee and sat down.

Anne looked surprised. "When he came back, it was tearing me up. I guess I hadn't thought much about what this was doing to you."

"Let me finish," he said sternly. "I kept telling myself that our lives would return to normal when we finally buried him again, but it hasn't." He stood up and paced across the room. "Tommy returned again today, through a young girl who was part of his past. Anne, now I am faced again with his ghost!" He rubbed his brow. "I don't mean to be, but I am fed up!" He felt the tension leave his shoulders. *There. At least I said it,* he thought. He took a deep breath and reached for her hand.

Anne noticed the sadness in John's voice. She squeezed his hand. "I'm sorry, honey. I didn't realize . . . "

But her reply was cut short as John let go of her hand and stood. "I'm going to bed," he announced. He didn't bend to kiss her lightly on the lips as part of his nightly ritual. Instead, he slowly walked away from her, ignoring the tears forming in the corners of her eyes.

After he closed the bedroom door, she stared silently into the aloneness of their living room, as her mind raced back through the years. How happy she and John had been as sweethearts in high school. Their lives were so uncomplicated. As sweethearts they knew it was meant to be. Everyone had given their blessings. Their future together was secured so that after high school, they'd marry and settle in the suburbs of Atlanta, raise a family and live happily ever after.

But the American dream was not to be theirs. She smiled, remembering the Sunday afternoon she first met Staff Sergeant Thomas Aquinas McGlynn. Her thoughts stopped at that fateful day when she was so taken by Tommy's self-confidence, and what she later learned to be his Irish blarney. He had won her heart from the very beginning. He looked so fit and dashing in his uniform. His paratrooper Jump Boots were polished to a high gloss. She remembered the butterflies in her stomach when he came over to her table, giving her his rakish smile and she'd shyly looked away.

When he reached the booth where they were sitting, Tommy McGlynn had surprised her. He didn't say anything to her. Instead, he spoke to her mother to ask if he could take their order. Then he gave her mother a sob story about how he and his friends were in Atlanta for the weekend, and they'd run out of money. He was waiting on tables at the VFW to earn enough gas money to get back to Fort Benning. It was an unbelievable tale, but her mother ordered drinks anyway and giggled like a young girl charmed by a handsome soldier.

Tommy soon returned to their table with the sodas they'd ordered, set napkins in front of them, and put the beverages down. Then he placed another napkin at the empty seat beside Anne and placed a bottle of beer on it, so he could scoot in close beside her, as if he had been invited all along.

When her mother asked how much her bill was, he said he didn't know and changed the subject by introducing himself. From that moment on, he turned on the charm. He looked at Anne's mother. "Ma'am, I've fallen in love with your daughter and would like to get to know her better. May I?"

Her mother, never having met the likes of Tommy McGlynn, soon composed herself, told him it was up to Anne, but to keep in mind that Anne's father was a career First Sergeant. If a problem arose she was sure he could handle it.

When Tommy looked at Anne, his smile was replaced by a solemn look on his face. He asked her to dance.

Her heart pounded. She nodded.

The song that played on the jukebox the first time he held her in his arms on the dance floor became *their song*: "Too Young," by Nat King Cole. He swept her off her feet.

John Bath, her high school sweetheart quickly became a faded memory, shattered by the dashing Tommy McGlynn, a paratrooper stationed at Fort Benning.

As Mrs. McGlynn, I'd had a good life despite the difficult years when Tommy was a junior NCO. When the children came, it was even better. Life was as close to ideal as the occasional military separations would allow. Then Tommy and Mitzamuri volunteered for a dangerous mission into Laos.

Suddenly she had a flashback, remembering. . . years ago . . . the loud knock on her door in the early morning hours. Even now she felt again the cold fear grip her heart. It was the night she learned her husband was missing. The words of Tommy's Group Commander were as vivid as they were when she first heard them.

She tried to shake the memory of that dreadful morning from her mind but she couldn't. It was that morning she also a lost near-term baby who would have been their fourth child. . . .

Now Anne sat alone in the quiet room and wept softly. She wiped the dampness from her eyes, and returned mentally to the living room of her home with John Bath. There she turned off the lights. She climbed the stairs slowly, as her joints were aching, and went into their bedroom. John was snoring in his light, soft comforting sound. She wanted to touch him or to say something to him that would heal any wounds. Instead, she changed into her nightclothes, got into bed, and turned on her side with her back to her husband. She closed her eyes, hoping to erase the disturbing images, but the flashback of that dreadful night was vivid, and her mind forced her to live it again.

John never leaves the house without kissing me. Good Lord! He doesn't leave for a short trip to the hardware store without kissing me good-bye, Anne thought as she finished her breakfast.

At breakfast, June sensed the tension between her parents. When her stepfather left for work without kissing her mother, June knew something was not right. "What's wrong, mamma?" June asked.

"Nothing, honey. Why do you ask?"

"Oh, I don't know. There's something out of tune between you and Dad this morning. He didn't kiss you when he left for work."

"Oh," Anne murmured. She busied herself clearing the dishes from the table. She felt tears come, perhaps to wash away last night's vivid dream and for the hurt she was causing her husband. She tried not to let June see her tears.

The tears welling up were not lost on June, and she was suddenly unsettled. *What's happening that I don't know about? What did I do? What's upsetting my family?*

Chapter 36: Anne's Social Call

At home alone, Anne couldn't put the thought of Tommy's other woman out of her head. *What is she like? Is she younger than I am? Prettier?*

Anne opened the telephone book to search for a name she thought she remembered. She had no idea of its spelling, or if it was in the phone book at all.

Now determined, she concentrated on the name she was seeking rather than any plan of action.

What was it Tommy always said? she asked herself. *Stay flexible. The best laid plan of mice and men, and so forth....* She smiled inwardly as she remembered Tommy never finishing the quote. He probably had long forgotten its ending or its source.

All Anne could remember about the last name of the young girl who had visited the day before was that it sounded much like the name of a Canadian city, which began with an 'S'. Saskatchewan came to mind immediately and stayed in her mind, although she knew that name was wrong. She turned to the pages containing the 'S' listings. Then, followed her finger as it skipped down the list of names.

Saban, Sabatino, Sadler, as she muttered to herself, "No, no, no," until her finger stopped at Sangsuwan. "Ah, here it is."

I want to know how and why this Sangsuwan family came to Marietta. I'm going to face the other woman head on—Let the chips fall where they may. Anne copied the street address and phone number onto her notebook, said a quick prayer, and headed for the car.

At the same time, when June was leaving school, she made a quick decision to confront Sirion's mother, Mrs. Sangsuwan. June assumed she'd somehow caused this upheaval in her family's life.

As June drove around the corner of the Sangsuwan's street, her jaw dropped. *Why's my mom knocking on the front door of Sirion Sangsuwan's home?* Dumfounded, June pulled her car to the curb and watched, *What should I do next? . . . Wait. . . I won't do anything, yet. I'll have to see what happens next.*

As Anne continued to knock on the door, she suddenly doubted herself. *Could the woman even speak English? If not, how could we possibly communicate? I should have called first. I should have asked Mitzi for advice. He might know the answer to my question.*

The front door opened. From behind the door, a pleasant voice asked, "May I help you?"

Quickly gathering her thoughts, Anne answered, "Hello. My name is Anne Bath. I'd like to speak with you. May I come in?"

Phin look confused and paused before answering, but she moved slowly to the side to allow room for Anne to enter. *Who is this woman? What does she want from me?*

Although it wasn't obvious, the two women were appraising one another, each waiting for the other to speak. Anne reached into her purse and brought out a picture of Tommy and quietly passed it to Phin. Anne saw the look of recognition on her face and noticed Phin's hand begin to tremble.

A tear dropped onto Tommy's picture as Phin silently stared at it. Phin tried to blink back the tears spilling from her eyes. "You knew my American husband?"

Shocked by the question, Anne found it difficult to answer. She nodded her head as she managed to whisper, "Yes." Then gathering herself, she added, "He's the father of my children."

Anne's answer frightened Phin. *This must be first wife! She has come to take Sirion!* Her mind raced. *What can I do to stop this woman from taking my daughter?*

The fear of losing her only daughter to this stranger at the door was even stronger than her Buddhist beliefs. Buddhists pretty much accept life as it is, and she was inclined to say in her native Lao, *Baw pen nyang,* which literally translates to "It doesn't matter" referencing the belief that all life is preordained. A life where, in doing good things, she would become an *arhat,* a "sage", and attain enlightenment, never to be born again. Otherwise, she'd be doomed to being reborn to suffer again and again.

She invited Anne to sit down in the living room. Silence permeated the room as both women tried to think of what to say, until Phin took the initiative.

"After my American husband had been with us for almost 5 years, his memories began to return. Sirion was a little girl then. Both my children were very attached to him. He was good to us, and respected by the village elders. But one day, he began to act strange. He held his head a lot. That night after we'd gone to the sleeping mat, he got up and gathered his things. I stood in the darkness and watched as he left us. My heart cried out for him to return, but I remained silent. I watched and listened until the sounds he made as he paddled away stopped.

"He came back to you, but then the gods took him away. He was lost to both of us." Phin sat straighter, and said, "Now, my Kumpang has joined your army. Must you take my Sirion? I beg you not to take her from me. She is all I have left of him."

Anne stared at Phin in disbelief. Finally, Anne stammered, "I . . . I didn't come here to take your daughter away from you. I only came to, to . . ." *What have I come for? To make this poor woman miserable? To see if she was pretty? What was I thinking?* Finding her voice again, Anne forced it to remain steady. "I came over to meet you, and to say I met your lovely children yesterday. Your son, Tom, is a very handsome young man, and Sirion is such a pretty young lady." As soon as she uttered the words, she knew her words sounded terribly lame.

"Kumpang?" Phin replied. "You met my children yesterday?"

Anne felt a twinge of panic as she wondered how she could extricate herself from this terrible situation she'd created by coming here in the first place. Then she realized Phin had said something.

"I don't understand," Anne told her, with a quizzical look on her face.

"Kumpang. My son's name is Kumpang. He is called 'Tom' only by Americans, a name he uses to honor his American father."

Anne knew, because of the age of the young man, that her Tommy McGlynn couldn't possibly be the father of Tom, or "Kumpang", or whatever he was called. She felt resentment building up inside. *Tommy had been* my *husband, not* this woman's. *Even if Tommy had fathered the girl, it wasn't because of an act of love. Tommy was the victim in this sordid affair. And a victim of that damned war, and his damned sense of duty.*

Outside in her own car, every so often June glanced at the Seiko watch Tommy had sent her. She'd become lost in memories of her father, when she heard a tap on the car window.

"June? Is that you?"

June jumped. She looked toward the voice. Who had startled her? She saw Sirion standing beside her car.

"What are you doing sitting here?" asked Sirion.

Thinking quickly, June answered, "I just dropped off a friend over on Water Street, and I thought I'd drive the long way home. That's when I saw my mother's car, or at least I think it's my mother's car, parked up the street. I decided to see what she's up to."

"The one parked in front of my house? Is that your mother's car?"

"Your house? What is *my* mother doing at *your* house? I didn't think our mothers knew each other," June said.

Sirion grinned. "Let's go see." They took off toward Sirion's house.

The sound of the door opening broke the awkward silence between Phin and Anne. In came a cheerful Sirion and a somber looking June. Sirion greeted Anne with a pleasant smile and a courteous "Hello", but June could only nod toward her mother. She completely disregarded Phin.

Sirion was the first to speak. "June and I saw your car, Mrs. Bath, and wondered if you knew my mother. We came in to check."

Anne was thankful for the interruption. She managed to give a plausible explanation for her visit to Phin. "I just came by to meet your mother, and . . . tell her what wonderful children you and your brother are! She should be very proud of you! . . . I'd also love for you all to come over to our house for a cookout soon. Maybe next weekend."

"That would be super! Wouldn't it, mother?" Sirion said, giving her mother a nod and a hello hug.

On the other hand, June didn't think it was super because she didn't think her mother's invitation was genuine this time. When her mom was distressed, June knew she'd say, "Lets have a cookout!" Almost the same way Scarlet O'Hara might say, 'I'll worry about this tomorrow.' She'd heard her mother make genuine invitations that were well-received. This was neither.

Phin nodded in reply to June's question, not knowing what she was agreeing to, or what to do, or how to feel. *After these people leave, I'll call Maria to ask her advice.*

Thinking quickly, June asked, "Mother, have you forgotten your dental appointment?"

Inwardly sighing a breath of relief, Anne glanced at her Seiko wristwatch. "My goodness, I'd forgotten about it completely. Thanks, honey." Then she turned toward Phin. "I'm sorry, but I better get going. I'm afraid that I'll be late for the dentist." She moved slowly toward the door. "It was nice meeting you, Mrs. Sangsuwan."

Anne gave June a grateful look. "June, I'll see you at home. Don't be late for dinner now."

"I won't, momma."

Chapter 37: John and Anne McGlynn Bath

Anne turned into her drive and pressed the button to open the garage door. She was surprised to see her husband's car in its usual place. It was too early for him to be home. He hardly ever left work early. The last time was when she had the flu, and he'd been worried about her. Well, she had no symptoms of any kind today. She went into the house, feeling some apprehension.

From the living room, she heard the melodic voice of Frank Sinatra singing, "You're My Girl." Expecting the worst, she steeled herself and walked boldly into the room.

A dozen long-stemmed roses were carefully arranged in a vase on the coffee table. Before them, stood a contrite husband. John's first words to her were about his tirade the night before. "I'm so sorry, honey. It was selfish of me to unleash that tirade on you last night. I was overwhelmed with this situation we're all going through, and I'm sorry I unfairly took my worries out on you."

Anne was tempted to ask what else he was sorry for, perhaps failing to kiss her this morning, but the apologetic look was enough to tell her he was truly sorry. She opened her arms to him, and they embraced.

"I just couldn't take it any longer," he said. "I had to come home early." He kissed her deeply. "I love you, Anne, I'm truly sorry about the way I acted. I don't know what I'd do if I lost you again."

"John, there's not much of a chance of that. I love you, too. You know I do. Yes, I was hurt, especially when I came to bed and found you asleep. I wanted to tell you that I was so sorry for what I put you through before Tommy's death. It was terrible of me."

John put his finger to her lips to stop her apology and told her again how much he loved her. He took her hand and led her to their bedroom.

They hadn't finished their lovemaking when they heard someone coming up the stairs.

"One of the girls," Anne whispered. "Did you lock the bedroom door?"

"No, I thought you did," John answered.

Anne giggled, and then whispered, "We'd better be quiet." She moved her hips up to him. "Really quiet," and she moaned softly.

They showered together and dressed in fresh clothes before coming out of their room. Smiling, Anne knocked on Kim's bedroom door as they passed it.

"Kim, honey, dad and I are going grocery shopping. Do you want to go?"

The answer was almost immediate. "No thanks, mom. I've got to finish my homework. Dad came home awfully early, didn't he? I could hear you two giggling and carrying on like a couple of teenagers."

Anne's face reddened as she tried to think of a reply, but she suddenly thought better of it and joined John at the head of the stairs.

They stole out of the house, quietly, until the car door was closed and John burst out laughing. He shook his head. "I thought I was going to choke holding back that laugh. Honey, your face was red as a beet."

She playfully jabbed an elbow into his ribs and laughed seductively. "We'd better go shopping before I drag you back up to the bedroom and make you sorry that you embarrassed me."

"Suits me!" her husband exclaimed as he turned the engine off and groped her knee.

"Oh, you! Start the motor," Anne said as she jabbed her elbow into his ribs again. "We'd better get started, or I'll never get dinner fixed."

In a voice as sexy as he could make it, he said, "Forget dinner, baby. Let's get a motel room. We can make all the noise we want. How does that sound?"

"Never mind any motel rooms. I was really embarrassed."

"I'm sorry. I know you were, honey, but don't we have things reversed? It's the teenagers who don't want to be caught in the act, not their parents."

John then backed from the driveway as he looked over his shoulder. He had not failed to see the smile on Anne's face and the twinkle in her eye as she thought about the motel room. She felt the car lurch forward toward the grocery store. They really were an old married couple. The kids were nearly all grown. He sat on his side of their full-sized family car, and she was worried about getting dinner started. They were getting older, but this afternoon they'd proven that they still had the hots for each other.

She reached across the seat and placed her hand on his thigh.

"The room?" he asked.

"Just drive to the store. Besides, I need to tell you what happened to me today." She told John about going to the Sangsuwans' earlier and about how June had rescued her from what was becoming a sticky situation.

"What was June doing there?" he finally asked.

"I have no idea, but I intend to ask her when I see her."

"Well?" John asked.

"Well what?"

"What are we going to do about having a cookout?" he asked.

"We?"

"Oh, stop fooling around. I'm serious. I think we should have one," he said as he felt his stomach grumble.

"Okay, honey. We'll have a cookout." She gave his thigh a pat and removed her hand.

"I wonder what they'd like. I guess we could ask Brian to get Kumpang to suggest a menu?"

"How did you remember his name?"

"It's easy when you pay attention when you're introduced," John told her. "Why don't we have barbecued ribs, potato salad, and whatever else you can come up with?"

"Because, dummy, we don't know what they like. There are cultures that don't eat the foods we do. Are you aware of the Jewish dietary laws, or that cows are sacred in India?"

"Sweetheart, please, spare me Foreign Diets 101. The people we're discussing aren't Jewish, and they aren't from India. The point I'm trying to make is, from what I understand, the family wants to Americanize. That, my dear wife, calls for hot dogs, hamburgers, cole slaw, baked beans, and potato salad. And don't forget beer." John softened his tone. "Of course, we'd be better off playing it safe by asking Kumpang. Agreed?"

"I guess it would be a good idea," she said. "I'll call Brian tonight."

CHAPTER 38: Finding the Facts

Tom answered the phone on the first ring. "Lieutenant Aquinas here."

"Hey."

"Hi, Brian." Tom had recognized Brian's voice.

"You busy?"

"Not really."

Brian read coldness in Tom's reply, but he went ahead with his reason for calling. "Do you want to meet me at Belford's on West St. Julian Street? I've got a few things I need to talk to you about."

"I'll bet you do. What time do you want to meet?"

He ignored Tom's strange answer. "How about eight? I've got to meet Mary at nine."

"I'll be there."

What the hell is going on? Brian wondered.

Brian was at the bar at Belford's sipping his drink when Tom walked in. Seeing Brian at the bar, he walked over and sat beside him. Strangely, he ordered a beer before he acknowledged Brian.

"What's so important that it couldn't be said over the phone?" Tom asked without looking at Brian.

Taken aback, Brian put his purpose aside for the moment and asked, "What's wrong, Tom. You don't seem to be your usual self. Are you in some sort of trouble?"

"Not me, my family."

"What's wrong? Is it anything I can help you with?"

"You sure can." Still not looking at Brian, Tom took another sip of his drink and answered, "Tell your family to leave Sirion where she is."

"And just what is that supposed to mean?"

Tom ignored the question and continued to avoid Brian's. "Brian, I'm really disappointed. I thought you were a friend I could call brother."

Tom picked up the beer can and killed it. He started to move from the bar, but was stopped by the strong grip Brian had on his wrist.

"You're not leaving until I find out what the hell you're talking about. Let's get a table where we can talk privately." He let go of Tom before he took off toward a table over in the corner, assuming that Tom would follow.

Tom stared after him a moment, shrugged, and then followed.

Brian sat down. "What brought on all that crap a minute ago?"

"I had a call from my mother today. She was crying," Tom answered.

In a sympathetic voice, Brian asked him what was wrong. "Bad news from Laos?"

"No. She was crying because she's afraid." Brian asked.

"For cripes sake, get to the point. Why is she afraid?"

"Your mother visited her today, and she's afraid your family will take my sister away."

"What in the hell would cause her to think that? My mother told me she just went over to meet your mother and to invite her to a cookout. I plan on inviting Mary to come. Now is as good a time as any for my family to meet her. My mother even asked me to find out what kind of foods your family likes."

Tom felt a sudden flash of shame. "I guess there was a breakdown in communication somewhere along the line. My mother is frightened and she's not one to scare easily."

"Well, we'll fix that mix up by calling my mother when we get back to the B.O.Q. Drink up, buddy!"

Brian glanced at Tom as he dialed his mother's number. "We'll get to the bottom of this crap right now."

"Hey, mom. Brian here. I've got a question for you. Did you say anything to Tom's mother about wanting to take Sirion away from her or did you threaten her in any way?"

"Of course not. Where did you get that idea?"

"She told Tom you were there and showed her a picture of my father. She said you were going to exercise rights of the first wife or something . . . something about taking Sirion away."

"What?! . . .I showed her the picture as a means of identifying him. It was a way of telling her who I was. I never dreamed it would be taken as a threat or mean something else."

"Unfortunately, it has, and we've got to do something to rectify it."

"Honey, as I told you earlier. I invited Phin and Sirion to a cookout. I was going to call you tomorrow so we could set a date for it, so we could work it out for you and Tom to be here on leave or something. Whatever the Army calls it these days."

"Okay. Hey, I want to ask if I can bring the love of my life? I think it's about time she meets my family and vice versa. Would it be all right if I brought her?"

"Of course, child, we'd love to meet her . . . Would you please tell Tom that I'm really sorry there was such a misunderstanding."

"I will, mom. Say hello to everybody for me. I've got to run. I've got a heavy dinner date. I love you. Bye."

Brian hung up and told Tom what his mother had said about showing his dad's picture. "I guess when your mother saw dad's picture, she put two and two together, but it didn't add up to four. Did she say anything to you about the cookout?"

"No, she didn't. She wouldn't know a cookout from a plate of grits." Tom smiled shyly.

"Hey, you want to come to dinner with me and Mary?"

"Sure! Are you buying?"

CHAPTER 39: Brian and Mary

The waitress brought a dessert cart to their table and asked what the three of them wanted. Both officers refused, but Mary couldn't deny herself the chocolate éclair that lay so close to her.

"Yes, I'll have the éclair, please."

Brian moaned inwardly as he thought of having to wait a while longer to say what he'd rehearsed. He had planned to take the small velvet box from his pocket and ask, "May I offer dessert, Mary." He had thought it would be a unique way to propose. Much better than getting down on one knee in front of all these people.

Mary was too busy to notice but Tom did. "Is something wrong, Brian?"

"No. Why do you ask?"

"You seem to be on edge."

Brian gave a sheepish smile and stirred his coffee. "I've been wondering about the weight our pretty nurse will gain from her dessert."

Mary didn't comment on Brian's remark. She simply broke a piece of her éclair off with her fork and smiled at Brian as she exaggerated the pleasure of its taste. She blotted her lips with her napkin.

"Now, Brian, what's bothering you?"

Suddenly, he felt awkward as questions rose in his mind. *How will she react? Is this the right time and place? What if she says no?*

Then throwing caution to the wind, he ignored his doubts. Brian took the velvet-covered box from his pocket. He hesitated only for a moment, and then opened it and held it out for her to see.

"Mary, this may not be the right place but it's the right time. Will you marry me?"

Mary gasped at the unexpected question. She stared but said nothing.

Thoughts raced through Brian's mind. *I should have waited for a better time. I truly love this woman, and I don't know what I'll do if she says no. The diamond is too damn small. She doesn't like it. Have I embarrassed her?*

Drawn away from his thoughts, Brian saw tears begin to form in the corners of Mary's eyes, and he mentally began to kick himself until she said something.

At first it was just a soft, "Yes" and then as she took his hand in hers and said, "I love you, Brian, and yes, I'll marry you."

Those at nearby tables were startled as Brian rose and brought his love to her feet and kissed her a long, lingering kiss.

Tom started clapping and shouting, "Well done! Well done, Brian! And yes, I'll be your Best Man."

The other diners seemed to take Tom's comments as a cue. They, too, began to applaud.

Tom took their kiss as his cue to leave. After he congratulated them both, he walked to the bar alone, leaving them to enjoy the moment.

When they left the club, Brian couldn't remember being this happy. However, it was short-lived when Mary told him he'd have to ask her father for her hand in marriage— to get her father's permission to do what he'd just done, propose to her.

"Isn't that custom a bit dated?" he asked.

"Brian, my father is only being protective of me. He and I had a father/daughter talk when I was accepted as an Army nurse. He knew I'd be sent to many places and meet handsome devils such as you. It bothered him to know I'd be too far away for him to protect me or to be there when I needed advice. Brian, I love my mom and dad, and I would never hurt them. You may think my dad is old fashioned, but he's my dad and I love him too much to disappoint him. Can you understand what I'm trying to say?"

"Yes, I do. It looks to me that we have the same type parents. We don't need my parent's permission to get married, but I'm sure they would prefer knowing you before we set a date."

He took her hand and continued, "I haven't told you, yet, about a picnic my folks are planning in Atlanta to welcome Tom's family."

"To welcome Tom's family?"

"I have a lot to explain to you, don't I? It's a long story."

"Brian, I want to know everything about you and your family."

"How much time do you have to listen to our story?"

"Our story?" Her eyes were wide with curiosity.

"Yes, our story." He pointed toward Tom.

Mary nodded. "All night, honey. We can go to my place and I'll put on a pot of coffee."

Brian sat on the sofa and watched as Mary measured out the coffee for her automatic coffee maker.

This is the woman I want to spend the rest of my life with. I feel so comfortable with her, he thought, as he imagined them together like this in their own home.

"What are you so quiet about?" Mary asked.

Brian didn't need time to consider his answer. "About how lucky I am to have met you before it was too late."

"Too late for what?"

The coffee machine beeped, signaling the coffee was ready.

Brian began his story from the beginning. He told her about watching the plane taxi down the runway as it carried his father and Major McGrath toward a distant land. He told about going to bed at night after night, eager for morning to come so he could sit down to bacon and eggs, loving the comfortable feeling of having his dad back home. But the mornings brought disappointment. His dad never returned.

She heard the pride when he spoke about his father going into harm's way to save another warrior. His eyes were agonizingly sad when he spoke of losing his father, the terrible feeling of being abandoned and the loneliness he felt during his formative years.

Mary wanted to hold him, to comfort him, to never let him go. Hours passed and still Brian had much story to tell. He finally finished as he told her about how he accepted the folded flag the morning they buried his father. He told her about the words the Captain said to him, "This flag is presented on behalf of the President and a grateful nation, as a token of appreciation for the honorable and faithful service rendered by your father."

She thought she saw a hint of a tear in his eye, and it was then, at that time and place, that she really fell in love with him. Gone was the crush. Her love had deepened and she knew she would never leave him.

"Brian Bath here," he spoke into the phone which had awakened him at B.O.Q.

"Lieutenant Bath?"

Not recognizing the voice, Brian simply answered, "Yes, sir." His grogginess was fading. He wondered what was coming next.

"This is Mary's dad. How are you this morning?"

He was instantly, totally awake. He glanced at his watch.

"Good morning, sir," he said to Mary's dad.

"Did I awaken you, Lieutenant? Mary gave me your phone number."

"No, sir. I was just laying here thinking about what Mary and I could do today. And, sir? Please call me Brian."

"Okay, Brian, if you'll drop the 'sir'."

"I'd feel a bit uncomfortable doing that, sir."

Mary's father chuckled, but added, "Mary told me she had a helluva time getting you to stop calling her 'ma'am.' I could never think of my little girl as a 'ma'am.' Now, I may be old fashioned, but I still believe I should screen my daughter's suitors. Don't you agree?"

"Sir? Did you just say suitors as in the plural?"

Mary's dad made a noise that could have been a laugh. "Yes, Brian, I did. But to make things easier for you, I'll drop it to one suitor. You. Now let's get down to business. When Mary told me you intended to fly here to ask me for her hand in marriage, I thought, 'This sounded like something I would have done to win her mother.' Would you really have flown up here to ask me?"

"Sir, I would have walked if necessary." It was that important to Brian. He'd do anything to have Mary.

"I don't expect you to drop what you're doing and fly here. What I'd like you to do is tell me something about yourself. I understand you're a West Point graduate and a Ranger officer who parachutes from perfectly good airplanes."

"Guilty on all counts, sir. Well, not quite. I had to cut short my time at West Point when my father was dying, but I am an Airborne Ranger officer."

"If I understand correctly, Rangers are volunteers who may be called upon to do the impossible; or to put it in another vein, they go willingly into harm's way at a more dangerous level. Am I right?"

This man has hit it right on the button, Brian thought, but he answered, "Yes, sir. But with all things considered, we *are* volunteers who are better trained and equipped than you may think."

"That may very well be, Brian, but I don't relish the thought of my daughter becoming a widow at an early age. Especially, a widow with children to raise. Can you understand that?"

"Sir, I understand what you're saying, because I have no desire for her to become a widow at any age; and I don't say that lightly."

There was a pause in their conversation as Mary's dad considered Brian's reply. "Brian, instead of flying all the way here and sitting stranger to stranger, what do you think of using the mail to get to know one another? Then, at a date somewhere down the line, we can reconsider plane reservations."

"That sounds reasonable to me, sir," Brian answered, but thought, *I'll go along with your plan, old man, but I intend to marry your daughter come hell or high water.*

"It was nice talking with you, son. Thank you for going along with a father who wants the best for his little girl."

"I understand, sir, and you'll soon get a letter extolling my better points and reasons why I'm the man for her." Then he heard a soft chuckle on the other end of the line before the connection was broken.

Brian had no sooner replaced the phone onto its cradle before it rang again.

Damn! I'll never get to Mary's at this pace, he thought. He lifted the phone and was rather curt in identifying himself. "Lieutenant Bath here!"

"You don't have to bite my head off, Lieutenant," Mary said.

He knew she was miffed, and it was probably because he was running late. Mary almost always called him Brian unless she was upset about something he had done that upset her.

"I'm sorry, honey. I know I'm running late, but I just hung up from another call when your call came through."

"Who was the other call from? Or should I ask?"

"It was your father, honey."

Mary was alarmed. "My father? Why did he call you? To let you know the rules regarding marriage to his favorite daughter? Did he ask a lot of personal questions?"

"No, sweetheart. Calm down. I'll tell you all about it on the drive."

MEETING THE FAMILIES

Brian told Mary about the phone call from her father as they drove to Savannah. He ended by telling about how he'd promised to write her father a letter.

"And it won't be a short note, honey. I'm going to convince your dad that I'm the only man for you."

Mary smiled and reached for his free hand and squeezed it gently. "You are, you know."

"You know it," he said as he rubbed at her fingers in his hand and told her that he loved her.

Brian was in a very good mood when he drove up to The Pirate House, one of Savannah's finest restaurants. He accepted the ticket from the parking valet and watched as the man drove his car into the parking lot.

The diningroom hummed with conversation from other diners as the receptionist showed Brian and Mary to a table by the window overlooking the Savannah River. They were no sooner seated than an attractive young woman came to their table. Her lightly starched white apron did well to offset the black of her short uniform.

The waitress smiled and said in a soft voice, "Good evening. My name is Alicia, and I'll be your server this evening. May I get you something from the bar?" She placed menus on their table.

"What would you care for, honey?" Brian asked.

Looking toward their waitress, Mary said, "Oh, I don't know, maybe a vodka martini. Please have the bartender add a few drops of olive juice."

"Good. A dirty vodka martini for the lady, and I'll have a vodka gimlet, please," Brian told the waitress.

Mary raised her eyebrows. "A dirty martini?"

"That's what it's called, sweetheart."

Brian and Mary made small talk as they sipped their drinks and read their menus.

"This better be good. My taste buds are all set for the châteaubriand," Mary said.

"That, sweetheart, is what I was about to suggest," Brian said, and signaled the waitress.

"Alicia, do you think the chef would mind if I asked for a particular menu?"

"I'm sure he won't. He's a nice guy." She smiled. "Let me ask him. I'll be right back."

"This is a great restaurant," Mary said.

"I love French food." Brian toyed with his napkin and sent Mary one of his most winning smiles.

The waitress came back to their table. "The chef looked out the kitchen door, saw that you're a Ranger. He told me there'd be no problem."

"How did he know I'm a Ranger?"

Mary laughed as she answered for Alicia, "Brian, it's the hair cut."

Brian wiped his hand across his closely cropped head with its Ranger haircut and said, "It is obvious, isn't it? I'm so used to it now that I don't feel like I've ever had it cut any other way."

"Yes, it's obvious, silly. Now give Alicia our order. I'm starving."

"Yes, dear." Then turning to the waitress he ordered châteaubriand for two and onion omelets with fried potatoes on the side. "And French bread if you have it. If not, rolls will do."

"That's an odd combination," Mary said.

"I hope you like it." Brian lifted his drink in salute before taking a sip.

When he finished, Mary slid her hand across the table to hold his and asked him about her father's phone call.

"I told you all about the call on the way here," Brian replied.

"Not all of it. I want to know what you thought about my dad, your first impression, and what you were thinking when he called."

"I liked him. I heard a chuckle or two on his end of the conversation, so he must have a sense of humor. But most of all, I liked his reason for calling. Before we hung up, he thanked me for going along with a father who wants only the best for his little girl."

Mary blushed at being referred to as 'daddy's little girl.' She asked, "Did you like him?"

"I didn't hear anything not to like. We both have your best interest at heart and we both love you. In different ways, of course, but we both do love you."

She smiled as she squeezed his hand and told him she loved them both, too, and then added, "In different ways, of course. Now tell me why you chose this restaurant. I know you are taking me out to a special dinner for some purpose."

Brian thought for a moment before answering. "Okay, I've been thinking a lot about my biological father. More so today. Probably because of your dad's phone call. It reminded me about how fathers want the best for their children. I know that is how my father felt, too. This particular meal, the one I just ordered, was my dad's favorite. I guess I wanted to bring him back for the moment. To be here, to eat his favorite food, is sort of like sharing a meal with him."

Brian paused just long enough to remember how happy he was as a child. Happy, that is, until his dad went away for the last time.

"Dad never told us about the combat he experienced. He talked more about the people he'd met and about the countries he'd visited. He used to tell us about eating onion omelets, fried potatoes, French bread, and châteaubriand. He and Uncle Mitzi used to order it all of the time."

"Your Uncle Mitzi? Was he in the Army with your father?"

"Uncle Mitzi wasn't my real uncle. His name is Sergeant Major Joseph Mitzamuri. He was dad's best friend, but I'll tell you about him another time. I have no doubt you'll meet him at our wedding."

He looked up as the waitress approached their table, expertly weaving around other tables as she balanced the tray which held their food. When she reached their table, she deftly opened a folding tray stand with one hand and set the tray on it. She placed their full plates on the table.

"Will there be anything else?" she asked.

"Yes, please. A bottle of Cabernet Sauvignon would be nice."

"I'll be right back with it," she said. "Enjoy your dinner," she smiled and added, "or breakfast."

"*Bon appetit.*" Brian smiled at Mary.

As they ate, Brian continued to talk about his father. "Mary, keep in mind that back in those days when my dad was in Special Forces, they ate whatever the people they were there to advise ate. Actually they still do, but my father's diet in the Laotian jungles was mainly glutinous rice and water-buffalo jerky."

"Sounds appetizing," she said sarcastically.

"Not according to my dad's tales."

"Your dad's tales?" She looked up as she took another bite. "Can you remember one for me?"

"Sure. I think I'd like that."

Mary smiled. She knew he wanted to talk about it, that it would be therapeutic for him somehow.

Brian began his dad's story as he spoke about a small restaurant in Savannakhet, Laos.

"Dad and Uncle Mitzi found a small restaurant owned by an expatriate Frenchman and his Lao wife. The Frenchman had been with the Foreign Legion. Dad and Uncle Mitzi went there whenever they came in from an Operation, to eat the same meal that we're eating tonight. Dad told me that he and Uncle Mitzi used to think that they were the only American G.I.s who knew about the place. Later, it was discovered by other G.I.s found it a popular place for camaraderie, a good meal, and *Biere LaReu*.

"Mai Lin was the bookkeeper-office manager there and that's where she and Uncle Mitzi were introduced. That marriage has certainly lasted a long time and they both have been important in my life.

"Anyway, at that establishment the first time they saw another GI there it was Mike McDougle, a non-com in one of the other Airborne units. Mike hadn't recognized dad because of the weight dad had lost while on his glutinous rice diet, and because of the handlebar mustache dad had grown. Mike's sweetheart of the moment was called the 'Tiger Woman of Savannakhet.' Dad never said how she earned the title and we didn't dare ask."

"Savannakhet?" Mary asked. "Sounds like one of the exotic names James A. Michener used in his *Tales of the South Pacific*." She used her napkin to pat her lips.

As she did so, Brian envied the napkin. He suddenly wanted to kiss her. She was so patient to listen to him as he rattled on about his father. He poured them both another glass of wine and watched as the waitress came to take their plates away.

Mary slid her hand across the table to hold his. "Do you feel it?" she asked.

"Feel what?" he asked.

"The comfortable feeling, the warmth—the feeling . . . "

Brian interrupted to complete her sentence, " that we are meant for one another?"

"I love you, Brian." Mary said softly.

"I love you, too, honey." He squeezed her hand. "I've never felt more comfortable with anybody I can think of— except my mother." He looked down. "Speaking of my mother, she's planning a cookout for Tom and his family, and she said to ask you to come."

"When is it planned?" Mary asked.

"No date has been set yet. It depends on when you, Tom, and I can get a free weekend. I think it's time you met my family, don't you?"

"Yes, I'd like that. Then we'll plan a visit with mine when you feel up to it, of course."

"I think it's time we set a date for our wedding. I hate it every time I have to leave you at your quarters. We belong together," Brian replied.

Still holding his hand, she turned toward the window and looked out at the river. They'd agreed from the onset of their relationship that their first time would not be in the back seat of a car or in some motel room. It would be with license in hand and in a honeymoon atmosphere.

Mary turned back toward him and let her eyes meet his. "Brian, I want you, too, but we agreed to wait and it's important to me that we do. It's what I was raised to believe, and I want to honor that belief. Brian, I love you more than I ever thought I'd love anyone, and I don't want our love to be tarnished in any way. Don't you understand?"

Brian took both her hands in his and kissed her fingertips. "Honey, you are everything to me, and I'll love you to my dying day. I don't want to rush you for the wrong reasons."

"All right, Brian, we'll start the wedding arrangements as soon as we can. But," she added, "the wedding arrangements will be our secret until you speak to my dad. You have to ask him formally. I wouldn't hurt him for the world."

Brian smiled and released her hands. He reached for his wine glass and raised it in a toast. "I love you," he whispered, and read the same words on her lips as she whispered them back.

Eager to set the date for their wedding, Brian and Mary took a short leave and drove to Memphis to visit her parents. They wanted to have things settled with her father before going to the picnic at the Bath's house.

Their visit was fruitful in that Brian and his future in-laws hit it off right away. Brian presented a good case in asking for Mary's hand. He pretty much covered all the major points in his young life, but he purposely omitted the story of his real father being missing in action and what it did to his family.

In giving his approval, Mr. Monaghan added, "Young man, now that we've met, there's no doubt in my mind that you'd have really walked here to argue your case. Take good care of my little girl and be happy."

Brian and his future bride were happy when they left the Monaghans' home. They'd received the traditional blessing and set a tentative date for the wedding. Next, they needed to coordinate the date with Brian's family.

On the way back, Mary was fine until they approached Marietta. *Will Brian's family like me enough? Will they welcome me as my family has welcomed Brian?*

Brian broke through her thoughts. "We've arrived at the Bath plantation."

"What did you say, honey?" she asked.

"I said, 'We're here.'" He parked the car and shut off the ignition.

Mary looked up and saw the front door open. Brian's family was coming out onto the porch to greet them.

After the introductions were made, Mary asked, "Is there anything I can do to help with the cookout, Mrs. Bath?"

"No thank you, hon', and please call me Anne. We're not a family who insists on formalities."

"Anne? I had forgotten that we had the same name," she said to Brian, as she playfully jabbed her elbow into his rib cage.

Startled by the action, Anne Bath could do no more than stammer, "Y-yes, it is." She saw an impish smile on her son's face.

"It's really nothing, mom." Brian said, maintaining the grin that was so familiar to his mother.

"Nothing? Nothing?" Mary feigned anger toward Brian. She looked at him and then back at his mother. "Would you like to hear what your son said when we first met?" Not waiting for an answer, she continued, "When I first met him, he asked my name, and I told him. If I remember correctly, he asked me, 'Is there a reason the name is synonymous with beauty, because your name and my mother's name are the same?' All the while he kept smiling complacently. I fell for his malarkey."

Mary gave him a fake punch on the shoulder.

"Ouch, that hurt," Brian cried out, sounding truly wounded. "It worked didn't it?" His smile was even more impish than before.

At home for the weekend of the planned cookout, Tom sat at the table with Phin, waiting for Brian's phone call and trying hard to allay his mother's fear of losing Sirion. He was convinced her fears were all a part of not knowing the laws of this country or how the people did things. Back in Laos, it might have happened, but here it was different.

The ring of the telephone interrupted their conversation. "I'll get it, mom." He answered the phone on the second ring and recognized Brian's voice immediately.

"Hi, Tom. Brian here. I'm just calling to make sure you got home all right and to tell you the picnic is on for tomorrow afternoon. One o'clock if you can make it. If not, we'll change the time to be more convenient for your family."

"One o'clock will be fine for us, Brian. How was your trip to Memphis?"

"I'll tell you all about it when I see you tomorrow. You know where our house is, right?"

"Sure, we'll be there with bells on," Tommy answered.

He turned toward the table expecting to continue the conversation with his mother but she was already in the kitchen seeing to their dinner.

Tomorrow came early for the Sangsuwan family. Tom's mother had spent a restless night worrying about the picnic imagining different scenarios being played out in her mind. The family of her American husband would win Sirion away from her by showing her a better way of life, or she'd bring shame on her children by embarrassing them with her old country ways. She feared the Americans would present a document ordering Sirion to serve the first wife or to go away.

As they rounded the corner and neared the Bath's house, Phin could hear laughter coming from their yard. She got out of the car, and her attack of anxiety felt much like the one she'd experienced so many years ago, the day her American husband was buried. She remembered wanting to cry out to the driver to go on, not to stop at the cemetery but to keep going, but she hadn't. Today, she would also maintain her silence for the same reason—for the sake of her children.

Tom sensed his mother's discomfort and had a sudden urge to take her and Sirion home before disaster struck. Noticing his mother's resolve, he continued into the backyard thinking he'd keep an eye on the situation and be ready to leave if necessary.

Brian's family greeted them warmly. Tom thought they were very gracious to his mother. Phin replied, *"Sabadee"* with her finger tips together at her waistline. Phin handed Anne a folded silk scarf. "I make for you," Phin said.

Anne thanked her graciously, then asked, "You made it. How could you make this?"

Phin replied, proudly,"Found small loom at Thrift store and used silk thread to weave." He could tell that Phin was starting to relax. Then Phin pointed to the Mulberry Tree in their yard. "That tree feed silkworms. You raise silkworms, yes?"

Anne was amazed. "No, we don't raise silkworms, but yes it is a Mulberry tree. You're very observant. Did you make your skirt?"

"Thank you. My skirt is *Plaine de Jarres* sunflower design. Don't have big loom here, like at home."

Tom realized his mother and Anne were chatting as if they were old friends. "Let me introduce you to our guests." Anne led her to a group of women standing in the shade.

Tom spotted Brian lighting the charcoal grill for his dad, and he went over to them. "Good to see you again, Mr. Bath," he said as they shook hands.

"Hello, Tom. How have you been?"

Before he could answer, Brian asked, "Would you like a beer? They're over there in the cooler." He nodded his head toward it. "Help yourself. I've got something I want to talk to you about."

Tom glanced apprehensively toward his mother before going to the cooler, wondering if it would upset her if she saw him drinking beer, but she seemed lost in conversation with Brian's mother and with Mary. He took two beers from the cooler. He opened his and sipped it as he walked back to the grill where he opened Brian's beer and handed it to him.

"Hey, Tom, would you consider being my Best Man? After all, your being in the hospital is what caused Mary and I to meet."

"What does Mary say about it?"

"She agrees that you were responsible for us getting together and that you deserve to be the chosen one," Brian answered and gave a hearty laugh.

"What does a Best Man do?" Tom asked.

"Nothing you can't handle. I was an old friend's Best Man once, and I got all the information I needed from Captain Rice who had the same honor for Major Mitchell. I can write out a few notes for you, and we'll go from there." Then, with a nod, he added, "Your most important duty will be to lay on the bachelor party."

"The bachelor party?"

"Yep, the bachelor party. I'm sure you'll get more than a few tips on how to set it up."

Tom was listening to Brian, but his mind was on his mother. As much as Tom wanted his mother to have an enjoyable afternoon, he was still uneasy for her. This was the woman who had rice at every meal at home. He held his breath as he watched her take a small portion of potato salad on her fork.

When she put it in her mouth, the scowl on her face relaxed and she chewed it slowly. She popped in another bite.

Sirion came up to her and handed her a paper plate with a hotdog and a hamburger. This would be the mother of all tests.

Phin delicately picked up the hotdog and gave it an appraising look.

"Taste it," instructed Sirion.

Phin's eyes grew large as she brought the hotdog closer to her mouth.

Tom killed the rest of his beer.

Phin took a small bite and smiled.

He could tell that she found it to her liking. His mother wasn't good with change, but he was proud that she was making the effort. Tom relaxed and felt he could step away for a few minutes while she finished eating. He needed to dish up a plate of food for himself. He headed for Sirion to ask where she'd found the hotdogs and burgers.

Sirion was talking easily with June and Kimmie in a group of giggling girls. Seeing his sister laughing with the girls made him feel good. He remembered Sirion being shunned by the other children of his village. Life here in America was so much better.

Tom started to turn away to get his food, then go look after Phin when the girl next to Kimmie turned toward him.

Their eyes met and she smiled, and turned back to Kimmie.

He felt a thousand needles as they played along his body. He hadn't seen that face since high school.

Patti nodded to Kimmie, waved her fingers to the other girls, then left the group to walked across the lawn toward Tom. Patti smiled again.

Tom regained his composure and moved toward her. "Is that you, Patti?"

She linked her arm through his. "Sure is. Catch me up, soldier!"

He grinned at her. "You've changed. You were pretty then, but now you're absolutely beautiful."

"Miss Georgia Peach just last year!"

He felt as if he'd always known her. "Come with me. There's someone I'd like you to meet." He took her hand and they walked over to Phin.

The bitterness he'd felt . . . when his village had rejected him, when first his real father and then man who'd raised him had deserted—All this bitterness fell away. Here, in Georgia, he'd found acceptance. Here, he had been asked by Brian to be a member of his wedding in a position as family. The invitation came from Brian McGlynn Bath, the man he had once envied and swore to best. With the old bitterness behind him, he could feel that the score had been settled. He could put all that rejection behind him.

He even felt that somehow the promise had been kept. The promise made that night in Laos when he had listened to his mother weeping over the American who'd left them— when he'd promised himself he'd do all he could to bring joy back into her life.

"My family did the right thing in coming to America," he said to his mother but smiled at Patti. "The right thing." Then he introduced them.

Phin looked at Kumpang and then Patti, then back at Kumpang. "My boy, Kumpang, must like you lots. You very pretty girl."

"Mother, my name is Tom."

"Not to me . . . You have very big smile."

CHAPTER 40: Planning the Monaghan-Bath Wedding

Brian and Mary sat across the table from each other, each with a glass of Cabernet Sauvignon. It was now their favorite wine since their dinner at the Pirate House.

"Did you and your cohorts have a good time last night?" Mary asked.

"Yes, as a matter of fact, we did."

"Did a dancing woman pop out of a large cake?" she prodded.

Brian grinned. "I'm not telling. Self-incrimination you know, the Fifth Amendment, and of course, my right to have a lawyer present."

"Well, I hope all of you had a good time." She smiled prettily at him. "You and I have a few things to discuss."

"Okay, shoot."

"First a question. Have you made up your mind about whether you want to wear a tuxedo or your dress uniform?"

"I have given it a great deal of thought and find I'm best suited for a uniform. Is that okay with you? Do you have a problem with that?"

"Of course, not. I happen to be a member of the same military," she answered. "Would you object to me wearing white?"

"All right, but I insist it be a white flowing gown and a veil."

"I know that would also please my father."

"It will please me, too, honey. After all, this will be the only marriage either one of us will ever have. When we're old and gray, we can take the wedding pictures, wipe off the dust and relive the finest days of my life."

Mary smiled as she interrupted, "*Our* lives; but please, I pray, continue. I can picture it now—you and I lying on the carpet by the fireplace looking at our photos and sipping a fine wine as we remember our wedding day, the births of our children, and the many other happy moments of our life together. Can you picture that far ahead, Brian? Will we have a happy family?"

"Mary, I swear to you that I'll give our marriage all that I have or will have to make it one of those really great marriages that lasts seventy-five years." He reached across the table and held her hand.

"Brian, do you remember meeting Ruth? One of our nurses?"

"You mean the red-head with the big . . . you know . . ." Brian gave her a mischievous grin.

Ignoring this, she said, "She's one of our best nurses, and she graciously loaned me two pamphlets to use in planning our wedding. One covers the military wedding, the second concerns religious requirements."

"That was nice of her," Brian said. He shifted uncomfortably in his seat.

The way he said it prompted Mary to ask him, "Do you have any doubts, or as they say, cold feet?"

Brian took a sip of his wine. He loved this woman who sat across the table from him. He loved her with his very being, but he knew it was time to make her understand how his chosen career could cause problems. He met her eyes and thought how fortunate he was to have a woman who cared so much about him.

"Cold feet? Not a chance sweetheart." He blew her a mocking kiss. "I love you much too much . . . but . . . I've been asking myself if our marriage will be fair to you." *I'm subject to immediate deployment at any time where I stand a chance of being wounded or killed. Would it be fair for her to live under those conditions?*

Suddenly, he could not look into her brown eyes any longer. He lowered his head to stare at the wine glass he held in his hands.

The silence of the room bore into him. His heart pounded. He swallowed hard.

"Brian Bath, I'm an Army Nurse by choice." With a startlingly calm voice, she continued, "I'm well-aware of the hazards of being in the military. I'm also well-aware of the hazards of your duties. More importantly, I believe in our love. If you were deployed, you'd know that you had someone who loved you and was praying and planning for your safe return. I'd be there for you to come home to. You wouldn't have to come back to an empty room at your Bachelors' Quarters."

Seeing tears forming in her eyes, he stood up and went around the table. He pulled her to her feet and held her close. He attempted to kiss away her tears. "You're right, Mary, you usually are. Don't you dare think I intend to let you get away from me."

She buried her face in his shoulder. "Do you want to postpone the wedding?" came a muffled question.

"No, let's make the plans. Let's do it now."

She looked up as he brushed the tears from her cheeks.

"Where were we before I interrupted with my stupid insecurities?" he asked.

"The uniform. What uniform do you intend to wear?"

He guided her back to her chair, and he went to his seat. He leaned across the table and took her hands.

"I'd prefer wearing my Dress Blues and have the Best Man and ushers in Dress Blues. Now, it's your turn . . . a long white gown with a veil. But what about the rest of the wedding party? I bet your bridesmaids will all be Army Nurses. How do you feel about them wearing their Dress Blues too?"

"Oh no, Ruth will kill me. Her's are too tight. They're too uncomfortable. They'll wear pastel dresses and can choose the colors that suit them. It will look better in the wedding photos if the guys are in uniform and the bridesmaids are in dresses. I'll still be wearing white," she said.

"Okay, that's settled. What's next on the agenda?"

Mary took the pamphlets from her handbag, and they began to plan in earnest, covering everything from the engagement, to the announcements, to making decisions on what to call their in-laws.

Mary pointed to the pamphlet covering religious ceremonies, and opened to the page for Catholic ceremonies. "I've read through this pamphlet, honey, and I'd like to point out a couple of things before I give it to you for your comments. Is that all right?"

"Sure, honey. You're the boss."

"I've marked the pages. Look at the first page that I dog-eared, the last paragraph. It has a reading that I think would be great to do at the wedding. Tell me what you think; read it to me aloud."

> We need have no fears. To love others outside the family, to give in the right way will not harm the love between husband and wife. When you began to love your partner, you gave, but in the giving you gained more. So, as a couple, your love and giving to those outside the home will enable your own love to grow stronger and deeper. Our God is faithful and keeps the word given to us.

Brian turned the page.

> And God blessed marriage, so that when man took her to himself, she would be glorious, with no speck or wrinkle or anything like that, but holy and faultless. In the same way, husbands must love their wives as they love their own bodies; for a man to love his wife is for him to love himself.
>
> A man never hates his own body, but he feeds it and looks after it; and that is the way Christ treats the Church.
>
> To sum up; you too, as a man, must love your wife as you love yourself; and let every wife respect her husband.
>
> This is the word of the Lord.

"So, what do you think about it?" Mary asked.

"I liked it but isn't there something missing? Where's the love, honor and obey parts?"

"Obey? Obey? You seem to forget that you're a mere Lieutenant and I'm a Captain. The obey part in this marriage is going to be the other way around."

Knowing how to push her buttons, he answered, "Yes, Captain, ma'am. Will I have to request a kiss at the end of the ceremony or must I salute you first?"

"Neither," she said. She reached across the table and pinched his arm. "What did I tell you about calling me 'Captain' or 'ma'am'?" She blew him a kiss.

"What do you really think about the reading?"

"I liked it and if it's what you want, we'll have it in the ceremony."

She yawned and glanced at her watch. "Good Lord! It's after two. I think we'd better continue this in the morning. Before I forget, do you think Tom will be all right as the Best Man? I doubt if he knows anything about Catholic weddings or any wedding for that matter."

"Let me put your mind at ease, sweetheart. You can rest assured that he has already visited the library to read as much he could about weddings. He is like that. The man lives at the library, I swear. And he is a perfectionist when it comes to doing for others. I wouldn't doubt it if he knows more about his duties than anybody I could have picked."

"Tom's not familiar with the Mass."

"Mary, I have no doubt in my military mind that Tom will know all there is to know in plenty of time for the wedding.

They went back to her place as it was too late for him to go to the B.O.Q. They left the restaurant arm in arm.

Waking to the smell of brewing coffee, Brian sat up on the couch she'd made up for him to sleep on and thought, *She's right again. This will be much better than coming home to an empty room in the B.O.Q.*

"Hungry?" Mary had noticed that he had stirred awake.

"I'm famished, but I'd like to clean up before we eat."

"There's a clean towel and wash cloth on the towel rack. There's a spare toothbrush in the medicine cabinet."

As Brian toweled himself dry, he thought about how nice it would be if he didn't have to sleep on the couch. He dressed and went into the kitchen, sniffing at the bacon that sizzled in the skillet. He walked up behind Mary and put his arms around her, kissed her on the cheek, and told her he loved her.

"How many eggs can you eat?" she asked.

"I could eat a dozen but two should do it."

"Two eggs coming up. Would you make the toast?"

When their breakfast was finished, they cleared the table together, and she washed the dishes as he dried them with an ease that felt natural.

Brian remembered the other words written in the pamphlet, words that spoke to his heart. These words described perfectly how he felt toward Mary.

Love is always patient and kind; It is never jealous; Love is never boastful or conceited; It is never rude or selfish; It does not take offense, and is not resentful. Love takes no pleasure in other people's sins but delights in the truth. It is always ready to excuse, to trust, to hope, and endure whatever comes. Love does not come to an end.

His love for her overwhelmed him.

THE GROOM'S PARTY

Each of the officers brought a small gag gift, explaining, with great hilarity, what it was, and how to use it. One Lieutenant brought a pair of lace panties with a "Follow Me" shoulder patch from the Infantry School sewn on the back.

After the laughter died, Brian stood and raised his glass in a toast. "Gentlemen, I thank you and salute you," he said, and then still standing with his drink raised, he mimicked the Irish brogue he remembered from his grandfather McGlynn. "Gentlemen, your attention please! I propose a toast to you all in the true Irish spirit and in Gaelic, a language my grandfather brought to our country many years ago. *'Croich Honorah!'"* he shouted as he drained the drink.

"What's that mean Brian?" someone asked.

Lieutenant Brian McGlynn/Bath glanced slowly about the room as if looking for the questioner and soberly said, "May you die with honor." He watched as the officers raised their glasses in toast, a sign of their approval, and drank every drop.

Then another, in a voice slightly louder than normal, said, "Rangers, lead the way!"

THE NUPTIALS

When Brian heard the organ begin the wedding music, he turned toward the back of the church. He strained his neck to see her walk down the aisle holding the arm of her father. A beam of light from the stained glass window gave her face and red hair a radiance, even under the veil. Mr. Monaghan looked very proud. Even with the halting step of the wedding march, Mary was so beautiful and graceful. Suddenly, he wondered why he was nervous. Was he afraid Mary would bolt from the chapel or was he finally aware of the responsibilities he faced?

Then he remembered the words of the liturgy: *When one finds a worthy wife, her value is far beyond pearls, . . . her husband entrusting his heart to her has an unfailing prize. . . . She brings him good in all the days of her life. . . .* The words reassured him.

When Mary reached the altar, she handed the bouquet of white lilies to her Maid of Honor. When she turned to Brian, he lifted her veil and looked deeply into her eyes. He wanted to kiss her, but that had to wait. She smiled and they held hands. Then the priest began the introductory prayers of the liturgy.

"Father, hear our prayers for Brian and Mary, who today are to be united in marriage before your altar. Give them your blessing and strengthen their love for each other. We ask this through Christ our

Lord." The chaplain directed them to two chairs sitting to the right of the altar where they would sit during the Nuptial Mass.

As Tom turned to sit with the ushers for the Mass, he touched his pocket to be sure the wedding ring was there to hand to Brian later. Tom noticed his mother and sister in the front pew sitting with Brian's family. *Why are they sitting there?*

There was no way for him to know that Brian's mother had insisted they *sit with the family.* Had he known, he would have been pleased rather than bewildered. Although he'd never been to a Catholic Mass, he was interested in what he watched. However, the idea of his family sitting together with Brian's family continued to intrude on his thoughts until the Mass ended. He looked back toward his mother and sister once more, and then took his place alongside Brian for the wedding vows.

Tom noticed Brian's hand was a bit wobbly when he handed him the ring for Mary. The ceremony unfolded exactly as practiced. Brian and Mary kissed and then turned to start down the aisle, now as husband and wife. Eileen, the Maid of Honor, accepted Tom's arm as they followed the Bride and Groom. They walked beneath the arch of sabers toward the waiting limo, which would take them to the Officers' Club for the reception.

THE WEDDING RECEPTION

At the O Club, the emcee introduced the happy couple, and the room gave a thunderous applause and a chorus of hurrahs.

"And now, the bride and groom have the first waltz," the emcee announced. They danced to rich tenor voice of her Uncle Leo serenading them to the *Irish Wedding Song.* The Bride and Groom held hands and gazed into each other's eyes at they stepped onto the dance floor. Uncle Leo's words echoed through the room, and Mary and Brian danced to this traditional waltz. With the repeat of the last chorus, the gathered guests broke into a round of applause.

Soft music filled the room, and the Emcee announced it was time for the father and daughter dance.

Mr. Monaghan rose and took Mary's hand. "May I have this dance, beautiful lady?"

"You most certainly may, Daddy." Father and daughter danced to the tune of "Daddy's Little Girl."

Mary looked into her father's face. The tears on his cheeks matched her own.

"Be happy, sweetheart, and if you ever need me, you know where I am."

"I know, Daddy. I love you."

When the song ended, Mr. Monaghan escorted Mary to the groom. She kissed the tear running down her Daddy's cheek and held him tightly for just a moment. . . .

As Best Man, Tom asked the Maid of Honor for the next dance. "I know you're the Maid of Honor, but I don't think I know your name."

She giggled. "You don't remember me at all. You haven't got a clue."

"How come you look at me so funny. Don't you believe I'm Brian's brother?" Tom asked.

"No. It's not that. It's because we met before, and I don't mean at the rehearsal. But obviously, you were in no shape to remember."

Tom felt embarrassed, but he didn't know why. "Well, are you going to tell me or not?"

"I'm glad you're here. I saw your chopper go down in Operation *Urgent Fury*, but there was nothing I could do, then. Later, when Garcia and Brian pulled you out of the wreckage, you were loaded onto my chopper to go to the *Guam*. You must be a very tough guy to have survived."

Tom missed a step, and looked her in the eyes. 'Thanks, but I don't understand. How did *you* see it?"

"The two Black Hawks were ahead of me. I was the pilot of the third chopper. You were in the first."

"But women aren't allowed in combat!"

"Maybe that's what the Pentagon line is, but I sure was there in the thick of it. Altogether, 200 American women were in that fight."

"I was sure I heard the Pentagon spokesman say 'There were no women in combat'."

"Yeah, that's what the top brass says. So we don't get our ribbon, our combat pay, or recognition. There are 200 women who are hoppin' mad about it. I'm going to apply for a transfer to the astronaut program. Maybe I won't be so invisible there."

"Were you the one Sergeant Henning ordered to land on the *Guam* when the Navy said no?"

"You got it!"

"He said you made a perfect landing despite rough water and the moving deck."

"Just another day. No big deal."

"Well, I'm glad you thought so. How did you get here? How do you know Mary and Brian?"

"Mary and I go way back. Kindergarten, in fact."

As the music ended, Tom took a step back from her. "Good luck. I wish you well."

When the music stopped, Tom aimed straight for Patti to ask for a dance. When he put his arm around her waist, he felt an electric sensation. As they began to sway to the music, he looked down into her eyes, "I've been too wired to eat. How about you."

"I've been helping Mary behind the scenes and only had time for a handful of Georgia peanuts," she smiled.

"Promise me you will come find me when we send off Brian and Mary. I'd like to take you to my favorite restaurant for châteaubriand. Or if that's not alright, we can go wherever you'd like. We have a lot of catching up to do."

She smiled, and her eyes sparkled. She nodded her head and moved closer to him just as the dance ended.

Tom danced with Phin, and Brian danced with Anne. Then the boys exchanged mothers for the next dance. When the beat picked up, John came across the room, "Mind if I dance with my wife?" Tom bowed to Anne and put her hand in John's hand.

Brian asked Mai Lin for the next dance, and it was Mitzi's turn to dance with the bride. By then, most of the guests were dancing.

After several more fast dances, and the couples had returned to their seats, a chair was placed in the middle of the room and all bachelor guests were invited to stand in a group, facing the chair. They knew what was next on the program. They were about to take part in the ritual of giving the single men and women the opportunity to meet by chance, in the throwing of the bridal bouquet and tossing of the bride's garter.

There were good-natured whistles and comments as Brian reached up under Mary's gown and removed her garter. Standing and turning toward the group of men, he smiled as he looked, about selecting the one man to toss it to. He turned his back and tossed the garter over his shoulder. The garter flew until Tom caught it unintentionally. He had no idea what he was to do with it until he was told by one of the others. Wishing he had studied more on the wedding reception and its customs, he turned and walked to his seat as the single ladies took the place just vacated by the young men.

Mary held her bouquet with both hands. She smiled at Brian and then surveyed the eager faces of the young ladies. She turned her back and threw the bouquet behind her. One of her nurses caught it. There were squeals of delight as the lucky young lady sat in the chair beside Tom.

The men at the reception began calling for Tom to do his duty. "Get up there, Tom. Put the garter where it belongs," one yelled.

Tom wished he were back in Ban Hin Leek Fai. *Crazy American customs*, he thought. His embarrassment obvious, Tom braved it out in the spirit of the occasion. The crowd whooped its hurrahs, catcalls, and applauded, but it quieted as Tom knelt in front of the young lady.

She coyly raised her dress to her knees and more catcalls ensued. The lady in front of him lifted her foot from the floor so he could slip the garter onto her shapely leg. He slid it to her knee and started to stand up, when there were a few shouts of "Higher, higher."

But the lady saw his embarrassment. She whispered, "It's all right, Tom; slide it a little higher." She pulled the hem of her skirt higher, and he slid the garter to the hem of her gown. Then he stood up, and quickly kissed her cheek. He took her hand and walked her to her seat amid applause.

Tom's heart was still pounding. His role as Best Man wasn't over, yet. He took several deep breaths, trying to calm down, and waited as waiters poured champagne at each table. He stood and tapped a knife against an empty water glass to catch everyone's attention. He turned toward Brian and Mary.

"I propose a toast to the newlyweds, two people I think the world of." Then turning toward the just married couple, Tom raised his glass. "May you be poor in misfortune, rich in blessings, slow to make enemies, and quick to make friends. But rich or poor, quick or slow, may you know nothing but happiness from this day forward." Then taking a sip of champagne, he swallowed hard, and said, "I love you both."

Mr. Monaghan and Brian's mother both took turns, as they stood to thank Tom for his toast. Brian's mother remarked that Tom's toast had an Irish sound to it.

After dinner one of the ushers brought Brian his sword so he could cut the cake in true tradition. Everyone expected them to squash the cake as they fed each other a piece, but Brian delicately fed Mary a bite of cake, and Mary's response was the same. The gentleness between the couple was touching to witness.

When it was time for the send off, Tom made sure that their car was in place at the bottom of the steps leading into the club. Their bags were loaded in the trunk and ready to go. He stood off to the side and watched the couple come down the steps amid a shower of birdseed and shouts of congratulations.

Ducking the thrown birdseed as they rushed to their car, Brian spotted Tom. He took Mary's hand and walked toward him. Mary kissed Tom on the cheek and thanked him. Brian put an arm around Tom's shoulder, and grinned. "Thanks, brother. I owe you one."

Tom waved as he watched the car drove away. His thoughts were spinning. He kept thinking, *Brian called me 'brother'— not Tom, but 'brother' — I like the sound of it!*

Just then, Patti came up behind him and put her hand on his arm.

He grinned at her. "Has Kimmie told you she's my sister?"

Patti gave him a quizzical look.

"You remember that night on the mountain when we took Kimmie Bath home? She's my sister and I didn't know it. We've got a lot to talk about," Tom said. "Kimmie and June are both my sisters."

"That makes Brian your brother?" Patti raised her eyebrows. "I thought he was your rival."

"Yes, my brother. That's so much better than my rival! And besides, I am the Best Man.

THE END

Appendix

A. Original wording: "A Plan of Discipline by Major Robert Roger"

1. All Rangers are to be subject to the rules and articles of war; to appear at roll call every evening on their own parade, equipped, each with a firelock, 60 rounds of power and ball, and a hatchet, at which time an officer from each company is to inspect the same, to see they are in order, so as to be ready on any emergency to march at a minute's warning; and, before they are dismissed, appoint the necessary guards and scouts . . . for the next day.

2. Whenever you are ordered out to the enemies' forts or frontiers for discoveries, if your numbers be small, march in a single file, keeping at such distance from each other as to prevent one shot from killing two men, sending one man or more forward, and the like on each side, at the distance of 20 yards from the main body, if the ground you march over will admit of it, to give the signal to the officer of the approach of any enemy and of their numbers, etc.

3. If you march over marshes or soft ground, change your position, and march abreast of each other to prevent the enemy from tracing you (as they would do if you marched in a single file) until you get over such ground. Then resume your former order and march until it is quite dark before you encamp. If possible, encamp on a piece of ground which may afford your sentries the advantage of seeing and hearing the enemy some considerable distance. Keep one half of your whole party awake alternately through the night.

4. Some time before you come to the place you would reconnoiter, make a stand, and send out one or two men in whom you can confide, to look out the best ground for making your observations.

5. If you have the good fortune to take any prisoners, keep them separate, until they are examined. In your return, take a different route from that in which you went out, the you may better discover any party at your rear, and have an opportunity, if their strength be superior to your, to alter your course, or disperse, as circumstances may require.

6. If you march in a large body of 300 or 400, with a design to attack the enemy, divide your party into three columns, each headed by a proper officer, and let those columns march in single files, the columns to the right and left keeping 30 yards distance or more from that of the center. If the ground will admit and let proper guards be kept in the front and rear, and suitable flanking parties at a due distance as before directed, with orders to halt on all eminences, to take a view of the surrounding ground, to prevent your being ambuscaded, and to notify the approach or retreat of the enemy, that proper dispositions may be made for attacking, defending, etc. And if the enemy approach in your front on level ground, form a front of your three columns or main body with the advanced guard, keeping out your flanking parties, as if you were marching under the command of trusty officers, to prevent the enemy from pressing hard on either of your wings, or surrounding you, which is their usual method . . . if their numbers will admit of it, and be careful likewise to support and strengthen your rear-guard.

7. If your are obliged to receive the enemy's fire, fall, or squat down, until it is over; then rise and discharge at them. If their main body is equal to yours, extend yourselves occasionally; but if superior, be careful to support and strengthen your flanking parties, to make them equal to theirs, that if possible you may repulse them to their main body, in which case push upon them with the greatest resolution with equal force in each flank and in the center, observing to keep at a due distance from each other, advance from tree to tree, with one half of the party before the other 10 or 12 yards. If the enemy push upon you, let your front fire and fall down, and then let your rear advance through them and do the like, by which time those who before were in front will be ready to discharge again, and repeat the same alternatively, as occasion shall require; by this means, you will keep up such a constant fire, that the enemy will not be able easily to break your order, or gain your ground.

8. If you oblige the enemy to retreat, be careful, in your pursuit of them to keep out your flanking parties, and prevent them from gaining eminences, or rising grounds, in which case they would perhaps be able to rally and repulse you in their turn.

9. If you are obliged to retreat, let the front of your whole party fire and fall back, until the rear hath done the same, making for the best ground you can; by this means, you will oblige the enemy to pursue you, if they do it at all, in the face of constant fire.

10. If the enemy is so superior that you are in danger of being surrounded by them, let the whole body disperse and everyone take a different road to the place of rendezvous appointed for that evening, which must every morning be altered and fixed for the evening ensuing, in order to bring the whole party, or as many of them as possible, together, after any separation that my happen in the day. But if you should happen to be actually surrounded, form yourselves into a square, or if in the wood, a circle is best, and if possible make a stand until the darkness of the night favors your escape.

11. If your rear is attacked, the main body and flankers must face about to the right or left as occasion shall require, and form themselves to oppose the enemy, as before directed; and the same method must be observed, if attacked in either of your flanks, by which means you will always make a rear of one of your flank-guards.

12. If you determine to rally after a retreat, in order to make a fresh stand against the enemy, by all means endeavor to do it on the most rising ground you come at, which will give you greatly the advantage in point of situation, and enable you to repulse superior numbers.

13. In general, when pushed upon by the enemy, reserve your fire until they approach very near, which will then put them into the greatest surprise and consternation, and give you an opportunity of rushing upon them with your hatchets and cutlasses to the better advantage.

14. When you encamp at night, fix your sentries in such a manner as not to be relieved from the main body until morning, profound secrecy and silence

being often of the last importance in these cases. Each sentry, therefore, should consist of six men, two of whom must be constantly alert, and when relieved by their fellows, it should be done without noise. In case those on duty see or hear anything which alarms them, they are not to speak, but on of them is silently to retreat, that proper dispositions may be made; and all occasional sentries should be fixed in like manner.

15. At the first dawn of the day, awake your whole detachment; that being the time when the enemy chooses attack, you should by all means be in readiness to receive them.

16. If the enemy should be discovered by your detachments in the morning, and their numbers are superior to yours, and a victory doubtful, you should not attack them until the evening, as then they will not know your numbers, and if you are repulsed, your retreat will be favored by the darkness of the night.

17. Before you leave your encampment, send out small parties to scout round it, to see if there be any appearance or track of an enemy that might have been near you during the night.

18. When you stop for refreshment, choose some spring or rivulet if you can, and dispose your party so as not to be surprised, posting proper guards and sentries at a due distance, and let a small party waylay the path came in, least the enemy should be pursuing.

19. If in your return, you have to cross rivers, avoid the usual fords as much as possible, lest the enemy should have discovered and be there expecting you.

20. If you have to pass by lakes, keep at some distance from the edge of the water, lest, in case of an ambuscade or an attack from the enemy, when in that situation, your retreat should be cut off.

21. If the enemy pursue your rear, take a circle until you come to your own tracks, and there form an ambush to receive them and give them the first fire.

22. When you return from a scout, and come near our forts, avoid the usual roads and avenues thereto, lest the enemy should have headed you, and lay in ambush to receive you, when almost exhausted with fatigue.

23. When you pursue any party that has been near our forts or encampments, follow not directly in their tracks, lest they should be discovered by their rear-guards, who, at such time, would be most alert; but endeavor, by a different route, to head and meet them in some narrow pass, or lay in ambush to receive them when and where they least expect it.

24. If you are to embark in canoes, battoes, or otherwise by water, choose the evening for the time of your embarkation, as you will then have the whole night before you, to pass undiscovered by any parties of the enemy on hills, or other places, which command a prospect of the lake or river you are upon.

25. In paddling or rowing, give orders that the boat or canoe next the sternmost, wait for her and the third for the second, and the fourth for the third, as so on, to prevent separation, and that you may be ready to assist each other on any emergency.

26. Appoint one man in each boat to look out for fires on the adjacent shores, from the number and size of which you may form some judgement of the numbers that kindled them, or whether you are able to attack them or not.

27. If you find the enemy encamped near the banks of a river or lake, which you imagine they will attempt to cross for their security upon being attacked, leave a detachment of your party on the opposite shore to receive them, while, with the remainder, you surprise them, having them between you and the lake or the river.

28. If you cannot satisfy yourself as to the enemy's number and strength from the fires etc., conceal your boats at some distance and ascertain their number by a reconnoitering party when they embark or march in the morning, marking the course they steer, etc., so when you pursue, ambush, and attack them, or let them pass, as prudence shall direct you. In general,

however, that you may not be discovered by the enemy upon the lakes and rovers at a great distance, it is safest to lay by, with your boats and party concealed all day, without noise or show, and to pursue your intended route by night; and whether you go by land or water, give out parole and countersigns, in order to know one another in the dark, and likewise appoint a station for every man to repair to, in case of any accident that may separate you.

B. Modern modified wording of "Rogers' Rangers Standing Orders" by Major Robert Rogers, 1759

1. Don't forget nothing.
2. Have your musket clean as a whistle, hatchet scoured, 60 rounds powder and ball, and be ready to march at a minute's warning.
3. When you're on the march, act the way you would if you was sneaking up on a deer. See enemy first.
4. Tell the truth about what you see and what you do. There is an army depending on us for correct information. You can lie all you please when you tell other folks about the Rangers, but don't ever lie to a Ranger or an officer.
5. Don't ever take a chance you don't have to.
6. When you're on the march, we march as a single file, far enough apart so one shot can't go thru two men.
7. If we strike swamps or soft ground, we spread out abreast, so it's hard to track us.
8. When we march, we keep moving until dark, so as to give the enemy the least chance at us.
9. When we camp, half the party stays awake while the other half sleeps.
10. If we take prisoners, we keep 'em separate until we have had time to examine them, or they can cook up a story between 'em.
11. Don't ever march the same way. Take a different route so you won't be ambushed.

12. No matter whether we travel in big parties or little ones, each party has to keep a scout 20 yards ahead, 20 yards on each flank and 20 yards in the rear, so the main body can't be surprised and wiped out.
13. Every night you'll be told where to meet if surrounded by a superior force.
14. Don't sit down to eat without posting sentries.
15. Don't sleep beyond dawn. Dawn's when the French and Indians attack.
16. Don't cross a river by a regular ford.
17. If somebody's trailing you, make a circle, come back onto your own tracks, and ambush the folks that aim to ambush you.
18. Don't stand up when the enemy's coming against you. Kneel down, lie down, or hide behind a tree.
19. Let the enemy come until he's almost close enough to touch. Then let him have it and jump out and finish him with you hatchet.

C.   Ranger Creed

Recognizing that I volunteered as a Ranger, fully knowing the hazards of my chosen profession, I will always endeavor to uphold the prestige, honor, and high "esprit de corps" of my Ranger Regiment.

Acknowledging the fact that a Ranger is a more elite soldier who arrives at the cutting edge of battle by land, sea, or air, I accept the fact that as a Ranger my country expects me to move farther, faster, and fight harder than any other soldier.

Never shall I fail my comrades. I will always keep myself mentally alert, physically strong, and morally straight and I will shoulder more than my share of the task whatever it may be. One hundred percent and then some.

Gallantly will I show the world that I am a specially-selected and well-trained soldier. My courtesy to superior officers, my neatness of dress, and care for equipment shall set the example for others to follow.

Energetically will I meet the enemies of my country. I shall defeat them on the field of battle for I am better trained and will fight with all my might. Surrender is not a Ranger word. I will never leave a fallen comrade to fall into the hands of the enemy and under no circumstances will I ever embarrass my country.

Readily will I display the intestinal fortitude required to fight on to the Ranger objective and complete the mission, though I be the lone survivor.

D. The Airborne Creed

- ★ I am an Airborne trooper! A PARATROOPER!
- ★ I jump by parachute from any plane in flight. I volunteered to do it, knowing well the hazards of my choice.
- ★ I serve in a mighty Airborne Force—famed for deeds in war—renowned for readiness in peace. It is my pledge to uphold its honor and prestige in all I am—in all I do.
- ★ I am an elite trooper—a sky trooper—a shock trooper—a spearhead trooper. I blaze the way to far-flung goals—behind, before, above the foe's front line.
- ★ I know that I may have to fight without support for days on end. Therefore, I keep mind and body always fit to do my part in any Airborne task. I am self-reliant and unafraid. I shoot true, and march fast and far. I fight hard and excel in every art and artifice of war.
- ★ I never fail a fellow trooper. I cherish as a sacred trust the lives of men with whom I serve. Leaders have my fullest loyalty, and those I lead never find me lacking.
- ★ I have pride in the Airborne! I never let it down!
- ★ In peace, I do not shrink the dullest of duty nor protest the toughest training. My weapons and equipment are always combat ready. I am neat of dress—military in courtesy—proper in conduct and behavior.
- ★ In battle, I fear no foe's ability, nor under-estimate his prowess, power and guile. I fight him with all my might and skills—ever alert to evade capture or escape a trap. I never surrender, though I be the last.
- ★ My goal in peace or war is to succeed in any mission of the day—or die, if needs be, in the try.
- ★ I belong to a proud and glorious team—the Airborne, the Army, my Country. I am its chosen pride to fight where others may not go—to serve them well until the final victory.
- ★ I am the trooper of the sky! I am my Nation's best! In peace and war I never fail. Anywhere, anytime, in anything—I AM AIRBORNE!

In Memoriam

Publication of this book is in honor of the author Raymond F. Flaherty, a soldier's soldier and Pulitzer Prize Contender, and to our warriors who died in Operation *Urgent Fury* in Grenada.

There were 19 known dead and 116 wounded. Here is a partial list in no specific order, of the U.S. Servicemen killed in action during Operation *Urgent Fury* or as a result of wounds sustained. The Operation was successful in rescuing and evacuating all the American medical students and their families from three university campuses in Grenada.

SGT Philip S. Grenier

SGT Kevin J. Lannon

Kenneth John Butcher

SGT Randy E. Cline

SSG Gary L. Epps

USMC Major John P. Giguere

CPT Keith J. Lucas

SGT Sean P. Luketina

QM1, MM1 Kevin E. Lundberg

PFC Markin R. Maynard

HT1, HP1 Stephen L. Morris

SGT Mark A. Rademacher

CPT Michael F. Ritz

PFC Russell L. Robinson

ENCS Robert R. Schamberger

USMC Captain Jeb F. Seagle

USMC 1st Lieutenant Jeffrey R. Sharver

SGT Stephen E. Slater

SPC Mark O. Yamane

MM1 John Butcher,

QM1 Kevin Lundbergh,

HT1 Stephen Morris, and

ENCS Robert R. Schamberger

MAIN SOURCE: http://www.pow-mia-kia.org

References & Resources

Periodical
- Berry, William, et. al. "Ten Days of *Urgent Fury*" *All Hands* 807 (May 1984): 18-27.

Books
- Alighieri, Dante. *The Divine Comedy*.
- Flanagan, E.M. *Airborne: A Combat History of American Airborne Forces*. New York: Ballantine Books, 2002.
- Mill, John Stuart. *On Liberty*. London: Longman, Roberts, & Green, 1869.
- Tanaka, Chester. *Go for Broke: A Pictorial History of the Japanese American 100th Infantry Battalion and the 442nd Regimental Combat Team*. Novato, CA: Presidio Press, 1997. Chester Tanaka, a Japanese-American, was a member K Company, 442nd Infantry.

Government documents
- U. S. Army   **Oath of Enlistment,** Uniform Code of Military Justice (Title 10, US Code; Act of 5 May 1960, replacing the wording first adopted in 1789, with amendment effective October 5, 1962.) Oaths. <http://www.army.mil/CMH/faq/oaths.htm>
- U. S. Army   **Oath of Enlistment of a Commissioned Officer,** DA Form 71, August 1, 1959 for officers. **Uniform Code of Military Justice** (Title 10, **US Code**; Act of 5 May 1960, replacing the wording first adopted in 1789, with amendment effective October 5, 1962.) Oaths. <http://www.army.mil/CMH/faq/oaths.htm>

Electronic Resources
- *Abram's Charter*
  <http://www.specialoperations.com/Army/Rangers/default2.html>
- Cobb County Courts, Cobb County, GA. *Application for Change of Name*.
  <http://lawlibrary.cobbcountyga.gov/downloads/NameChangeAdult/AdultNamePacket.pdf>
- "The FReeper Foxhole Remembers Operation *Urgent Fury* — Grenada—Jan. 26th, 2003." Free Republic, US. Military History, Current Events and Veterans Issues. Posted January 26, 2003. <http://www.fas.org/man/dod-101

/ops/urgent_fury.htm> "In total, an invasion force of 1,900 U.S. troops, reaching a high of about 5,000 in five days, and 300 troops from the neighboring islands encountered about 1,200 Grenadians, 780 Cubans, 49 Soviets, 24 North Koreans, 16 East Germans, 14 Bulgarians, and 3 or 4 Libyans. Within three days all main objectives were accomplished. Five hundred ninety-nine (599) Americans and 80 foreign nationals were evacuated, and the U.S. forces were successful in the eventual reestablishment of a representative form of government in Grenada."

- "Grenada: Operation *Urgent Fury*" (23 October-21 November 1983) <http://www.history.navy.mil/faq/faq95-1.htm>
- "Military Women in Operation *Urgent Fury* and Just Cause." <http://userpages.aug.com/coptback/panama.htm>
- "The Ranger Creed" <https://www.benning.army.mil/75thranger/index.asp>
- Robert Rogers' "Standing Orders," Major Robert Rogers, 1759, 75th Ranger Regiment. <http://www.soc.mil/75thrr/75th_home.htm>
- "A Plan of Discipline" **Journals of Major Robert Rogers**, 1769 Dublin edition, transcribed by M. Christopher New. <http://reactor-core.org/rogers-rangers.html>
- "US Army Ranger Training." <http://specialoperationsmilitary.com>
- "Silver Star Awards for Gallantry in Grenada during Operation *Urgent Fury*." <http://www.homeofheroes.com/valor2/ss/6-PostRVN/05-Grenada.html>

About Raymond F. Flaherty

Master Sergeant Raymond F. Flaherty was born August 6, 1927, the eldest of nine children. Raised in Boston, Ray attended public school until World War II interrupted his education. He served aboard ship with the Merchant Marine until he entered the U.S. Army in 1945.

During the Korean War, he was a member of the 9th Airborne Ranger Company and saw ground combat with Company L, 15th Infantry Regiment. There he was awarded the Silver Star, Bronze Star, and Purple Heart Medals and his first award of the Combat Infantryman Badge.

In 1962, Flaherty went to Laos on Operation *White Star* as team sergeant of a Special Forces 'A' Detachment from the 7th Special Forces Group. His first tour in South Vietnam was as a team sergeant of an 'A' Detachment from the 1st Special Forces Group in 1963, where he was awarded his second Combat Infantryman Badge. Ray returned to South Vietnam in 1965 to serve as intelligence sergeant of the 4th Battalion, 173rd Airborne Brigade, then as operations sergeant of a 'B' Detachment of the 5th Special Forces Group.

According to Col. Richard O. Sutton, M. D., author of the book "Operation *White Star*," he based the character called "Flag" on Master Sergeant Raymond F. Flaherty.

Raymond F. Flaherty retired to Florida in 1967. **He Didn't Say *Good-Bye*** was his first novel to be published. It's about the U.S. Army Special Forces in Laos, MIA, and the resilience of military families. **Strangers Brothers** is the exciting sequel portraying the lives of the next generation who became Airborne Rangers, participated in Operation *Urgent Fury* in Grenada. It also deals with the challenges of blended families, confronting the question of 'Who is our family?'

By the time of his death on Patriot Day, September 11, 2006, Ray had produced three novels, most of which he created on his laptop even while undergoing weekly chemo treatments and frequent hospitalizations. After the oncologist reluctantly told Ray he had only two weeks to live, Ray said he didn't have time to die because he was determined to see his first novel in print and it was part of the doctor's job to keep him alive to do it. That novel **He Didn't Say *Good-Bye*** became a contender for the Pulitzer Prize in Letters (fiction) in 2006. He lived an additional 13 months. Ray was a soldier's soldier, a man of courage and determination. He's also an inspiration to all of us who may feel we don't have time to write or to accomplish our dreams.

About Pat McDonough

Pat McDonough was a Pulitzer Prize Semi-Finalist in 1997 for **Without Keys: My 15 Weeks With the Street People.** Recently she co-author **Kazik's Polish Navy.** She's a freelance writer, editor, publisher/owner of Terra Sancta Press, and sometimes ghostwriter. Her publication credits include **A New Draft Constitution for the State of Maryland, Solid Waste Management, Gaining and Maintaining Public Acceptance in Solid Waste Management**, as well as numerous articles and short stories. At various times, Pat was a grief counselor, a real estate sales person, a mortgage banker, a builder, a housing inspector, and a consultant. She's the mother of two and grandmother of three boys.

Terra Sancta Press Catalog

- **Strangers Brothers** by Raymond F. Flaherty with Pat McDonough. ISBN: 978-0-9653467-8-8 $21.95 USD.
- **He Didn't Say *Good-Bye*** by Raymond F. Flaherty .ISBN: 978-0-9653467-7-1 $24.95 USD. *Pulitzer Prize contender in 2006.*
- **Kazik's Polish Navy** by Kazimierz J. Kasperek with Pat McDonough. ISBN: 978-0-9653467-2-6 $21.95 USD. *Pulitzer Prize contender in 2009.*
- **What Made Us Who We Are Today, World War II Oral History** by Mary Timpe Robsman. $19.95 USD. ISBN: 978-0-9653467-4-0
- **Without Keys, My 15 Weeks With the Street People** by Pat McDonough $24.00. Use ISBN 978-0-9653467-1-9 for hard cover with dust jacket; ISBN: 978-0-9653467-0-2 for soft cover, perfect binding. *Pulitzer Prize Semi-finalist 1997. Winner of five MIPA Awards of Merit.*

E-mail	books4you@cfl.rr.com accepts Visa or MasterCard.
Our website	http://www.terrasanctapress.com accepts PayPal, and most credit cards
Phone	321-254-9672 (11 a.m. - 8 p.m. EST)
Fax	321-259-9242 (a 24-hour number)
Mail order	**Terra Sancta Press**, 304 Royal Palm Dr., Melbourne, FL 32935-6955. For bulk orders or special discounts, query by email or phone.

Terra Sancta Press SAN: 854-1388

The *Strangers Brothers* Story

Strangers Brothers, sequel to Ray Flaherty's **He Didn't Say** *Good-Bye*, tells the story of the coming together of two brothers, from different cultures, and raised separately by the same father. While the brothers, both Airborne Rangers are involved in Operation *Urgent Fury*, the rescue mission to Grenada, a secret is revealed and their lives unravel. Living in the same Georgia town, how can two disparate families come to grips with one man's "other life"?

What others say

I thoroughly enjoyed **Strangers Brothers**. Truthfully, it made me think, long after I put it down. It gave me insight into things I'd heard but didn't really understand: for instance, the training. I have always known it was hard, but had no details. The comradeship was there, too.

CAROL SALZMAN

A great read! **Strangers Brothers** show how the practical and emotional understanding of one man ("Tom Aquinas") can bring goals, success, and two culturally disparate families together. **Strangers Brothers** has an emotional immediacy that never leaves. . . . It carries right to the last page. The ending brought a tear to my eye. In fact, many passages brought tears of sorrow or joy.

MARIE E. ROMAN, educator

Master Sergeant Ray Flaherty's **Strangers Brothers** is a well-written novel that allows you to follow Kumpang (Tom Aquinas) from childhood to manhood. It's a story of a young boy who has set almost impossible goals for himself in order to honor the man who was the father figure in his life. Flaherty's unique storytelling transforms the reader into the mind of Kumpang (Tom Aquinas) as he goes from an immigrant Lao lad on through the rigors of Basic Training, Jump School, Airborne Ranger Training and on through the invasion of Grenada.

You re-live the pain of the 'M14 thumb' (mine was the 'M1 Thumb'), and the fear of standing in the door of a mock-up on the 34-foot tower, staring down at the 'Black Hat.' Thirty-four feet seemed like a thousand when you stood there knowing you were to leap out into space, and the only things that would keep you from plummeting to the hard Georgia ground below were those two, thin, risers connected to your harness and a thin cable. You prayed to God that none would snap. You screamed out your number and leapt into space with eyes squeezed shut, and arms flailing in the wind, even while your fingers gripped the reserve parachute pack on your chest. The fall, that seemed to go on forever, suddenly jerked to a stop as the risers reached the end of the slack, and you coasted slowly down the cable.

There was the panoramic view as you were hoisted to the top of the 250-foot towers. When you stared out across the horizon, you swore you could almost see the curvature of the earth. Then, the click of the lock when the ring which held your parachute engaged the release, and you felt the chute break loose.

The instructor's voice drummed in your ears. "You have the dirty arm, Trooper. Slip to the right. Slip to the right!"

And yes, there were a couple of incidents where jumpers had slipped into the towers. . . .

War is war, whether it be World War II, Korea, Viet Nam or Grenada, and Flaherty's description of the invasion of Grenada places you with those Rangers aboard the Black Hawks as they approached the landing zone. You can almost feel the heat as the choppers are hit, burst into flames and crashed to the ground. Only someone who has been there can know the fear of coming under fire for the first time. Then events happen so swiftly that you react, not because you're thinking, but because the training you had made you do things out of instinct. The screw-ups before and during the invasion, no maps, no beacons to guide the choppers in, unknown assessments of the enemy troops, all contributed to an almost disastrous engagement but created the scenario for the final outcome of the story. **Strangers Brothers** is a novel well-worth reading.

MSG. CHARLES G. JAMES (ret.)